SWEPT AWAY

The desert warrior of her dreams came galloping toward her like a shadowed promise. She dropped her shovel in fright, recognizing the tall, veiled figure. Jabari. Her legs trembled and she stepped back, leaning against the boulder. A wicked-looking sword flashed silver in the moonlight as he held it aloft.

Even in her terror, she marveled at his magnificence, his proud fierceness like an ancient warrior. The sheikh looked like a dark, avenging angel.

Instinctively, she knew he intended to kill her. She had violated some sacred ancestral burying place. Any last vestige of strength fled her. Tears formed in her eyes as she contemplated the specter of death approaching swiftly.

Elizabeth bowed her head, waiting for the killing blow. Then raised her gaze for one last look at life. And let out a startled gasp as he whirled the blade in the air, and sheathed it.

He stopped his horse in front of her. In one powerful motion, he leaned down and as easily as a falcon plucks prey from the sky, scooped her into the saddle.

THE FALCON & THE DOVE

BONNIE VANAK

LEISURE BOOKS  NEW YORK CITY

A LEISURE BOOK®

November 2002

Published by

Dorchester Publishing Co., Inc.
276 Fifth Avenue
New York, NY 10001

Cover art by John Ennis.
www.ennisart.com

ISBN 0-8439-5132-X

Printed in the United States of America.

Visit us on the web at www.dorchesterpub.com.

For my parents, Marian and Harold Fischer, who taught me to dream; and Frank, who kept the dream alive.

Special thanks to my critique partner and "sister," Julie Sloane; the Mood Swing gals for their constant cheerleading; Vanessa Tirado for her prayers and amazing faith; Beebs, Jill & the "loopies," for all their friendship; Gina Fontana, my friend and co-worker through sixteen years of slogging through drug raids, prisons, insane asylums, slums, jungles and Slurpee runs; and my editor, Chris, for taking a chance.

THE FALCON & THE DOVE

The Legend

The sands of Akhetaten hold a secret.

Deep inside the ancient city's dusky earth lies a large gold disk called the Almha. Created in Egypt's eighteenth dynasty by one of pharaoh's wives to venerate the sun god Aten, it became a symbol of power and destruction.

When Queen Kiya showed the Almha to her husband, Pharaoh Akhenaten marveled at its beauty. He used the disk to draw crowds to Aten's temples. Akhenaten rewarded Kiya by building a temple for her to worship privately with her priests, the Khamsin warriors of the wind.

But Akhenaten's primary wife, Nefertiti, envied Kiya's power. She whispered to the pharaoh that he was a god himself, and he used the Almha to demand worship for himself instead of Aten.

Furious with her husband's sacrilege, Kiya stole the Almha and buried it. She commanded the Khamsin to guard its hiding place for all eternity, knowing she would not long survive her husband's fury and Nefertiti's jealousy.

That night, she retired to her chambers with her lover, the Khamsin leader, wanting one more chance to be held in his strong embrace. With her soft lips, she silenced Ranefer's protests that he could protect her from Akhenaten's wrath. The sweet torment in his kiss echoed her own sorrow.

Seizing the opportunity to eliminate her rival, Nefertiti convinced Akhenaten to execute Kiya for her theft. As the pharaoh and his guards marched toward her room, Kiya whispered an impassioned good-bye to her lover. She watched him vanish into the night, cherishing his promise that his spirit would wait through the ages to reunite with her.

The pharaoh threatened and cajoled, but Kiya remained silent. When the flash of the sickle sword hovered above her neck, she calmly bowed her head to its blade, praying for her lover's courage and surrendering her life instead of the Almha's secret.

The Khamsin took their revenge upon Nefertiti, killing her and scattering her ashes to prevent her soul from entering the afterlife. They mourned their beloved Queen Kiya, but knew that not even death's sting could separate her from her true love.

Legend says three signs of the white dove she cherished so much will herald Kiya's return to Ranefer. The Khamsin leader will marry her and peace and prosperity will again reign over the tribe.

He breathed slowly, willing his emotions to calm. One palm tightened around his scimitar's ivory hilt. The sheikh withdrew the blade and touched his hand to his heart and then his lips in the Khamsin gesture of honor before battle.

Jabari smiled, then let loose a loud, undulating cry. Now.

Time to attack.

Riding a donkey for three miles from the village of Haggi Quandil to the Amarna dig site had to prove her dedication to archaeology. Elizabeth Summers rubbed her sore behind and cursed. Couldn't the beast plod along any faster?

She flicked the donkey's reins. No use. The animal was more stubborn than Uncle Nahid. And it stank. No, it reeked.

No matter. Her senses had already adjusted to Egypt's overpowering sights, smells and sounds. Sour sweat of unwashed bodies, fragrant spices, the delicious odor of roasting lamb on a spit. The babble of Arabic, stunning pink skies at sunset, shimmering heat that wrapped around her body like a warm cloak.

But nothing compared to the exhilaration of walking over sand that hid thousand-year-old mysteries. Elizabeth glanced at the lonely desert, wondering what awaited her at the excavation. Flinders Petrie had discovered the city once called Akhetaten, now called Amarna after the local village. Centuries of dirt coughed up history and she would participate in the discoveries.

Bordering the Nile, Amarna nestled in a flat valley eight miles long. Three miles to the east, steep limestone cliffs marked the beginning of the Arabian Desert. Sunbaked mountains and valleys stretched for miles beyond the cliffs to the Red Sea.

Heat seeped deep into her bones. It felt good after Boston's winter chill. Sleepy from the sun's warmth, Elizabeth slipped into a familiar daydream. She was an ancient Egyptian royal returning from worshiping with her priests in the temple. Straight, blunt-cut black hair swung to her linen-draped shoulders. Dusty black kohl lined her sloe eyes. The cloying scent of myrrh clung to her clipped, rounded nails.

Her dream vanished as she remembered the reality. Uncle Nahid's telegram said the team uncovered a plaster pavement about twenty-five feet long in Akhetaten's central palace. Flinders had preserved the floor by coating it with tapioca and water using one finger. Uncle Nahid persuaded him to let her draw it. If her sketches impressed him, perhaps he would let her do more. Maybe Flinders would even hire her as an artist for other excavations.

Then her shoulders slumped as she remembered the rest of Uncle Nahid's cable. The rules: "Walk to the excavation. Flinders wants no animals onsite. When riding offsite, do not ride astride. Only men can excavate. Women aren't strong enough. No swearing. No showing off your knowledge of the eighteenth dynasty. You're only twenty-two years old and it isn't polite to brag. No mention of any of those despicable suffrage activities in Boston. Above all, you must act like a lady."

Already she had violated Rule Number One. Elizabeth glanced down at her bunched-up skirt and the very unladylike position of her legs. So much for Rule Number Two. Rule Number Three lay in wait. That one she was determined to break. Women weren't strong enough to excavate? *I can do anything a man can do. I'll prove it.*

Across the flat plain she saw a distant bustle of activity at the dig site, like black ants crawling over white frosted cake. She frowned. Black ants? Workers usually wore white . . . not black . . . and the sounds coming from the site echoed with frantic screams, not the singsong rhythm of picks and axes.

What in the name of heaven was going on? At the dig's perimeter, Elizabeth jerked the reins, bringing her slow progress to a complete halt. Her jaw dropped at the chaos erupting before her. Dozens of indigo-robed men yelling blood-curdling cries trampled over the site.

Veils draped across their faces, they overturned wheelbarrows of dirt and tables holding artifacts. A paraffin lamp slid to the ground, splotching the tawny sand with oozing fuel. One warrior brandishing a long sword hacked at earthernware jars, sending precious quarts of fresh water gushing out. Stunned archaeologists scrambled out of their determined paths. Terrified diggers ran screaming from the fierce desert warriors. "Run for your lives," one yelled. "The Khamsin!"

Her mouth went dry as she wildly surveyed the scene, looking for Uncle Nahid. Nervous fingers twisted stray locks that escaped the loosely pinned chignon at the nape of her neck. Earth flew up in miniature sand tornadoes, clogging her nostrils and making her sneeze. And then she saw it and her heart stilled. The palace floor. The delicate plaster Flinders had preserved flew in a dusty cloud as a warrior pulverized it with his horse's flaying hooves. A shorter man watching from horseback twirled a long scimitar in the air, hooting with glee as he did the same.

This deliberate, malicious destruction infuriated her. How dare they? They were destroying history! Useless now to sketch it, for nothing remained. The one chance she had to prove herself to Flinders disappeared under the pounding hooves. This last thought made her kick the donkey into action. It gave a protesting bray, but trotted toward the taller raider. Elizabeth stopped short of the pavement, sliding off the donkey and running up to the warrior with white-knuckled anger.

"Stop!" she screamed in Arabic. "What in the name of Allah are you doing? You are destroying the pavement! Oh, stop!"

The indigo-robed man whirled his mount around to face her. Probably he never had anyone, let alone a woman, tell him what to do before. *Good! It's about time someone did!*

The indigo veil hid all but his eyes, black as the desert night. Elizabeth recoiled, flustered. She had never seen such intense, penetrating eyes before. For a minute she stared into them and felt as if she glimpsed a mirror into her own soul.

Then she saw the destroyed floor. Deep gouges scarred

the beautiful design. Elizabeth sank to her knees with a loud wail. "Oh, look! It is all ruined! Ruined!" She sifted through the crumbled plaster.

The sword-wielding warrior leaned over his saddle, pointing his long, wicked blade at her. "Jabari, what do you want with this woman? Shall I take her captive? Or at least gag her mouth shut?" The man sounded bewildered yet menacing.

"No, Nazim, leave her be." His deep, sensual tones caressed her. Elizabeth shivered at the raw power and command in that husky voice. The leader. Which made him responsible for this barbaric act. Her temper sailed out of control.

"How can you do this? Stupid, senseless destruction! Weeks of work, ruined! Haven't you a brain in your head? Don't you realize this is your past?" Arabic tumbled out of her mouth in a steady stream.

Then with a loud curse, she broke Uncle Nahid's Rule Number Four. The leader's dark eyes widened. Finely arched black brows rose as if her words bemused him.

"Jabari, did she just call you a donkey?" the one called Nazim asked in a wondering voice.

"No, I called him an ass!" she said in English. Elizabeth recoiled as Jabari fixed her with a steely look. Several warriors rode up, surrounding her like wolves salivating for a fresh kill. Suddenly she felt very small and very alone.

Then she looked at the ruined floor. Elizabeth picked up fragments of plaster. Hot tears stung her eyes. "How could you do this? You have no right invade and destroy this find," she whispered, cradling the shards in her palms.

"No, my lady, you are wrong. We have every right, for this is our ancestors' sacred city. You are the invaders," Jabari stated with quiet dignity.

She looked up at him, frustrated grief mixing with a mystical sense of awe. There was something about the proud way he sat upon his horse, his long ebony hair spilling almost halfway down his back—as if he once ruled the sacred city with a firm hand. And the archaeological team was a horde picking everything clean like vultures tearing apart carrion. His erect posture reminded her of a powerful king capable of destroying enemies with one uttered command to his men.

Piqued by her odd reaction, Elizabeth stood and flung the plaster at him. It sprayed a white cloud over his blue robe. She lifted her chin skyward, daring him to react.

His piercing black eyes narrowed, but he snapped an order to his men and they whirled their horses around, racing away. The leader's mount snorted and danced with impatience.

Elizabeth's courage wavered as he withdrew his sword. He twirled it gracefully, then lowered it to her. Sharp steel kissed the air near her face. She stood motionless, not daring to breathe as the blade's dull edge stroked her throat. Then he drew his sword back and rumbled in a low threat. "Beware. You have not seen the last of us. I, Jabari bin Tarik Hassid, sheikh of the great Khamsin warriors of the wind, leave you with this warning. Leave our holy city now, or you will suffer the consequences. This I promise."

Elizabeth watched him ride off into a cloud of dust, then vanish, like a hot, dry desert wind.

"What in the name of Allah was that?"

His second-in-command echoed his own bewilderment. Jabari shook his head as they rode through a dry riverbed that cut through the immense limestone cliffs sheltering Akhetaten. Pale gray rock formations passed as they pressed deeper into the *wadi*.

"Never have I seen a woman display such spirit. Or foolishness. Or passion . . . other than in bed," Nazim marveled.

Jabari felt awed and angered. Such a woman! Fire in her heart and those haunting eyes, as lapis as the clear Egyptian sky. Her gaze had locked with his as if boring deep into his innermost soul. He took a long, calming breath to quell the emotions raging inside him. As leader of the Khamsin, he required a keen, alert mind at all times. Emotions were a luxury he could not afford. Emotions made one fuzzy-minded. Emotions diluted strength needed to wage war.

"Riding a donkey! She had courage while the *samak* ran like frightened sheep." Nazim laughed and slapped his thigh.

Jabari smiled beneath his veil in agreement. Nazim called the English *samak* because they were as white as a fish's belly. And equally soft and weak. But the woman, she was no fish.

"She called me an ass," Jabari stated, still astonished. No woman in his tribe would dare raise her voice to the sheikh, let alone call him an insulting name.

"She would have called you worse if she spoke better Arabic," Nazim pointed out. "At least she did not call you a donkey."

"Why do you think she was there?" he asked.

Nazim gave a shrug barely decipherable under his *binish.* "Who knows why these Westerners do what they do. Perhaps they tire of playing in the sand and are starting their own harem."

"I thought you said the Western men knew not how to make love to a woman. That they did not know the secrets of one hundred kisses or to rub her soft skin with perfumed oils, but flopped about like *samak* out of the water," Jabari quipped.

"*Flopped* is the word. Their manhood is as soft-bellied as they are!" Nazim laughed.

Jabari snorted in shared derision as his stomach pitched and rolled. A woman among the infidel invaders.

The law was clear. Death came with swift swords to those disturbing the sacred hiding place of the Almha. Jabari and his men had no qualms about doling out the punishment with sharpened scimitars to foolish men who dared to try.

But a woman . . . that was another matter. Entirely.

"Do you think they will leave now?" Nazim asked.

"Every time I see them picking at the earth, I feel sickened."

Jabari looked at the hope in his amber eyes, understanding his best friend's anguish.

"No, Nazim, they will not. They are stubborn, these English. It will take more than destruction to make them leave."

"Perhaps my blade can convince them more." Nazim withdrew his scimitar. Sunlight bounced off gleaming steel as he swished it through the air in an arc.

"Not unless they begin digging near the Almha. They are not even close. I want no unnecessary bloodshed," Jabari ordered.

Nazim sheathed his blade, nodding. "Especially now that we know there is a woman present."

Jabari closed his eyes, remembering the image the Englishwoman burned into his brain. She was a mirage in the distant heat that beckoned to him like a ripe pomegranate tempting a man mad with hunger. Her long, lacy white dress did little to disguise generous curves. A man could put both hands around that tiny waist and pull her into a tight embrace. Wind had reached beneath her straw hat and grasped in its fist strands of hair pale as golden sand.

He drew in a harsh breath, remembering her softness, the full lush lips and high cheekbones. Such proud elegance.

Opening his eyes, Jabari suppressed a groan of desire. The Western woman was an oasis for the eyes, but it wasn't merely her body that made him long for her. It was her manner that captured his heart. Her regal confidence spoke of a woman as dignified as the ancient Egyptian royals.

Nazim broke into his thoughts with a lusty laugh. "And such a woman too. Those breasts. Did you see them? Huge!"

"I saw them," Jabari said tersely. "I also saw how upset she was when I smashed the floor."

"Heretic art in the palace where Nefertiti and Akhenaten

lived. An obscenity to our people." Nazim shook his head. "She is a foreigner who does not understand the history of our tribe's hatred for Nefertiti and reverence for Queen Kiya."

"Nefertiti was a power-hungry whore." Nazim removed his veil, leaned over and spat on the ground in disgust. He tucked the face cloth back into his turban, adjusting the headpiece.

This time Jabari let himself laugh. "My friend, if Nefertiti were alive, you would offer her to the English as a sacrifice."

"And hand them my sword to do the deed." Nazim's amber eyes flashed with sudden humor. "She was beneath Kiya and should have never been appointed first wife."

Nazim, like many of his fellow tribesmen, still held a formidable loyalty to Kiya. Lately Jabari found himself questioning that devotion to a long-dead queen. He had sworn a sacred oath to obey Kiya's edict and kill whoever disturbed the Almha. But days like today, he felt the tug of duty pulling him two ways—as leader of his people and as the Almha's chief protector.

He cast a sideways glance at his friend. "Nazim, do you believe in the legend of Kiya returning to us? That she will lead us to peace and prosperity?"

Tiny lines formed at the corners of his eyes as Nazim scrunched his brow. "I believe in the power of true love. Is it not what founded our tribe—love for only one god? And Kiya's love for Ranefer."

Jabari snorted with impatience. "I believe more in the Almha's powerful influence than in any love story. The Al-Hajid know it exists. If they find it, our enemies will have the power to rule my people because they cling to superstition that he who claims the Almha is worthy of worship as an ancient god."

"That is why we guard it, Jabari. Why every time we see those English dig, my blood boils. They know nothing of the tremendous power of the disk or the agony our ancestors suffered in guarding it! Those grounds are sacred." Nazim's voice trembled with angry frustration.

"Steady my friend. I, too, hate what they are doing. Perhaps we did scare them off. Musab is there in disguise as a digger. He will report back to me if our plan worked."

"If not, we will attack again," Nazim said, calmer now.

Attack again, when so many more problems plagued their tribe? When his people faced hunger in the coming summer because of poor crop harvests last year? Staggering burdens of responsibility and leadership weighted his mind.

"I need to meet with the elders about breeding new horses for the season to increase our income," Jabari half-muttered, tugging at the reins. His exquisite white mare, a product of one such breeding, seemed to sense her master's discomfort. She shook her head, making the blue tassels covering her muzzle dance.

"Easy, Sahar," he crooned, patting her withers. "Soon, we will be home."

"Home. Fresh camel's milk. And dinner. I am starving and my mother promised to cook couscous for dinner," Nazim complained.

"Your mother's couscous could poison a dung beetle," Jabari mocked.

"May the fleas of a thousand camels nestle in your crotch for insulting my mother's cooking," Nazim shot back.

"Better the fleas off one thousand camels than one flea off the backs of the English," Jabari replied and both men laughed.

"Except that woman. I would not mind a flea off her back nestling in my crotch." He gave his sheikh an amused wink in shared male camaraderie.

Jabari did not smile. His friend's display of indifferent lust filled him with a jealous, disquieting anger. Her regal grace demanded dignity, not a crude inventory of her body parts, as becoming as those parts were. He shook his head, confused by the inner turmoil of emotions. Why was he so taken by a foreign woman when so much beauty rested within his own people's tents?

She possessed a reckless courage and acted assured and highly intelligent. Jabari thought about this. Such a woman would never be quiet and meek, like the women in his tribe, but assertive and independent. Defiant even.

And dangerous. Jabari lost his mother when she asserted her independence. Better for him to have a submissive woman, who would obey and let him protect her, than to face another heartache.

He stared at the walls of rock, thinking of what a woman of fire the blond beauty was. Would she shiver with delight as he caressed her arms and led a trail of kisses down her neck? Or fight like a spirited horse that needed taming? Jabari's loins tightened at the idea of that pleasure.

While studying in Cairo, he heard jokes that Western women living in the city were as fierce as warriors when bedded. Only the strongest men could handle them. This only intrigued Jabari.

He shifted in his saddle, tugging beneath his indigo *binish* at trousers that suddenly seemed too tight. Inwardly, he groaned. How long had it been since he'd allowed himself the pleasures of a woman in his arms?

A hesitant cough next to him drew his attention. Nazim gave him an odd look.

"Are you all right, sire? Is something binding you?"

"Fine," he snapped. "You ride too slow. Come, let us hurry."

Jabari was glad his friend couldn't read minds. Daydreaming about love play with a Western woman! Such fantasies were beneath a Khamsin chieftain.

But as they galloped off toward the high desert, he found himself dwelling on her. Clearly she shared with the English the same burning desire to discover what lay below the sand. Otherwise, she would not be there.

What would it be like to bed such a passionate spirit?

* * *

"Elizabeth, I praise Allah you arrived safe and sound and those jackals did not harm you."

In a rare display of affection, Nahid Wilson hugged her. Born in Egypt, he returned there to live after receiving a science degree from Oxford University. Nahid devoted his life to studying ancient Egypt, working with archaeologists like Flinders Petrie. He rarely traveled to Boston, except for a recent visit to help move his mother into a tuberculous sanatorium.

Releasing Elizabeth, he scratched his salt-and-pepper beard. Hooded brown eyes swept over the ruins of the upturned camp. Nahid gestured toward the destroyed floor.

"At least Flinders sketched the pavement before they destroyed it. So you see what we face here. You must be very careful, Elizabeth. This is no ordinary dig."

So Flinders had refused to wait for her artistic talents. Elizabeth nudged aside keen disappointment, worried more about the dig's future than her moment of glory.

"Uncle Nahid, what is Mr. Petrie going to do? I can't see him abandoning the dig. Not now."

"We had no time to react. They rode like the wind. . . . I couldn't even grab my gun. Recently I met . . . a sheikh of a tribe not far from here. The Al-Hajid are the Khamsin's worst enemies. If I hire a few to patrol the site, we will be protected. Those jackals will think twice about attacking again if the Al-Hajid guard our dig! When I see Flinders, I shall tell him."

Elizabeth twisted a loose strand of hair around one index finger. Finally, she would meet the great man. This made her more nervous than confronting that desert warrior. Flinders had carved out a reputation as an austere eccentric with a demand for exacting detail. Every artifact, even rubbish, was cataloged. The eccentric part came from his odd behavior. At Giza ten years ago, he took to wearing only trousers and a pink vest. Outside the pyramid, that was. Inside . . .

"Is Mr. Petrie wearing . . . clothing?" she whispered.

His bushy brows contracted. "Elizabeth!"

"Well . . . you were the one who told me he measured the inside of the Giza pyramids totally . . . naked!"

"It was hot and he was alone. Elizabeth, mind your tongue. Here he comes."

To her relief the eminent archaeologist wore the same clothing as her uncle—white shirt with the sleeves rolled up, khaki trousers and sturdy shoes. Flinders's bearded face looked brooding and his eyes bulged in a curious manner. His gaze roved around the site, until settling on her. Even after her uncle made introductions, his expression did not change.

Then his sight swept over her straying donkey, munching on the remains of a digger's lunch of flatbread and cheese. Those large, inquisitive eyes bulged even more.

"He's mine," Elizabeth explained, lifting her shoulders. "I know you said no animals on the site, but I was so excited I couldn't walk. I couldn't wait to get here and see . . ."

"This?" Flinders gave a grudging smile as he gestured toward an overturned table. "Plenty to see before this fiasco. Fortunately, I preserved the pavement on paper."

"The Khamsin will not attack again, Flinders," Nahid stated. He outlined his idea as the archaeologist nodded.

"Excellent plan, Nahid. I heard of the Khamsin warriors of the wind. They veil their faces before enemies and strike as swiftly as the killing windstorm they are named after. Why they are interested in this site, I have no idea."

"They are bloodthirsty cowards," Nahid growled.

"But, Uncle Nahid, they didn't hurt anyone. If they were bloodthirsty, why did they spare lives?" Elizabeth thought of the way the sheikh's blade caressed her throat and shivered.

"They will," he grumbled ominously. "The sheikh has waited until now to attack but he will return. I sense it."

"He said his name was Jabari," Elizabeth mused out loud. "He warned me, us, to leave or suffer the consequences."

As Nahid went into a sputtering fit about the consequences the Al-Hajid would deliver to Jabari, Elizabeth silently rolled the word on her tongue. Jabari. Ancient Egyptian name meaning "brave." She suspected the sheikh deserved his name.

Why did she defend him? The man destroyed what she revered, then threatened her. Beware. Elizabeth scowled. Was she one of those romantic, starry-eyed girls who turned to mush over a man with an aura of danger about him?

She forgot the sheikh as a digger trotted over, bearing fragments of pottery recovered from the muddle. Elizabeth plucked a piece from his palms. A delicate shade of pink clay, its decorative edges reflected the style of early Aegean pottery.

"From Cyprus, probably. Proof that Egypt traded with other Bronze Age cultures," Elizabeth murmured. She glanced up into the men's faces. Flinders looked intrigued. Uncle Nahid—furious.

"Elizabeth, come with me. I want to talk with you."

She handed back the relic and followed Nahid to a shaded field table that survived the destruction. He turned over two crates that served as chairs and beckoned her to sit.

He frowned in patriarchal disapproval. "Elizabeth, I'm quite disappointed in you. I didn't bring you here to show off. You must maintain a low profile."

"All I want is to join the excavation." Elizabeth fumbled with a sketchbook and pen left on the table. "Why else would I have studied so hard? Besides, when we start digging for . . ."

Elizabeth stopped short as Nahid put a finger to his lips, imploring her silence. His gaze darted around the camp. She studied his face, guileless and smooth of expression. The dark, hooded eyes were adroit at concealing secrets from the rest of the archaeological team.

"Thank Allah the Khamsin dogs did not destroy all the palace. And they did not touch the temple," Nahid said, changing the subject with an oily smoothness.

Elizabeth picked up a pen and dipped it into a well of India ink that had survived the destruction. She began doodling a pharaoh's face with an elongated skull, fleshy lips and slanted eyes. "The temple is a wonderful find. We can tell so much about the culture from the way they built their temples. They worshiped Aten, the sun god. Their temples were built open to the sky."

"Akhenaten was not a typical pharaoh. He worshiped only Aten and moved the capital from Thebes to here to do so," Nahid reminded her. "His enemies destroyed Aten's temples and the entire city after he died. They even erased all memories of him from Egypt's records. They called him a heretic."

"Heretic or not, he built a fabulous city. Imagine what it was like in ancient days. Nobles living in columned houses with carved, gilded chairs, thick rugs and cushions. Priests offering worship in open-air temples to Aten. And Akhenaten himself, racing in his chariot down the road," Elizabeth said dreamily.

"Imagine the wealth of gold they had," Nahid replied in a hardened voice.

Elizabeth's pen paused and she glanced upward. Seeing a covetous gleam in her uncle's eyes, she suppressed a shiver. Time for her to change the subject.

"If I gain field experience here, I could get a job as an artist with another expedition." She looked hopefully at Nahid.

"Don't count on it." His voice held a note of sympathy. "It's men's work. You're something of an anomaly."

She bent her head, unable to keep her lower lip from trembling. After a formal education at Vassar, the hard work, the fight to prove herself as an equal to the male students, and now Nahid crushed her hopes like bugs under his heels? She fought to keep her voice even.

"I grew up going with Daddy on digs all over the world. I can recite ancient Egyptian history better than half the men here. My Arabic is better than most, and my artwork is excellent. Why can't I do what I love?"

Her uncle sighed. "Elizabeth, just because your father was an archaeologist doesn't guarantee you a space as an artist in the field. Conditions are harsh in the best of circumstances and few women have the stamina for it." He patted her hand in an avuncular manner. "Your studies will serve you well as a librarian. That's a fine job for a woman."

A librarian. A destiny resigned to shelving musty volumes in dimly lit spaces instead of the thrills of unearthing ancient history in the sunshine. Elizabeth felt all her hopes and dreams crumble into dust as fine as the Egyptian sands.

Nahid glanced around and lowered his voice. "You'll have your chance later. When we find what we really came here for."

Elizabeth nodded with resignation, but reprimanded herself. Her own dreams must yield to their real mission here.

"If the paper I found is correct, then Amarna is the place . . ." she started to say.

"Shhhh." Nahid cut her off. He put a finger to his lips.

Elizabeth leaned over the table, whispering, "I pray we find the cure for Nana."

In contrast to other sites, Amarna, located halfway between the ancient capital of Thebes and its modern capital, Cairo, had no treasures of gold and precious gems. Or so everyone thought.

Everyone but Elizabeth and Nahid.

And they'd be damned before they told anyone how Elizabeth found a piece of papyrus tucked away in a secret compartment of her grandmother's treasured mahogany chest. A very interesting papyrus that told of the Almha, a golden disk as bright as the sun, buried in an ancient city called Akhetaten.

It was, after all, a family matter.

Chapter Two

Elizabeth headed for the Nile that afternoon, desperate to escape tormenting thoughts.

You must concentrate on Nana and not your own selfish concerns. Doctors had banished Nana to a tuberculous sanatorium in New York. Nahid, her mother's brother, was her only other relative, and thus Flinders had been persuaded to let Elizabeth join the dig.

Her throat closed tight with sudden grief. Crying wouldn't help. Finding the Almha might. The papyrus indicated ancient remedies for respiratory diseases were inscribed on the disk.

The papyrus she'd found in her grandmother's trunk while cleaning out her attic had been yellowed with age but well-preserved. Nana had kept it locked up with a lovely white *kuftan* trimmed with gold embroidery that looked like a wedding garment. Elizabeth also found an ankh on a leather strip of necklace.

When she asked her grandmother about the items, the older woman had gotten so upset Elizabeth vowed to never bring it up again. She suspected it had to do with the Bedouin tribe in Egypt Nana left behind long ago. Every time Elizabeth asked about her past, her grandmother refused to talk about it.

The trunk's contents indicated Nana hadn't rejected all her Bedouin memories. How ironic if the Almha, hidden within the sands her grandmother abandoned, had the remedy for her illness.

A trickle of sweat, like a single tear, beaded at her temple and then slid down past her neck. At the river's edge, under the cooling shade of date palms, she felt her spirits lift. A *felucca* caught her attention as the ancient boat sailed serenely past on its way to a distant location. The quiet waters slushing against the riverbank soothed her.

Inhaling the damp, earthy scent of the river's perfume, Elizabeth let the romance unfolding before her eyes wash over her in a gentle flood. The mighty Nile kept mysteries tucked into her deep breast, whispering to Elizabeth of proud queens and powerful pharaohs who had bathed in her silky embrace. A soft wind caressed the palms. Leaves rustled as if agreeing with the water's revelation of ancient secrets.

"All you need is a handsome stranger on a white horse, carrying you off to his tent," she said aloud, laughing, then stopped. Elizabeth had no idea what happened between men and women behind closed bedroom doors . . . or in the privacy of a desert tent.

The desert bandit she encountered certainly did. *Jabari.* Elizabeth suspected the confident manner he displayed in controlling his horse applied to everything he did. She shivered, thinking of his broad shoulders and piercing eyes. A strange tingling she didn't understand filled her lower belly.

She imagined him galloping up to her, pulling her onto his steed and racing off into the vast desert together. Then she shook her head free of the image and scowled.

"Ridiculous! Love is for silly girls who adore waiting on men. I will not be some man's slave," she grumbled as if her words could break the magic of the Nile's charm.

Elizabeth sighed and turned to head back, almost running headlong into Nahid.

"There you are. Time to go back to work."

She grimaced. The dig site had been restored and work resumed. Flinders had ignored her after that brief flash of interest. Now she couldn't sketch. Nahid ordered her to catalog finds because of her "excellent penmanship."

"I can't wait to record more notes about what *men* find."

"You know how important your job is," Nahid said in a low voice. "I need you to let me know if you see any clues about the location of a small temple. Once we find it, we'll start our own secret excavation."

"The papyrus said the Almha was buried by Kiya in an ancient place of great rejoicing. It mentions Akhenaten gave Kiya the Maru Aten as her private temple to worship the Aten, but why would she bury it there?"

"Why wouldn't she bury it there?" he replied.

"I think there's another place more sacred to her, a place the pharaoh would never suspect. He needed that disk and probably dug everywhere for it. 'Stripped of the Almha, the symbol of Aten's power, the great pharaoh lost influence, for the temples lay in waste, the people no longer worshiping the Aten or Akhenaten,' " Elizabeth quoted the papyrus.

Nahid shielded his eyes and glanced skyward. "We'll find it. Moonlight's the best time to dig. Can't say you've excavated for buried treasure then, eh? Too romantic for words."

Remembering her earlier daydream, Elizabeth frowned. "Romance? Not for me. I'd rather belly dance naked in a river full of hungry crocodiles."

She could care less about treasure and love. She only wanted to find a treatment to save Nana's life.

But she could not totally banish thoughts of the mysterious Jabari spiriting her away. Taking her far away from responsibility, duty and the heartache of lost hopes to a place where she would be free to do as she wished, to indulge every desire.

Her dream was a silly storybook fantasy. Elizabeth refused to allow her practical mind to dwell on it for long.

Besides, such a thing would never happen to her.

An excellent day for a hunt. His prized peregrine falcon had downed two hares. They swung now from his belt. Jabari's boots stirred a small dust cloud as he strode through the pebbled sand, passing the long line of black tents. Women nodded in respect. Warriors called greetings, but he barely noticed. Normally hunting cleared his mind. Not today. He felt drugged by the woman at the dig site. She haunted his thoughts.

Next to his tent, a tall acacia tree provided sprawling shade. Jabari settled his bird upon a perch beneath its branches. With a loving hand, he absently stroked Ghazi. The woman's regal pride echoed the bird's. Both were independent spirits. Ghazi was tame now, but it had taken Jabari several weeks to gentle the falcon. The bird had fought him fiercely. He suspected the Western woman, if captured, would react the same.

"Jabari, I must speak with you."

He settled the leather glove back onto its nail and glanced at Nazim, standing protectively in front of a woman. Wearing a black *abbaya,* she clutched three young children to her as she bowed before him. The woman hung her head, refusing to look up.

"This woman needs to ask something of you." Nazim's jaw tensed beneath his beard as he glanced at the youngest child.

Jabari looked at the little boy, his mouth turning to dry sand at what he saw. Huge brown eyes swimming with tears engulfed his thin face. A dirt-streaked mouth encircled an equally dirt-streaked thumb. Jabari squatted, taking the boy's small hand into his large one. It felt paper light. The child acted listless. Patches of coarse black hair had fallen out of his scalp. A tiny belly protruded from beneath his garment.

Malnutrition. He saw the signs years ago in Cairo. Jabari

glanced up at the mother's hollow cheeks, the despairing blankness in her eyes as she finally lifted her head.

"Sire, I come from Haggi Quandil. My husband died and his family threw me out because there was not enough food." She lowered her voice. "The men, they paid me to . . . pleasure them. But the village elder heard and threatened to stone me. I heard of your great generosity. If it pleases you, I will share your bed. I beg you. I will do anything to save my children."

Jabari's heart twisted with grief as he stood. He struggled for words. Silently, he unhooked the hares from his belt and handed them to the woman. He glanced at his second-in-command.

"Nazim, see to it that they are housed and have one of my cousins care for their needs. I will provide food from my stock of sheep and goats and anything else required."

Turning to the woman, he gave her his gentlest smile.

"Never again will you submit to a man's lust to feed your little ones. I take you into my clan as a sister and place you under my protection. Nazim will speak with the village elder about this. If anyone dares to harm you, they face my wrath."

The woman clutched the dead hares as if holding the gold of the pharaohs. "Thank you. Bless you, sire," she whispered.

He rubbed his chin, watching as Nazim led her away. Already the hunger began. First in the village. Next it would spread to his own tribe. A shrieking gaggle of children chasing one of the dogs that guarded the flocks passed by. Jabari stared at them, his stomach clenched from worry. How long before they began looking as desperate?

Although lacking an appetite now, he settled onto a hand-woven red carpet before the campfire as his female relatives began dinner preparations. Asriyah, his aunt, and her four daughters diced vegetables and tossed them into in a large copper pot where water bubbled over a crackling fire.

Their rhythmic movements soothed his troubled mind. Clad in indigo long-sleeved dresses, their heads covered with scarves to protect against the sun, they swayed with an inherrent grace that made every movement a dance. Silver earrings caught reflections of the setting sun and jingled as the women moved. The women of his tribe had a fluid suppleness like river water. Yet even they could not rival the lovely stranger's elegance. Gazing upon her beauty had refreshed his weary spirit. Jabari closed his eyes, remembering it now.

"I saw what you did. It was a good thing, my nephew, although now we have no meat for dinner. Unless you want me to slaughter one of the sheep," his aunt said.

Opening one eye, he glanced at her. "It will serve us well to forgo meat for one dinner," he said, feeling an instinctive need to begin rationing food.

Asriyah lowered herself to the ground in one graceful motion. "We could always borrow from Nazim's mother, although she is cooking couscous again and it tastes horrible."

Jabari threw back his head and laughed. His good humor restored, he lazily stretched his legs before him.

"Why do you not join the other men while we prepare the meal? I am sure the Majli are eager to talk with you."

"I will talk with the elders later," he said, giving a dismissive wave.

"As long as you are here . . ." Asriyah's eyes surveyed the grounds. Small fires glowed where the other families had set up their evening meals before their black goat-hair tents. A circle of older men sat under a date palm, talking.

Finally, Asriyah seemed satisfied that no men were within hearing distance. Her aging brown eyes lost their usual merriment and became serious.

"Jabari, forgive me for bringing up the subject, but the women in your harem wish to learn to read. Especially Badra."

The peace he'd felt earlier slipped away. Jabari's brow furrowed as he looked his aunt directly in the eye. "No."

The word came out as direct and biting as he intended.

"But Badra pines to learn. Farah would not mind as well. Farah says if you marry her, her reading would prove useful to you," Asriyah pressed, still keeping her voice respectful.

"I will never marry any of my concubines. Khamsin law states a warrior must have only one wife and she must be pure. Farah and Badra were not virgins when I rescued them," Jabari retorted, troubled that Farah kept hoping he would marry her.

He thought of the women under his protection, kept in a guarded compound in the village of Amarna. Beautiful, exotic and meek, not daring to present their requests to him, but using his aunt instead. The Western woman would not be so timid. He suspected she was highly educated as well.

I have plenty of things I would enjoy teaching that woman, Jabari thought, a smile tugging at his mouth. *And none of them have anything to do with reading.*

He imagined her clad in a flowing silk gown of lapis to reflect her eyes. Her slender form reclined on his bed against several plush cushions, waiting for him to begin the lessons.

He caught his aunt looking at him with an air of expectation. Jabari tightened his jaw.

"Women are to be cherished and protected by our men. Our warriors' strict code of honor calls for it. That is the way of our people. They do not need an education."

"If that woman you just helped were educated, perhaps her son would not be so ill. She could find a job and help herself," Asriyah said softly.

She had a point. Why did he cling to ancient customs when he prided himself on being a man of vision? Jabari treasured his own education, for it taught him valuable tools to help his people. His heart struggled between past traditions and present problems. And then he remembered and narrowed his eyes at his aunt.

"Do you forget what happened to my mother? If she

never learned to read, she would still be with us today." Jabari's rage intensified. He clutched his hand into a fist as the grief surfaced again. Slamming it down, he glared at her.

Asriyah heaved a sigh from deep within her chest, "No, I could never forget. I see your wisdom in this." She bowed her head in respect to his words.

Troubled by her sad expression, Jabari squeezed her hand, for he truly loved his aunt. "Trust me, it is for the best. Nothing good can come of women becoming educated. The council would agree with me on this."

Hope dawned in her eyes. "The council respects you. They follow your word. If you changed your mind, so would they."

"All but one. And here he comes. More problems, I am certain." He could not help releasing a frustrated sigh.

She gave him a troubled glance. "Jabari, you are as honorable as your father, Allah rest his soul. You are a fearless warrior and one of the most powerful leaders our tribe has known. But you are only twenty-six. So much rests on your shoulders at such a young age. I worry about you."

He smiled, trying to reassure her. "Do not. I walk with the spirit of our ancestors and they give me strength and might."

Asriyah opened her mouth to respond but shut it as a shadow fell over them. Jabari looked up to see his grandfather, Nkosi, standing before him.

"My grandson, you must meet with the Majli on a matter of grave importance. Musab has returned as well." The elderly man, proud as a lion and as dignified, spoke in reverent words justifying Jabari's role as sheikh, but the tone brooked no quarter. Jabari nodded and stood. He bid his aunt good-bye and walked with his grandfather to the men, who stood upon his arrival. The circle had grown to include his commanders and Nazim, he realized with dismay as he sat. It had gone from a friendly informal group to one signifying something more ominous. His gaze shot over to a struggling man brought forward by two warriors.

Jabari recognized him as one of the tribesmen who cared for the animal flocks.

"This . . . dog was discovered digging for the sacred Almha," said Nkosi, his dark eyes flashing with anger. "Every person in the tribe knows the penalty."

One of his own people? Jabari held up a hand. "Wait. I wish to know why someone would risk his life. Why did you do it?"

"I did no such thing," the man whined. "Your men are mistaken. I only was trying to protect it from the English."

He lied, Jabari realized as he watched the man avoid his gaze and the pulse jump in his neck.

"Why should you protect it? Now that the English are here, we have a market for it. I will ask the council to discuss giving up the sacred oath. It is too valuable to leave in the sand."

The man's beady eyes shone with avarice. "The English will pay much for it, I know, it is gold . . . and I deserve a share."

Jabari's stomach churned with disgust. He turned to the elders. "Should we give up our sacred oath and sell the disk?"

The Majli scowled and said in unison, "No."

Nkosi leveled a look at the prisoner. "As chief elder, I uphold the ancient law protecting the Almha. I decide the fate of those of our people foolish enough to unearth it." He turned to the warriors holding the man. "Kill him," he said briefly.

The guards turned to Jabari for confirmation. The sheikh gave a grave nod.

The man shrieked as they led him away. Jabari watched, repulsion rising in his throat. The English brought more than tools with them. They brought greed and it infected his people.

When Nkosi suggested retiring to the ceremonial tent for a formal meeting, Jabari's alarm intensified. They headed for the small black tent, rolling the sides down to guarantee privacy.

"*Assalaamu Alaikum,*" he said. Jabari settled onto the carpet as they returned his traditional greeting of peace. He analyzed the mood of the Majlis. Each elder represented one of the twelve Khamsin clans. Although he ruled the Khamsin, the elders held great influence. As a group, they had the power to strip him of power and vote for a new sheikh if they thought it best for the tribe. Individually, if displeased, a Majli could resign, causing a break in the clans and the tribe's solidarity. It was Jabari's job to maintain unity as well as govern his people.

This was why his grandfather resigned as sheikh years ago. Nkosi had nearly split the clans when he gave away one of the tribe's secrets. He relinquished power to Jabari's father, ensuring the Hassid clan retained leadership. However, the clans respected him so much they asked Nkosi to become chief elder.

The Majlis' gray-bearded faces looked disturbed. He realized why as his most valued spy sat before him. Musab's bushy brows furrowed. He tensed every muscle in his thin frame.

"Sire, I have troubling news. The raid did not work. Indeed, the infidels have retaliated by bringing in Al-Hajid warriors."

A tremendous intake of breaths sounded as if all on the honored council were gasping their last. The thought would have amused Jabari if he weren't so shocked himself.

"How could this have happened? The Al-Hajid have not dared to venture to this part of the desert since their last raid on our camp a year ago," Nkosi demanded.

"We spilled enough of their blood then to frighten them away for good. So I had hoped," Nazim muttered.

"We have problems from those jackals mounting *ghazus* against the caravans in the south," Izzah, one of his commanders, added.

Jabari held up a hand. "All of you, quiet. I need to hear from Musab exactly what has occurred. Continue. Why do the English dig in our sacred city?"

Honest bewilderment flickered through Musab's dark eyes. "Sire, I am ashamed to inform you I do not know. My English is too poor to understand them. I have failed you." The warrior hung his head, his shoulders slumping in apparent disgrace.

Guilt coursed through Jabari. He'd sent his finest spy, who understood a smidgen of English, to do the work of a lowly servant. Musab was trained to report the movements of enemy camps, to select the weak points for raiding parties. Jabari had given him a task destined to fail. Not only wasn't Musab's English fluent enough, he also had to perform the very task they despised the team for—disrupt their ancestors' sacred city.

Jabari laid a hand upon Musab's shoulder and spoke in a firm voice. "Be of good cheer, Musab. You have not failed me. I do not need you to echo the words of the English, but to be my eyes. You are the best eyes I have. You are my desert hawk who sees all."

The older man straightened with pride. "There are at least ten Al-Hajid warriors armed with rifles. They guard the diggers during the day and the site at night."

Bad news indeed, for it made nighttime raids too risky. He looked at Nazim. "Rifles. Men of honor fight with blades."

"Men of modern times fight with rifles," Nazim replied. "We lack sufficient ammunition for an attack. We must purchase some."

Thinking of the economic problems plaguing the tribe, Jabari frowned. "I do not like the idea, but I agree. Use the funds from the last sale of mares. Hopefully, it will be replaced."

He did not voice his fears that it would not. The Al-Hajid sheikh, Fareeq bin Hamid Taleq, had been raiding caravans and barricading the southern trade routes to the Red Sea. Jabari suspected the Al-Hajid's terrorism had another purpose—to block access to the Khamsin's southern camp where they sold their purebred Arabian mares. If the campaign continued, they'd lose valuable customers. The horse-breeding business was their economic means of survival.

"In the meantime, I will risk no more of my men in a battle we cannot win. First we will discover what the infidels plan. If they do not dig near the Almha, its secret remains safe."

He glanced at his grandfather's face, carved with age much like well-worn rock. "We are bound to protect the Almha first."

"The blood oath must be honored. Your father once held fast to this, before that she-devil he married weakened and dishonored him." Nkosi made the sign against the Evil Eye.

Familiar grief and anger returned. Tarik had been killed by a British soldier in a raid barely six months after Jabari's mother left him. In the three years since, Jabari had shouldered the responsibility of leading his people.

Nkosi put an affectionate hand on his grandson's shoulder. "So many responsibilities assumed for one so young. You have done well. I am proud to call you my kin. I know when you choose a bride, she will be as respectful as a sheikh's wife should be. Tarik made a grave mistake by teaching your mother to read."

A flush of pride swept through Jabari at the rarely given praise. Although Nkosi was his wisest counselor and his advice rarely discarded, he often clashed with his grandson.

"We must find out what the English plan. I am the Almha's chief protector, and I speak excellent English. I will spy on the infidels." He glanced at Musab, not wanting to dishonor him. "Musab will continue his work at the dig site."

Protests greeted his words. Nazim gave him a worried look.

"I will go with you. It is much too dangerous with the Al-Hajid there. I will not violate my oath to protect you." Nazim touched the right sleeve of his *binish*. A falcon, the symbol of Jabari's clan, was tattooed on his upper right arm.

"You are my second-in-command, Nazim, as well as my guardian. I need you here to assume command while I am gone," Jabari responded.

"Sire, we cannot risk losing you," one elder protested.

"I must uphold my oath. It is a matter of honor," he stated.

He glanced at his grandfather, who frowned. "You are my only grandson. I see this as an unnecessary risk to your life."

"Do not fear. I will be most careful. I will go down to the dig site and hire myself out as a worker. I can blend in as effortlessly as a shadow. I shall be Asim, humble digger." Jabari smiled at the joke. *Asim* in Arabic meant "protector." And who better to protect Akhetaten's secret?

His best friend gave him a sly glance. "So be it. However, there is only one way I will remain here. Shave your beard and cut your hair to perfect your disguise."

"Cut my hair?" Jabari felt the locks that grew past his shoulder blades. The thought bothered him more than shaving his beard. His hair was the longest in the tribe, just a fraction longer than Nazim's. He eyed him with suspicion.

"To your shoulders. Then you will not stand out among the other diggers." Nazim's amber eyes sparked with mischief.

"You say this only to finally win our bet," he accused him.

Nazim shrugged. "Does it matter now whose hair is the longest? I am only concerned for your safety."

Nkosi waved his hand in an impatient manner. "Enough of this silliness. Nazim is right. Cut your hair and shave your beard. I will respect your decision to spy, although I do not like you working for the infidels. You are a warrior of the wind. Such work is beneath you. And the British are sly, treacherous dogs."

The old man hated the British as much as he hated the

Al-Hajid. Rage and grief constantly stoked his burning anger. Once Nkosi had dared to fall in love with a member of the Al-Hajid. He had arranged to wed her in a secret ceremony. But she had run away to Cairo instead and married a British officer.

Jabari's shoulders stiffened. "Nothing is beneath me if it means upholding my blood oath as a warrior for our people."

The old man nodded in approval, his lips thinned to a tight slash. "Indeed. Do as you must. Just take care. Who knows what tricks the infidel Westerners will play?"

Westerners. So many problems haunted him that thoughts of the Western woman offered a pleasant distraction. His body flooded with warmth as he remembered her soft curves. Was he truly holding fast to his blood oath to protect the Almha?

Or did a deeper, more passionate reason drive him to the dig site?

Chapter Three

Spine stiffer than a drapery rod. Corset squeezing her waist into waspish slenderness. High-collared, long-sleeved white dress draped in proper prudishness over her legs. Beneath a shaded canopy, Elizabeth sat on a crate at the field table, ready to loan her "excellent penmanship" to the cause of archaeology.

A passing worker ogled her. His gaze roved to her bodice, then he gave her a suggestive smile riddled with lust. Elizabeth returned the look with a cold stare.

Another one. Diggers, field workers and the Al-Hajid warriors guarding the camp accorded her no respect. They either gave her leering stares or made condescending remarks. Even her uncle refused to let her do more than record artifacts.

Sitting across from Elizabeth, Nahid wrote in the field catalog and called out specimen numbers to her. The catalog, a book with pages secured by a clamp, was one of the most important documents on the site. Flinders, unlike his predecessors, insisted on recording every single artifact, no matter how insignificant the find.

With meticulous precision, Elizabeth wrote in black ink about each artifact. She recorded the specimen number Nahid assigned to it as he jotted it down in the catalog.

They worked until Nahid snapped the book shut with a satisfied sigh. One of the Al-Hajid warriors, clad in a flowing crimson robe and loose white trousers, approached. Elizabeth resisted a shiver. The Al-Hajid warriors looked crueler than the Khamsin, although this one acted friendlier than the others.

He placed a cage fashioned from bamboo on the field table and looked at her uncle.

"Soon it is time for the noonday meal. Fresh meat, captured this morning by a villager," he said with a greedy look at the beautiful white dove. Elizabeth could almost see him drool.

"No!" She stood, grabbed the cage and peered inside. The gentle bird cooed, unaware of its impending doom.

"I'll pay you for her. Good cash," she offered.

Nahid glanced at her. "Elizabeth, it's just a dove. Egyptians eat them all the time."

"I know. But this one . . . it's beautiful. You used to own a dove. We could use her, train her to take messages back and forth like Isis did." She quoted a price to the warrior, who quoted another. They bartered until he seemed satisfied.

Elizabeth gave her uncle a pleading look. He dug into his pocket and gave the money to the warrior. Reaching between the bars, she stroked the dove's feathers.

"The day grows hot. Why don't you go back to the village and rest a while and bring the dove with you? I won't need you until much later." The suggestion was more of a command. She nodded, filling with resentment at being shoved off the dig site.

As she shuffled south to her hut in the village, Elizabeth's thoughts wandered to the dashing desert bandit. What did he look like beneath that veil? As she entertained the possibilities, an idea formed. Elizabeth smiled and picked up her pace.

About two hours later, she returned, minus the dove. And this time no one could leer at her or praise her penmanship.

Clad in a white turban, the trailing end of the cloth veiling her face, and a long shirtlike garment called a *thobe,* she blended in with the diggers. Elizabeth glanced around the busy dig site, then swiped an abandoned *turia,* shovel and wheelbarrow. She choose her spot away from the others—southeast of the Great Temple, just outside the *temenos* wall. The mud-brick wall marked the beginning of the temple. Layers of sand mixed with rock presented a challenge. Excavation required great skill, for she had to loosen earth while trying to prevent her short-handled hoe from shattering something that lay below the surface.

This was life. Dust in her hair, sweat streaming into her eyes, history in her hands. She sang a song in Arabic her Egyptian mother had taught her in childhood. Since she was little, Elizabeth had dreamed of visiting Egypt and unearthing her secrets. Beautiful Egypt. *Ta Meri,* the Egyptian phrase for land of love. Hauntingly barren desert rippling colors of amber, gold and sepia. Ever-present sun beating like a wild heartbeat in an azure sky that was scimitar sharp in its raw beauty.

She rolled the filled wheelbarrow to a mesh tray. Elizabeth used a small spade to shovel fill into the tray. Sifting through the earth, she found nothing.

Disappointed, she repeated the process, again finding nothing until only a bucket of fill remained in her wheelbarrow. Disgusted, she sucked in a quivering breath through the veil.

"Of all the sites, of all the areas, you had to pick one that was a complete and utter waste," she muttered aloud.

As she tilted the tray, something caught her eye. She picked it up and reached for her brush. With exquisite care, she swept the object free of dirt.

Large lips and a protruding nose. Part of a statue carved from indurated limestone! The great pharaoh himself rested in her hands. Her hands, hands that men thought good only for scribbling numbers, trembled with emotion. Elizabeth's throat closed tight with suffocating joy. Tears blurred her eyes.

She wanted to run up to the rugged limestone cliffs sheltering the valley and shout out her discovery. Her heart leaped in her chest, thudding thunderously with happiness.

Elizabeth turned the fragment over in her left palm. She gazed upon it and let history work its magic. She could almost smell the sour sweat as the artist grunted with concentration at his task, chiseling the statue to please his king. She closed her eyes and folded her palm over the specimen and found herself lost, drifting, back in time and space . . .

Pharaoh Akhenaten approached, a phalanx of bare-chested royal guards with sharp sickle swords protecting him. The king's fleshy lips curled upward into a ruthless smile. He would destroy all who stood in his path, including the one who dared to bury the Almha, the symbol of his power. . . .

Elizabeth gasped from the images in her daydream. Her eyes flew open. She staggered like a drunken sailor wheeling about on deck. Woozy and lightheaded, she desperately grabbled for balance. Arms pinwheeled madly for purchase. Still clutching the fragment, she succumbed and fell to the ground.

Was the earth spinning madly? Or was it her? What happened? Elizabeth closed her eyes, sickened by the revolving sensations as if she'd stepped off a fast-moving carousel. All she wanted was this nauseating feeling to stop. Dimly she heard murmuring overhead and a deep, resonating voice say into her ear in Arabic, "The sun has overcome this one."

A calloused but soothing hand rested gently on her brow. Her eyelids fluttered and she reluctantly opened them. And found herself looking up into a pair of black, piercing eyes.

She'd attracted a large crowd of workers, judging from the mass of sandaled feet near her head. But it was her rescuer who claimed her attention. Elizabeth's breath hitched and she found herself unable to tear her eyes away from his penetrating gaze. Coffee-colored eyes, as dark and liquid as the thick Arabian brew, scrutinized her. Those eyes reminded her of the desert raider Jabari. But this man was no sheikh, for he dressed like other diggers and his hair was much shorter.

He had a strongly chiseled face with a firm, clean-shaven jawline. Thick ebony locks of hair curled about his shoulders from beneath a white turban. She closed her eyes again, wondering if she were still dreaming.

Lightly, he ran a thumb across her upper cheek. The feather-light touch made her heart race as crazily as it had just a few minutes earlier. Elizabeth opened her eyes and saw his fierce brow furrow into a baffled frown. Her breath came in shortened gasps beneath the veil's cloying thickness.

"A digger with eyes as blue as the desert sky. And soft cheeks for such a hard worker," he mused.

She was unprepared for his next move as his hand touched to the vein throbbing in her throat. The dark stranger checked her pulse, resting his arm in an intimate place no male had ever touched before. Black eyebrows rose in shocked surprise as he encountered a round softness instead of a man's firm chest.

Damn. The corset had been tightened to its fullest capacity, but not enough to flatten what nature had bestowed on her.

She shuddered, and saw his eyes gleam with amusement. Firm, sensual lips curved into a wicked smile.

He knew.

The handsome field worker reached over and pulled off her veil. He sat back on his haunches with what seemed like a satisfied sigh.

"A woman. Playing games by dressing up as a man to do a man's work," he said in English. He shot Elizabeth a blistering look of pure contempt.

Elizabeth glared at him as she tossed the turban aside. She sat up, struggling against waves of nausea washing over her in a sickening flood. Her throat ached with thirst. She cradled her head in her palms, hoping to steady herself. A firm hand grasped her shoulder.

"Lie back. You are not strong and the heat has weakened you," he commanded. Although spoken with a deep, almost musical accent, his English was flawless.

Another condescending male! He assumed that she had swooned in weakness. "I'm fine," she growled, letting anger feed her energy. "I didn't faint from the heat. I'm stronger than I look." She thrust aside his hand with rude impatience.

His dark gaze narrowed. "Such strength," he said mockingly. "I suppose since you are so strong, you then have no need of this water." He withdrew the canteen he'd started to proffer.

She stared with longing at the container, licking her parched bottom lip. Suddenly Nahid's voice cut through the crowd with shocked disapproval.

"Elizabeth! What in the name of Allah are you doing?"

A rush of guilt overcame her. Elizabeth reached for the hand her uncle extended and let him pull her to her feet. The digger rose at the same time.

"If you won't let me dig dressed as a woman, I thought I'd try it dressed as a man." Her shoulders tensed with pride.

The stranger frowned, glancing at the diggers making signs against the Evil Eye as they backed away from her. "You should have dressed as a mummy, for you frighten the workers. Women dressing as men are like jinn, spirits that haunt the desert."

Annoyed, Elizabeth looked up at him. And up. She craned her neck. He was much taller than the diggers. Taller than many on the archaeological team. His majestic stature intimidated her almost as much as his good looks did.

"Elizabeth, what are you gawking at?" Nahid grunted.

The hard curves of the limestone clutched in her left hand restored her sense. She turned toward Nahid, hoping to soften his anger. Elizabeth opened her palm to reveal the fragment.

"I found this. Look! Akhenaten himself, it must be! Probably smashed after his death at the same time the cartouches were erased!" Elizabeth bubbled with excitement.

Her uncle plucked it from her palm and examined the fragment. Something tugged at the corners of his lips. It looked like an approving smile. She hoped it was.

"An excellent specimen. Flinders will be pleased. How did you find this?"

"I figured the *temenos* wall a logical place to find statues of Akhenaten, since the pharaoh worshiped himself as much as Aten." Elizabeth folded her arms, feeling smug that she, not the field experts, had thought to dig there first.

"Well, you certainly did hit upon something here."

"All the more reason to let me dig," she suggested.

"In men's clothing or as a woman?" the stranger asked.

"Touché. Who are you anyway? What business do you have here?" she demanded in a haughty tone. Inwardly, she cringed at her lack of manners. But Elizabeth cared more about showing him she was in control. Judging from the way his eyes narrowed, he grew angry that she dared to question him. Somehow she had the feeling this man wasn't used to interrogations. Elizabeth shrugged off the odd feeling they had met before.

He started to speak, but Nahid looked up and cut him off. "Asim is our new site supervisor and translator. He'll be taking over for me so I can concentrate on the palace. He's very skilled and good with the workers. Since no one on the team besides me speaks decent Arabic, we're fortunate to have him."

To her surprise, Asim gave Nahid a look of dark contempt as if the praise meant nothing to him.

"And who are you and what are you doing here?" Asim returned Elizabeth's rude inquiry, but his proud manner made it sound as if he had the right to question her. Control threatened to slip again. Elizabeth squared her shoulders, determined to stand up to this imposing man. She held a higher status than he did.

Nahid waved a hand, chopping off her opportunity to speak.

"This is my niece, Elizabeth Summers. She helps me record artifacts." Her uncle's words shrunk her to a position lower than an inconsequential basket boy. Someone called her uncle, and Nahid wandered away, murmuring an excuse.

"Which crew will you oversee?" she asked in Arabic, disproving that only Nahid spoke the language.

Asim gave her a long, thoughtful look. "This one. I will translate orders from the field directors, supervise and handle all *baksheesh* payments for this crew," he replied in English.

A wicked idea suddenly surfaced. Maybe she could use this man to get what she ultimately wanted. "Good. I'll take my *baksheesh* now instead of later," she told Asim in English.

His eyes widened and his arched black eyebrows drew together in a thunderous scowl. Normally *baksheesh* was paid at day's end. At dusk, she and Nahid lit the lantern and sat under the canopy with the site supervisors while diggers lined up before them. All the artifacts were examined and their value recorded in the notebook under the finder's name, then the tips were handed out.

"*Baksheesh,*" she said, thrusting her chin upward. "You're in charge of paying all the workers who find artifacts here. For my payment, I'll take four hours of digging and sifting through fill instead of cataloging."

Elizabeth absently wrapped a strand of hair around her index finger, waiting for his answer.

He said nothing, inspecting her with a velvet gaze that brushed from the top of her mussed hair to the tips of her scuffed sandals. What a rude boor! She did her own assessment. His tight, powder-blue *thobe* and knee-length sleeveless white vest profiled an athlete's body. Long slits up the *thobe*'s sides revealed dark, loose-fitting trousers. He radiated a commanding presence strikingly different from his fellow workers.

Asim scratched his chin. "The men will not work with you. A woman is considered bad luck." His arrogant tone indicated *I will not work with you either.*

She thrust up the sleeves of her garment, which started to droop in the heat. "I can work just fine by myself," she stated. Elizabeth's bottom lip jutted out in stubborn protest.

He stared at the sweat running in a steady river down her temple. "You have not the ability to endure the desert sun."

She wiped her forehead with her sleeve. "I can handle it."

Her uncle returned, frowning at the exchange between the two of them. "Elizabeth, what are you doing?"

"Bargaining, Uncle Nahid. I want to dig."

"No. I forbid it. I told you earlier."

"If you do, I'll just keep slipping back here at night and dig anyway." Her threat suggested she would do so instead of helping him dig for the Almha. Of course she wouldn't, but it was her one advantage with Nahid.

It worked, for he made a low growling noise in his throat and looked at Asim. "All right. I'm putting her under your care. No more than two hours of digging a day. I don't want her overtaxed."

Asim glanced at Nahid, as if he were a mosquito buzzing about in the conversation. How interesting. He looked annoyed, as if Nahid had overstepped his authority. As if he were Nahid's superior, not vice-versa.

Then a blankness fell over his features. His broad shoulders lifted, as if he couldn't care less. "We shall see if you can stand up to the task or if you will faint again, like a girl. If you do, then you go back to your uncle." He smiled in a smug manner as if to say *I doubt you will last one hour in the sun.*

She couldn't back out now. Something inside spurred her to knock that smug smile off Asim's face. Show him that a woman could do a job as well as a man.

"Good." She held out her right hand. Nahid grumbled and walked away again, barking at the diggers to return to work.

Asim looked at her hand as if she held a scorpion.

"I offer to shake hands on our arrangement, as a man would in my country. Or do you fear doing business with a woman?"

His jaw tightened. "A most strange British custom. I have no fear of a mere woman," he replied.

"I'm American. Not British," she corrected.

"Indeed," he murmured. "I have heard of American women and how they are as fiery as a hot desert wind. I see that such legends are not myth but fact."

Asim took Elizabeth's outstretched palm, enfolding it in his enormous hand. His touch was assured and firm. She tried to withdraw her hand, but he held it, rubbing his thumb gently over her skin. She suppressed a shiver at his caress.

"Such a dainty hand, this one. So pale and delicate. Such a shame to subject it to the harshness of the desert sun." Those liquid black eyes pierced hers, two pools of darkness that she felt herself falling into and drowning. "Women were not meant to toil like a beast of burden, a stupid donkey. Allah created them to grace the hearth with their beauty and to bring forth new life." He gave her a smoldering look, as if to hint that he would like to help her fulfill that part of womanhood.

Elizabeth felt her knees weaken and sway like two palms in a strong wind. She was glad the *thobe* concealed her legs. Her heart pounded faster than when she'd found the artifact. One suggestive glance from a handsome man and she felt as nervous as a debutante encountering her first suitor.

She was a logical woman of science, for heaven's sake! She struggled for the correct Arabic words, feeling the need to meet him on his level, even though her Arabic was not as good as his English. Elizabeth racked her brain. Oh yes.

"Don't judge me by my reproductive parts. I am stronger than your toughest . . . ass." She looked at him bemused as he threw his head back and laughed. A deep, throaty sound that had no restraint. White teeth gleamed as he flashed her an impish smile.

"*Homarah.* Donkey. Not ass. You are mixing body parts with donkeys. Do not call yourself a donkey. It is a grave insult," he corrected in English. Elizabeth felt a furious flush skate up her chest to her cheeks.

"Donkeys are very stubborn. I have expertise in taming such creatures. They fight the bit, but eventually they submit to my will and are honored to let me ride them. Such is the case with women. Women need men to rule over them," he said softly.

The double entendre filled her with cold fury as much his attitude did. "In case you haven't heard, this is the nineteenth century and women no longer need men to dictate their lives." She lifted her chin with justified pride. "In my country, women are fighting for the right to vote. I am a proud member of the National American Woman Suffrage Association." Elizabeth drew in a deep breath. Whew. That title was a mouthful enough in English and she could not began to think of the Arabic translation.

In response, Asim bowed his head, folded his hands and brought them to his lips.

"Now what are you doing?" she asked, astounded.

"Thanking Allah I do not live in your country," he responded, lifting his head. Black eyes twinkled with teasing mirth. She grit her teeth. He heaved a deep breath. "So be it. *Inshallauh.* As my people say: If Allah wills it, it will come to fruition."

Elizabeth let out the half-breath she'd been holding. Hopefully, Allah would be on her side. She'd need all the help she could get to stand up to the strong-willed Asim. Elizabeth had won the first battle. But as she watched him walk away to talk with her uncle, she had the nasty feeling her victory would be short-lived. He didn't seem like a man accustomed to losing.

That afternoon, Jabari watched his men sift through dirt at the Great Temple. He squatted on his haunches, resting his chin in his hands. Nearby, teams of diggers shoveled and hacked at the sand in near unison.

His mind drifted back to the earlier encounter with Elizabeth. When he'd seen the worker lying on the ground, he'd been mystified that a man fainted from the heat.

When he'd laid his arm upon her soft breasts, he'd concealed his shock. Her beauty enticed him, threatened to make him lose good sense. And then she opened her mouth. Sense regained.

He scolded himself for thinking of her. As beautiful as she was, Elizabeth was an unwelcome distraction. His duty to his people and the Almha demanded his full attention.

Rising, he surveyed the site. Honest bewilderment surged through him. What reasons had these Westerners for uncovering the earth? What purpose did it serve?

Perhaps if he could understand their motivations, it would arm him with a better means to fight their intrusion. He preferred straightforward war. The infidels were armed with *turias* and shovels, hardly the weapons he was used to battling. Right now he felt as if he were fighting jinn in the dunes, swinging his sword at the dry winds.

A digger looked up, asking for water. Jabari brought over a small canteen, looking on as the man drank. The workers violated everything he vowed to protect. As much as he wanted to despise them for their sacrilege, he could not. The ancient city was sacred to the Khamsin only. And the money these men earned put food on the table for their families.

The English paid them generous *baksheesh*. Little chance then to sway them to quit. Frustration swept through Jabari. Desert life was harsh and few opportunities existed for the diggers to earn the type of money in one month they were earning in one week from the dig site. Such dilemmas plagued his tribe as well. The old ways were failing to adequately provide as society advanced more and more.

As he went to place the flask on a nearby table, a figure in black and scarlet neared. Al-Hajid. Not of the milder Farris clan, but the Taleq, the clan with the cruelest reputation. Every muscle tensed. Jabari fought to rein in his emotions.

"This work is easy for you, no? Like a woman watching children." The Al-Hajid warrior shifted the rifle on his shoulder, gave a mocking laugh. Jabari's hands trembled with rage, itching to hold a blade instead of a canteen. He took a deep, calming breath and set down the water.

Jabari forced an agreeable note in his voice. "What do you think they look for?"

The warrior relaxed, loosening his grip on the rifle. Leaning one booted foot on a crate, he gazed at the dirt flung into the air by busy diggers.

"Who knows? Probably something to ease their manhood as they have no women with them. Except for that girl. She is a strange one, that fair-haired woman."

"She acts like no woman I know." Jabari hated to agree with his enemy, but the man was right in this case. He felt his loins constrict, thinking of how she'd challenged him. Jaded by the pampering caresses of docile women who sought only to please him in bed, Jabari discovered his sexual hunger aroused by Elizabeth's spirit. This annoyed him as much as her defiance did.

"She has a battling spirit like the goddesses of old. I would not mind her sharing my tent. She would forget the pale-skinned English when she sees what it is like to have a real man bed her," the warrior boasted, his lips curling in a lusty sneer.

Shooting a sideways glance at his enemy, Jabari drew his brows together. *I would see your head rolling in the sand, dog of the desert, before your filthy hands touched her.* A deep, possessive rage shook him. His body stiffened into a warrior's stance. His right hand shot automatically to his left side and touched only thin cotton. Of course, he was not armed. Stupid of him to forget. The warrior's eyes narrowed with suspicion. He saw the move. Recognized it, probably. Jabari cursed inwardly and forced calm and an amused smile to his lips.

"She is quite beautiful. I would fight you for her, but alas, I have only *turias* for weapons and I desire money from the Westerners more than the pleasures of their women."

A grudging chuckle joined his hearty laugh. Jabari gave a respectful nod as the warrior examined him. His friendly grin must have fooled the man, for the Al-Hajid warrior walked away. But his grip tightened again on the rifle and he kept looking back.

A slow, steady hiss escaped his lips. Too close. He had nearly betrayed himself before his enemy. He must be more careful to control his emotions. And lovely Elizabeth presented the biggest challenge of all, for she brought every one raging to the surface. She threatened his safety.

A calculating smile spread over his face. He'd let her dig and twist that pride of hers to his advantage. Break her. She'd faint. He'd send her trotting back to her uncle like a good little girl, out of his sight and thoughts.

His smile faded as he remembered her feisty spirit. This one, she would not surrender easily. Jabari brushed the folds of his *thobe.* He had the feeling that locking swords with an Al-Hajid warrior offered an easier conquest than the war he saw on the horizon with the blue-eyed Elizabeth.

Much easier.

Chapter Four

"You came here to dig. So dig." Asim thrust his hands on his hips. His gaze flicked to the small pile of fill in Elizabeth's wheelbarrow.

"I am digging. Just adjusting my hair," she said in a low voice filled with fatigue.

Elizabeth pushed away an errant lock of hair, keeping her temper in check. Only one hour on the job and already the sun was taking its toll. Perspiration plastered her chignon to her neck. Soaked, too, were the striped cotton blouse and khaki skirt, freshly laundered the night before. But she couldn't stop now. She had to pretend the heat didn't affect her.

Of course it didn't help he'd put her to work during the hottest part of the day. She swore he wanted to push her into succumbing to the heat.

The jaunty straw hat, which seemed so perky and fashionable before, now proved useless in the blistering sun.

"This is what you wanted, so stop complaining," she told her aching back. Every muscle in her torso quivered and jumped in a bizarre ballet of pain. Worse were the tiny blisters now forming in the webbing between her thumb and forefinger.

"Too much? The heat saps your strength. You need not do any more. Leave the work for the men." Asim gave her a slow smile, calculating and shrewd.

She glowered at him. He stood there like a caliph above the trench she was digging. His long white *thobe* was drier than the Sahara and his face cool and clean. Didn't the man sweat at all?

"I can do this," she snapped, and placed her trembling hands around the pick ax's handle.

Excavation now concentrated on careful clearing outside the Great Temple. The remains of the temple had been sketched. Diggers removed the overburden, the fill that had piled up, to clear any artifacts at floor level.

Elizabeth had expected Asim to assign her to the temple itself. Instead, the beast relegated her to digging a trench that ran the perimeter of the outside walls. Amarna was built on a desert surface of sand and gravel, but beneath lay stony earth. Digging a trench felt like shoveling boulders.

She hoisted the heavy pick ax by its wooden handle and carefully let it swing. It bit the sand, breaking up the dirt with a satisfied thud. She picked up her shovel and dug. Pinpricks of dizziness swam before her eyes. She could not faint. She'd show him. The digging had shifted beyond a mere desire to find artifacts. Now it was a pure battle of wills.

To divert her mind from the heat, every time she dug her shovel into the earth, she pretended she was hitting Asim instead and knocking that smug smile off his face.

The beast.

Her spirit seemed as gritty as the sandy earth she flung into the wheelbarrow. Coated with perspiration, Elizabeth looked ready to drop in the blazing sun. But she refused to surrender.

Jabari felt admiration mixed with annoyance for her

stubbornness. She was so determined to prove herself that she'd work until dropping from sheer exhaustion. Her fearless determination equaled his own resolve. Both would do whatever was necessary to accomplish their goals.

Her body swayed like a river reed as she bent in rhythm to the shovel. As much as he hated disrupting his ancestors' sacred city, his spirits lifted. It was quite entertaining watching Elizabeth's lovely body in action.

Bending over, she sifted through the dirt to see if anything interesting had surfaced. His appreciative eye followed the curve of her form. Generous breasts accented a slender waist.

Beads of perspiration formed at his temple, but not from the sun. As she moved with sinuous grace, Jabari felt a familiar stirring beneath his trousers. He silently cursed and swallowed hard, wishing she'd stuck to dressing as a man.

Elizabeth removed her hat, fanning her face. It fell from her hands. Suddenly he noticed her flushed face and swaying body. Finally, the heat had won. He felt no sense of victory, only alarm. Jabari grabbed a canteen, a small vial and leaped into the trench.

"Here, take this," he urged in Arabic, urgency making him switch back to his native language. He uncapped a container of salt pills and pressed one into her dirty palm. "Your body is losing water. The salt will allow you to retain moisture."

She stared at the round tablet as if he'd handed her a snake. "I don't need it. I can take the heat." Elizabeth replied in Arabic and handed the tablet back to him.

He narrowed his eyes at her. Would there be no end to this woman's mulishness?

"Listen to me," he said carefully in English, hoping use of her native language would penetrate that thick layer of pride. "I speak with truth. Your body is rapidly losing precious moisture. You will become sick if you do not cool down and keep water in your body." He tilted her trembling face up with one hand. Jabari looked straight into her blue eyes, hoping she'd see reason reflected in his. "Take it. Now."

Elizabeth knit her brows and opened her lips, to protest, most likely. Jabari seized his advantage. Gripping her mouth gently, but firmly with one hand, he popped the salt past her parted lips with the other. He closed her mouth with his fingers.

"Swallow."

Huge lapis eyes turned colder than ice, but she obeyed. He handed her the canteen. She drank and handed it back. He slung it over his shoulder.

"Good girl. Now go under the shade."

She opened her mouth again, but saw his expression and closed it. "Now," he said sternly. Jabari climbed out of the trench and held his hand out to her. She considered, then placed her hand into his, allowing him to help her scramble out.

She climbed out with more vigor than expected and collided against his chest. Instead of jerking away, Elizabeth sighed and sagged against him as if that sudden move sapped her strength. Startled, Jabari looked down at the lithe body pressed against him. Her head tucked neatly beneath his chin. He inhaled her scent—freshly washed hair that smelled of rosemary.

Elizabeth lifted her face to his, her blue eyes large, questioning and as innocent as a child's. Transfixed, he gazed down at her luminous skin. The earlier response he'd had returned, betraying his masculine reaction to holding her close.

Allah help him, this woman angered and enchanted him as no other. Many had thrown themselves at his feet, or into his bed. He'd grown to regard women as an easing of his manhood. He knew he'd have to take a wife soon. It was his duty as Khamsin Sheikh to father sons and pass leadership on to them.

Jabari regarded the task as a necessary obligation. Still, part of him longed for something deeper. He wanted a woman who would not serve him with slavish adoration, but love him with all her heart. A woman with passions that ran as deeply as his own.

He stroked her golden tresses, marveling at their silky texture. Suddenly he realized he had run straightforward into his fate. For some reason yet unknown to him, this American woman's path and his were destined to cross.

A journey together had begun. But what the outcome would be, ah, that was the question yet unanswered.

What was happening to her? Elizabeth tried to shake free of her lassitude. How could one man claim so much power over her?

She gazed up into his dark eyes. They were deep, captivating and spoke of mysteries, passion and unbidden pleasures. And a new emotion was reflected there—concern for her welfare.

She found herself staring at his lips, curved and inviting, full and sensual. Hastily she yanked her gaze away, trailing it down to the breadth of his muscled shoulders. As Elizabeth leaned against his firm body, she felt him stroke her hair. His touch had a certain comfort. A delicious scent of spices and sun-dried clothing clung to him. Then something hard nudged her belly. It felt like a steel sword, prodding her as if asking a question. But he wore no sword. . . .

She followed the direction of the probing object. Elizabeth choked back a shocked gasp. An odd, fluttering feeling surfaced between her legs. A flush flamed her cheeks. Looking up, she saw his face was equally reddened. And angry. Elizabeth stepped back and nearly toppled into the trench. Asim grabbed her arms, steadying her.

Her gaze darted away from him. What did this reaction mean? Did he find her as intriguing as she found him? She resented that she had no idea about what happened between men and women.

"Come. A few moments' rest in the shade and some water will refresh you." He stated it as a command. Asim took her elbow and guided her to the shade of a nearby canopy.

Crates surrounded a makeshift table littered with tools and some potsherds. He steered her toward an empty crate and she sank onto it.

"Here. Water." She took the canteen he offered, watching as he sat across from her. Of whom did he remind her?

"It's warm. Can't I get a glass of cold water?"

"Warm water is best. Your body is too overcome by the heat. If you drank cold water, your stomach would constrict and it would merely come right back up."

"Oh." She sipped some more. "I guess you're right."

He raised one eyebrow, amusement dancing in his eyes. "After some years of living in the desert as a simple herdsman, I have come to know such things."

"You speak English beautifully for a 'simple herdsman,' " she observed. Something about this man did not add up.

A look of alarm flashed over his face, then vanished like a desert rain. "My father thought it would be useful for me to speak English because of the British occupation of our country."

Elizabeth had the feeling he'd just evaded telling her the whole truth without actually lying. She licked her lips and set down the canteen. The flush of heat exhaustion was quelling a bit and she could finally think straight. Or was it because he sat a comfortable distance away from her?

Her feet ached. Elizabeth pushed her seat back, fetched a smaller crate and propped up her boots on it, facing Asim. His dark eyes narrowed as they focused on her feet.

"Do not do that," he said quietly. "It is considered very rude to show the soles of your feet to others."

"Oh? Sorry." Elizabeth set her feet down.

Asim stared with unabashed frankness. "Now it is my turn to ask questions. How do you come by your knowledge of my land?"

"I went to college at Vassar and learned. My father was an American archaeologist. My mother was Egyptian and I loved hearing about her native land. I wanted to explore it."

"Why do you dig then? Why not do as your heart desires?"

She squinted at him. "I don't understand."

"Explore," he said patiently. "Perhaps my English is not that good. When you explore, you journey to another destination, yes?"

"Oh!" Elizabeth smiled. "Yes, you are right. But in this case, my destination is the past. Egypt's past."

"The past? How can one journey to another time?"

Now the smile spread over her face like a brushfire. She felt the bubbling excitement that always came whenever she discussed archaeology. Elizabeth sat on the smaller crate closer to the table and picked up a potsherd. "By unearthing it. When you excavate, you uncover the past. Look at this piece. Flinders Petrie wants every single artifact recorded. Why? Because each discovery is a clue. Like a big puzzle piece. With every specimen, you take a journey through history to ancient times."

"Ah, I understand," he said, not sounding as if he did. "Was this passion of yours for taking this journey into the past encouraged by your mother?"

"She helped my father when they went on digs," Elizabeth explained, toying with the pottery piece.

"Among my people, a father would never allow his daughter to visit another country unescorted, although he must have given your uncle the responsibility of protecting you."

Elizabeth felt her lower lip quiver with unexpected emotion as she remembered how she followed her blond-haired, blue-eyed father around with a small brush, mimicking his actions. He used to call her "my little archaeologist."

"He's dead," she said bluntly. "When I was twelve, he and my mother were killed in England. The cave they were exploring collapsed." Elizabeth fought tears burning in her throat.

Jabari's warm palm encircled hers as it rested upon the

table. "I am sorry," he said softly. "I, too, lost ones I loved dearly."

His eyes echoed his words, for they were filled with some hidden anguish. For a moment, they sat, saying nothing, letting the silence of shared grief fill the empty space between them.

She withdrew her hand and propped her chin up, regarding the seemingly endless flat desert stretching beyond the dig site. Rising heat caused the sullen air to shimmer like silver dust plumes dancing above the earth.

"Mama taught me to love deserts long before I ever set foot in one." Elizabeth smiled. "She told me so many stories when I was little. The desert was a magical place, full of enchantment. So mysterious and yet simple compared to the material greediness of the city. She used to call it her spirit place because she could hear the silence of her soul in its sands."

"Do you know that when you talk of her, your face becomes as tranquil as quiet pools of silver moonlight?" He gazed at her with an intensity she found both exciting and disturbing.

Flustered, Elizabeth stammered, "Uh . . . she . . . was an exceptional woman."

He took the canteen of water and drank deeply. Fascinated, she watched his Adam's apple bob up and down. Asim set down the container and wiped his mouth with the back of one hand. "And now that you have seen the desert for yourself?" he asked.

"It is everything I've ever imagined it to be. Such raw, honest beauty that takes nothing and gives nothing."

He considered her words and gazed out into the sands. His eyes lost their usual intensity and turned wistful. "Honest, yes. But the desert is so much more. It gives life and it ravages it. It can be breathtakingly beautiful with crimson sunsets that make your heart ache, or bitterly cruel as it lashes your soul and strips it bare until it weeps with sorrow. On some nights it is so lonely it feels as though every living being has fled the earth and you alone remain."

His husky voice filled with sadness. Elizabeth felt an odd longing to ease his melancholy. "Sometimes it's good to strip away your soul until it weeps with sorrow," she quietly replied.

Any trace of anguish fled his eyes, replaced by hardened obsidian again. "Such is not the way for men. Weeping is for children and silly females. Tears are a display of weakness. Men must be strong, like a towering pyramid."

Her sympathy evaporated. One sentence of empathy and he became all arrogant male again.

She glared at him. "Silly females? I'd rather think that a man who is brave enough to cry is stronger than one who pretends he feels nothing."

His nostrils flared and he leaned across the table, as if to spring over it. "Brave? What would happen to such a man? A man who shows fear or cries is a weak leader. He loses his sense and makes his people and himself vulnerable to enemies."

Two black brows drew together as he pinned her to the seat with the force of his gaze. "Such a man is no warrior. It is better for him to die alone in the desert than to be exposed to such shame. You are a woman and know nothing of these matters. Such talk could be dangerous for you," he growled.

She leaned back in alarm, his anger a hot wind pressing against her body. Her hands trembled. Elizabeth folded them into her lap, lest they betray her sudden nervousness.

This was no humble digger hired as a pleasant fellow to translate. Something jostled her memory as she took in the proud lift of his head and the straightness of his spine. He sat on the crate as if it were a throne and she a lowly peasant who dared to address him. Suddenly it clicked. The desert warrior she'd seen!

She narrowed her gaze, studying him with skeptical eyes. Just as swiftly as it arrived, the scowl fled his face, replaced with a charming smile.

"Forgive me please. I am too opinionated at times. I did not mean to frighten you. It is not my place to say such things to a lady," he said in a courteous tone.

His abrupt change of mood was like watching sunshine break through dark thunderheads. She'd rather have the storm clouds. The anger was more honest than this sudden congeniality.

"You didn't scare me," Elizabeth lied. "But I am curious as to why you are so clearly impassioned about such matters. If I didn't know better, I'd say you were speaking from experience about being a warrior of the desert. Not opinion."

She had to see if her hunch proved correct. Was Asim the dark horseman called Jabari?

But the mask did not slip from his face again. He gave an indifferent shrug. "In my country, there is a little of the desert warrior in every man, even the humblest digger such as myself." He glanced at the sun's position in the sky. "Your two hours of digging are nearly passed, my lady. If you wish to receive full *baksheesh* payment, you need to return to work."

Clever fellow. He'd closed the subject so neatly she could almost hear the door shut. Elizabeth watched him as he led the way back to the trench. Funny. She didn't recall that shuffling, hesitant walk before. Didn't his step have a confident stride?

What kind of games was this man playing? And what were the stakes? Asim had suddenly become as much of a enigma as Amarna. Fine with her.

Elizabeth adored solving mysteries.

Fool. He'd let a woman nearly uncover his charade. Bested by a woman! It couldn't get any worse. Jabari felt horrified by the idea as he poured water into a bowl on an empty crate outside his mud-brick hut. Still, Elizabeth's knowledge proved more beneficial than the little he'd gathered from eavesdropping on the English. He learned more about the excavation from her in one hour than he'd learned in one day from them.

He lathered his hands with soap, scrubbed his face with more vigor than necessary, then rinsed and blindly groped for the towel. A soft cloth was thrust into his hand. Jabari swiped his eyes and blinked at the grinning face of Nazim.

"Now I know my day has gotten worse," he muttered.

"Are you not pleased to see me, sire?" Nazim had a woven cloth bag over one shoulder and was clad in the standard outfit of a digger. The only difference was the lavender turban perched upon his head like a large, colorful flower.

Jabari grimaced as he dried his face. "I ordered you to take charge while I was gone. Is this your idea of obeying?"

Nazim's even white teeth flashed like diamonds in the dying sunlight. "I am obeying your orders. You said to take charge during the day and here it is, nearly nightfall. Did you truly think I would not come to check on you? I am your guardian."

Tossing the towel down, Jabari looked at his friend's headgear. He nodded at the turban. "What is that?"

Nazim's eyes rolled upward. "My disguise. I thought this would help me blend in with the English. Do they not like colors of the rainbow? I have read of these . . . what are they called? English fops?"

"Fops?" Jabari groaned. "My friend, your turban is wound too tightly around your thick skull. This is a color for women. You resemble that girlish man who bought horses from us last summer. The one who winked at you?"

Nazim tore the turban off his head with disarming speed. He gave it a look of pure disgust.

"Disguise or not, I refuse to look like a female or a man who does not like females." He rubbed his head ruefully.

His mood lifted and Jabari laughed at his friend's woeful expression. It felt wonderful to laugh after such a disastrous day. With a jerk of his head, he beckoned Nazim to follow him inside the hut.

As a site supervisor, he'd been given mud bricks to build

his own hut. A carpet covering the sand was strewn with plump pillows. Jabari, still chuckling, and Nazim sat on the carpet facing each other. The sheikh slapped his friend's knee with mirth.

"I am most glad you came. After what I have been through today, I needed to laugh."

"Anything to serve my lord," Nazim said, bending forward in a mock bow. His expression sobered. "What has happened with you?"

"First, your news. How is everything? And my Ghazi? Are you taking good care of him?"

"All is well with the tribe. Your falcon." Nazim pursed his lips. "You know no one else can handle him. I've sent him out on several hunts, but . . ." He glanced at his right hand, which bore a recent crescent-shaped scar. "I do believe he misses you."

"That's my Ghazi," Jabari said proudly. "I apologize for my bird's poor behavior."

"The meat he brought back was worth it," Nazim said. He reached into his bag, withdrew a folded cloth and handed it over.

"I brought you this. Asriyah figured they would starve you."

Jabari tore open the gift with great eagerness to find a large flat cake inside. His aunt's speciality—made with millet and tiny seeds and baked with just a bit of honey for sweetness. He broke off a sizable share and offered it to Nazim. Custom dictated the guest be served first. Nazim took a small piece and handed it back to Jabari.

Sighing with pleasure, Jabari chewed the bread with relish. Suddenly the day didn't seem that bad after all.

"So tell me, what tortures have these English infidels designed for you? You have a private room, comfortable sleeping quarters, fresh water. Do they force a dozen virgins upon you each night as well?"

"Until I plead for mercy," Jabari replied. He waved a hand at the entrance. "They beat down my door to serve my every need."

Nazim chuckled. "And the woman we saw the other day? Does she serve your every need?"

Elizabeth would eat sand before serving his needs. Jabari tore off another piece of bread and shook his head. "That one . . . she is vexing. Never have I met a more stubborn woman. I do not understand her."

"You have met her?" Nazim leaned forward with avid interest.

Jabari pulled out a chest filled with male pride. "I am her—what do they call it?—boss. She obeys me."

"She does?" Nazim's eyes widened. "That one did not appear as a woman who obeys. What does she do for you?"

"I have her digging in the dirt."

Nazim groaned. "And you say I have a thick skull. You would have a luscious treasure like that slaving in the sun?"

"It was her choice," he replied, his chest deflating.

"Strange creatures, these Westerners." Nazim shook his head. "Do all their women wish to dig in the dirt?"

"I think it is just her. She has such a passion for finding things. When she sees something in the sand, it is like she has discovered priceless jewels." Jabari smiled. Elizabeth took such obvious pleasure from excavating that he almost wanted to plant objects in the sand just to witness her childlike glee.

"What about the Almha? Is this . . . woman . . . helping to search for it as well?"

Jabari frowned. Nazim had hit upon a point still bemusing him. "I do not know. From What I have gathered, they do not even suspect its existence. Since I have been here, all they talk about is what a find the city is."

"Why do they dig then?" Nazim's bewilderment echoed his own.

Jabari paused, remembering the glow on Elizabeth's face as she mentioned how archaeology opened a door to the past. "Perhaps it is something deep within them that craves to know. A thirst for knowledge of ancient times."

Nazim snorted. "They have a queer thirst, these Westerners."

"Not half as queer as your strange turban, my friend."

"True," Nazim agreed and both men laughed. It was good to be among friends again.

"I still do not like leaving you alone. I have business in the village. I will stay there, away from the dig site but close enough to keep an eye on you. Izzah can manage tribal affairs."

Jabari started to protest and then saw the stubborn jut of his friend's jaw. Nazim only did his duty as he did his. To refuse dishonored him. He nodded.

"I will be glad of your company," he admitted.

"My company? I would think you would prefer the woman," Nazim teased. "Just for her intellect alone, of course."

"Elizabeth is quite intelligent and knowledgeable. If I coax information from her, I learn more about the dig than by eavesdropping on the English," Jabari mused aloud.

"A good plan. But do not get too close to her. A woman can be more dangerous than the sharpest sword," Nazim said quietly.

Jabari scowled. "Do you think my father raised a fool, Nazim? I am in full control of my emotions and my ability to control her."

But Jabari wondered. Was he?

Elizabeth paused in her task and wiped her forehead. Still, the heat was more bearable that day, perhaps because she and Asim reached an amicable understanding.

Neither had mentioned the previous day's exchange. Instead, they approached each other in a polite, respectful manner. He was quite curious and kept asking her pointed questions about archaeology and the dig site, which she loved to answer.

He had stopped her when she winced and flexed her fists. Asim jumped down into the trench and grabbed her hands.

"Your hands," he said in dismay. With extreme care he cradled their slenderness in his broad palms. Asim turned her hands over and examined the large, reddened blisters.

She yanked her hands out of his. "It doesn't hurt much."

He appraised her thoughtfully. "I will dig and fill the wheelbarrow and you can inspect anything I find. And explain to me what you are looking for. I wish to learn," he ordered.

Elizabeth started to protest and saw the determined look on his face. She nodded.

He added, "First, I have a salve for those blisters. If you do not treat them, they will become infected."

She admitted to herself that his plan provided relief to her burning palms while salvaging her pride at the same time. Such consideration was something she hadn't expected of him.

And the gentle way he'd applied the ointment with his assured touch made her wonder what kind of man he really was.

The team broke for lunch. Asim sat across from her on a packing box at a large crate used for a table and set down a cloth-wrapped package and a small pot of honey. Sighing, Elizabeth picked at her rations and eyed his meal with interest. The delicious smell tempted her far more than tinned meat.

"What's that?" she asked him.

"*Tameya.* Fried bean patties. Would you like one?"

"Thank you. I didn't come all the way to Egypt to eat tinned meat," Elizabeth said and bit into the patty he offered. "My grandmother used to make these. But yours taste much better."

He gave an affectionate smile at the napkin containing his meal. "My cousin Layla is a good cook." His dark eyes filled with curiosity. "Your grandmother is Egyptian?"

"Born here, somewhere in the desert, but, like her religion, it never left her blood. My grandmother is Muslim. So is my uncle. To marry my mother, my father had to convert. He did, but was rather lazy about following the faith. Although he once went with Uncle Nahid to Mecca during the Haj and threw stones at the three pillars representing Satan," she told him.

Asim considered, gazing toward the horizon with a thoughtful look. "I have never been to Mecca. My people are also not strict Muslims. We practice many of the tenets, but also have our own . . . religious customs dating back several thousand years."

How curious. "Your people? You mean the villagers?"

A startled look came into his eyes and then he blinked. Perhaps it was the sun because now he looked as impassive as before. "There are two villages near here. Haggi Quandil, near the river, and Amarna. Some of my . . . people . . . live in Amarna. It is a smaller village to the south of Haggi Quandil."

"The village the site is named after," Elizabeth said, remembering. "A villager from Amarna found tablets near here. They were letters from Pharaoh Akhenaten to other kingdoms."

A muscle jumped in his cheek as he looked away. "Yes, that woman. She was digging for dried mud brick to use as fuel and found them and they ended up in the hands of . . . foreigners. She disrupted the past."

"And so are you. You're here. What's wrong with disrupting the past? You can learn so much from it."

He frowned as if to disagree, and then he smiled. "Perhaps you are right. I am eager to learn about this dig."

Elizabeth had the feeling he again expertly evaded the truth without lying. She shrugged and continued eating. Between bites, she began to sketch the artifacts they had recovered. Elizabeth glanced up to see his dark eyes narrow and followed the direction of his gaze to a nearby table.

"I don't like them." Her voice dropped to a whisper as she talked of the Al-Hajid warriors settling a brass teapot on the table. "Not those ones. They . . . look savage. The others, in the red and white, are nicer. But they aren't here anymore."

Asim said nothing, but continued eating. His intense, brooding look reminded her of a falcon she saw once in a zoo. Its round eyes had quietly watched visitors as if each were an enemy and it longed to sink its talons into them.

"The Al-Hajid have two clans, Farris and Taleq. The Farris wear red and white, the Taleq red and black. The Taleq ordered the Farris off the site. I think they wrested away control of the tribe from the Farris," he observed, swiping at his mouth.

"Why would the two clans fight if they are in the same tribe? I don't understand. Aren't they like family?"

"Family, yes. But like families, clans sometimes squabble. It is the sheikh's duty to resolve the quarrels, if he cares about his people and the tribe's unity. A strong leader will not tolerate cruelty in his tribe or the larger clans preying upon the smaller ones to seize power."

"How do you know so much about them?" Elizabeth asked.

"It is wise to know all one can about those one works with," he murmured, his gaze following the men as they joined the lunch line. He drizzled honey over flatbread and offered it to her. Elizabeth declined. Asim ate the bread. She watched his tongue slowly lick honey from the lush curve of his upper lip. It was a perfectly natural gesture, yet he made it seem naughty. An odd, sensual excitement coursed through her.

Asim caught her staring and arched one brow. Flustered, she looked back at the table the Al-Hajid abandoned, wanting to deflect his attention. "They scare me," she admitted, shivering.

"They are dull-witted and not true warriors. Guns give the weakest men the illusion of power," he stated with authority.

Then his mouth tugged upward in a crooked grin. She melted a bit. Really, he was quite good looking and that smile . . . it spoke of something mischievous.

"I will show you how stupid they are," he told her, his black eyes twinkling with mirth. He unfolded his large frame and rose, taking the honey pot. He dabbled a bit on their cup handles, then sprinted back to his own seat.

Soon after, the warriors returned. Elizabeth snickered as the men picked up the tin cups and drank. Their customary scowls turned to expressions of frank bewilderment as they tried to shake their hands free.

She sputtered with laughter. It was a silly prank she never expected of him. Asim looked at the Al-Hajid with a smug grin.

After lunch, they returned to work. He unearthed a few interesting potsherds. Now, sitting at the table, she examined them. Gingerly, she brushed the specimens free of dirt. Life didn't get any better than this.

"Elizabeth."

The sharp rasp of her name shattered her joy like a hammer against glass. She glanced up to find her uncle staring at her.

Nahid leaned down and whispered, "I found it. The Maru Aten. Tonight we look for the Almha. Meet me at my hut at midnight."

"I'll be there," she whispered. Nahid strode off as if he'd merely stopped to see what she'd found.

She glanced around. Asim was a few feet away, but she doubted he overheard. So be it. Tonight began the real search.

What would Elizabeth say if she knew what he'd learned from living in the desert? For in addition to learning to survive in a harsh environment, the desert's deep silence taught Jabari to listen. He could hear music in sand dunes shifting meters away . . . and the sharp whispers of traitorous women making plans.

Cold fury filled him as he stared at her. Jabari had begun to believe that she only wanted to uncloak Egypt's past. Elizabeth was the most complex female he'd ever met. Charming, extremely bright and funny, she had a resilience that nearly equaled his own. He enjoyed talking with her.

Conversation with her took the edge off his constant loneliness.

But in the end, she proved herself just as greedy as the other diggers. Desiring wealth and riches above all else. She didn't treasure the past, but the treasure itself. And he'd allowed her to take advantage of him!

What papyrus gave them knowledge of the Almha? The only one in existence belonged to his tribe. Nkosi, in a rare moment of foolishness, gave it as a gift to his secret lover and resigned his position as sheikh in shame over the act. How had these Westerners found it? Jabari clenched his fists. It didn't matter. He had to stop her.

If she even knew where to look. The Maru Aten was far from the Almha. Yet his heart burned for revenge. The Maru Aten was Kiya's ancient temple where the Khamsin once worshiped with their queen. It was one of his people's most sacred spots.

Elizabeth ran over to him, her face radiant. She carried a small artifact in her hands and held it up for his inspection.

"Look! Part of pot that probably contained perfumed olive oil." She caressed the specimen lovingly, oblivious to his quiet rage. "When I touch it, I feel like I am one with your culture."

He sniffed with displeasure. *You will never be part of us,* he vowed silently. *You are a curse to my people.*

She glanced up. "I thought you liked finding these."

Reining in his temper with careful control, he forced a civil reply. "It is your concern, not mine. I must leave. I have business with the other diggers and cannot waste more time"—he searched for the correct words—"playing in the sand with you."

The stamp of hurt in her eyes eased his pride somewhat. Jabari turned on his heels. He was a fool for letting his guard slip. Like a wild horse, Elizabeth had galloped into his life and overcome his natural wariness with her beauty and sparkling intelligence. Just when he trusted her, she kicked and sent him careening into the sand.

His spirit roared for retribution, but Jabari quelled the longing. His honor as a warrior of the wind demanded silence, for the mission to protect the Almha came first.

Revenge would come later and its taste would be sweet, indeed.

Chapter Five

Egypt cloaked in moonlight had an exotic, mysterious beauty, but Elizabeth was too upset to appreciate it. Questions raced through her mind as she lowered her pick ax to the dirt.

Her uncle took her to the ruins of the Maru Aten a few miles from the dig site. Little chance for discovery existed. The Al-Hajid patrolled only the excavation. Elizabeth had felt quiet delight upon reaching the site. Now an unsettling guilt came over her as if they unearthed remains best left alone. Nahid shoveled fill alongside the trench to use as backfill later.

Elizabeth thought about Asim's astonishing mood change. He must have overheard them. But even so, why would a mere digger be offended by a secret excavation? Unless he was no mere digger.

A chill skittered up her spine at the idea. Elizabeth threw down her pick and grabbed up a shovel, leaning on it.

"Elizabeth!"

She jumped as Nahid whispered her name. "Standing around dreaming won't find anything! Stop woolgathering! Every second counts if we're going to find the blasted thing and smuggle it out of here before the archaeology team gets wind of it."

She set down her shovel, deeply troubled by her uncle's words. "But the most important thing is finding the ancient remedies. Right?"

He didn't reply, but grunted as he continued to dig with relentless determination. Elizabeth wondered about her uncle's churlish attitude. Lately he upset her. But he was family, and she had so little of that.

She thought of her grandmother, a woman as enigmatic as her son. Jana had left her tribe and married a British soldier stationed in Cairo. Nahid and Rasha, Elizabeth's mother, grew up in Egypt. Their only link to the desert was the language.

As she wiped her forehead, Elizabeth pondered her grandmother's decision. Why had Nana left her tribe in Egypt? If for love, why had she totally rejected her culture as well?

"Uncle Nahid, what tribe was Nana from? Wasn't it one in the Arabian Desert?" Elizabeth racked her brain for what little Nana had revealed about the old days.

Moonlight reflected his dilated eyes and surprised reaction. Nahid stopped digging and leaned on his shovel.

"That was in the past. My mother never wished to talk about it, so I suggest you do the same. Don't forget why you're here."

"You're right. We must hurry to find the cure for Nana."

"There is so much at stake," he muttered half to himself. "My mother is only part of this."

Her uncle's cryptic words worried Elizabeth. Was he truly interested in finding a cure to save his own mother? Or had money replaced his original intent to find the Almha?

She couldn't bear it if Nahid's greed motivated him. The thought agonized her so much that she had to dismiss it.

Better the Almha remain buried beneath the sands than in the hands of a treasure hunter.

* * *

As expected, they'd found nothing. He watched as the American girl and her avaricious uncle dug for three hours. Then they carefully erased evidence of their crime.

Still, the knowledge didn't ease Jabari's turmoil the following day. He thought himself a better judge of character. Elizabeth seemed so honestly passionate about discovering ancient Egypt. How could she have swindled his feelings so completely?

Mulling over these thoughts, he shuffled his feet in the rocky sand as he journeyed east toward Wadi Abu Hasah el-Bahari, the main wadi leading away from Amarna. The wadi, a dry riverbed that cut through the mountains, was sacred to his people. They believed their ancestors' spirits dwelled there.

One could almost hear the whispers of the dead there.

Certainly the whispers of the dead were intimately preferable to the nagging thoughts in his mind.

Heat as intense as the emotions raging inside him poked at his flesh. The air smelled of dust and ancient longings. Tugging his veil across his face and tucking it into his turban, Jabari pressed on, walking over the stony ground. Curving southward, then cutting abruptly north, then south again, the wadi was strewn with numerous pebbles, boulders and rocks. Sheer limestone walls rose on either side of him.

After about four kilometers, the canyon walls began to narrow. Jabari paused before a large boulder near the entrance of the royal wadi, the canyon locating royal tombs and secret catacombs where his ancestors were buried. He stared at the rock in silence. Alone. So alone. No one in the world understood the heavy weight upon his shoulders. He had no helpmate, no partner with whom he could share his burdens. Not even his closest friend and confidante, Nazim, fully comprehended the multitude of problems facing their tribe.

Silence flowed over him in a peaceful wave. Then a flap of wings broke the quiet. Jabari glanced skyward and saw a white dove fly overhead. He stepped back, marveling at the sight. Was it a sign from his ancestors that his days of loneliness would soon end? He craned his neck and watched the bird fly toward the west to the Nile until she vanished from sight.

Then he fell to his knees and sat with his legs tucked beneath him. He rested his hands upon his lap and closed his eyes. Bowing his head with great respect, he recited aloud in ancient Egyptian the sacred words his father had taught him.

"Homage to you, my honored ancestors. May the Lord of Eternity whose glory is revealed now to you, forever keep you in his embrace. I come before you, a warrior of the wind, my heart pure and my spirit strong. I humble myself before you and plead your guidance. Guard my heart against evil. Guard my tongue against falsehoods. Renew me with your strength of ages. Make me one with the desert. Grant me victory in battle, honor in defeat and wisdom to lead our people. May your sacred memories remain forever written on the four winds."

A welcoming sense of peace and harmony flowed through him as he performed the age-old ritual. Jabari found comfort in the old ways and customs. Silence echoed throughout the canyon. The earlier desolation he'd felt vanished. He was alone but lonely no longer. His ancestors walked with him.

Jabari scooped up a handful of earth and tossed it into the wind. "May Allah guide my footsteps and lead me on the pathway to do His will, not mine."

He rose in one motion, bowed his head again, and removed his veil, feeling peaceful and optimistic. And then he heard it. A slight, muffled sneeze. Jabari sniffed the air. A delicate scent of rosemary floated in the breeze.

He wasn't alone, after all.

He mustn't see her.

Elizabeth cursed the dust she'd kicked up in her frenzy to hide from Asim. It tickled her nose like a feather duster.

She had tried in vain to stifle the sneeze. No use.

She hadn't meant to eavesdrop. She had taken Isis out for a training session to have her fly back to camp. For some odd reason, Elizabeth felt compelled to take the dove to this section of the wadi. She had seen Asim approach and immediately released Isis. Then she ducked into a narrow cleft and watched.

All day he had been avoiding her and every time she tried to talk to him, he'd pleaded work as an excuse. He looked vulnerable and lonely, his stately shoulders slumped as if burdened by heavy sorrow. Her heart ached to comfort him. Of course, he'd be furious if he found her there.

So she remained frozen to the sand, enthralled by his husky recitation, though she understood none of it.

Surely he knew someone had followed him. She peeked out. He stood still for a moment, staring at the rocks in front of him, then started toward her. Her pulse galloped in a wild frenzy and she desperately squeezed herself farther into the cleft. She heard his sandals scrape against the rocky ground. And she saw his tall, muscular body stride past her hiding place.

She waited a full minute, then risked a peek. Gone.

Elizabeth stepped out. Relief made her legs shaky. She walked to where he'd uttered his prayer and spoke softly, feeling she had to apologize for disturbing the privacy of such a sacred spot.

"Please forgive me for intruding. I meant no harm," she said, placing her hand upon the boulder.

Her palm tingled with a sudden warmth. Elizabeth jerked her hand free and looked at it, confused. She glanced around. Why did this place seem so familiar? As if she'd been there before. The call of ancient memories sang in the wind, and she held out her hands as if to let them brush against her fingers.

It's nothing. Just my imagination.

She shrugged off the feeling and walked quickly away, but she could not dismiss the overwhelming notion that the royal wadi was of great importance. Maybe even greater to her than Asim.

At midnight, the traitors continued their dig.

A shadow in the moonlight, he lay on the sand some meters from the ancient temple. He noticed Elizabeth worked more slowly than her uncle, as if her heart balked at such a task. From time to time, he saw Nahid pause and gesture angrily at her. Then, shoulders sagging, she'd resume digging.

This time, Jabari did not check his wrath. He let it fill every pore of his being. Let it blacken his heart against her. Let its fierce heat consume him lest he weaken with pity for Elizabeth. Sympathy for the enemy struck down a man as quickly as a scimitar slicing through air.

He narrowed his eyes. Elizabeth had spied upon him as he'd performed the sacred ritual earlier. He'd sensed her presence from her delicate scent. But he had ignored her and his own rage and passed by. He needed to be a wraith in the desert dust.

Sounds of earth being shoveled carried across the sand. Jabari laid his head down and smiled to himself. He could afford to sleep. They would not cease for yet another hour.

True to his prediction, the digging stopped an hour later. Jabari raised his head and chuckled softly as he watched Nahid backfill the area with angry zeal.

To his surprise, Elizabeth did not join Nahid in walking back to camp. Instead she picked up a small bag and headed in his direction, toward the river. He watched her as she made her way through the cultivated fields and scatterings of palm trees.

He had to find out what she planned. Jabari followed her with the stealth of a lion tracking his prey through tall grasses. Ducking behind a tall palm just a few meters from where she stood, he squatted down to wait.

What she did next made him choke back an astonished gasp.

She looked around as if to check no one watched. Then

she dropped her bag and began undressing. The dirt-stained blouse first, then the skirt. Now she was clad only in some kind of restraining device that looked quite uncomfortable upon her chest and a white, dresslike undergarment. Her long slender arms gleamed in the moonlight.

If she took anything else off, his heart would leap out of his chest like a startled gazelle. His conscience nagged at him to leave. Pure male instinct urged him to stay.

Elizabeth lifted her face to the sky and smiled at it like a lover. Her breasts rose and fell in a gentle wave. Her hands unpinned the bun at her neck nape. Long blond hair spilled down her back. She reached down and fiddled with the bodice of the restraining device. Jabari's heartbeat quickened.

She unfastened it. Her breasts spilled out. They were large, shapely and firm. He felt himself reaching out, hypnotized, longing to cradle one in his palm, to feel its plumb texture in his bare hand. Blood pounded in his temples. She pulled the apparatus off and let it fall to the ground. His pulse thundered.

Elizabeth unbuttoned the undergarment and slid out of it as if shedding an outer skin. She turned, exposing luminous skin below the veil of straight golden hair.

He watched her dig into her bag, withdraw a bar of soap and wade waist deep into the river. She faced him, dipped into the Nile, then rose, droplets clinging to her delectable round breasts and slender, curved limbs. Her body glistened like ivory in the silver moonlight.

How he wished he were one of those droplets right now, rolling down her satin skin, tasting its softness. Unable to tear his eyes away, Jabari held his breath. Despite the night's chill, sweat formed at his temple.

With erotic slowness, Elizabeth slid the soap over her arm, trailing a path of bubbles in its wake. Desire, hot and fierce, flooded his loins. He wanted her. Never had he wanted a woman as fiercely as he wanted to take her right now. Kiss that long, graceful neck. Capture her in his arms and possess her.

What was wrong with him? Women had stripped before him, wishing only to pleasure him with slow, alluring movements designed to fully arouse him. Yet this American woman's innocent bathing seduced him faster than their exotic dances ever did.

He gazed upon her as she scrubbed her lithe form, then ducked into the water. Standing, she took the soap and lathered her hair.

Mere minutes ago, his wrath mounted against her. He longed to slice through her pride, to humble her as he did with the men who dared to cross him. Now she stood before him, the lovely lines of her body revealing every inch of the woman.

She couldn't disarm him any more than if she'd walked up to him and stripped away his dagger and scimitar. So he thought.

Then she slid below the water and rose like a nymph emerging from a frothy sea. And began to sing in a low, lush voice.

Jabari recognized the tune as an Egyptian lullaby his own mother once sang to him. He closed his eyes and recalled the tender love his mother lavished on him throughout his childhood. Jabari's chest ached with a crazed longing he didn't understand. Desire mated with a comforting feeling of being cherished. Listening to Elizabeth's sweet voice speak to him in song, he allowed her spell to wind around his heart.

Jabari's eyes flew open. What in the name of Allah was he doing? Lusting over some naked girl like a lovesick youth. He bore the title of Khamsin Sheikh. He, Jabari bin Tarik Hassid, descendent of honored warriors of the wind, feared by many, respected by all, was softening over a woman!

He scowled at his manhood throbbing beneath his trousers, wishing *that* would grow soft instead. "You are getting me into trouble. I will not listen to you!" he whispered.

Disgusted, he stood and stole one last look at Elizabeth. She lay on her back, peacefully frothing the water with lazy kicks of her long legs. He turned his back to her and fled into the night back to his hut. No sleep would ease his restlessness that night. Morning could not come soon enough.

Elizabeth floated on her back, feeling shy at being naked in the open. She wanted to leave on her chemise, but one couldn't bathe in clothing. Besides, no one saw but the moon. She stared at the silver globe caressing her with its gentle light.

Stroking the water with long leg kicks, she appraised her body. Not too bad. Flat stomach, breasts a little too large, but firm, long legs. Automatically her hand drifted down to the unusual birthmark on her right hip. The rose-colored splotch resembled a dove descending to the earth. Her mother used to say it was her mark of honor and would lead to her destiny.

Closing her eyes, she listened to the stillness of night, wanting to hear the deepest desires of her soul. Her thoughts doubled back to Asim reciting the prayer in the wadi. It seemed like a sacred place. A place where one would worship . . .

She slipped below the water at that startling thought. Choking, she paddled frantically to the surface and then stood, gasping for air.

Excitement surged through her. She knew exactly where to look for the Almha. She thought about rushing back to tell Uncle Nahid. Her instincts said no. Let her surprise him.

This time, she'd do it on her own. Tomorrow night. She, Elizabeth Summers, would uncloak the secrets of the treasure that had lain undiscovered for more than three thousand years.

He could no longer tolerate his enemies violating the sacred sands. The Al-Hajid must leave. The following night, Jabari summoned Nazim and Musab. They dressed in their indigo *binishes.* Slid their scimitars into metal sheaths at their waists. Checked their short daggers and tugged soft leather boots over loose cotton trousers. Wound the indigo fabric around their heads in tight turbans and draped veils across their faces. Nazim and Musab picked up their rifles and shouldered them. Jabari took a blanket, bedroll and goatskin of water and carried them outside.

After Jabari tied the supplies to his mare, they led their horses away. A good distance from the sleeping camp, they stopped and mounted. The trio rode nearly to the dig site, then dismounted, walking with great stealth. But no sign of the Al-Hajid. Not until they reached the actual site.

Lazy dogs, Jabari thought in contempt. Rifles leaned against the table as six men lay on the ground, snoring. Jabari beckoned to Nazim, who silently swiped the guns, laying them out of reach.

Then the trio made the Khamsin gesture of honor before battle and stood before them, letting loose the Khamsin war cry.

"I am Jabari bin Tarik Hassid, sheikh of the great Khamsin warriors of the wind. I will tolerate your presence in this sacred city no longer. Leave now or your spirits leave you!"

They jumped up, groping for rifles no longer there.

"Khamsin jackal. You guard a dead city and pay tribute to Kiya, the whore. You leave priceless gold lying in the sand, stupid dog," one sneered as they withdrew their swords.

Nazim growled at the insult, but Jabari remained silent. No emotion. He tensed his body in a warrior's stance as they attacked. Steel bit steel as they battled the Al-Hajid. It was over in a few minutes. He glanced at the dead bodies.

"Musab and I will take care of this," Nazim offered. "Shall I leave them as a warning for the English?"

"No. I want them to think they abandoned the site. I need to visit the sacred wadi before spying on the girl. My spirit is restless. Go back to the village with Musab when you finish. I am not returning. I want to sleep under the stars tonight."

Jabari ran to his mare and then rode toward the main wadi. As he neared the canyon's entrance, distant movement caused him to stop short. He narrowed his gaze. Someone ran into the valley. At this time of night? No innocent soul for certain. He clucked to his mare and rode a little farther.

When he reached the entrance of the main wadi, Jabari slid off Sahar and let her reins trail, signaling her to stay put. He hugged the craggy rock walls, his keen eyesight aiding him in the dark shadows. Silently he made his way through the canyon, nearing the sacred spot of worship.

Sounds of scraping assaulted his eardrums. Jabari's pulse quickened. Someone was digging near the entrance to the royal wadi. One of the *samak* had discovered the Almha.

He slid his scimitar out of its sheath, keeping it lowered. Displeasure mixed with the metallic taste of anger over the task he was forced to carry out.

Killing an unarmed man was dishonorable. But duty called for it. He swore a blood oath to uphold the law passed down through the ages. *He who dares disturb the Almha's resting place will see death approach on the wind with a sharpened sword.*

With great caution, but added haste, Jabari moved among the rocks. He rounded the bend and saw the boulder where he paid tribute only the day before.

Elizabeth flung a pick into the rocky earth.

Jabari nearly dropped his scimitar in anguished shock. Please Allah, not her, he prayed. He closed his eyes, hoping for a miracle. Opened them. There was no mistaking that figure. He had seen every delectable line and lush curve of it the night before.

Rage, confusion, remorse and agony flooded his soul. As much as Elizabeth had angered him and violated the very principles his people revered, he could not take her life.

But the law required it. Jabari, like all desert tribesmen,

lived by a strict code of honor. He had sworn a sacred oath. Breaking it meant not only banishment but dishonor to his family's name. When word leaked out, other tribes would see the Khamsin as weak.

Jabari slashed his scimitar in an arc, listening to it whoosh through the air. He envisioned the act, a sudden slice, without warning. She would feel no pain. The killing blow would part her spirit from her body in one swift motion.

He felt sickened at the thought of laying steel against that graceful neck.

There had to be another way. But what? He could not let her go. She would find the Almha. And then trot back to camp with her treasure. Sell it to the highest bidder, unaware of its awesome, dangerous ability to influence his people.

Jabari did something he had never considered before killing an enemy. He dropped to his knees and prayed for a way to spare her life. He begged Allah for wisdom. He pleaded with the spirit of his ancestors for guidance.

Just when he thought there were no answers, he knew what he must do. Jabari stood, clutching his scimitar, and headed for his horse.

So enthralled was she by her vision, Elizabeth dug in a frenzy she never knew she possessed. Alternating between pick and shovel, she flung pebbles and dirt left and right in a mad energy that did not come from her alone.

Pleading a headache, she'd succeeded in stalling Nahid from digging at the temple for one more night. Before midnight, she'd dressed in only sandals, skirt, blouse and a thin chemise beneath the garments. Her hair hung down her back. She had dressed so quickly the unbuttoned blouse gaped open at her throat.

Elizabeth had avoided the dig site by hugging the sheer cliffs, but she saw no warriors patrolling. She knew this place was sacred from the way Asim had revered it the other day. She felt it was important to her as well. Now she understood everything. With every fiber of her being, the Almha called to her. It sang out, crying to her from beneath its ancient burial place. She wanted to stop and stuff her ears with her fingers, its music was so disturbingly lovely, but her hands refused to stop working. Moonlight spilled over the rocky sands. The scent of night and tangy herbs growing nearby filled her nostrils.

Suddenly a new sound cut through the melody of the Almha calling out to her. Thunder softly growled in the distance.

No, not thunder. Hoof beats pounding over pebbles and hardened sand. Elizabeth jerked her head up, horrified.

The desert warrior of her dreams came galloping toward her like a shadowed promise. She dropped the shovel in fright, recognizing the tall, veiled figure. Jabari. Her legs trembled and she stepped back, leaning against the boulder. A wicked-looking sword flashed silver in the moonlight as he held it aloft.

Even in her terror, she marveled at his magnificence, his proud fierceness like an ancient warrior. The sheikh looked like a dark, avenging angel.

Instinctively, she knew he intended to kill her. She had violated some sacred ancestral burying place. Any last vestige of strength fled her. Tears formed in her eyes as she contemplated the specter of death approaching swiftly.

Elizabeth bowed her head, waiting for the killing blow. Then raised her head for one last look at life. And let out a startled gasp as he whirled the blade in the air and sheathed it.

He stopped his horse in front of her. In one powerful motion, he leaned down and as easily as a falcon plucks prey from the sky, scooped her into the saddle.

Chapter Six

She had lingered on the edge of death and lived. Too shocked to speak, Elizabeth felt her heart gallop as swiftly as the horse's hooves.

Anger, relief and confusion swept over her. The dark angel of death did not part her life from her body. Instead, he spirited her away with him.

She must be dreaming. Elizabeth clung to the high pommel, bouncing up and down with the horse's gait. No, not dreaming.

Jabari's arm encircled her waist in an unyielding grip as they galloped through the main wadi. Air slapped against her naked calves, for he forced her to bunch up her skirt and ride astride like a man. His body felt harder than marble against her back. Warm breath tickled her ear as he leaned over her shoulder, giving the reins a light flick.

He was kidnapping her. What right did he have?

Instinct urged her to struggle to escape. Logic said she'd fall and break her neck. He would stop. Eventually.

They slowed to a canter, passing steep canyon walls until reaching the open valley. Elizabeth wished she had stayed safely ensconced in her crude hut in Haggi Quandil. This whole Egyptian adventure had rapidly dissolved into a nightmare.

A short distance from the limestone cliffs, two dark-robed figures on horseback waited on the sandy plain. Elizabeth's dread heightened. This wasn't a spontaneous act.

He stopped and held up a hand in greeting as the other men bowed their head like a subordinate before the master. "Musab. Nazim. Near the royal wadi. Get the shovel and pick and cover the earth. Remove any trace of her digging." He spoke Arabic in a firm, commanding voice.

"Yes, sire," one said. "Then what are your orders? Shall I accompany you?"

"No, Nazim. Musab, I need you to appease the *samak* with a story about her vanishing. Tell them that Elizabeth grew tired of the dig and went to Cairo for a while. She asked me to be her guide. Do not speak of this to anyone else in the tribe."

"It will be done as you say." Two men galloped past them into the canyon. Jabari clucked to his horse and they rode south.

"Be my guide!" Elizabeth shook with fury as she cried out in Arabic. "I'll be your guide on the pathway to—to—heaven if you don't let me go right now!"

She jabbed her elbow into his stomach and met solid muscle. The beast didn't even flinch.

"Hell," he corrected. "Pathway to hell. I cannot release you. It would be advisable for you to sit quietly while we make our journey. Be thankful I spared your life. For now."

"I'll be thankful when I get off this blasted animal. What do you think you are doing! You can't kidnap me!"

"Can I not? I just have." His arrogant tone infuriated her.

He jerked the reins, stopping the horse, then grasped Elizabeth's chin with one strong hand, forcing her to face him. Slowly he unveiled, revealing a clean-shaven, handsome face.

Elizabeth gasped. Asim! She knew it! And yet did not trust her own instincts. She cursed her naiveté.

Ebony eyes pierced hers with fierce intensity. "I am Jabari bin Tarik Hassid, son of Tarik the honored warrior, slayer of traitors, descendent of nobility, sheikh of the great Khamsin warriors. I warned you to leave. You did not."

If his objective was to make her quake with fear, he failed. Elizabeth sniffed as if he'd just announced he sold fake Egyptian artifacts at the *souks*. "I'm not afraid of you."

"You should be," he said softly. "I do not deal lightly with those who cross me."

Her mouth went dry. "What are you going to do with me? Cut my head off?"

Jabari continued to grip her chin, his eyes nearly hypnotizing her with their excruciating scrutiny. "If I wished, your head would be rolling in the sand already," he said in a chilling tone. "For now, you are my captive."

"I don't think so," she replied, and taking advantage of his momentary release of her waist, she suddenly twisted. Grabbing the pommel for purchase, she went to throw her leg over the saddle and jump.

"Not so fast, my lady." He grabbed her around the waist again, this time trapping her with both arms. She felt like a mouse in the coils of a giant anaconda.

"Do that once more and you will force me to bind your hands. It will make our ride much less pleasant," he spoke harshly into her left ear.

"Then I'll scream."

"I am prepared for that as well." Jabari continued to hold her with his left arm while he removed a cloth from his belted waist. He dangled the shimmering silk fabric before her. "Do you promise to remain quiet, or shall I gag you now and save the trouble of doing it later?"

Her eyes followed the gag as he swung it back and forth like a pendulum. "I won't scream."

"Good girl." Jabari tucked the cloth back into his belt.

"But I promise you, you are stupid if you think you can pull this off without anyone missing me."

"I would not be too certain of your status at the dig site." Jabari pulled her against him again and clucked to his mount. They trotted southward, hugging a path closest to the cliff walls. "You will not be much missed except by your uncle."

"You're a liar!"

"I speak truthfully. Has anyone missed you these past few days we have worked together?"

It dawned on her he had a point. Her shoulders sagged with humiliation. She might as well have walked off into the desert alone and let the sands cover her.

"Why are you doing this?" Elizabeth asked with dull resignation.

"You violated my ancestors' sacred grounds," he growled.

Elizabeth gulped and placed a hand protectively around her neck. "Is that all? I had thought you wanted to kill me for something else. Like the Almha."

He jerked on the reins and stopped the horse so suddenly her head snapped forward.

"Who else knows of this?" Jabari grabbed her and twisted her toward him. Black brows drew together in a menacing scowl.

"Just un . . . no one," she fibbed.

"Your uncle of course. I saw you digging with him."

"You spied on us!" Elizabeth's mouth dropped open.

"But of course. I was merely performing my duty."

"Does your duty include removing people's heads?"

His eyes glinted dangerously. "I am a Khamsin warrior. I swore an oath at manhood to protect the Almha from discovery by killing treasure-hunting thieves such as yourself. It is sacred to my people."

In dignified outrage, Elizabeth drew herself up. "I am no treasure-hunting thief! I'm a woman who happens to excel in the field of archaeology!"

"Yes, you are a woman," he murmured. She didn't care for that look on his face in the brilliant light of the nearly full moon. It was . . . ominous. As if she were a cornered gazelle and he a lion eyeing her for dinner. A very hungry lion.

"So you see, I understand now. The Almha is sacred to you. Very well, I promise I won't dig it up. You may let me go now." She folded her arms, vainly hoping he'd see reason.

In response, he settled an arm around her waist again, clucked to his horse and they galloped off into the night.

Too bad Elizabeth kept her promise not to scream. He wished he could gag her. Every time she opened those lovely lips, part of him wanted to choke her.

He'd spared her life and she acted angry about it!

Jabari swore under his breath as they rode south, hugging the cliffs to avoid the village where the archaeology team slept.

"Where are you taking me?"

He growled. "To the top of the cliffs. I only spared your life for a brief time. I must now take your body and hurl it off the edge as a sacrifice to my gods."

Her sudden gasp made him chuckle softly. She heard him, for she muttered, "Beast."

"You know what's wrong with you?" she continued. "You're emotionally impoverished. You have no feelings at all."

Oh, you are so very wrong, my lady. On the contrary. My problem is I have too many feelings. If he had not, Jabari would be riding free as the wind instead of with a lush, lovely problem molded firmly against him.

Moonbeams cast shadows on towering walls. Ghostly grayish sand stretched for miles. He inhaled the fragrance of rosemary-scented skin pressed against his body. She made him dizzy with a heated combination of desire, anger and frustration. He was furious with her for putting him into the predicament now facing him—what would happen when they reached his home? How could he ever explain this to the Majli?

Kidnapping women was acceptable among his people. The Khamsin code of honor demanded they be treated with great respect. But no code of honor existed for kidnapping a Western woman who dared to disturb the Almha. What in the name of Allah was he going to do with her?

They rode in silence for a while. Jabari's thoughts whirled about his head like sand kicked up by the fierce Khamsin wind his tribe was named after. When Elizabeth finally spoke, he gave a sudden start.

"You aren't really going to throw me off the top of the cliffs, are you?" she asked in a small voice.

He pulled her tight against him. Her body was slender, lithe and quite tempting. "No," he said quietly, recognizing the fear in her words.

Her breasts rose and fell, rubbing against his arm. The sensation felt disturbingly erotic. "What then are you planning for me?"

"I do not know," he answered honestly.

She glanced over her shoulder, knitting her brows in a puzzled frown. "You come galloping through the wadi as if to kill me, then you kidnap me and you have no idea what you are going to do? Seems like a very well-conceived plan," Elizabeth drawled.

Jabari ground his teeth. "I may save you for as a treat for my grandfather. I will have my people boil you in oil and then serve you with couscous. My grandfather prefers white meat."

She seemed to ponder the idea. "I have only one request."

"What?" he snapped.

"Put the couscous on the side. I hate couscous."

He shook his head, a reluctant smile tugging his lips. By the grace of Allah, she vexed and amused him! "Why?"

"It tastes like gritty sand. Disgusting. I had it in a restaurant in Cairo before I arrived in Amarna."

"A restaurant." Jabari snorted with derision. "My aunt's couscous would shame them."

"Your aunt? What about your mother? Can't she cook?"

Jabari did not reply. When a few minutes passed, she repeated her question.

He stiffened and loosened his grip around her waist. "I lost my mother four years ago."

"Lost? Do you mean she died?"

"She is dead to me," he replied shortly.

"What was she like? Do you think she'd approve of your running around the desert kidnapping women?"

Old emotions surfaced like ancient demons. He closed his eyes, thinking of his mother. How she loved his father with every breath she drew. *It was not enough. She wanted something more than simple tribal life.* Jabari bit his bottom lip, recognizing the truth. He still missed her.

"I have no need for anyone's approval, certainly not a woman's," he snapped.

"You talk as if women are inferior to men."

"And your point is?"

She stiffened. Jabari felt as if he embraced wood. "Women are equal to men. We can do anything you can."

"You cannot. Women are for bearing sons and satisfying a man's needs in bed," he stated in clipped tones.

Elizabeth's stubbornness eerily echoed his mother's. He closed his eyes, grief and anger tugging at him, remembering the warmth of his mother's embrace, her gentle smile.

His heart had ripped in two when she left his father and shamed him. Jabari let his temper rise against Elizabeth. No more of this bewitching attraction for her. She scared him and he had to assert control.

"If you are equal to a man, then how can I hold you captive? For a man would struggle like a lion to escape," Jabari taunted.

"If I were a man, you would not have spared me. I cannot see you riding into the desert with a man," she responded.

True. If she were a man, he'd have no qualms about taking her life. Jabari could not deny his growing feelings for Elizabeth. She threatened his good sense just as she did back at the dig site. Only this time he risked more than being uncloaked by an Al-Hajid. His honor and strength as a leader hung precariously in the balance. Jabari remembered how his father's love for his mother stripped him of power in the eyes of his men when he returned from Cairo without her. He should have brought her back kicking and screaming rather than face such disgrace. A man who could not control his woman is a weak leader, his grandfather had said. He should kill Elizabeth now and end this madness. Jabari fingered his scimitar's handle.

His mind felt fuzzy from lack of sleep. A few hours would clear his befuddled brain. And then he could decide.

Pressing his knees into Sahar's sides, he urged her forward and they rode on, shadows in the night.

Up and down. Back and forth. Her favorite rocking horse had a soothing motion. She giggled as her body swayed with it. Then suddenly her horse stopped rocking. Dimly she heard it snort. *Funny. Rocking horses don't snort.*

Her skin felt chilled. Elizabeth shook off the dazed feeling. She'd dozed off and they had stopped.

She sniffed the air and smelled the dank scent of river water. They must be just south of the village of Haggi Quandil, next to the Nile. Jabari dismounted behind her and walked the horse over to a large rock, dropping the reins. Deprived of his body's warmth, she rubbed her arms in the suddenly cold night.

"Why are we stopping? Are we there yet?"

He did not answer but began untying a bedroll from behind the saddle. Jabari unrolled it and spread it out so it was wide enough to accommodate two people. She eyed the bedding with some apprehension, remembering what he had said earlier.

"The hour is late. We will rest here for a few hours." He reached up and beckoned to her. "I will help you down."

"I've been on horses before. I don't need help," she said, and swung her leg over the saddle as she dismounted.

"Sit," he ordered, pointing to the bedroll. Unfastening a bag from the saddle, he offered it to her.

"Water."

She took a long swallow and handed it back to him. Jabari didn't drink but replaced the bag on the saddle. The thin bedroll provided more comfort from the hardened ground than she would have thought.

The moon had shrunk in the sky, although it still lit the desert with pale, grayish light. Distant stars peppered the thick richness of the night sky, mocking her with the romance of their twinkling dances. Moonlit night. Starshine. All alone with a handsome desert warrior.

Who had a steel sword at least three feet long.

Elizabeth recalled her earlier fantasies about being spirited away and shook her head. What a romantic fool she was! Her fantasies never included being held prisoner. Certainly not by an arrogant, proud sheikh who acted as if he'd done her a favor by not beheading her. She clutched her neck as she watched him stroke his horse's muzzle with great affection.

His manner of dress authenticated the dangerous air about him. A high-collared, loose-fitting indigo robe draped to mid-thigh. The robe had long slits on both sides, wide sleeves and was secured by a leather belt. Sword and dagger dangled from his waist. Dark, loose trousers were tucked into soft leather boots.

"Why do you wear this clothing? Or is this robe what your tribe wears when kidnapping women and raiding dig sites?"

Jabari turned from his horse with a scowl. "The *binish* is worn by all our warriors. We receive this sacred garment, our turbans and scimitars when we are initiated into manhood."

She couldn't help the small smirk creeping over her lips at the proud tone of his voice. "So, what else does your initiation into manhood include? Small animal sacrifices?"

His dark eyes gleamed with sudden intensity. Fingering the dagger at his waist, he gave her a diabolical smile. "Not small animals. Humans. Americans over British. Less blue blood."

Elizabeth couldn't tell if he joked and gulped.

Jabari cocked his head at her. "I need to water Sahar. The river is only a short walk from here, but I cannot keep an eye on you while I do so." He reached up into a small woven bag tied to his saddle and withdrew two braided plaits of cord.

Elizabeth shook, realizing what he intended.

"I won't run away. Please don't do this," she said, panicking at being trussed like a chicken for a roast.

In the light of the moon, she saw a flicker of regret pass over his face. "I am sorry, but I must," Jabari said quietly. He grasped her hands and bound them with one of the ropes. He eyed her ankles, tucked beneath her as she sat cross-legged.

"Stretch out your legs. I must tie your ankles together."

"Do you really think I can go anywhere like this?" She held out her imprisoned wrists.

"Yes," he said curtly. "Now stretch out your legs."

She lifted her chin in a stubborn gesture. "No."

Jabari heaved a sigh. "Elizabeth, I am a patient man, but you are wearing that patience thin. It is very late and I am very tired. Either stretch out your legs so I may bind them, or I will remove all your clothing and prevent your escape that way."

She blinked once in amazement. "You wouldn't dare."

"I would," he said in a hard voice. "And if you think running to the village would help you, let me assure you there are less than honorable men there who would not hesitate to satisfy their lust with a naked American woman."

Elizabeth swallowed, thinking about what he said. She stretched out her legs, yanking her skirt down. With grim irony she wished for the confines of stockings to hide her bare skin from his intense gaze. Jabari bound her legs gently at the ankles, leaving the rope slack enough, tying an intricate knot she had trouble following.

Abruptly he stood, nodded and walked over to the waiting horse. "I will not be long."

Elizabeth shuddered. The desert night embraced her with its bitter cold. Jabari looked at her, frowned, then untied a striped blanket from his saddle. He squatted next to her and draped it over her shoulders, drawing it around her like a cape.

"Thank you," she whispered. He gave an abrupt nod, turned and began walking Sahar toward the Nile.

As soon as he did, she shrugged off the blanket and started working on untying her bonds. With her right hand at an awkward position, Elizabeth picked and tugged at the rope around her ankles. Desperately, she glanced around for a sharp object to cut the rope. A nearby rock caught her eye. She picked it up and with the sharpest edge, began sawing against her bonds awkwardly.

It was like trying to cut steel with a butter knife. Still, she persisted. *Have to try. Maybe at least free the ankles, I can run fast, the camp isn't far . . .*

The sound of approaching hoofbeats erased her hopes. Elizabeth tossed aside the stone. She forced her face to relax in a winsome smile.

Jabari picked up the discarded blanket and fingered it. He bent down and inspected the rope around her ankles and gave her a questioning look.

"What did you expect?" She shrugged.

"Nothing less," he stated. Jabari unfastened both ropes with ease and she stretched her hands out gratefully. Barely had she begun to rub her wrists when he tied both ropes together, then secured one about his waist.

"Now what are you planning?" She gestured toward the rope.

His answering smile filled her with tension, which grew when he knelt next to her. Reaching under her arms, he circled her waist with the other end.

She put her hands against his shoulders and tried to push him away in vain. "What are you doing?"

Jabari tied the rope in another complicated knot. "Now I can sleep," he said in a satisfied voice.

"So you're going to tether me to you like a dog to a

post?" Elizabeth squealed. "You don't trust that I'm tired as well? That I need sleep more than I need to escape?"

He raised one eyebrow. "No. Why would I? Would you?"

She admitted grudgingly that he was right. She wouldn't.

He removed the long scimitar and a sharp dagger from his belt, placing them at the bedroll's edge. Sitting next to her, he unwound his turban, shaking his shoulder-length hair free. Transfixed, she stared at the gleaming black satin. She wondered what it would feel like beneath her fingers, the kinked curls against her bare skin.

Jabari dropped the cloth and threw the blanket over his legs. "Lie down," he ordered.

Lie down? Next to him? A finger of fear touched her spine. Glancing at him, Elizabeth wondered what he wanted. She'd heard stories of desert bandits and how they treated female captives. She shivered again, this time not from the cold, and scooted a little away from him.

"What are you going to do?" she asked, hating the quiver in her voice.

He must have read her mind, for his fierce expression softened. "Elizabeth, I have no intentions of ravishing your body tonight, as lovely as it is. You have nothing to fear from me," he said quietly.

On the contrary, she had everything to fear. Most of all, she dreaded the disturbing feelings her kidnapper brought out in her. "I'm not afraid," she said. "I'm just not . . . sleepy."

"As you wish." Jabari shrugged. "Whether or not you sleep makes no difference to me." He laid down on the bedroll, turned his back to her and pulled the blanket over him, leaving her sitting up, exposed to the chilly night air.

Barely two minutes later, her body started trembling from the cold. Elizabeth cradled herself with her arms. Pride prevented her from lying next to him and sharing the blanket.

Her body began cursing her pride. A needle-sharp wind

blowing through the valley pricked through the thin covering of her blouse and began numbing her toes.

She had no idea the desert could be so cold. Memories of the own soft, warm cot and sheepskin blanket teased her.

"Elizabeth." Jabari's sudden calling of her name startled her. He rolled over to face her. "Stop being so stubborn. Come, lie down and share the blanket before you freeze to death."

"Freeze to death in the desert," she said through chattering teeth. "What an ironic way to die. Although I admit I prefer it to having my head cut off."

Jabari lifted the edge of the blanket, a tempting invitation. Oh, how she longed to curl beneath its soft warmth.

"Elizabeth," he repeated.

She wiggled a bit away from him. He sighed heavily. "I have told you, you will be safe tonight. On my honor as a warrior of the wind. Do not be afraid."

Her frozen toes shoved aside pride and she gave in, lying as far away from him as the rope permitted. Jabari threw the blanket over her.

She raised her head and saw him study her with quiet concentration. Ebony eyes captured hers, mesmerizing her. No hard anger or cruelty lurked there, only dark turmoil, as if the man wrestled with unseen demons. Almost against her will, Elizabeth moved closer to him.

What was she doing?

She stopped and forced herself to look away from his hypnotic gaze. Her eyes traveled down the slope of his smooth cheekbones and drifted to the full lower lip. A strong yet sensual mouth invited her to draw close . . . to brush her lips against it and excavate the mysteries that awaited her in the richness of his kiss.

Elizabeth flipped over and presented her back to him. Let him stare at that.

She closed her eyes and tried to relax, an impossible task. Even under the thick blanket, her body felt like chunk of solid ice. She tugged at the cloth and shuddered.

"What's wrong?" he asked softly.

"I'm cold." She hated herself for complaining but was unable to stop. Shaking, she curled herself into a tight ball, trying to find warmth.

Suddenly his warm, solid body pressed against her back. Her breath hitched as a firm arm draped across her waist, pulling her back. As Jabari spooned himself next to her, Elizabeth's muscles suddenly tensed, like a rabbit frozen to the ground as it sensed a falcon circling overhead.

"I told you, you have nothing to fear from me. Let my body keep you warm. Just lie quietly and sleep," he whispered, his heated breath tickling her ear.

But she knew it wasn't Jabari she feared. It was her own inexplicable physical reaction to this mysterious desert warrior.

She closed her eyes and tried to let sleep claim her.

The slender figure in his arms finally relaxed. Elizabeth's quiet, even breathing told him she'd fallen asleep at last.

Not that he could.

Jabari closed his eyes again, trying to summon elusive sleep. Each time he did, Elizabeth's face swirled in his thoughts. The long lashes sweeping up from large, questioning eyes, her mouth as innocent and tempting as a lush pomegranate. He had hidden his surprise when she started to advance toward him. It was a relief when she'd turned over and he could no longer gaze upon the temptation of her lips.

He'd promised he would not touch her that evening, more for his benefit than hers, for he needed to distance himself from her. Jabari always kept his word. But this promise was a hard one to keep. Especially with their bodies forced together as protection from the cold. He'd thought the chilly air would serve as a welcome distraction to the allure of the beguiling woman in his arms. But one section of his lower body throbbed and demanded release. Not every part of him was exhausted!

Aware of his body's growing response to holding Elizabeth, Jabari broke contact and moved away.

What was he going to do with her? He couldn't bring her back to his people. They couldn't roam the desert forever, either. Killing her offered the only logical solution. If only there was a safe place to keep her, away from all eyes, until he managed to decide what to do.

She stirred in her sleep, shivering. With some reluctance, Jabari moved closer. He enjoyed how well their bodies molded together. Her long blond hair shimmered in the moonlight. Gently he smoothed an errant strand back from her brow.

Why had she come into his life? What destiny brought them together time and time again? Clearly their fates were locked together tighter than he now held Elizabeth in his arms. For all his practical ways, Jabari could not ignore his culture's age-old beliefs. He believed in Kismet as much as he believed in the power of modern machines. Like his Khamsin brethren, Jabari embraced an odd mixture of faith in Allah, desert spirits and superstitions. It was bred into his blood and bones.

His pondering of their interlocked destinies broke when Elizabeth sighed in her sleep. And began moving against him, rubbing her body up and down against his. He groaned. The delicious friction created a natural response. It had been a long time since he'd held a woman in his arms and now he could do nothing about it. He wished he'd made time to visit his concubines before spying on the dig site. His body ached for release.

With the sudden force the solution hit him. His harem, housed at Amarna. The spacious quarters were extremely private and well guarded.

He glanced down at the woman slumbering in his arms and smiled. Let her rest for a while. And now he could too. Soon enough, they would ride to her new sleeping quarters—among the ladies of his harem.

Chapter Seven

Elizabeth's head bobbed as the horse trotted down the main street of Amarna. When Jabari stopped before a large walled enclosure, encircled in a protective manner by villagers' mud-brick huts, her chin drooped on her chest like a wilted flower.

They stopped before a massive gate. Jabari dismounted, withdrew a key from his robe, unlocked the gate and led Elizabeth on the horse into a courtyard ringed by a building that encircled it. He locked the gate again and let the horse's reins drop. He dismounted and leaned against the animal. Jabari held out a hand to Elizabeth.

"Come."

Come. Sit. Water. His tyrannical attitude exasperated her. Elizabeth ignored his hand and dismounted, pausing to pat the horse's withers. She frowned, realizing the animal's sex. "A mare? Doesn't suit you. Why don't you ride a stallion?"

He hesitated as if divulging secrets. "Khamsin . . . and other desert tribes, do not ride stallions, only use them for breeding. Mares are better for riding into battle, for they do not whinny at other horses and alert the enemy. They are more docile."

"And easier to control, which you like," she grumbled. Elizabeth looked at the graceful animal. "You'll just leave her here? Don't you tie up her reins?"

Jabari caressed the mare's nose tenderly. "Sahar is my beloved friend. I do not tie up my friends."

"No, you just tie up women." She didn't suppress a yawn. Her eyelids drooped. Jabari became a blurred blue figure.

A strong arm encircled her waist, supporting her as they walked. For once, she did not struggle. She was too tired.

He crossed the courtyard to the building. A stout wooden door barred their way. Jabari gave a series of cryptic knocks, which led to sounds of a bolt being slid back.

The door swung inward and she followed Jabari inside. A muscular and powerful-looking man, nearly as tall as Jabari himself, bowed before him, then shut and bolted the door.

"Welcome back, sire. I heard your horse approach." He held a small glass lamp in one massive hand. Shadows danced across his blue vest and white shirt. Black, loose-fitting pants belted with a thick leather cord did not hide stocky legs that she swore were larger than her waist. A dagger and two long, deadly looking scimitars dangled from his belt. The man was armed to the teeth as if expecting an invasion. What could he possibly be protecting in Jabari's empty apartment? Jewels? Gold?

The servant barely glanced at her. His lack of curiosity perturbed Elizabeth. If she were Jabari's servant and he arrived in the middle of the night with a strange woman, she'd gawk to say the least.

She glanced at their surroundings. Soft lamplight showed her a room with plush pillows settled about low tables, thick carpets on a marbled floor and intricate mosaic tile work on the walls.

"Sire, we were not expecting you. Shall I prepare a meal?

A bath? What do you desire?" The man's tone was respectful.

"Just something to drink and some fruit for now, Aziz," Jabari replied. "We are quite tired and wish to rest."

"Yes, sire."

Carrying the lamp before him, Aziz led them down the twists and turns of a hallway lined with many closed doors. Elizabeth rubbed her eyes. Jabari glanced at her. "I am certain your sleeping quarters will meet with your satisfaction."

Good. Sleep to clear her mind and figure out an escape. If she weren't so exhausted, she'd kick and scream the whole way.

They stopped at the end of the hallway before a large door. The servant reached for a ring of keys around his waist and unlocked the door. He opened it and bowed low again.

"Welcome back, master. May your night be eased with all the delights you so richly deserve." Before Elizabeth could puzzle over this odd greeting, the man stepped inside. He crossed the room silently, lighting lamps scattered on several low tables.

Elizabeth forgot her exhaustion and looked around with unease. It was a squarish room with elaborate tapestries hanging from ceiling to floor. Persian carpets covered the floors in a riot of deep crimson and gold. Dominating the room was an enormous low bed covered in red silk piled with several plush pillows of crimson and gold. Several gold embroidered cushions with backs like legless chairs were scattered around a long, low sandalwood table surrounded by large, plush pillows. Clearly, Jabari slept there. Elizabeth's distress grew. Did he expect her to as well? With him? She hadn't the strength to fight him off. Not now. But he promised he wouldn't touch her that night . . .

Jabari led her to the straight-back cushions. Elizabeth sank into the plushness, studying him warily. He stood proudly, a king comfortable in his home. She had never met anyone like him before, so confident, so handsome. So annoying. He removed his weapons, unwound his turban and shook his hair free.

She started when Aziz went down the hallway, pounding on the doors and calling out, "The master has arrived!"

She heard doors creak open and watched as two of the loveliest, most exotic women she'd ever seen stumbled into the room, rubbing sleep from their sloe eyes. Wearing richly embroidered diaphanous gowns of lavender and emerald, both had shapely bodies and long black hair spilling past their shoulders.

Anxiety replaced her exhaustion. Elizabeth turned to Jabari, who stood beside her with a broad smile.

"Badra, Farah, peace and blessings to you," Jabari said as the women lowered their heads to him. "This is Elizabeth."

As her mouth dropped open in shock, he turned to Elizabeth and gestured to the women. "Welcome to my harem."

Sitting on the carpeted floor, resting against a tall stack of cushions, Jabari accepted a tall glass of sweet fruit juice from Aziz. He selected a date from an assortment the servant offered on a silver tray and watched Elizabeth's dumbfounded reaction. Her blue eyes widened as she watched the women settle themselves around Jabari on the floor like graceful flowers draped about a vine. Farah sat behind his back and suddenly he felt her soft hands begin to massage his neck.

He allowed Badra to pull off his leather boots and she made a clucking sound of disapproval. She went into the attached bath chamber, returning with a small basin of water and some thick towels, then knelt and began washing his feet.

Aziz offered a glass to Elizabeth. Suspicion tightened her face as she took it, sniffing it as if he'd given her poison. She declined the dates he proffered, but finally drank the juice. Aziz shrugged and placed them on the table.

"I should have expected you to have a harem," she said, glaring. "Why did you bring me here?"

Jabari put his glass on the table and leaned back, enjoying the feel of Farah's accomplished fingers kneading the tired muscles in his shoulders.

"It should be obvious to you, my lady," he replied, meeting her hostile stare with an amused chuckle. "You're my prisoner. Relax and enjoy it. Have a date. Are you not hungry?"

"I am not your prisoner, and I am not staying here!"

"You have no choice." Jabari sat straighter, narrowing his eyes. "You are not in a position to argue. You will stay here and be well cared for, as are my concubines."

"Your concubines." She made a moue of distaste saying the word. "Your slaves. You are a barbarian for imprisoning them!"

Elizabeth's words grated on his tired nerves. In the back of his mind, he knew she lashed out from fear and shock. Jabari forced himself to adopt a mild tone.

"My concubines are not slaves. Their every need is met. I care for them just as I care for the needs of my people. Know this, Elizabeth: Your world is far different from mine. These women need my protection. I am honorbound to give it to them. Do not let your Western ways judge what you do not understand."

Farah settled closer to him, rubbing her breasts against his back in slow strokes meant to seduce. Jabari smiled, but his eyes were on Elizabeth. Despite his exhaustion, he felt a stab of piercing desire at the sparkle in her eyes, the lovely cheeks flushed with anger, the way her breasts heaved with the passion of her emotions. So different from his concubines, who doted on him with meek submissiveness. Her fiery spirit raised his ardor. He wanted her as he never wanted another woman and that desire shamed him, for had he violated his blood oath because of it? Honor was everything to Jabari. Without honor, he could not rule as sheikh or even live as a man, let alone a warrior of the wind.

What would his grandfather say if he discovered Jabari let her live because he desired her in his bed? He inhaled deeply.

"Oh, my Western ways can judge what is going on here. I understand. You said you would not ravish me tonight. So you are saving me for another night? You spared my life and brought me here just to bring me to your bed. Why kill me with your sword when my body can suit your needs? Or does your sacred oath make allowances for a man's lust? Where is the honor in that?"

Elizabeth could not have hit him in a more vulnerable spot. Jabari reeled from the truth of her accusations. Defensively, he struck back, determined to demean her as she had belittled him.

"Women were made to love men, to bear children and serve men. My concubines desire to please me, and they delight in doing so. Unlike you, they know all about being a woman," he taunted.

Elizabeth folded her arms and that lovely mouth tightened with anger. "I am not a whore like them. Or any of the other women in your tribe. I stand on my own two feet." She leaned forward and showed him the soles of her feet.

Badra shrank back as if Elizabeth were a deadly snake spitting. Farah stopped her ministrations and gasped.

Rage filled him. She knew how this gesture insulted him. He checked his temper and took a long, controlling breath. Out of the corner of his eye, he saw Aziz whip around. His servant's hand went to the silver dagger he kept belted to his waist. Jabari held up a hand for him to stop. He gave Badra a tender, reassuring smile before turning his full fury on Elizabeth.

"These women are honorable, as are all the women in my tribe. You insult me and those in my own household. Do not do lash your tongue at me again, Elizabeth, or you will suffer its loss." He spoke in the low, threatening tone that intimidated his strongest warriors. Never before had

Jabari spoken to a woman thus, and it angered him even more that she forced him to do so.

She lifted her chin with an air of proud disbelief. "You would actually cut out my tongue?"

"Not me," Jabari said in chilling tones. He snapped his fingers and Aziz silently glided forward. "Him."

Her eyes widened as she glanced at the dagger at Aziz's belt. "You wouldn't dare. My uncle . . . he'd get you!"

"Elizabeth, perhaps I should speak slowly for my words to penetrate to your brain. You are no longer under the protection of your uncle. No one knows where you are."

Jabari gave her the steady, piercing look that terrified men who dared to cross him. "You are my captive. You have no rights here. You will learn to obey me, my lady."

Her chest rose and fell with the force of her exhaled breathing. Two dark blue icicles bore into his eyes. "I will not."

Jabari felt torn between exhilarating desire and deep wrath by her rebellion. Part of him wanted her to fight him and demonstrate that passionate spirit that attracted him. Part of him, the traditional sheikh who could not look powerless before a woman, needed to assert his authority. Her disobedient attitude could cause substantial problems. Women in his tribe obeyed men. Period. They trusted the men, knowing a Khamsin warrior treasured and protected his woman at all costs.

"Yes, you will. You are my captive. I have the power to do with you as I please," he growled. Badra looked up at his angry tone. She nestled close to him, her eyes glazing over with fear. He flashed her a reassuring smile to let her know he harbored her no ill will and smoothed her hair in a loving gesture.

Elizabeth's dirt-streaked face grew crimson with fury that almost bordered on jealous rage. Just as he was marveling over this, she picked up her glass.

"I am fed up with you ordering me around. You have no power over me!" she shrieked and flung the contents in his face, dousing him and Badra in a sticky wash of citrus. Badra gave a startled cry and hid her head, shaking with sobs.

Aziz whirled toward Elizabeth, his dagger drawn and ready. No one dared to strike the sheikh. Penalty for doing so was death. Jabari held up his hand again to stop him.

Icy black rage filled him. In the past two months, Badra had finally opened up. The constant terror that had plagued her since she came to his harem had ceased. She had even begun to laugh and the music of her singing filled him with great joy, for she had begun to heal from the wounds of her past.

Now Elizabeth had disturbed his harem with discord and violent words, filling Badra with fear once more.

Jabari took care of his first concern and motioned for Farah to reassure Badra. He took the towel, wiping his face. He uncoiled his body like a cobra ready to strike and approached Elizabeth. Her outraged face contorted into an ugly mask.

Instead of the harem being a solution, it only added to his problems. Word would spread that Jabari had a new woman in his harem, a disobedient one.

Glancing at Aziz, he saw his servant's scowl turn into puzzled expectation as he regarded Jabari. Aziz waited to see what action his master would take to put Elizabeth in her place. If he took none, word would seep back to the tribe that Jabari's new woman had made a fool of him. Just as his mother made a fool of his father. His men would regard him as weak. He'd lose respect among his warriors as his father lost respect. They would refuse to follow his orders and he could lose leadership.

He had to punish her to save face. Bend her stubborn pride and make her obey. Like a wild colt that kicked out with flaying hooves, he had to bring her under control. Such defiance called for a beating. Jabari never hit animals or women.

But there was another way of stripping pride from those slender shoulders and making her totally vulnerable. He hated what he had to do, but she forced him into it.

"Elizabeth, you have exhausted my patience with your behavior. I will no longer tolerate your rudeness. You leave me with no choice as to what I must do."

Jabari took her hand and pulled her to her feet. Uncertainty clouded her eyes. As he withdrew the sharp blade at his belt, her breathing quickened. Elizabeth's arms went limp, dropping as if suddenly losing all muscle control.

Hooking one finger into her partly opened blouse, he pulled it outwards. Then he plunged his dagger into it and slowly tore it open to her waist. She closed her eyes as he cut the skirt in a long rip that thundered in the silent room. The skirt fell to the floor, leaving her clad in blouse and undergarment.

He looked at her a moment, judging her reaction. Elizabeth's eyes flashed defiance and she lifted her chin. Not enough, then. Jabari tugged the blouse off, let it fall to the floor. She began to shake. Her breath came in sharp, ragged pants. He took the dagger and traced a line over her breasts and belly and down to her thighs. He did so very gently so the blade did not touch her, only the undergarment. Standing, he cut the cloth at her shoulders. Jabari pulled out the undergarment from her chest with one hand and slowly slipped the dagger between her breasts, careful not to touch her skin. White cloth split in two as the knife glided along the fabric down to the hem. The last of her clothing fell to the floor. Elizabeth now stood naked before him. Her breasts rose and fell rapidly in rhythm to her quickened breaths, but he took no pleasure at their sight. She turned scarlet, covering herself with her hands.

"Apologize to Badra. Then kneel and bow before me with your head to the floor," he commanded, gesturing to the floor with his dagger. "In your proper place."

To his immense relief, she stammered a quick apology to his concubine, then sank to her knees and placed her forehead on the floor, remaining at his feet.

He stood for a minute, looking down at her, feeling disgusted with himself, then turned and left the room.

* * *

He was going to rape her.

Elizabeth trembled at Jabari's feet, knowing what would happen next. How horribly right he'd been. She had no power in his harem and he could do as he pleased.

Jabari had lied to her. He would use her for his pleasure that night. Why else would he strip her naked?

She bit her lip, willing her body to stop shaking. His eyes had filled with a murderous fury, and it tempered her own anger with terror. Instinctively she knew that she'd made a mistake and foolishly misjudged his limit on tolerance. He was a proud man and she'd humiliated him. Now he'd pay her back.

She knelt at his feet, not daring to raise her eyes until she heard the door slam. Elizabeth cautiously looked up and raised her head a bit. But for the women, she was alone. She sat back, feeling a curious mixture of relief and bewilderment. She did not understand this man. She wondered if she ever would.

The two women stared as if Elizabeth were a mummy rising from the dead. She gave them a cheerless smile. Probably if she had been a corpse springing to life they couldn't have been more shocked. She doubted they dared to utter a peep against Jabari. The one called Badra had stopped crying. Her gaze roved curiously over Elizabeth's naked body, alighting on her dove birthmark. Lovely almond-shaped eyes widened. Elizabeth cringed, covering herself, feeling vulnerable and shaky.

"Get up." Aziz grabbed her arm with such force she cried out. He yanked her to her feet. His hostile glare told her that this man wasn't merely outraged by what she'd done, but would have gladly killed her if Jabari hadn't stopped him. Still gripping her arm, he led her from the room.

"Where are you taking me?" She wondered if Jabari had delayed his reaction only to devise a more sinister punishment. The servant grunted and opened a door down the hallway.

"In there, you will sleep." Aziz all but shoved her into

the room and shut the door. A lamp cast shadows about the room, which was large enough only for a narrow bed, writing table, chair and tapestries on the walls. A soft white gown lay on the bed.

A key turned in the lock. Imprisoned. Elizabeth noticed a small door off one wall and she quickly ran to it. Only a washstand, a slop jar and some linens inside. Elizabeth felt futility claim her courage. She donned the gown and laid down on the soft bed. Too exhausted to think of what the morning would bring from her actions that night, she drifted off to sleep.

Chapter Eight

She awoke to a room filled with dawn streaking through the latticed window. Two faces stared at her with avid curiosity.

Her heart thudded in her chest and she sat upright, scattering the women around her like frightened cats. Elizabeth had suffered through a restless night. Caught in the throes of her usual childhood nightmare, she dreamed of her parents walking through the cave. They turned and waved. Elizabeth had opened her mouth to warn them, but they did not hear. She stared in horror as the ceiling collapsed upon them, and then she screamed.

Dimly she remembered someone comforting her in the middle of the night, caressing her temple and soothing away her fear. It must have all been part of the dream, she reasoned.

Seeming to gather their courage, the women crept back to the bed again. One reached out and touched Elizabeth's face.

"Why are you doing that?" Elizabeth asked sharply in Arabic. She backed away from the woman's fingers as if they burned.

"Never have I seen a woman speak to the master thus or dare to strike him. Aziz should have killed you for such disrespect. Yet you are here. Are you a jinn come to haunt us?"

A jinn. If so, she could vanish at will and Jabari would have no power over her. She wanted to laugh. But the woman's very real trepidation stopped her.

"I am no jinn."

"But you are so insulting to the master. Why do you speak to him that way?"

She glanced at the speaker. Thick black hair curled down to her waist. Kohl outlined her sloe eyelids. The woman wore a diaphanous crimson gown with a short red silk jacket embroidered with silver thread. Her exotic beauty suddenly made Elizabeth aware of her own dirt-streaked state.

"Who are you? How long have you been here?"

The woman lifted her head with a flush of pride. "I am named Farah. I have served the master faithfully for three years."

Enslaved for three years in this luxurious dungeon. Elizabeth swung her legs off the side of the bed.

Farah reached out and fingered a strand of Elizabeth's hair. "So straight and thin. The master will not like this. He prefers women to have hair as thick as sheep's wool." Her lovely eyes gave Elizabeth a look recognizable in any culture—one woman's scorn for another.

She pushed Farah's hand away. "Then he can have your sheep's wool and leave me in peace with my thin hair."

Farah's slender brows arched and she curled her lips. "You do not desire the master in your bed? It is a great honor to be chosen to serve him thus!"

"I'd rather drown in the Nile."

"I do not understand. The master's touch is like that of the sun. It fills me with burning desire. When he chooses me for the night, I am proud. When I lie beneath him, I glory that Allah made me a woman and created my body to receive him."

She cast a critical glance at Elizabeth. "You will find he is unlike any other lover."

Elizabeth sniffed. "I have no intention of taking him or any other man as my lover."

Sudden understanding dawned on Farah's face. "Ah, now I know why he has brought you here. You are untouched!"

Elizabeth felt a flush creep up her neck to her cheeks. She folded her arms and lifted her chin. "I am a virgin," she stated with as much pride as she did when declaring her beliefs as a suffragette.

A knowing smile tugged at the corners of Farah's beautiful mouth. "You will not stay one for long."

Farah turned to her companion and began an intimate discussion of sex. Farah compared Jabari's manliness to their former captor, Sheikh Fareeq. She outlined in explicit detail exactly what kind of prowess Jabari displayed in bed. Elizabeth felt the flush darken until her face burned in a raging inferno. She had a vague idea of what the various parts were but could not envision what went where. Now Farah gleefully filled in all the details, leaving nothing to the imagination. Elizabeth's lower belly trembled as she contemplated Farah's words. An unbidden image of Jabari's powerful body straddling hers sprang to mind.

Farah held up her thumb and forefinger barely an inch apart. "Fareeq was but like this."

Her smile broadened with sly satisfaction. "Our master is a strong man. He is like this!" She threw apart her hands, stretching them farther, making Badra laugh.

She cast a devious look at Elizabeth's scarlet face. "I do not envy you being a virgin. The first time is painful even with small ones such as Fareeq. But our master is . . . quite . . . large."

Elizabeth gulped. She saw Farah smirk and realized the woman deliberately baited her. *You have a brain. Remember you are educated and have an advantage these women never had.* Pity for Farah flickered through her.

Elizabeth rose from her bed with as much regal elegance

as she could muster. She looked at them with scorn. "Large, small, what does it matter? Whatever the size, men are all the same. They think with that instrument of their manhood. Not me. I have an education, and I thank Allah I don't have to rely upon a man as if I were a dog begging for favors!"

She walked into the bathing chamber and slammed the door. When she emerged, Farah had vanished. Timid Badra remained, sitting on her bed. Wide sloe eyes looked at her in admiration. She gave her a shy smile that dimmed Elizabeth's anger.

Elizabeth joined her on the bed, feeling suddenly lonely. She could use a friend now. Unlike the haughty Farah, Badra seemed a possible candidate. She touched her hand.

"I am sorry Badra for . . . calling you that name and hitting you with the juice. I never meant to hurt you."

"I have never seen anyone act that way. You have a powerful *ka* to have such courage," she said with a little sigh.

"My life force is not courageous, only stubborn. I can't stand Jabari ordering me around! And I will not be his prisoner!"

"But Jabari is gentle. He never gives orders. And we are not prisoners. I am allowed to come and go as I please. Perhaps he treats you differently because he can't control you."

Elizabeth wondered at the girl's insight. "And he never will. I'll escape from here." She looked at Badra. "How did you get in? The door was locked."

The dark-eyed girl fumbled in her gown's pocket and withdrew a golden key. "I am allowed outside the compound if I wish. Sometimes I go back to the Khamsin camp. I miss the women there, especially Jabari's aunt."

"By yourself or with others?"

"I have a Khamsin warrior who lives in Amarna escort me for my protection. It is not safe for me to go alone."

Elizabeth stared at her. "Badra, why don't you leave?"

"Leave?" The girl's brown eyes widened to the size of

dark grapes. "Jabari asked me the same thing once, if I wanted to go. But to where? Who would care for me? I love it here."

Pity coursed through her. The teenager seemed to accept her captivity. Perhaps she convinced herself it offered more comfort than the terrors of the unknown outside world.

Something about Jabari's harem puzzled her, though. Many harems consisted of concubines passed down from generation to generation. Sons inherited their father's concubines. She asked Badra about this.

"Oh no, the Khamsin are not like other tribes. Because Ranefer, Kiya's high priest and founder of the Khamsin, was so devoted to Kiya, he vowed that all warriors could have only one wife to love for all eternity. The sheikh may have concubines only while he remains unmarried. When he takes a wife, arrangements are made to marry off the concubines."

Elizabeth hid her surprise. Such devotion to a wife was not what she expected of Jabari's people. Certainly not of men who vowed to chop off heads of those who dug for their sacred Almha.

"Badra, what do you know of the Khamsin? Where do they camp? They seemed to appear out of nowhere, my uncle said, when they raided the dig site."

Badra hesitated and looked around as if fearing eavesdroppers. "The Khamsin live deep in the Arabian Desert to hide the tribe. But a few warriors live in Amarna in disguise. The Khamsin call them the *saqrs*."

"Why are they called the falcons?"

"The symbol of my master's clan is a falcon. The *saqrs* are like birds who keep watchful eyes on the city. If they see suspicious activity, they report to the camp. If they catch anyone digging for the Almha, they execute him. Except in rare cases of a tribal member. Then the offender is brought before the Majli, the council of elders. The chief elder has the right to either terminate his life or grant clemency."

"How far is the camp?" Elizabeth asked.

"It is about three hours. I am to visit there today."

Badra, her only hope, was leaving. An idea blossomed. Elizabeth gazed around the tiny room. A small writing desk sat shoved up against the wall. She scrambled to it, found paper and pencil and scribbled a note.

"Badra, I need your help. Please. Make an excuse to your escort that you need to visit the village. Bring this note to Nahid Wilson in Haggi Quandil. Please. Can you do that?"

She smiled shyly. "My *saqr* is devoted to me. He hopes I will marry him when Jabari takes a wife. He will do anything for me. But this," she tapped the paper, "what does it say?"

"You can't read?" Elizabeth watched her sloe eyes fill with tears of frustration.

"I wish to learn." Her tiny sigh filled Elizabeth with compassion. "Jabari will not permit it."

Probably because he used their ignorance to keep them with him, she thought with anger. "He is cruel for denying you this."

"Oh no! Jabari is very kind. It is against Khamsin custom for women to learn to read."

Elizabeth felt her anger against Jabari waver, seeing the worshipful look on Badra's face. "Maybe I can teach you to read," she offered.

Badra's eyes filled with such excitement that Elizabeth felt guilty for taking her own education for granted. "When you return from the camp. And make sure my uncle takes care of my dove," she said, twisting a lock of hair. "He may have forgotten about Isis. She hasn't been fed in nearly two days. If you do this, I will teach you to read. Until I can escape here."

Hope faded from Badra's beaming face. She pouted. "Leave us? Where would you go?"

"Back to the dig site. Then home, I guess."

"Leave Egypt! But, but, our land has so much to offer. How could anyone leave *Ta Meri*?" Badra's lip quivered.

"I don't really . . . I love Egypt, but . . . I have pressing business back home." She did love Egypt. The rich barrenness of the desert and the ancient history tugged at her heart.

"What kind of dove is it?" Badra asked, after Elizabeth gave her instructions on how to find her little hut.

"A white dove. She is quite gentle." Elizabeth squinted at the mysterious smile curving Badra's lips. "Why do you ask?"

"No reason." But Badra's smile only widened. Truly, she was quite beautiful. Elizabeth admired her exotic looks and sighed.

"As long as I'm here, why don't we begin now?" She walked to the little desk, fished out some paper and began to draw out Badra's name. For the next hour, she taught Badra to write the letters, pleased to see the girl's delighted smile.

At the sound of a key turning in the lock, she shoved pencil and paper away. As Aziz walked in, Badra scrambled out. Elizabeth said a quick prayer that the girl's love for learning would outweigh her loyalty to Jabari, and her note would be delivered.

"You will bathe now, then eat. The master has ordered it."

The mere mention of a bath made Elizabeth feel refreshed, but stubborn pride made her resist. Perhaps if she stayed filthy, Jabari would avoid her. But the big man fingered his dagger.

He led her down the corridor and opened a door revealing an oblong room. The room opened to a large outdoor courtyard featuring a lavish garden filled with flowering acacias, mimosa and flame trees with small stone benches set beneath them. A large mosaic pool stretched from the shaded room into the garden. And the flowers! Stalks of pink and red roses, white jasmine bushes, towering pink oleander shrubs, even small purple violets peeking their shy heads up from rock-lined beds. A small gurgling fountain burbled in the center of the courtyard. Such opulence amid the barren desert made Elizabeth's jaw drop in wonder.

Nestling against one wall was a large, sarcophagus-sized copper tub filled with water. Steam filtered off the top.

"Take off your clothes," Aziz said. "Bathe now."

Her eyebrows shot up. "I undress before no man."

He scowled. "I am the master's guardian of the harem. It is my duty to see that all his women are cared for and meet with his approval. You will bathe now!"

"Aziz." An older woman in an indigo, long-sleeved dress approached. Her manner had dignity and her smile held only gentleness. She laid a hand on the fierce man's arm. "She is new. Please, be patient. I will deal with this one myself."

"As you wish, my lady." Aziz gave Elizabeth one last scowl and turned on his heel.

"Who are you?" Elizabeth turned to her savior with a smile of gratitude.

"I am Layla, Jabari's cousin and the mistress in charge of his harem. Do not be afraid. I am here to assure your comfort."

"Comfort." Elizabeth frowned. "My only comfort lies in escaping this prison."

Layla looked surprised. "Prison? Jabari's women are treated like royalty. They only need ask for something and receive it."

Elizabeth bit off a crude remark and allowed Layla to lead her over to the tub. She stripped and sank gratefully into the steaming warmth, letting the woman wash her shoulders and back and soap her hair, rinsing it with a lotion that carried the delicious fragrant scent of the rosemary she loved so much.

After she'd dried off, Layla combed her long hair and gave her a long azure gown of the sheerest gossamer fabric. Elizabeth glanced at the robe, fingering its lovely folds. She held it up to the light and saw Layla's face peering back through the gauze. She handed it back.

"I can't wear this. You can see right through it."

"Ah, yes. I had figured as much," Layla disappeared a minute and returned with a beautiful powder-blue silk gown so light it almost floated on the air as she handed it over. Elizabeth shrugged it over her shoulders. It skimmed her bare ankles and clung to her full breasts. Without her corset, chemise and stockings, she felt wanton and naked despite the covering.

She felt a pang of homesickness for the good, old-fashioned feminine garments of restraint.

"How lovely you are, my lady. My cousin will be quite pleased when he takes breakfast with you."

"Jabari is dining with me?"

"He has requested it," Layla replied. "He has ordered to see you as soon as you are dressed and bathed."

Suddenly Elizabeth itched to cover her face with mud. Perhaps if she remained dirty Jabari would back away from her.

"Come." Reluctantly Elizabeth followed Layla out of the bath chamber down the winding corridor to a room that opened onto the garden. Seated before a low table spread with an assortment of fruit, Jabari studied a document. He had discarded his indigo *binish* for a simpler wardrobe—a long white robe, loose-fitting white cotton pants and sandals. A thick black cord belted his waist, where an ivory-handled dagger hung. Eggshell white contrasted sharply with his bronzed skin. He radiated authority and regal might. Freed from his turban, his shoulder-length, curled hair shimmered with wetness as if he also had recently bathed. Elizabeth cursed the fact that he was so devastatingly handsome, for he aroused unsettling feelings in her. She wanted to hate him.

Her eyes involuntarily shot down to the space between his legs. Thankfully, the object Farah had mentioned remained hidden. Was it truly as large as she had indicated? Elizabeth felt her cheeks flush and forced herself to gaze elsewhere.

Looking up, he spotted her and turned his scrutiny from the document to her, expressionless. He might as well have been inspecting a horse or another possession. Possession.

Elizabeth's anger returned, thinking how he regarded her as one.

She hung back, reluctant to approach him, unsure of what he expected. She felt a soft hand squeeze hers. Layla gave an understanding smile. "Come, it is all right." She started to lead her over to the table, but Elizabeth tugged her hand away.

"Thank you. I can manage on my own." She squared her shoulders, thrust her chin up and marched over to the table.

Jabari's eyes had never left her. "Thank you, Layla." His gaze bored into Elizabeth with dark intensity. "Please sit," he said to Elizabeth, indicating a space directly across from him.

Elizabeth nodded and lowered herself to one of the plush cushions, tucking her legs beneath her.

"Fruit?" He politely offered her a basket. She selected a fig and bit into it, enjoying the juiciness. Jabari set the basket down as Layla busied herself with a silver coffee service.

Layla poured strong Arabic coffee from a *dallah* into two small cups. Elizabeth smiled her thanks and sipped the bitter brew, relishing the spicy taste of cardamom.

Layla glided out of the room and Elizabeth and Jabari studied each other with wariness, two warriors sizing each other up before battle. She bristled with mutinous fury, remembering how he'd humiliated her the night before. *He will not win,* she vowed.

Jabari rolled up the document and frowned as if puzzling over a problem. He tapped the paper on the table's edge.

"Elizabeth, I realize that last night you were quite exhausted and in shock. I am willing to concede that your rude behavior was a result of that. Therefore, I have decided to forgive you. However, from this moment on, I expect you to act civilized while you are here and not shame my household again."

Laughter bubbled up through her throat as she set down

the fig. "Civilized? I am not the one running around demanding everyone call me 'master' and 'sire' and threatening to cut out their tongues!" She ran her hands through her drying hair. "This is absurd. You can't be serious, Jabari!"

His lips pulled together in a tight slash. "Elizabeth, do not laugh at me," he said in a low voice. "This is my culture. These are my people. You know nothing of us."

Instinct warned her she stepped on dangerous ground. Never very diplomatic, she struggled for words that conveyed her feelings but would not insult. She could not find any. Everything that caused her to march for women's right to vote raged against Jabari keeping concubines.

"I understand. You feel you are perfectly within your right to kidnap a woman, take her to your harem and bind her to your ways. You do this cloaked in a veneer of 'culture' and 'custom.' You are so enamored of these ancient traditions that are quite convenient for men but enslave women!"

"I protect what is my own. These women are sheltered from those who would harm them, safe from other men who would abuse them. My concubines are not slaves. They desire to stay here. They are free to go at any time."

She wrinkled her nose. "You would let them all go?"

"Of course. As I told you, I am a man of my word."

"So you said." She sniffed. "You said you would not touch me last night, yet you ripped the clothing from me like an animal."

Ebony eyes glittered with animosity. "I kept my word. I did not touch you, but you needed to be taught humility and to keep that wicked tongue of yours in check. I have been quite lenient, Elizabeth. Among my people, the penalty for striking the sheikh is death. For what you did last night you could have easily lost your life. Aziz was quite prepared to deliver that punishment."

She swallowed hard, remembering the glint of hate in the servant's eyes and his disdain for her earlier.

He seemed to gauge her reaction and added in a softer

tone, "My concubines choose to remain here under the shelter of my protection. They are wise women. They know that there is nowhere they may go without a man to guide their steps. Without a man, they are as helpless as a dove hunted by the falcon."

"If they were educated and taught to relish freedom and use their brains, perhaps they would fly away faster than a falcon," she challenged. *Maybe even Badra.*

He lifted his broad shoulders. "You have a point. But it is not a woman's place to live apart from man. She needs him."

"You are so hopelessly archaic! Do you really believe that? An educated woman has no need of a man."

His mouth tightened as he looked at her. Then his expression softened. Jabari reached across the table and picked up her hand. His thumb caressed her skin with deliberate slowness, shooting a prickling sensation up her spine.

"Educated women," he murmured. "Does such schooling milk life from women leaving them dry as desert sand? Do not they still harbor the same yearnings and desires? Their minds may be sharp and clever, but their desires are cloaked. They are still women, and their bodies still burn with hidden passions only a man may satisfy."

She tried to tug her hand away. "Not me. I have no such need of a man." Her own words soured in her mouth. Did she? Elizabeth never gave marriage and children a second thought. She was too busy trying to carve her way into a man's world.

His eyebrows lifted with mock disbelief. "You do not."

"Of course not. Men are shackles around a woman's ankles."

"Is that what we are to you? My poor little Elizabeth, so much denying herself as a woman."

"I don't deny myself anything. I'd rather have a career and independence than passion."

A sudden sensual gleam lit his eyes. She leaned back from the power of his gaze. "Ah, so you say. You are willing to live without passion, digging in the dirt for your fulfillment."

"My career would be my passion."

"You would deny your body what it longs for?"

"I have no such feelings. You are mistaken," she said, hoping to convince herself.

He fingered his chin and studied her, his dark brows drawn together in a puzzled frown. Now she knew what the insects she'd studied at Vassar felt like, pinned to a board and subjected to thorough examination.

"Why are you looking at me like that?" she demanded.

"Like what?"

"Like . . . that! As if I have horns growing out of my head!"

"I am not looking at your head," he murmured.

She followed the direction of his gaze downward to the breasts the silk gown did little to disguise. Elizabeth cursed herself for leaving behind her corset at the camp when she'd dug for the Almha. So much for women's freedom!

"So you say you can live without passion. But of course you have never experienced it before. Or have you?" he asked, his gaze piercing hers.

"I . . ." she dropped her head, feeling suddenly shy and embarrassed, "I have never been with a man before."

She peeped up at him through her lashes and saw his lips curve into a beguiling smile. The smile of a hungry wolf discovering a sheep had wandered into his den.

"Such a rare flower I behold before me, with the greatest of riches to offer a man," he said softly.

Elizabeth tensed her body against his seductive lion's purr. "I am not a flower. I warn you, Jabari. I'm more of a cactus with very, very sharp thorns."

"Cactus plants are no threat to me. They provide succulent refreshment. I love the challenge of conquering a prickly exterior to claim the sweetness inside," he murmured.

Elizabeth lowered her gaze, flustered and a little afraid of his intentions. She thought again of what Farah had said and her breathing hitched. If she looked into his eyes, she'd lose her soul and he'd see the reflection of the desire she desperately tried to hide from him.

"Elizabeth, look at me." His voice was a velvet caress against her skin.

She focused on his hands splayed against the dark wood of the table. Such powerful hands, with fine black silk hair feathering the backs.

"I see it in your eyes when I gaze upon your face. You hide much inside, but your eyes do not lie. Your body longs for mine."

A gurgle of laughter bubbled from her lips, but it came across as a frustrated sputter. "How can you say such things? You are making arrogant assumptions." But she did not look up.

His hands vanished from the table. She heard the scraping of sandals cross the room. Felt the air press against her as he sat down. One thumb hooked under her jaw. Jabari tilted her chin up, forcing her to meet his gaze. She looked into his eyes. They told a thousand tales of ancient passions and future longings. It was like staring into the burning sands and seeing a shimmering mirage. Their dark mystery pulled her into the vortex of his hunger for her. Jabari removed his thumb and picked up her hand. Elizabeth cursed its telltale trembling.

"So if I touch your soft skin, you do not feel anything. You are as impassive as one of your precious artifacts?" Without waiting for an answer, Jabari caressed her palm, the masculine roughness of his fingers evoking a shiver from her.

She jerked her hand away and scooted back.

"Elizabeth," he said slowly, "you cannot deny there is such passion between us."

"I deny it," she said, choking the lie from her lips.

"Ah, your clever tongue says one thing, but your body tells another. You quiver at my touch. Your body sings to me."

She turned from him, staring at the exquisite handiwork

of the wall tapestries. Counting all the intricate whorls would help her regain control. Elizabeth felt two strong hands on her shoulders gently forcing her to turn back to face him.

"Don't fight it, Elizabeth. I will have you." His deep voice held the supreme confidence of one accustomed to getting what he wanted. Instinctively she knew Jabari would hunt her down with ruthless patience if she managed to escape the harem. He would track her across sand and storms and claim her as his own. His fierce possessiveness shook her self-assurance.

Her choking sob of protest turned into a tiny whimper.

"I have so much I can teach you." Jabari's voice dropped to the barest whisper. He cradled her cheeks with his hands. "You are the most exciting woman I have ever met. I long to show you what true passion is between a man and woman."

His touch rippled across her skin. It felt so intimate, possessive and captivating. Elizabeth did not want this. She wanted to run away, escape the new, exciting and frightening sensations that made her oblivious to everything but him.

One arm encircled her waist, drawing her close. Jabari softly slid his thumb along her jaw, then drifted down in a feather-light touch to the sensitive part of her neck. Elizabeth gasped. She tried to pull away, but he held her trapped in his firm embrace. Her heart pounded an erratic cadence as heat rushed through her veins.

"So you see, you are not a cold stone object lying in the dust for thousands of years. Or a cactus," he murmured.

Mesmerized by the glow of desire reflected in his dark brown velvet eyes, she could not move. Elizabeth's mouth parted as he bent down to kiss her, even as logic urged her to seize the advantage and flee.

All thoughts of doing so fled as his lips softly brushed against hers. Strong arms encircled her waist as he clutched her to him. She closed her eyes, her lower belly quivering with an aching need. He explored her, tasted the contours of her mouth. The tip of his tongue glided over the curve of her lower lip and lingered there. Jabari deepened the kiss and she felt his tongue gently prod her mouth, then slip inside. She tasted sweet dates and fierce desire as his tongue flicked over hers. His kiss became more urgent, a sand tornado that blinded her to everything but him. Spinning out of control now as his mouth claimed her and he leaned against her, gently lowering her to the pillows.

Elizabeth struggled weakly as his body pressed against hers. His scent filled her nostrils: cloves, sandalwood, clean skin. She became aware of the softness of the plush cushions beneath her and the hard urgency of the man pressing her against them. Heat coursed through her as he slid a warm palm under the gown, caressing her rounded thigh. She wondered how his fingers would feel stroking her bare skin against the arch of her spine.

Jabari released her mouth. He bent his head and teased the soft skin at her neck with a light flick of his tongue. Elizabeth moaned, bending her head back. She was losing the battle against this man. Teeth grazed her sensitive skin, alternating with soft licks. The sensation deeply aroused her.

"Oh my *kalila,*" he murmured.

She felt his body suddenly lift off, freeing her as he broke their embrace. She stared up in shock at his furious scowl.

Beloved? Why did he call her that? Touching her swollen lips, Elizabeth sat up, totally flummoxed.

No affection from him now, for those ebony eyes turned into ice. Jabari's nostrils flared. If she weren't so shaky, she'd swear he was angry at himself. He drew in a deep breath and then a humorless, knowing smile tugged at his lips.

"You were correct in what you said last night, Elizabeth. Your body does suit my needs. I will spare you, for I have not experienced the delights of a virgin in a long time," he said softly, the dangerous glint returning to his eyes.

She squared her shoulders, desperate to know what he planned. "What will you do with me?"

"I warned you. You violated holy ground. You will stay here . . . until I talk to the tribal elders."

"And then? Do they decide my fate?"

He fingered his chin as if pondering her question. His gaze swept up and down her frame with impassive frankness. "If they learn of your sacrilege, yes. My grandfather is the chief elder and dispenses punishment on those who dig for the sacred Almha. Trust me, it is safer for you here."

She might as well just hand her head over . . . or her body. The man was as unpredictable as a desert wind. Would he imprison her forever inside his harem? Or let the elders kill her?

Jabari clapped his hands and Layla appeared at the door. He picked up the abandoned document and unfurled it, perusing it once more. The dismissal was curt. "You will go with Layla now. You are free to explore the grounds and do as you please. If you desire anything, she will see to your needs."

Elizabeth hesitated, feeling as helpless as a trapped animal. "What are your plans?" She winced at the pleading note in her voice.

"That, my lady, is not for you to know. You will remain here and if I desire to call you to my chamber later, you will be prepared for me." Jabari finally looked at her. She shivered at the black passion in the depths of those dark eyes.

She let Layla lead her from the room, feeling a thin thread of hope snipped by his implied threat.

He needed to clear his mind. First he met with his *saqrs* about the dig site activity. The English continued to excavate in the same area. Then he pored over accounts with the village elder. The winter drought threatened that the crop harvests would to be as meager as last year. Burdened with this problem, he retreated to the Nile's bank for peace. For two hours, Jabari sat on the riverbank, meditating. No use. Every time he tried to reach the sacred space, Elizabeth's sweet mouth came to mind. Finally, he gave up. Alone, he rode back to the Khamsin camp, a swarm of problems buzzing about his head like angry bees.

Elizabeth, Elizabeth. Bewildering. Frustrating. Full of passion and excitement, as strong as the desert sun and as vulnerable as a child. She angered and intoxicated him. Horrified by the tenderness he felt during their kiss, he had to leave. He could not let affection weaken him as it had weakened his father.

Jabari mentally rehearsed the words he planned to say before the Majli as he explained his predicament. As Sahar came onto the wide, open valley of the Khamsin camp, he squinted at the sight. No guards flanked the camp's northern entrance. Anger curdled his surly mood as he rode into camp. Then he noticed a crowd clustered together and talking with great excitement. It filled him with dread. Suddenly they spotted him and shouted. Like a massive wave, they rushed toward him. Jabari struggled to rein in Sahar, then slid off his horse.

Jabari clutched the reins and walked through the crowd, trying to make sense of the babbling voices around him. To his great relief he saw Nazim threading an impatient path through the blue-cloaked bodies. He scowled at his second-in-command.

"Nazim, why were my guards not posted at the entrance? Who is responsible for this?" Jabari shouted above the din.

"Sire, I cannot begin to tell you how relieved we are for your return!" Nazim's voice, filled with urgency, gave him pause.

"What happened?" The last thing he needed was more problems.

"Come see. The entire tribe has been talking of nothing else all morning. Near Ghazi." Nazim took Sahar's reins and passed them over to a waiting warrior, who led the horse away. He jerked his head toward Jabari's own tent as the two men wound through the excited, murmuring crowd.

On the wood perch in his usual place sat Ghazi. Jabari's anxiety that something happened to his beloved friend and falcon vanished. And then he saw it—tied to the left side of Ghazi's post, no fear of the bird of prey that sat at its side.

His heart hammered and his mouth went dry. Dear Allah, it could not be. But it was . . . after all these millennia . . .

"She is here," Nazim announced in a somber tone as Jabari stared at the beautiful white bird. "At last, the white dove has returned to us."

Chapter Nine

"She flew in from the west, as it was written." Nazim sat on the thick carpeting of the *maharama,* the men's formal quarters of the tent used for ceremonial purposes and war council meetings. His friend's voice rose above the twelve Majli council members murmuring as they sat in a circle. The elders had called for an emergency meeting to evaluate the situation. Stale air inside the tent mingled with excited anticipation over the bird's arrival.

Troubled by this new tangle of events, Jabari stared at the crimson carpet and traced its patterns with one finger. He had hoped to hold a quiet meeting with the Majli, plead for Elizabeth's life with the excuse she was a mere woman, and do it with a minimum of fuss. Instead, he faced a council foaming at the mouth with nervous energy. How could he even begin to justify Elizabeth's actions when the tribe had witnessed signs of the prophecy coming true? It cast her treachery in a dangerous light. Now the Majli would never forgive her digging for the Almha, not with the arrival of their queen foreshadowed by the white dove.

If he told them of Elizabeth's sacrilege, Nkosi would not hesitate to kill her.

Jabari banished thoughts of Elizabeth. She was safe enough for now in his harem; no one need know of her existence. She'd remain a phantom tucked away behind massive mud-brick walls.

He turned his attention to the council and held up a hand for silence. All eyes turned toward him.

"I wish to know everything. Nazim, tell me what happened."

"Sire, I had just settled Ghazi on his perch this morning and was feeding him. Suddenly we saw her. She swooped in from the west and landed next to Ghazi. Ghazi did not attack her."

"Ghazi shares his perch with a bird he would hunt for food." Jabari mused over this. "What are the people saying?"

"They are overcome with great joy. They say the white dove is a sign that the storehouses will be filled again for the summer months. Many plan to celebrate tonight."

This news deeply disturbed Jabari. He could not bear to see his people hurt. Instead of carefully rationing food, the Khamsin would feast. By placing all their hopes in an ancient legend, they ignored the possible famine awaiting them. Jabari knit his brows. "Egypt is full of white doves. How can this be a sign?"

"Never has a white dove appeared in this section of desert before," Nazim pointed out. "It is too far inland. And there is little food in this area, as evidenced by her appetite."

"A sign our returning queen will be quite hungry. Perhaps I should send Ghazi out on many more hunts. Or will she magically wave her hands and make her own dinner appear?" Jabari's mouth twisted into a humorless smile. Nkosi grunted his displeasure.

"My grandson, why do you mock this? The prophecy has come to fruition. This is no time for jesting," he chided.

Jabari felt chagrined at the reprimand. "I am sorry, Grandfather. I mean no disrespect. But I am greatly troubled by what it means to our people. We must be absolutely certain. I am concerned that this bird will raise false hopes."

Nkosi's gnarled hand tapped his grandson's forehead. "That is why you must study the signs with your head as well as your heart. All will be made clear to you if you are willing to open yourself to it. The burden rests upon you, my grandson, and our people are depending upon you. Be wise in what you do."

His cryptic warning angered Jabari. "I am always wise when deciding our tribe's fate. I am worried more about our future than about this dove. Our people have suffered as of late with the competition from the Al-Hajid in horse breeding. Now that they are blocking the trade routes, it will suffer more. We have no caravans to raid for supplies."

"It is clear then. The time is right for Kiya's return. Our people need her vision and direction," Nkosi stated.

"Our people need hard and fast solutions and cannot wait for legends to give them answers," Jabari countered, keeping his tone respectful but not yielding.

"Kiya is no legend. Such solutions will come upon her arrival. It is written that our queen will lead us into the future. Do you not believe in the very reason why we have kept watch all these millennia? You are the Khamsin sheikh. Do you forget your duty?" Nkosi thundered back at him. His deep-set eyes flashed fury. The eleven other council members raised their eyebrows and even Nazim flinched.

"I do believe the prophecy and stand upon my oath as a Khamsin warrior in holding fast to protecting the Almha," Jabari said in a low voice. He set his face like stone and stared into the tent wall, wishing answers were carved there. Frustrated anger gnawed his insides.

"I would fall upon my scimitar if I failed to perform my duty. And my first duty is to my people, not to an ancient queen. There will not be enough food stores for the summer months. So you see, Grandfather, I will not stand by and wait upon a prophecy and watch our people slowly starve in the summer!"

He lifted his chin, meeting the old man's angry gaze with a steely stare. If he lowered his head in respect now, he'd lose standing among the council. As leader, he had to stand up to his grandfather and assert his authority. He could not let Nkosi's blithe dismissal of the Khamsin's problems influence the Majli. Jabari kept his breathing even and his hands steady upon his knees, refusing to give ground.

After a few minutes, Nkosi bowed his head and sighed so deeply the sound pierced Jabari's heart. "You are absolutely correct. What is your plan?"

Jabari exhaled in relief. "We must find alternative means of income for the tribe. Lady Anne Blunt's purchase of Arabian mares a few years ago stimulated interest for our horses among the Europeans. Our bloodlines have been highly recommended by our customers to others, who have made inquiries. I wrote a proposal for our southern tribe to sell Khamsin stock, including stallions, to the royal families of Poland and Germany."

Nazim's face contorted with anxiety. Jabari glanced at his best friend, empathizing with his emotional distress. The tribe sold only their mares, never their precious stallions. "Jabari, sell the studs? You know what this means?"

His jaw tightened. "Yes, I do. They will start their own stud farms and create competition. We shall lose business. Worse, they will dilute the pedigree. Our horses are finely tempered steel, swift of hoof and graceful. The Europeans will weaken the strain with impure blood. But we have no choice. We need the money now. The stallions will fetch a much higher price."

Jabari's heart ached with this painful admission. A deep sigh rippled through the tent, accompanied by regretful nods at his decision. Khamsin horses were Egypt's finest, purest Arabians. All warriors loved the tribe's horses and treated them with great affection.

"However, the immediate threat is the Al-Hajid. I suspect they will hinder the transaction. Indeed, I am certain they already know of the Europeans' plan to purchase our stock. That is the true reason for their terror campaign in the south."

"They will continue blocking the trade routes and frighten away customers," Nazim fumed, his amber eyes darkening as he unsheathed his dagger. He stabbed it into the carpet with a savage thrust. "We should attack. My blood thirsts for a *ghazu* upon those jackals."

Jabari plucked Nazim's knife from the carpet and handed it back. "In due time, my friend. But now is not that time."

"You will find answers, my grandson. I have great faith in this," Nkosi stated with pride.

Jabari regarded Nkosi with quiet pensiveness as the elders clucked and murmured their approval. "Thank you for your faith, Grandfather. I will not disappoint you."

Nkosi lifted his eyebrows and scratched his beard. "Such answers may not be so elusive. You forget the Almha. It would bring in enough income to feed our people for many summers."

His words caused a collective gasp among Nazim and the Majli. Jabari's stomach reeled with anger and grief. How could his beloved grandfather even think of such sacrilege?

"I would sell myself as a slave to the Al-Hajid before doing so," Jabari said in chilling tones.

His grandfather smiled. "I know this, my grandson. I merely test your loyalty, as is my right."

"You do much to test me, old man," Jabari growled affectionately. "Now about the dove. I wish to see it."

Nazim led the way to Ghazi's perch, parting the crowd. In the teeming throng Jabari spotted Badra next to his aunt. He smiled fondly at both of them.

Resolved to judge the situation with complete impartiality, Jabari found himself regarding the dove with the same reverent awe as the others. Agitated, the dove flapped her wings, trying to fly away. Her head swiveled to look straight at him. Immediately, she calmed. Shocked to find himself compelled by the beautiful dove, he stepped forward. She sat quietly with an air of expectation. As he stroked her chest, she greeted his caress with cooing sounds of pleasure. A deep feeling of peace settled over him.

"See how she tames under his touch! It is indeed a sign," one of the Majli said in awe.

"It is the prophecy," another elder cried out. "The white dove gentles under the strong hand of the Khamsin sheikh, foretelling of Kiya's submission to his will. He will mate with her and breed sons as strong and spirited as the desert winds."

Jabari's peace vanished upon remembering the prophecy. Honor bound him to marry the reincarnated queen. How could he when Elizabeth haunted him so? *Admit it. You cannot bear to let her go.* Jabari gave a philosophical shrug. He could not bother with details until he saw further proof.

"There are other signs. I will keep watch for them," Jabari promised the council members standing behind him. They gazed upon him as if he were a *jinn* materializing from the sands.

His head pounded from the assortment of problems plaguing him and the queer mysticism of the bird's arrival. Too much responsibility. Too many troubles. Suddenly he felt an urgent, nearly desperate need to see Elizabeth. Have her gurgling laughter soothe his troubled mind. Watch her blue eyes flash fire as he sparred with her. Aching need filled him, as if she were an oasis and he a man dying of thirst under the scorching sun.

Memories of her soft lips, dimpled smile and the spark in her eyes cheered him. Jabari wanted only to experience the force of her fiery spirit, to sharpen his wits against the whetstone of her sharp intelligence. Only Elizabeth's lively exchanges could ease the weight of responsibility from his shoulders.

Jabari fingered his chin and considered the council members. He motioned for Nazim to bring his horse. "I have no answers for now, but I assure you, they will come. I will not let my people starve, nor will I turn my back on the prophecy, should it indeed come to fruition. Urgent business calls me back to Amarna."

He mounted Sahar and rode like a man possessed, inflamed by the lovely vision of Elizabeth waiting for him.

Exhaustion claimed her, and Elizabeth slept deeply. When she awoke, the sun's position indicated late afternoon. Hunger drove her to explore her surroundings. She made her way down the winding labyrinth to the bathing chamber. In the garden outside, Layla sat in tranquil repose on a carpet on the ground weaving fabric on a wooden loom. Naked, Farah stretched out on some cushions beneath a tree. An earthernware pitcher, glasses and assortment of food sat on a low sandalwood table.

She gulped with embarrassment and turned away, but Layla spotted her. "Please, Elizabeth, join us. You must be hungry."

Elizabeth swallowed hard, trying to avoid Farah's nudity while her eyes widened at the sight of so much delicious food. But for the fig she'd consumed that morning, she hadn't eaten since lunch the previous day. She buttoned the robe to her neck. Her mouth watered and she helped herself to some cheese. Elizabeth ate several handfuls and an apple. She poured herself some citrus juice from the pitcher, then drank, sighing as she remembered how she'd tossed it into Jabari's face.

Layla smiled with contentment as she wove brightly colored thread in and out of the loom. Her indigo dress looked quite warm, but Elizabeth wished Farah were as conservative.

"Tell me, Elizabeth," Layla's low voice cut across her thoughts. It brushed across her frayed nerves like soothing velvet. "What brings you here to us? Were you also desiring to join the harem?"

Gurgling laughter bubbled up from Elizabeth's throat.

"Join? No. I was forcibly kidnapped by the 'master.' "

Layla's hands stopped moving. She pushed the loom aside and looked distressed. "Kidnapped? That is so unlike Jabari."

Elizabeth told Layla about digging for the Almha. Layla frowned.

"My cousin never hurts women. He is so kind and gentle."

Elizabeth thought of how he'd torn off her clothing and shuddered. "I find that hard to believe."

"But I speak the truth. Ask Farah."

Elizabeth glanced at Farah. "She is too blindly devoted to him to answer otherwise."

Layla gave her a thoughtful look. "Do you know how Farah and Badra came here?"

"No. Were they kidnapped as well?"

Layla shook her head. "Three years ago, my cousin led a raid against the Al-Hajid, our enemies. They had stolen the Khamsin's prized breeding stallion. It was but two months since Jabari's father, the sheikh, had died and Jabari led his men to recover the horse and avenge the tribe's honor."

Layla's gaze drifted southward, as if hearing the thundering hooves, seeing the warrior's scimitars slash the air.

"The Khamsin recovered the stallion. It is custom among our people during a raid to take women as captives. Jabari has never done this, for he will not break up families. However, as they turned home, two women ran to Jabari and begged for sanctuary."

She leaned forward, eager to hear why.

"The women were concubines to Sheikh Fareeq bin Hamid Taleq. They had escaped during the battle. They pleaded with Jabari and he offered them protection and brought them to our camp."

"He did?" Elizabeth's glance swept over Farah, seeing her nakedness anew, as if she were clothed in dignity. "Why didn't this Fareeq lead a raid to reclaim the women?"

"The Al-Hajid raided the camp, but Fareeq did not lead it. He fears Jabari. My cousin's skill as a courageous warrior is legendary among the desert tribes. The Khamsin killed many Al-Hajid and drove them away. Jabari feared they would attack again, so he brought the women here to protect them better. This building has always housed the sheikh's harem."

Perhaps if she learned more of his background, Elizabeth could better understand the man who held her captive. "Did Jabari's father have a harem?"

"Yes, he did, but tradition dictates that the sheikh must marry a pure woman. Traditionally, our sheikhs marry distant cousins to ensure family loyalty. Tarik fell deeply in love with a woman he met while visiting Cairo. She was not of our tribe."

Elizabeth asked about Jabari's father. Layla's mouth tightened.

"Tarik loved Jasmine. Although she came from the city, she adjusted well to our tribe. Until she begged him to teach her to read. Although it is against our tradition, Tarik indulged her."

A tightness clenched Elizabeth's stomach at Layla's look of anger. "She read all the time. Dinner was burnt and chores were not done, but Jabari and his father did not care. They wanted her to have that pleasure, for she was so joyful."

"What happened?"

"Jasmine grew restless. To appease her, Tarik took her to Cairo to visit her relatives. She told him she was staying there for a year, maybe more, to further her education. Tarik came back without her. Nkosi, his father, was furious and said she shamed him. Tarik said he loved her too much to force her to return."

"What a wonderful thing he did for his wife," Elizabeth murmured.

Layla's pretty face tightened. "Wonderful? His men mocked him for not controlling his woman. He lost respect. Six months later, he led a dangerous raid on an armed caravan to prove his valor. He was killed instantly."

"Oh no. Poor Jabari," Elizabeth whispered.

"If Jasmine never left Tarik, he would still be alive."

"That's unfair," Elizabeth protested. "She planned to return. How could she know her husband would react like that?"

"She should not have left him. Or forced him to break tradition. Traditions should not be broken."

"Tarik left her there, as I see it. How could his men say he was weak because he loved his wife? And if more men had broken the tradition, I daresay Jasmine's actions would have been seen as beneficial for the tribe."

"Traditions should not be broken," Layla repeated. She looked so distressed that Elizabeth wished she'd never brought up the topic. She glanced at Farah lying against the cushions. Perhaps deflecting the conversation to Jabari's concubines would allay Layla's anger. She asked about Badra and why she seemed so afraid, unlike the bolder Farah.

Layla's gentle eyes filled with more pain. "Badra was enslaved to Fareeq when she was eleven. She was barely a woman. She resisted his advances. He beat her."

Horrified, Elizabeth could only stare. "He beat her?"

"Even after she submitted. Each time she came to his bed, the whip waited for her. When she came before my master, she quivered like a frightened animal. She feared all men."

"How could he be so cruel?"

"Fareeq is a vile monster who receives pleasure from delivering pain. My cousin tried to undo the great damage Fareeq inflicted on her young spirit. He treated Badra with the most exquisite gentleness. He lavished every manner of kindness upon her, encouraged her, and when it was discovered she enjoyed singing, made her a *rebaba* from his own hands."

Elizabeth asked what a *rebaba* was. Layla explained the violinlike instrument was made from sticks of wood and a single strand of horse hair stretched across its base.

"He never . . . you know, she does not . . ." Elizabateh paused.

Layla smiled knowingly. "He never touched her. Badra is like a sister to him. Farah is the only one who shares his bed."

"I don't understand."

"You see him from your Western eyes with your Western ways. To you he is barbarian. To us," Layla's smile was kind but critical, "he is anything but."

"Layla," Elizabeth paused, searching for the right words. What Layla had told her made her understand Jabari a little better. Still, it did not justify what he had done to her. "Jabari is a kind man. To you, his people. But that doesn't excuse what he did to me. In my country, kidnapping an innocent woman is a crime."

"Ah, but you are not so innocent." The sweetness of Layla's smile fled. Her words made Elizabeth nervous.

"What do you mean?"

"You were stealing the Almha. It is most sacred to our people. Therefore, you are a thief deserving of punishment. Do you not see the difference?"

Her words made sense that Elizabeth struggled to justify herself. "I was not stealing it," she countered.

Layla's perfectly shaped eyebrows arched. "What were you doing then?"

Elizabeth realized her predicament. To these desert dwellers, digging up the tribe's ancient artifact constituted stealing. Even if the motive was innocent, the action was not.

"I see your point," Elizabeth conceded. "However, I was not after the Almha itself. I truly mean this."

Layla frowned. "But what then? The only other items on the disk are the ancient herbal cures. You with your modern medicine and doctors would have no need of that."

Elizabeth thought of Nana, alone and maybe dying. Tears filled her eyes. "You are so wrong," she muttered, looking away.

Silence reigned for a few moments. Elizabeth heard

plucking of fingers against strings and realized Layla had resumed her weaving. Elizabeth wiped her eyes and looked up.

"Do you know of the Almha's legend and why it is so sacred to our people?" When Elizabeth shook her head, she continued.

Enchanted, Elizabeth listened to tales of Akhenaten and his ways of worship, of the bravery of Queen Kiya who stole the Almha and was executed, the faithfulness of Ranefer, her lover, and how the Khamsin were sworn to guard the Almha with their lives.

"The wadi where the Almha is buried is most sacred."

"Because of the Almha?"

"Because Kiya buried it there. It was where she and Ranefer met and were lovers. It gave her cause for great rejoicing."

The papyrus made sense finally. Elizabeth laughed. Place of great rejoicing. Not for worship, but love!

"Why is your tribe called the Khamsin?" Elizabeth asked.

"We were a secret sect, Kiya's warrior priests, named after the deadly windstorm that sweeps through the desert each spring. Such storms kill the unwary. Our men are warriors of the wind."

How utterly appropriate. Elizabeth thought of Jabari's fierce, proud manner. "You are aptly named," she murmured.

She gazed at the pool with yearning. "Water in the desert. How did it get here?"

"Our master has devised a system for year-round crop irrigation so we are less dependent upon the annual Nile flooding. He pumps water to irrigate the fields and supply water for this pool. Jabari owns the land, and the people in Amarna cultivate the crops in exchange for a share of the harvest. The crops help sustain our people through the dry summer months. One of the villagers also tends this garden every week."

Elizabeth glanced at the flowers, itching to draw their

beauty. She fetched pad and pencil from her room and sat at the low sandalwood table. But instead of pink oleander blossoms, a man's rugged, dark looks surfaced beneath her strokes. She sketched Jabari, his long, silky hair blowing in the desert breeze. He stood perched on some rocks, like a falcon surveying the horizon. Pyramids rose skyward as he gazed into the distance, his tall frame as proud as the towering structures behind him. But she could not quite capture his eyes. Elizabeth thought about how expressive they were, cold as the desert night when looking at the Al-Hajid, warm with affection for Badra. And her? What were they when gazing upon her? Her pencil flew across paper of its own accord. She finished and stared at the results, blushing.

She turned the pad over and wandered over to the pool. Elizabeth knelt at the edge, testing the water with one finger.

"Go ahead," Layla encouraged her. "It is most refreshing."

"No, I am fine." The last thing she wanted was to bathe naked and chance Jabari wandering by in search of diversion.

Layla must have read her mind. "He had business with the elders and left earlier."

"No, I cannot." Elizabeth stood as Farah walked over.

"Are you afraid? I am. Your ugly Western body will blind me with its whiteness." Farah's lips curled in disgust. "Why does my master desire you? You have nothing to offer. Skinny pale-skinned weakling!" With a shove she pushed Elizabeth into the pool.

It wasn't deep but Elizabeth sputtered in indignation as she surfaced, glaring at the laughing Farah. Oh well. She did want to swim. Elizabeth clutched the robe to her. It clung to her with dead weight. Reluctantly, she shed it and put the wet mass next to the pool. She swam to the sunny end as Farah left the room, still laughing. Elizabeth's mind drifted to the levels of complexity in Jabari. Stubbornly clinging to ancient ways, yet modern in his economic approach. The man was a deep enigma. Like unearthing an archaeological find, she kept finding new strata to him. The layer of the powerful, arrogant leader determined to have his way peeled back to reveal a gentle man whose compassion saved an abused girl. What else would she unearth?

Elizabeth loved discovering mysteries below the sands. For the first time, she found a man to be as intriguing and compelling as the thrills of ancient secrets. It bothered her. She did not want to be attracted to him. Elizabeth shuddered, remembering his slow seduction. Jabari was too dangerous.

Flipping over on her back, she closed her eyes.

"I see you are quite enjoying my pool."

Jabari's husky voice cut across her thoughts. She flailed her arms and shot upright. Mortified, Elizabeth treaded water. He squatted by the edge of the pool with seamless grace for such a powerful physique. Mischief played across his handsome features as his lips quirked upward in a teasing grin.

"It is good to see you . . . so relaxed and at ease at last."

"You were supposed to be gone," she said, covering her breasts with her hands, horrified at being naked.

"I have returned." He knelt by the pool's edge, stirring the water with one finger. "Why do you hide yourself from me? You have nothing be ashamed of . . . indeed." He gave her a gentle smile. Elizabeth expected him to leer at her nakedness just as the diggers ogled her breasts on the field site. He instead focused on her face. His consideration bemused her.

"It isn't proper for me . . . to be seen like this."

"You struggle to prove yourself as a woman and do not realize the beauty Allah gave you is also part of being a woman."

"That's not the part I want men to respect. I'd rather be admired for my mind. All you care about are women's bodies. You said it. Women are only good for bearing children and satisfying men. You think only men are intelligent."

Jabari leaned forward with an earnest look. "You are much mistaken, Elizabeth. You catalog me with your artifacts. I am specimen number one, uncivilized desert dweller who regards women as useful only for pleasure or procreation. But that does not mean I cannot appreciate a woman for her other gifts as well."

She squinted at him, confused. "What gifts?"

A strange light glinted in Jabari's fathomless eyes. "Elizabeth, you have a college education. You are more learned than my men and you possess a formidable intelligence. In my tribe, your brilliant mind would intimidate most men."

"And what about you?" The question was a direct challenge.

"*I* am not most men," he stated with quiet assurance.

She looked away, feeling some distress that she had labeled him as unfairly as men had labeled her.

"The differences between men and women should be cherished, not scorned," he mused. "Each has strengths the other lacks, and this provides balance, as a tribe is balanced. Men should protect women, but if a woman has no man, no one at all, what good is that? Is she doomed to degrade herself to feed her children? Would she not be better assuming a man's strength in that case?"

"Of course," she shot back. But he didn't look at her.

"The old ways are much easier to accept and not question. But people who do not change become stale and remain behind as society advances," he said so softly she strained to hear him.

He didn't look arrogant or authoritative. Just confused and deep in thought as if troubled by a tremendous burden.

"So you think men and women can be equal?"

The question seemed to give him pause. Jabari frowned, rubbing his chin. "Women bear children. Men provide for the women. How can they be equal? These roles are best because they are dictated by how we were created."

He talked of physical equality. She talked of social equality. They stood on opposite sides of a huge chasm of culture and custom separating them. Jabari did not understand.

He glanced at her with a gentle smile. "The physical differences between men and women serve a useful purpose."

Two of the obvious differences rested in her sheltering palms. "Well, we couldn't be equal now anyway. You're wearing clothing. I'm not. It makes me . . . uncomfortable."

He considered this a minute, stood and began shedding his scimitar and the belt at his waist, dropping them to the floor. Jabari unfastened the buttons on his *binish.*

"What are you doing?"

"I am disrobing to make you more comfortable," he said, shucking the *binish.*

"I'm comfortable enough! I am, I am!" Elizabeth squeaked.

Next he yanked off the underlying black shirt. Clad only in black cotton trousers, he thrust his hands on narrow hips. Never had she seen a man's bare chest before. The splendor of male magnificence bewitched her. Jabari's broad shoulders and long arms studded with muscles, smooth chest and firm, flat stomach rippling with strength seemed sculpted from golden marble. Her breathing quickened as she bore witness to what he'd said. There were clear differences between men and women. Gorgeous ones, she amended, her glance darting down past his waistline to the bulge in his trousers.

Jabari followed the direction of her gaze. His eyes gleamed. She blushed, realizing her mouth hung open in spellbound fascination. When he reached for the drawstring around his waist, she swam furiously to the steps and scrambled out into the sunshine. Layla wrapped her in a large towel. She secured it at her breasts, relieved to have cloth stand between his eyes and her body. He strolled over, giving a mock pout of disappointment.

"Ah, so quick you are to cover yourself, like the sun hiding behind the moon. My day has grown dark because

Elizabeth shields herself from my sight." Jabari uttered a dramatic sigh as if he'd actually witnessed an eclipse. He bent his head and brought folded hands to his lips.

"What are you doing?" she asked, bewildered.

"Praying to Allah for my sunshine to return. Or for your towel to fall off." He lifted his eyebrows and peered up through thick black lashes, flashing her a devilish grin.

Elizabeth pressed a finger to her lips, but it did not suppress the laugh that spilled through them. He was an impossibly proud and arrogant man, but he had a roguish charm. Jabari's sense of humor captivated her as much as his good looks did. Unlike any other man she knew, he made her appreciate her femininity. He had an irresistible charisma. Her resolve to escape the harem slipped a few alarming notches. Elizabeth examined her emotions with brutal candor. The thought of never seeing him again was incredibly painful.

The realization brought her laughter to a grinding halt. What was she doing? The man kidnapped her! Was she becoming a starry-eyed ninny subjected to Jabari's capricious whims?

Frightened, she stepped back from the magnetic power he asserted over her. But his manner was inviting and friendly. He rested his elbow in one palm as he fingered his chin. The corners of his sensual lips quirked upward in a generous smile. She had never seen him this relaxed. Instinct told her the real Jabari, the one hidden from the outside world, stood before her revealing emotions as naked as her own skin had been minutes before.

So caught up was she in that beguiling smile Elizabeth forgot her fears. The cold mask worn by the proud desert warrior had vanished. She saw the compassionate man who protected a helpless girl cruelly beaten most of her teenage years. She saw the sophisticated, intelligent sovereign who brought economic viability to his people. She saw the tender lover whose kiss promised nights of passion and loyal devotion. The sun's heat began to seep into her skin. She closed her eyes and drifted into a dream, thinking about the symbol of his clan, the falcon:

He is the one for you, your lover destined for you. As the dove submits to the talons of the falcon, so shall you give yourself to him, but the falcon's grip is gentle with love.

Elizabeth's hands vibrated. She moaned, shaking off dizziness and the now-familiar sickly spinning sensation.

Jabari's smile vanished, replaced by tight-lipped concern. He caught her as she staggered forward. He picked her up in his strong, sure arms and carried her to one of the stone benches under a shade tree, easing her down upon it. Her head snapped forward. Leaning over her knees, she gasped for air, frantic to gulp in enough.

"Elizabeth!" Jabari's voice, sharpened by worry, seemed far away. She shook her head and moaned, clutching her belly and rocking back and forth. Tears flooded her eyes as panic took over. Two strong hands gripped her shoulders from behind. "Take deep breaths. Now."

Obeying him, she forced her lungs to expand and then exhaled slowly. After a few minutes the hyperventilating ceased.

Vaguely she heard him snap a command for water and became aware of him kneeling before her. He brushed the hair from her face and held a cup to her lips.

"Drink this. Slowly," he urged, tilting it upward. She sipped a little and pushed it away. Layla took the cup from him.

"It's gone now. I'll be all right." Elizabeth's lower lip trembled as she looked at him through a tear-veiled fog.

With a gentle hand he wiped tears from her cheek. "You must take extra care to avoid the late sun," he softly scolded her.

Jabari cradled her chin with one hand and brushed back a tangle of hair from her face with the other. "You are so fragile and the heat is too intense for you," he murmured.

"It wasn't heat stroke," she insisted. "Can't be. It just . . . comes on all the sudden."

He frowned, tracing her jaw with one finger. "How long have you had these episodes?"

"Not that long. They started just before . . ." She gasped, chilled by a sudden realization, and looked at him with dawning horror. "I met you. They've gotten worse since we met."

Brushing away his fingers, Elizabeth stood too rapidly and walked out of the shade. Her shaking legs wobbled like a newborn colt's. Immediately Jabari rose to her aid. Large, warm hands clutched her arms, bracing her as she swayed. His tall shadow fell over her, shielding her from the sun's brutal heat.

Jabari's powerful, yet gentle grip reminded her of the prophetic dream. *As the dove submits to the talons of the falcon, so shall you give yourself to him, but the falcon's grip is gentle with love.* She felt utterly powerless. Elizabeth's face tightened with anger as Jabari looked down at her with tenderness. His arms slid around her in a protective hug clearly meant to soothe and comfort.

It's all your fault. She had to erect a massive barrier between them. Better to face his antagonism than this solicitude. His loving affection would wear her down, seduce her with kindness and strip away her last bastion of freedom.

She vehemently denied the dream to herself. They must never become lovers. Elizabeth lashed out, knowing her words would anger him.

"It must be a psychological reaction to you," she snapped, struggling to free herself from his embrace. "Strutting barbarians disgust me."

Loving concern fled his face, and the cold blankness dropped into place again. Jabari momentarily tightened his grip around her and then let go.

"Have no fear, my lady," he said in a voice that chilled her to the bone with its iciness. "I will remove myself then from your presence so as to not sicken you further."

With ferocious might he tore away her towel, revealing her nakedness. She stifled a startled gasp. His eyes filled with mesmerizing intensity as they focused on her bare breasts. Elizabeth covered herself with her palms, but Jabari grabbed her wrists in a powerful grip, prying them apart with ease. Another difference between men and women: He was quite strong and could easily overpower her, she realized with growing panic. How moronic of her to forget that!

The smoldering look he gave her signaled his intent. "But make no mistake about it. If I desire you in my bed, no fainting spells will deter me from seeking my pleasure with you."

Elizabeth watched him stride away, his muscled shoulders proudly thrown back as if her rude rebuff had slid right off them. Her ruse backfired. She'd succeeded in widening the distance between them, only to step all over that arrogant pride. Elizabeth silently cursed herself. Now more than ever, Jabari had reason to force her to submit to him.

Chapter Ten

"And then what happened?"

Farah leaned forward eagerly as Jabari paused in his story. He pushed aside his empty plate and traced a line on his glass.

"I coated their cups with honey and they could not shake them free. The Al-Hajid were upset, being bested by sweetness."

She gave a girlish giggle. Jabari laughed as well, but his mind strayed to Elizabeth, remembering her deep, throaty laugh. Farah touched his hand across the sandalwood table.

"Do you wish me to stay with you tonight, master?"

"No, Farah," he said softly. "I am sorry. You are a beautiful woman, but my mind is with another."

"Why? Is she prettier than me?" Her lower lip quivered.

He smiled gently at her. "It is not a matter of beauty. It has to do with . . ." Jabari thought about it. Why did he want Elizabeth so badly? What deep hunger drove him to violate his oath, cause all sorts of problems in his harem?

Farah tilted her head, and he saw wisdom dawn in her eyes. "She challenges you. You like that."

Jabari leaned back against the cushions, smiling. "You are right," he admitted.

"The look in your eyes when you talk of her is the same as when you talk of besting the Al-Hajid. You are a strong warrior, master, and determined to win. Only you will not use honey to defeat her."

"Ah, you are wrong, dear Farah." He drummed his fingers on the floor. "I do plan to use honey, just as I bested the Al-Hajid with sweetness, so I will conquer Elizabeth with it as well."

Honey erased more than the pride of an arrogant enemy. He would use honeyed words on his desert rose. Determined to control Elizabeth, he opted for seduction. A most pleasant way to put her in her place. Tonight he would confess to her how much her beauty enticed him as he coaxed her into his bed.

Jabari thought of her fierce spirit and smiled, anticipating the evening to come.

Her tiny bedroom had become a cell. Elizabeth sat on the soft satin-covered bed, absently plucking at the coverlet. Earlier in the evening Aziz had locked her in the room. Later he brought dinner—mutton stew, camel's milk and figs. She had only picked at the food, her misery heightened by Jabari's deep laughter and Farah's shrill giggles echoing down the hall. Their lighthearted mood emphasized her loneliness.

All she wanted from her Egyptian trip was a chance to prove herself as an archaeologist and find a cure for Nana's pain. Nothing had gone right.

Some help you are. The Almha slipped through your fingers, you couldn't gain one smidgen of respect among your colleagues, and here you are, prisoner of a desert warrior who would just as soon chop off your head as make love to you. Elizabeth shuddered, unsure which prospect bothered her more. She recalled the predatory gleam in Jabari's eyes as he tore the towel from her body. This was no man to trifle with, but a proud warrior unused to women rejecting him. Her taunts did nothing to deter him. They only strengthened his resolve.

The lock clicked and her bedroom door opened. Elizabeth wiped her eyes and glanced up. Layla swept into the room, a gown in her arms, followed by Farah, her arms weighted by baskets filled with what suspiciously looked like oils and lotions. She toyed with a strand of hair and eyed the women as if they came armed with loaded rifles.

Layla laid the gown on the bed. She scrutinized Elizabeth as if she were an item for sale in the marketplace. "You know why we are here, my lady," she stated.

"Selling cosmetics from the *souks?*" Elizabeth hid her fear behind the joke. "I am not buying. You may leave now."

"We cannot," Layla said gently. "We must prepare you for Jabari. He has called you to his chamber for the evening."

She smoothed Elizabeth's hair, eyeing her critically. "The bathing chamber first."

No escape this time. In desperation, Elizabeth looked around, searching for an escape. She clenched and unclenched her fists. Against these two . . . she could hold her own . . . dash out the door, surprise them . . . Hope faded as Aziz entered the room and stood guard, wearing his customary scowl. And dagger.

"Come, my lady." Layla picked up the gown again and led her from the room down the hall to the bathing chamber as the other woman followed. During her bath, they poured a light rosemary scent over her hair, rinsing it, then vigorously toweled her. As Elizabeth stretched out on a long table near the pool, Layla uncapped a bottle and massaged her bare skin with warm rosemary-scented oil. Elizabeth's eyes closed from the delightful pampering. When Layla finished, Elizabeth flipped over, feeling shy as Layla rubbed her breasts and belly with oil. Elizabeth steeled herself against the wanton sensuality, not wishing to relax her defenses.

Farah entered the bath chamber, a silver tray on her outstretched palms. She offered Elizabeth a goblet. Elizabeth pursed her lips and shook her head.

"Please take the honeyed mead. It will ease your fear."

Elizabeth started to protest that she was not afraid and saw Farah's lips curl upward in a sympathetic smile. Elizabeth shrugged with pretended courage and sipped the sweet brew. It slipped down her raw throat, warming her stomach. Layla toweled her hair and combed it out.

A soft silk blue and green gown, light as a cobweb, was held out and Elizabeth wiggled into it. It felt delicate as air against her bare skin. Elizabeth fingered the silk and felt flushed again. She imagined Jabari, a lusty look in his eye, tearing it off as soon as she walked into his bedroom, ensnaring her like a falcon trapping a dove.

So much for innocence. Her hands shook a little.

Her eyes met Farah's. To her surprise, the woman offered a smile of understanding. Farah touched her arm in a hesitant gesture as if trying to make peace. "He really is . . . not *that* large. Jabari is quite gentle. Do not be afraid."

Elizabeth offered a halfhearted smile. As she followed the women back to her room, Elizabeth cast a wary glance back toward Jabari's bedroom, wondering what awaited her there.

Powder-blue silk slippers whispered down the hallway some time later as Layla escorted Elizabeth to Jabari's chambers. Elizabeth clutched the silk gown with one damp palm and wrapped a strand of her nearly dry hair around her index finger. Such a lovely gown, in varying shades of blue and emerald, the skirt billowing outward as she moved. A thin gauze veil stretched across her mouth.

Hunger grumbled in her stomach. She cursed the mead she'd sipped earlier, for it relaxed her as Farah had predicted. She wanted fear's sharp edge to keep her on guard.

Fear returned when Layla opened the door to Jabari's bedroom. Elizabeth fought the urge to bolt down the hallway and followed her inside.

Lounging on thick cushions on the floor, Jabari sat regally before a low sandalwood table spread with fruit and cheese. He looked up at Layla's greeting, stood and folded his arms. A black robe with wide sleeves embroidered with gold thread hung to his knees. Soft black cotton trousers clung to his muscled calves. He was straight of limb, well-formed and had the proud pose of a king accustomed to command. One did not say "no" to this man. Elizabeth could no more control him than she could stop the onslaught of a powerful Khamsin windstorm.

Layla pressed her arm and offered a consoling smile as she bowed out of the room. Elizabeth's lower lip pouted beneath the veil. Her body tensed with frustrated resentment more than fear. He'd violate her body. Overpower her easily, just to seek his pleasure. Then sated, he'd toss her away like a crumpled bit of paper. She seethed with anger against the upcoming intrusion.

"Please, sit. I am sure you are hungry. Aziz told me you ate none of your dinner." Jabari resumed his seat.

Her growling stomach confirmed his statement. With great caution, she inched her way toward the table and sat across from him. He offered a thick slice of cheese. She lifted her veil and nibbled at it, her eyes never leaving his face. As long as she ate, he would wait to attack her. Her body felt as rigid as the wooden table. Elizabeth summoned her fortitude and swallowed anxiety with the cheese. She remembered the *tameya* he had shared and wished he would slip back into that casual mood.

"This is good," she murmured, hoping to divert his attention from her to the food. "Do you make your own cheese?"

The corners of his lips twitched upward. "Yes, I made it myself from fresh goat's milk. Milked the goat, churned the milk, curdled the cheese. And when I was finished, I baked some flatbread to go with it." He stretched out his hands and gave a mournful frown. "My poor hands, I have worked so hard."

It took her a full minute to realize he joked with her. She set down the slab of cheese upon the plate. Elizabeth bowed her head and raised her hands to her face.

"What are you doing?" Jabari asked.

She lifted her head. "Thanking Allah that there is hope for you after all. Perhaps maybe you even clean as well as cook. I just might hire you myself."

Jabari guffawed, flashing even white teeth. He leaned back, putting his hands behind his bare head. His dark eyes sparkled with good-natured humor. "Alas, my talents are quite limited to simple tribal foods and none of your exotic Western dishes. They are too rich for my taste."

Sheer curiosity nudged aside her anger and fear. She leaned forward with avid interest. "Your tribe, are they Bedouin?"

"We have some of their customs, such as their famous hospitality, but we are not true Bedu, for the Bedu move from place to place as the seasons change. Our southern tribe, which conducts the horse breeding, is more mobile. Since we are sworn to guard the Almha, we remain in one place. However, this puts a great hardship on our flocks and food stores, so we cultivate grains and feed during the winter rains for the lean summer months. And we grow food for ourselves as well as cotton. It has been a dry winter and the food stores are quite low." He sighed.

"Where do you get your water from? A well?"

"No, a cave my ancestors discovered centuries ago when carving out alabaster for the pharaohs. The inside of the mountain had a hollow cavern with a bubbling spring. They hid the water source and decided to locate our people in the desert."

Elizabeth shuddered. Already nervous, she began talking rapidly. "I hate caves and rock tombs."

"Ah, yes. Your parents." Jabari murmured.

"I was with them and saw it happen. The guide grabbed me and ran. There was nothing I could do. Ever since then, I've been afraid of them. It's an awful, out-of-control feeling," she rambled. She knew she must sound like a babbling idiot. Elizabeth looked up to see his dark eyes fill with compassion.

"I am sorry," he said gently. "I sometimes feel the same way when I realize my people face going hungry."

Calmer now, his soothing tones pacifying her, she tilted her head and regarded him. "Don't you have a means to supplement your income? What of the horse breeding?"

"It serves us well, but business has been sporadic lately." He blew out a breath. "For many reasons."

"It must be frustrating for you seeing the large *baksheesh* payments the diggers receive, while your own people face hunger."

Jabari stared at her in frank admiration. "Yes, it is. You are very astute, Elizabeth."

"What about cotton? Do you grow enough to make a profit?" Elizabeth knew cotton was Egypt's best export. During the American Civil War, the South stopped exporting cotton, allowing Egypt and other countries to step in and fill the need.

"Prices have dropped severely in the past two decades since your country began exporting cotton again. And taxes have only gone up." He ran a hand through his dark, thick locks.

"Egypt has an immense foreign debt. I know the financial crisis of twenty years ago didn't help. But that's why the British came here. Foreign control to help repay the debt and straighten out the economy," Elizabeth pointed out.

Jabari grunted, lacing his fingers together. "So now we pay taxes to the British instead of the *khedive*. Even the foreign banks have not survived the financial crisis our country faces. Tell me how the British have helped Egypt any more than we can help ourselves."

"I can't," she said honestly. "But your *khedive* doesn't help. He keeps wanting more credit for his frills and personal pleasures and plunging Egypt more and more into debt."

"I have no respect for him or any of his men who bow before the infidels as if they were gods of old, only gods with money who can consolidate our debts." Jabari looked upward as if seeking answers from heaven. "Allah will provide a way. And in the meantime, we can always raid a caravan or two. Kidnap a few women. Hold them hostage in exchange for food and money."

Jabari's black eyes gleamed with mischief. "Now see here, you barbarian you, you will let me go at once, do you hear me? I shall not stand for your impertinence any longer! Where are my tea and crumpets?" He did such a perfect imitation in English of a British socialite that her belly hurt from laughing. Jabari's sense of humor charmed her.

"No tea. No crumpets today. All we have is goat's cheese. And I slaved so hard to make it. No water for tea. This is a desert. Do you think we have water in the desert?" She mimicked Jabari's deep, husky voice in English.

He chuckled and gave her a mock scowl, then switched back to Arabic. "I see now why I learned the language of the infidel, for sparring with your wicked tongue is most amusing."

"Where did you learn to speak English? And don't tell me from raiding caravans."

"My father thought it best I learned the ways of the West when the British took over ten years ago. He sent me to Cairo, to an English scholar he'd befriended while raiding a caravan. My father let his party go unharmed with a promise of payment—lessons for his son. I lived there for three years with my best friend, Nazim, and studied Western culture, among other things."

"Why?"

"The best way to defeat an enemy is to know how he thinks, to discover his weak spots," Jabari asserted.

Elizabeth considered. "Yes, that is how I approached archaeology and this dig. I knew the men thought me a stupid, helpless woman, so I disguised myself as a man to accomplish my goal."

He laid down on the cushions, propping up his head with one fist. "You would make an excellent warrior, for we do the same."

"I'm not sure of that." Elizabeth smiled, relaxing her shoulders. "I know how to use a *turia,* not a sword."

"Your best, most formidable weapon is your mind," Jabari countered. "An army of sheep is best led by a lion and will defeat an army of lions led by a sheep."

"That is very true," she marveled, pondering his words. "You are so wise! Who taught you this?"

Jabari gave her a charming smile. "Some old sheep."

She gave an exasperated moan.

"It is an ancient proverb."

"You see, much can be learned from the past. That is why I love history. Ancient tombs, cities, they all offer much wisdom into lifestyles of long ago!" Elizabeth tugged at a strand of hair. Could she make him understand?

"But your people do not respect my ancestors' grounds. They are sacred. Why not let the dead alone? Why must you corrupt the past?" Jabari sat up, frowning, but looked truly bewildered.

"Not corrupt. Preserve. There are those who would take the riches and plunder tombs for their own personal gain. But those like me only wish to re-create what once was. Jabari, your culture was the seat of civilization!" Elizabeth paused. Thought hard. Then smiled as she seized upon one thing she knew he understood.

"Doesn't preserving your culture's past ennoble it? Bring honor to your culture by setting it above others so we may learn from it? What greater honor than to display it before the world instead of leaving it buried in the sands?"

He nodded slowly. "I am beginning to understand. You talk of education. Teaching others. This can be a good thing."

"Of course! Even if it doesn't entail learning another language to exploit an enemy's weak spots."

As he laughed, she added in a mocking tone, "Of course you have no weak spots, for you are so brave and strong and know how to cook, in addition to your other numerous talents."

But Jabari did not laugh at her joke. Instead, his eyes

grew solemn. "I have many weak spots and my enemies know them all well. I am vulnerable because of my people. I am their leader and expected to act as such. I would give my life for my people. Yet it is not enough. Each time I see suffering, when there is not enough food to eat, when a child cries from hunger, it breaks me in two," he said, his voice laced with deep sorrow.

Elizabeth's defenses shattered as she took in the anguish in his face, the taut lips and tic of his right cheek. Jabari's proud resolve split in two. His dark eyes grew haunted. She felt a tug of tenderness for him, seeing the torment he faced, thinking of his tribe's future. Then he gathered himself together and his body grew stiff.

"Do I still act like the barbarian to you?" he asked. "Are you revolted by my appearance? Is that why you stare at me so?"

"No," she hesitated, studying his face. His confession deeply moved her. All her preconceived notions about this arrogant desert warrior shattered into tiny pieces. Elizabeth wanted to detest him to protect herself. She couldn't.

Propelled by feelings she didn't quite understand, Elizabeth abandoned the safety of the table between them and sat next to him. Jabari looked down as she placed her hand over his. Elizabeth gave it a tight squeeze and offered a consoling smile.

"You care a great deal about your people. I'm sure you are a good leader to worry about them so," she said in a gentle voice.

"I do care . . . a great deal," he agreed, looking directly at her with a strange intensity. Somehow she ascertained his statement had a double meaning. Flustered, she withdrew her hand.

He picked up her hand and examined it. Frowned at the traces of blisters caused by her excavating. His strong fingers, accustomed to wielding a scimitar with deadly ease against an enemy, felt comforting against her skin. Almost protective.

"Your hands are not as soft as when we first met. So

much digging. All for our sacred Almha. Yet you do not have the greedy air of a treasure hunter. Something tells me you did not want the Almha for yourself. Did your uncle force you to dig?"

Elizabeth said yes, cursing her stupidity as the word spilled from her lips. Lying to this man could be more dangerous than unearthing the sacred disk. *Fool! Just tell him the real reason! He will not harm you now.* But she could not trust him. Although she'd seen Jabari's compassionate side, she feared the fierce warrior in him would not demonstrate the same kindness.

"He is most unscrupulous, your uncle," Jabari observed, releasing her hand. He laid down again, propping his head on one elbow, and looked at her.

"He is all the family I have, besides Nana. I have no one else," she replied, feeling the deep longing surface. Elizabeth always yearned for a large family support structure.

"No one else?" Jabari's eyes widened as if he couldn't comprehend this revelation. The man probably had more relatives than a camel had fleas.

"Oh, friends. Plenty of those. One is a geologist and offered me a job assisting him, but my heart wasn't in it."

"Ah, your heart was buried in the sand instead." His eyes twinkled with amusement. "You wanted only to come to Egypt and steal away the past."

"Not steal," she protested. "I never intended to steal. . . ." Elizabeth paused as he sat up and placed one hand upon her cheek, caressing it softly.

"But you have," he said quietly. "Stealing hearts as if they were rare treasures. Will you steal mine now and march off with it as your prize?"

A slight smile tugged at the corners of her lips. "Only if it belongs to the eighteenth dynasty," she quipped.

He threw back his head and laughed. Even white teeth flashed against his bronzed skin. It was like watching a lion growl playfully. Enchanted, she drew in closer and tapped his chest with a boldness that surprised her.

"And what lies in here? Is it buried deep inside? What

would I find if I took my brush and swept away what covers it?"

Jabari caught her hand in his and brought it to his lips. He kissed it, captivating her with the arresting look in his midnight eyes. Her own heart skipped a few beats at the burning desire within that dark gaze.

"Once it was buried, but a lovely archaeologist dared to excavate for it. It quietly awaits your embrace. For only then can it be released from the tomb that imprisons it."

He reached into his robe and withdrew a slip of paper, unfolding it. Elizabeth inhaled, recognizing her drawing. Embarrassed, she looked away. She had forgotten about it.

"Is that what you see when you look at me, Elizabeth? My eyes, they are most unusual. And so are you," he said softly.

Her gaze darted back to the sketch. Elizabeth had drawn herself, a tiny figure in a silk gown that billowed in the breeze. One arm stretched out, beckoning with sultry allure to the distant man on the rocks. His eyes focused on her. They were not sharp with scrutiny for an enemy or warm with affection for a young girl. They blazed with the mysteries of the unknown, of hidden passions and acceptance of the invitation she offered.

He stood, pulling her up with him. Elizabeth's heart thudded harder as her sketch fell to the table. The lighthearted atmosphere had given way to something more intense. Dangerous.

"I wish to see your face," he said softly. Jabari unfastened her veil and gave it an impatient yank. It fluttered to the floor in a whisper of gossamer silk.

"Elizabeth," he murmured, "you know I did not call you here merely to talk, as enjoyable as our conversation has been."

She took a step backward, afraid. He advanced, a determined look on his face.

No more friendly camaraderie. He was a man who had only one thing on his mind: claiming what was his. She thought of what Farah had said about his size and panicked.

Elizabeth turned. Ran for the door. Locked. She jiggled the knob, her palms cold and clammy. A large, warm palm covered her hand and gently tugged it away from the doorknob.

Elizabeth backed against the door, her breath shooting out in ragged pants of fear and uncertainty. Hands curled into fists so tight they made her muscles ache. She looked at him, expecting him to seize her like a falcon seizing prey. Paw at her like a wild beast. But his face was filled with loving tenderness.

"Do not be afraid, my sweet Elizabeth. Ever since the first day we met, you have haunted my thoughts. Every time I close my eyes, you are there. You are the most beautiful woman I have ever met. Your sweetness reminds me of a precious desert rose."

She stopped pressing against the door, touched by his poetic confession and gentleness. Here was the Jabari whom Badra had talked of, the man lying beneath the cold arrogance.

"The fragile rose thrives amid the desert heat. Its beauty refreshes a man's weary spirit. As your beauty does to me. You made my heart stand still the first day I saw you."

"I felt the same," she confessed, staring wide-eyed at him. "Ever since I saw you looking down at me, I thought it was all a dream. And I did not want to wake up."

Jabari stepped closer. Gently, he cradled her face in his warm palms. He tilted her head skyward, then bent down and kissed her lips with the barest of touches, a light kiss fashioned from air, like spun cotton candy. "You are so beautiful, so sweet and innocent, you fill my heart with joy every time I am near you," he whispered against her mouth.

His words eased the rigidity of fear. Her shoulders lost their tension. He kissed her again, a little more forcefully, but still soft, this time a light rain drumming on her nerves.

Elizabeth uncurled her fists.

He took her hands, held them, their bodies barely touching as he kissed her. She leaned a little closer, curious at the richness of his mouth, the delicious taste of him. Needing to explore his lips. Wanting to unearth the delights that lay there.

Jabari pulled away. Broke the kiss. Stepped back.

Elizabeth felt frustrated disappointment. She stepped forward, tilting her pursed lips up with an air of expectation. Slid her hands up the coarse texture of his robe to his biceps, to his broad shoulders. Around his neck. Then she closed her eyes, pressed herself against him.

Kissed him. Nibbled at his lips, darting her tongue over them in an awkward motion. With a light grip on her upper arms, Jabari pulled back from her embrace.

A strange light came into those dark eyes. Tenderness, mixed with something else. Pride?

"Elizabeth, Elizabeth. How I have longed for this moment," he said softly, brushing a strand of her hair back from her face.

Jabari pulled her into his arms, wrapping them tightly around her waist and kissed her back. This time, not rain or cotton candy, but a sandstorm. A Khamsin, the driving, devilish hot desert wind his tribe was named for, engulfed her as his mouth sought hers.

She tightened her grip around his neck and opened her mouth to him as their tongues coupled in a frenzied mating. He was hunger and fury and need all pummeling through her, a thousand and one *turias* beating every single nerve in her body, demanding to free the passion buried deep inside her.

Breaking the kiss, he stepped back again, a gleam of satisfaction on his roguishly handsome face.

Elizabeth recoiled in shocked horror as she licked her swollen mouth. What had she unleashed in herself?

Jabari gave a knowing chuckle. She felt unreasonable fury at him. "You tricked me," she wailed.

"No tricks," he said softly, "for I only allowed you to feel what you have been fighting for so long. Do not fight me any longer, Elizabeth. Give in to your passion."

She opened her mouth to protest when he advanced again, his lips claiming hers once more. His tongue expertly traced the lower curve of her lip. Flicked between her parted lips. Breathed in her essence. Her life. Her longing for him.

And then he began a slow, stroking series of caresses up and down her back. His touch was fire and sun and sent raging sensations of need pulsing through her. She felt so awed by the feelings. Never had a man touched her this way before, made her skin feel so ultrasensitive. Filling her with sensual pleasure. Sagging against him as if her knees turned to sand, Elizabeth let him support her body weight. Jabari pulled away, then began kissing her most vulnerable spot. Her neck. She whimpered at the feel of his mouth claiming that sensitive place, the delightful softness of his tongue brushing against her bare skin.

"The time has come to make you mine," he whispered against her ear, then kissed her again, each kiss a tiny wildfire that hopped across her skin in a sizzling fire line.

She was helpless to extinguish the flames. She tried thoughts of marching with placards for suffragettes. Of her Nana, shaking her head in frowning condemnation. Nothing worked.

"Please," she gasped, battling him and her own urgent need of him. What had he done to her? Jabari had taken the shackles of her fear, unchained them and set her free, only to release the raging desire inside.

"I can't . . ."

"Do not resist, my little desert rose. Surrender to me. I promise I will be gentle," he said in a husky whisper and continued sending a fiery blaze down her neck.

Through the sheer fabric, she felt his hands slide over her body with assured, expert strokes. Jabari pulled her closer, the firm pressure of his body pressed against her. Elizabeth felt the male hardness between his legs. Shocked by the intimacy, and knowing what it would result in, she struggled in his arms.

"Votes for women," she cried out, pummeling him with her fists.

"You have already proven your equality, my love, with your sweet mouth." He chuckled against her neck. His laughter infuriated her. She let the anger rise, dominate the desire.

"I will fight you with all my might, Jabari," she vowed, even as her body burned from the fire of his touch. "You would force me against my will."

"I do not think so," he countered, brushing his lips against her earlobe, teasing it with a delicate lick.

She suppressed a low moan as he loosened his grip enough to run a possessive hand across her breasts, caressing her through the thin material. "I have yet to take a woman by force what she willingly gives to me, and thus it will be the same with you. Your body trembles at my touch. You will beg me to make you mine," he said in a deep, compelling voice.

Her independent streak finally reared its sleepy head in indignant protest of his words. Male arrogance!

"The hell I will! You can't make me."

Definite mistake. Never taunt male pride, especially if said pride was accompanied by more than six feet of hulking male muscle.

Scarcely had that thought crossed her mind when the hulking male muscle picked her up and scooped her over his shoulder. With an amused chuckle, Jabari crossed the distance to the bed as she muttered curses in English and beat his back with her fists. It was like striking a brick wall.

He laughed and dumped her gently onto the bed.

"So fierce! So wild! My beautiful Elizabeth, as spirited as a Khamsin colt!"

His eyes sparkled like diamond flecks in the flickering lamplight as he rapidly shucked his robe. His long, black locks spilled about his shoulders. Jabari stood before her proudly, letting her drink in the sight of him. His lean, sculpted body gleamed in the firelight. Tight black trousers molded to his heavily muscled thighs. Her gaze widened at the enormous protrusion in those trousers that demonstrated how very much he wanted her.

She scurried in the opposite direction across the massive bed, trying to escape. He laughed again and captured her in his determined embrace. Pinning her to the bed with his body, Jabari drove a knee between her thighs. He settled between the cradle of her legs and pulled both her arms above her head in a viselike grip. Strong, warm fingers laced through hers.

"I do not think you are going anywhere. Nor will you want to," he whispered and lowered his mouth to hers in a brutal kiss. His lips gentled as his tongue flickered over the rich bottom curve of her lower lip. Elizabeth writhed beneath him, horrified at the raging heat mounting in her.

A semblance of proper morality fled as she uttered a low moan of pleasure. Some of her body's rigidness eased. She answered the masterful thrusts of his tongue by opening her mouth to him. Tasting him. Breathing in his air, his spirit, his passion. A firestorm possessed her as she found it hard to breathe from the wild intensity of his demanding mouth. Jabari broke the kiss, letting go of her hands and sat up gazing down at her. Within the depths of his eyes she saw blazing passion reflecting in the lamp's flame. He desired her with an almost feral, primitive need to possess her.

He impatiently tugged the gown from her shoulders, then ripped the sheer fabric open with one mighty yank, baring her body. His hands encased her breasts. With a touch lighter than air, Jabari delicately fingered one tender bud, making it harden. She arched up, gasping with shuddering pleasure.

Jabari's laugh was rich with satisfaction as he lowered himself upon her, letting her feel the solid length of his body. Hot, ragged breath created warm waves upon her bare skin. He slid one knee up, rubbing against the soft curls at her juncture in a series of deliberate strokes that aroused her acutely.

Elizabeth gasped and arched her back and let out a low

cry at the searing heat, mortified at how easily he controlled her senses. The man's sensual power had a drugging effect.

He raised up on his hands and stared down at her. In the smoldering depths of his coffee-colored eyes she saw a mirror of her own burning need.

"Tell me, Elizabeth. I need to hear it from your lips. Tell me you want me or I will stop," he commanded.

"I-I want . . ." Desire and shame mingled, clashed. A flicker of morality corseted her passion, laced it up into a moment of doubt. She turned her head, feeling that if she gazed into his mesmerizing dark eyes she'd lose all sense. Jabari cupped her face and tilted it up, forcing her to meet his demanding gaze.

"I have told you I never force a woman. The choice is yours," he whispered to her, letting his fingertips trail down her neck to her breasts. He fingered her right nipple with exquisite slowness, and she gasped as it tautened with pleasure.

"Elizabeth, you have not answered. What is your decision?"

She struggled with the emotions claiming her. Ever since Jabari kidnapped her, Elizabeth fought to escape him. He fought equally hard to keep her imprisoned. She thought about his determination to subdue her and what Badra said, "I am allowed to come and go as I please. Perhaps he treats you differently because he can't control you." Here was the key that could set her free. If she wanted it . . .

"You said you would release your concubines if they no longer wanted to stay. If I make love with you now and promised I would never dig up the Almha, would you release me after and let me walk away?" she whispered, looking at his face.

Jabari had not imprisoned her inside his harem. He had imprisoned her inside newly awakened feelings for him. Deep down, her heart protested at leaving him. But she had to know if he would grant her freedom if she finally surrendered to him. She saw him struggle for answers. His eyes filled with haunting turmoil as he searched her face.

"No. Not after we make love. If that is what you truly want, then I will release you now," he said softly. "Do you, Elizabeth? Do you want to leave me right now? I will unlock the door and you may fly away, free as a bird. Answer me."

"No," she choked out in a throaty whisper. "I don't want to leave you now. You win."

Jabari looked surprised and then his face creased into the tenderest of smiles. "No, my lady. You have won."

She clung to him like sand to skin, feeling control slip away as easily as he kissed her. Her lips opened as his tongue teased, licked and excavated the depths of her mouth. Sharp, deep need assaulted her senses like a pick shattering hard earth.

Suddenly he released her mouth, bent his head, nibbled her neck, then sucked gently. The sensation was wildly erotic and she closed her eyes. Her hands explored the length of his back, kneading the hardened muscles, delighting in their firm texture, so different from her own soft femaleness. She reached down to cup his firm buttocks and pulled him closer.

Jabari's mouth rained a shower of kisses upon her skin. She shuddered as he cupped her breast and rubbed it softly as he kissed her. His lips roamed over her, kissing her in an elaborate ritual across her body. A soft kiss, claiming her skin, a delicate lick, a whorl of that delicious tongue. His mouth slowly caressed her skin, claiming every inch.

His touch became sizzling torture as he ravished her with his teasing mouth. He was relentless. Demanding. Ferocious in his need of her, his claim of her. Every nerve burned with heat as blazing as the desert sun. "What . . . are you doing to me?" she wailed, biting her lip.

Jabari raised his head and stared down at her, a wicked gleam in his eyes. "My warriors call this the secret of one hundred kisses," he murmured, lowering his mouth to her belly. "Shall I count for you?"

Silk spilled through her fingers as she ran her hands through his long, thick hair. Her eyelids fluttered closed as his mouth worked soft Arabian magic on her body. Jabari buried his face into her abdomen, continuing the slow torment designed to heighten her desire. Tasting her essence. Sampling her sweetness. Jabari's hands cupped the roundness of her backside in a demanding embrace. Wave after wave of pleasure rolled over her, stoking the fire to an increasing inferno. His expert touch spoke of a confident man who claimed her body with powerful sensuality. He lived it, breathed it as his mouth roamed over her with possessive intent. His kisses sent a trail of fire across her skin as he slowly moved to her right hip, pressing the flesh there with his lips, flicking his tongue skillfully over her naked skin.

And then he stopped. Confused, she looked down to find him gazing wide-eyed at her hip. He raised his head and she saw his eyes harden with some hidden emotion that frightened her with its intensity. She almost felt her hip burn as he stared at her birthmark. Jabari sat up and ran his thumb over it.

"Where did you get this? Who put this mark upon you?"

What happened? Elizabeth wrinkled her nose in bewilderment. "No one. It's a birthmark."

He stood rapidly and grabbed her arms, jerking her out of the bed so roughly she cried out. Jabari narrowed his gaze at her with such coldness her bare flesh broke out in gooseflesh. "Do not lie to me, Elizabeth, or I will have Aziz cut out your clever tongue this time. Who put this mark upon you?"

"I told you, I was born with it! Jabari, you're hurting me!" Why had he changed so suddenly? His mood change terrified her.

He released her, and resumed staring at the bird-shaped mark on her hip. "It cannot be," Jabari said in a dazed voice. "But it is there. The mark of the white dove." He rubbed the spot as if he could erase it with his touch. Then he glanced at her hair. Jabari reached out and wrapped a strand around his finger.

"Like Aten's beaming rays, her hair will be cloaked in sunshine as bright as purest gold," he muttered to himself.

"Why are you acting like this? What's going on?" Elizabeth clutched herself, feeling vulnerable in her naked state. The night air's chill and his bizarre behavior sent shivers through her body.

Releasing her hair, Jabari shook his head. "The council must be informed. But there is one more test yet to be determined," he mused more to himself than her. Grim determination now replaced the desire glimpsed earlier in his eyes. Jabari had turned into a deadly serious man facing a life-changing decision.

One minute the man kissed her with blind passion and posed a threat to her virginity, the next he acted as if possessed.

Jabari stared at the wall opposite, nodding thoughtfully. "It is so, then. The prophecy has come full circle. I was blinded before, but my eyes are opened now."

"I don't understand. What is going on?"

He glanced at her, as if finally noticing the woman and not the body part that had captured his interest. To her shocked amazement, he crossed the room, dug into a trunk and withdrew a large black robe. Jabari draped it across her shoulders.

"Cover yourself. Now," he ordered, turning his back on her.

Hurt and bewildered, she donned the massive garment. The sleeves dripped past her hands and she had to roll them up.

"You must leave now. Layla will escort you back to your quarters," he said in a harsh voice. Back still turned from her, he marched toward the door.

Elizabeth's cheeks grew hot with humiliation. Rejecting her for a birthmark? Confusion mingled with disappointment as she picked up the dragging hem of the robe and raced across the room to catch his arm.

"Jabari, you owe me an explanation," she said. Elizabeth bit her lip and summoned courage for her next words. "Why aren't you going to make love to me?"

He circled her like a bird of prey, his gaze critically sweeping up and down her body. Jabari put a warm palm against her hip. "I cannot love you the way I wish to, Elizabeth," he said in a rigid voice. "I am forbidden . . . now. The time will come, after the ceremony."

Ceremony? He hid something from her, something quite important. "Why didn't you remember this before you began ravishing my body?"

Did she see pity mixed with deep-seated desire in his eyes? Elizabeth couldn't tell. "Circumstances between us have changed," he said bluntly.

"What ceremony are you talking about?" Elizabeth wrinkled her nose as Jabari caught her hand in his. He squeezed it and his eyes glowed with a deep-seated sense of purpose.

"The ceremony binding us together as mates for all eternity. When I take you as my wife."

Chapter Eleven

He steeled himself for her response, prepared for the full force of her fury. He thought she would shriek with rage or strike out with her fists. Jabari took a deep calming breath.

Elizabeth's lower lip dropped and her eyes took on a queer blank expression. She opened and closed her mouth, looking indeed like a *samak,* a fish, trying to form words that did not come.

Then she squinted. Her lips trembled. She doubled over, shaking. Concerned, he took a step toward her to offer comfort, then realized she didn't cry.

Her body quivered with silent laughter. Elizabeth straightened, putting a hand to her mouth.

"Marriage! All the sudden you want to get married!" she sputtered, enunciating each syllable.

"I do not jest," he said, stiffening with pride. "I am most serious, Elizabeth. We must be married."

"Why? You're having a sudden attack of morality?"

Patience slipped a few notches. Jabari glared at her. "You do not understand. Things have changed between us, now that I know who you really are." He reeled in his temper and blew out a breath through his teeth. No one laughed at Jabari bin Tarik Hassid. Not even Queen Kiya herself would dare.

He gripped her hand and led her over to the bed, urging her to sit. She wiped her streaming eyes, amusement dancing across her face. "Jabari, please, you simply are not making any sense. First you say you will let me free and now you want to marry me?"

"I will explain then." Relief surged through him. She didn't laugh at him. Elizabeth was just confused. He wondered how to put it into words that she would understand. How could Elizabeth, raised with Western ways and ideals, even begin to comprehend the seriousness of what he was about to tell her? She had no connection to his people and their rigid code of honor. If only he could break down the barrier between their cultures . . .

Then it struck him. Elizabeth was half Egyptian. Surely it was bred into her blood, the ancient mysticism and connection to the past. Her fainting episodes. They must have a deeper meaning!

"Elizabeth, the strange dreams you have experienced since we met, can you tell me what you saw?"

She frowned. "Does this have anything to do with what you're going to tell me?"

"It could be. I suspect the two are tied."

"They were . . ." Her beautiful eyes clouded, as if she searched her memory. "The first one began at the dig, just before I met you when I held the artifact in my hand. And it was like I was transported . . . back into time. Like someone else was inside me." She gave a light laugh. "It sounds ridiculous."

"Go on. How many times has this happened?"

"Two other times. Once here." Wonder dawned in the depths of her blue irises. "And when I . . . saw you in main *wadi.* I touched the rock near where the Almha was buried and my hand tingled."

"Ah yes," he murmured. "No wonder you discovered

the Almha. What you experienced was a connection to the past. A memory."

"A memory?" Her brow wrinkled with confusion.

Jabari hesitated and reached for her hand, knowing she had to be told. He looked down at her soft skin and caressed it in a loving gesture. "Elizabeth, what I am about to tell you is most serious. Please do not be frightened. But it is important you fully understand what has happened to you."

"All right." Her expression was open and trusting.

"You experienced memories from the past. The reason the Almha called out to you is, why you so easily found it, was because you were its guardian. You buried it."

She bit her lip. "How . . ."

He squeezed her hand and looked at her with reverence. "You know the reason why the Khamsin guard the Almha?"

She nodded. "Layla told me the legend."

"It is not legend. Today a white dove flew in from the west to our camp, a sign that Kiya returns. My people have waited for three thousand years for our queen to come back. And now she has." He lifted her hand to his lips and softly kissed it.

Her eyes widened and she gasped. "You can't be serious! I am no queen!"

Jabari slid his hand possessively over her hip, tapping her now-hidden birthmark. "You have the mark of the white dove. There are three tests that prove the return of our queen. One—Kiya will carry the markings of the white dove upon her body. Two—her hair will be as gold as the sunshine sent down to earth by the Aten. Three—the dove will recognize her as its mistress."

He clasped both her hands in earnest. "It is you, Elizabeth. You have fulfilled two of the signs and I must bring you before my people to bring the prophecy to full circle and fulfill the third sign. You are the reincarnation of our queen and that is why we must marry. It is my duty to mate with you. Our sons will lead our people into prosperity."

Jerking her hands from his, Elizabeth shook her head, making her long blond hair fly back and forth. "But Jabari, I can't believe this! I'm not even familiar with your people!"

"How else do you explain your dreams? They did not happen prior to your arrival."

"No," she admitted. "It's simply too fantastic to believe!"

"Elizabeth, I speak the truth. Think back. You must have had some inkling this would happen . . . some link to your destiny."

Her eyes clouded over as if she fought the truth. "No, no, no. I'm an ordinary American citizen. I have no connection to you, your people or some fantasy about a long-dead queen!"

Jabari hesitated, knowing he had to break through that barrier she erected between them, either out of fear or simple denial. "Why did you come here?" he asked. "To seek the Almha. Surely you realize fate led you here at this time in your life."

"Fate." She gurgled with laughter. "Some fate. I came for other reasons. It's all coincidence. Timing."

"My people believe that there is no coincidence, only destiny. Elizabeth, you know your destiny called you here."

"It's too incredible to believe. But if you want to believe, you must." She shrugged. "It has nothing to do with me. And if you think I'd marry you . . . you think wrong."

His head began to pound. Somehow he had to convince her.

"Why are you set against the idea? Is it marriage itself that bothers you?" he asked slowly.

"I may not have any choice about being seduced by you, but I'll be damned if I marry. Marriage is for foolish women who would enslave themselves to men's whims." Elizabeth tossed her head, but he caught a tone of trepidation in her voice.

So she thought marriage only served as a shackle for women. Jabari shook his head in bemusement. Among the women of his tribe, marriage was a joyful event. No women were more revered than the wives of Khamsin warriors. He felt sorry for Elizabeth. She seemed so vulnerable, and her defiance reminded him of a terrified child struggling to maintain a brave front.

Jabari hesitated and plunged ahead. "Elizabeth, I want you as I've wanted no other woman."

Beautiful blue eyes narrowed with suspicion. "What about your concubines? What about Farah?"

He made a dismissive motion. "I am fond of Farah, but it is not the same. You are the only woman I want."

He said all this in a rush of emotion, waiting for her reaction with hesitation. Never before had he had ever risked admitting to a woman how very much he wanted her. Then again, never had he wanted a woman as much as Elizabeth.

She lowered her lashes and her lips quivered. A feeling of tenderness came over him. He did not fight his feelings this time, but allowed them to flow through him, to take over and claim him. Jabari cupped her face with his hands. Tears swam in the blue depths of her eyes and one spilled over his hand. Deeply troubled, Jabari traced a tear with the tip of one finger.

"I can't marry you. I could never marry you. I don't want to marry you!" The last sentence was uttered with a little more force, as if she dredged up all her strength to say it.

"Why? Is it because our cultures are so different?" he asked simply, brushing back the hair from her face. He ran his thumb along the lovely curve of her jawline.

"No. I mean yes, I mean, it's because . . ." She took a deep breath and continued, "You don't love me. You only desire me."

He opened his mouth to counter, and shut it. Love. His father once loved deeply, so much that he let his wife go. And it killed him in the end. Love weakened men. He could not afford to be seen as weak.

When he told her he'd let her walk out the door, Jabari meant it. He was willing to chance her leaving, for it was an acceptable risk. He had led Elizabeth to the brink of passion, showing her the pleasures awaiting her in his arms and she surrendered as he had anticipated. This was far different. Much more was at stake. Duty bound him to her now. He needed to marry her to fulfill the prophecy and restore hope to his people.

Feelings of deep confusion raged through him. He felt something for Elizabeth, but was that love? Jabari wrestled with his emotions. He had women in his bed before and they served only to ease his physical needs. Jabari realized if he were to consummate his desire for Elizabeth at last, it would not be enough. He could not bear the thought of her leaving. He was a man shut away in a deep cave who was finally allowed to feel the sun on his face. Without Elizabeth, the darkness returned.

He took a long, controlling breath. Jabari felt as if he stood ready to jump off the great limestone cliffs of Akhetaten, trusting she would catch him. He cradled her face, brushed his lips tenderly against hers, then whispered into her mouth, "You are so wrong, my lovely desert rose. You are the one my soul has waited for through the ages. I do love you."

She gazed up at him, her expression full of awed wonder. Her lips parted and she closed her eyes as he drank in the sweetness of that delectable mouth. Elizabeth clasped his neck as he kissed her, tasting her, then hunger overtook him and he deepened the kiss, wanting only to utterly and fully possess her. Jabari felt himself losing control and tore his mouth away. He smoothed her hair back and planted a light kiss atop her pert nose.

Then he saw her eyes narrow. A battle ensued inside his desert rose, a battle he realized he would lose.

"You're just saying that."

"I am not," he protested.

"I don't believe it. I can't marry a man who doesn't love

me for who I am, and only marries to fulfill some silly superstition. I can't love a man like you."

The last sentence sounded like a proclamation of doom. He had leaped off the cliffs, trusting she would catch him. Instead, she let him smash on the ground. If Elizabeth had taken his dagger and sliced his heart open, she could not have wounded him more. An ache so physical filled him that he wondered if the organ he had just handed to her still beat inside his chest. He inhaled and watched her blur as if she faded into the distance.

Anger offered the only defense against her rejection. He could never show her how deeply she had hurt him.

"You will marry me, and I will do my duty and fulfill the prophecy. I do not need your . . . love. Your body suffices enough."

He roughly yanked her robe open. His dispassionate gaze swept up and down her naked form, visually inspecting her as if purchasing an animal. Elizabeth flushed scarlet.

"You look strong enough to bear me many healthy sons. I already sampled some of your delights, so you will please me in bed. And you are a virgin, so you fulfill the requirement of purity for a sheikh's bride."

Giving her a look of disgust, he shoved her away.

"Tomorrow we ride for camp. You will marry me. Either as a willing bride or as my prisoner. There will be no escape."

Walking over to the door, he yanked it open and barked a command to Aziz to escort her back to her room. Jabari felt brief pain and realized his nails formed little half-moons in his clenched fists. Elizabeth watched him, fright clouding her clear blue eyes. Good. Let her fear him.

The last rays of sunshine in his soul vanished as the dark loneliness returned. Jabari watched Elizabeth walk down the hallway as loneliness descended into his heart.

Chapter Twelve

"Jabari, why do you bring before us an insolent woman who refuses to kneel?" One of the twelve elderly men seated in a semicircle on a luxuriant crimson carpet raised his eyebrows. He scowled. She resisted the impulse to make a rude gesture.

"She will. Elizabeth, kneel." Jabari pointed to the tent floor. "A woman's proper place before the Majli is the ground."

Elizabeth's lower lip jutted out. "No."

"Kneel," he said, a little more forcefully.

"I don't kneel before men," she retorted. Wild indignation bubbled up in a volcanic rage.

"Elizabeth," the word came out as an angry growl. Jabari's eyes darkened with anger. "Do as I say. Or you will regret it."

"What more can you do that I'll regret?"

"Up until now I've been quite lenient because you are a stranger to our ways. But we are in my camp. My territory. My people. Women do not look either the sheikh or the Majli in the eyes when presented before them. They bow their heads in humility and kneel. You will learn proper respect. Now kneel!"

In answer, she stared straight into his eyes, then swept her gaze over each elderly tribal member. She would not kneel before these men. Never.

Two strong hands settled on her shoulders. Elizabeth felt Jabari deliver a light kick to the back of her knees. Immediately her legs buckled and she fell to the ground.

"If you do not obey me, I will force you to do as I say."

Remaining on the floor, her arms folded in an attitude of defiance, she glared at the elderly men. Their jaws dropped in uniform incredulity. All wore indigo *binishes* and sported swords at their belts. They inhaled deeply as if shocked.

Oh, how she tired of men telling her what to do!

"Jabari, who is this woman who shows no respect? Is this one of the Westerners disrupting our ancestral grounds? She acts too bold and must be disciplined." The apparent leader, with a thick swatch of white hair curling beneath his blue turban, frowned.

Jabari kept a steady hand on her shoulder. He bowed his head. "Grandfather, I present to you the fulfillment of the prophecy told millennia ago. This is the woman who was promised to us—Elizabeth Summers."

"Truly? It cannot be! Not this one!" Jabari's grandfather fingered his chin in the same action she'd seen his grandson duplicate many times. "Are you certain?"

"I am indeed," Jabari stated somberly. "She fulfills two of the three tests." She felt him tug at the crimson silk scarf covering her head. Her hair tumbled out to more shocked gasps.

"Hair bright as the Aten," his grandfather stated. "And?"

"The mark," Jabari said. "The third test, of the dove, has yet to be determined."

"Let us see the mark," ordered a council member.

"Yes," Jabari murmured. "Stand up, Elizabeth."

Suddenly the floor seemed quite comfortable and much

safer. "Kneel, stand. Am I a puppet? You have spoken of the great hospitality of your tribe. I see none of it now!"

"Elizabeth, you must show the council your birthmark to prove who you are," Jabari urged.

"And you think I'm going to stand for that?" She touched her head to the carpet in an act of homage.

"What are you doing?"

"Paying my respects," she said, her voice muffled by the thick carpeting. "I've decided I am an unworthy woman and not fit to stand before the council."

She swore she heard a slight chuckle threaded through his low, impatient tone. "Elizabeth, understand that you are before the Majli. If you do not obey me and prove you are Kiya, they could take your life if they find out what you did."

She sniffed the mustiness of the carpet, mingled with the sourness of her fear. Elizabeth knew Jabari spoke the truth. Still, showing her nakedness before a group of old men . . . it was scandalous! Before she left that morning, Layla had dressed her in a beige *kamis* shirt and trousers. She completed the outfit with a long-sleeved cotton *kuftan* that draped to her ankles. The indigo *kuftan* had tiny yellow and green flowers embroidered on it. The peculiar outfit, which Layla said all the Khamsin women wore, felt comfortable.

Much more comfortable than the thought of stripping it off.

"You want me to take off my clothing before all these men? Am I to satisfy their lust or are they just curious about what a Western woman looks like before they boil me in oil?" she asked, her face still glued to the carpet.

She felt Jabari clasp her arms and let him pull her up to a standing position. With his thumb he tilted her chin up. The gentle smile lighting his eyes said "I am not the enemy." His gesture replenished her courage. "You will not be shamed. Trust me."

She had no choice. Her instinct said to trust him. Elizabeth nodded. "What do you want me to do?"

He snapped his fingers and a woman entered the tent, carrying a large indigo robe. She knelt before the council, rose and handed the garment to Jabari, who gestured with it to Elizabeth. "Go with my aunt Asriyah to my tent, take off all your clothing and put this on, then return."

More disrobing. Elizabeth tried to quell her stomach's churning. She glanced at the garment he gave her, then at Jabari, a question in her eyes. He smiled and touched her cheek lightly. "Do not be afraid. I will not let them harm you." Then he removed his hand as if remembering her words of the previous night.

She followed the silent woman out of the Majli's tent, pausing to don brown leather sandals as Asriyah did the same. Footwear was not permitted inside the tents.

The Khamsin camp marched across a narrow stretch of flat desert plain nestled against the mountains. Children shrieking and scampering stopped their play and gawked openly. Women carrying earthernware jars glanced with polite curiosity at her. Despite her anxiety, she smiled back at them. There was a certain peacefulness and simplicity in the camp, a leisurely attitude she never found in Boston. A few date palms and thorny acacia trees provided restful shade. She asked Asriyah about the date palms.

"Years ago, our people dug deep holes to reach the water source so the roots are watered," she explained.

They approached the largest tent of all, a veritable palace with many poles. Asriyah told her to remove her sandals, pulled the flap outward, and gestured for her to go inside.

Elizabeth paused, shocked into silence. Two birds clung to a perch just outside Jabari's tent. Sheltered from the sun by a thorn tree, the birds sat together peacefully. The brown peregrine falcon had a leather hood over its eyes. The other . . . Isis? She sucked in her breath. How would her dove have gotten here?

Elizabeth's breath hitched. No one must know Isis belonged to her. Jabari's people thought her a wild dove, the one that flew in from the west, the one that signaled the return of their queen. If Elizabeth played on their superstitions, the elders would proclaim her as this Kiya person. A legend come to life. And perhaps she could twist this new status to her advantage.

"What a gorgeous creature," she told Asriyah. "I've always loved birds." Elizabeth approached the perch and untied the bird. Then stepped back, beckoning. The dove flew to her, settling on her outstretched hand. It *was* Isis. She had taught her that move.

Asriyah murmured words to a few other women who had witnessed the scene. They stared as if she'd materialized before them. Elizabeth smiled inwardly, replaced the bird. She removed her sandals and ducked into the tent to change.

Jabari did not smile when she returned to the Majli's tent clad only in the robe. He turned her body, presenting her right side to the council. Hesitating for just a minute, he slid the fabric up her thigh to her hip. He did it skillfully, revealing only her right leg and hip, concealing the rest of her body beneath the robe's heavy folds.

Twelve men squinted, then stood and moved closer. A collective gasp rose from the group as they peered closely at the birthmark.

"She has the mark!" Jabari's grandfather said in awe. He reached out to touch it. She slapped his hand away.

"Touch me and I'll mark you," she snapped. "And trust me, it won't be your hip I aim for!"

He drew back, glowering at her. "This one is insolent! You need to discipline her, my grandson."

"She is right, Grandfather," Jabari replied, dropping the garment back into place. His dark eyes burned as he regarded the older man. Stepping in front of Elizabeth, Jabari's voice dropped to a low growl that surprised her with its vehemence.

"Do not touch her. Is that understood?"

As his grandfather muttered a sullen acquiescence, she puzzled over Jabari's protective attitude. Why was he defending her? The previous night he acted furious at what she'd said. Her barbed tongue had flogged his masculine pride with vicious precision. Judging from the possessive way he shielded her body, he disliked the idea of anyone else touching her, even if it were to confirm a sacred prophecy.

Perhaps he did love her as he had stated and did not merely say the words so she would marry him. Elizabeth reached for Jabari's hand. She gave it a quick squeeze in thanks. His skin was cool and unresponsive. Jabari looked away. His jaw hardened. He withdrew his hand from her grasp.

"My aunt awaits you outside the tent. Go back with her and get dressed," he ordered.

Her instincts were right. He married only to fulfill his duty to the tribe, she realized with sadness as she followed his aunt outside. Pausing to slip on her sandals, Elizabeth gazed at the camp. Tradition ruled the sands they called home. Tightly woven threads of honor and obligation bound Jabari to his destiny. He did not love her.

The jarring intensity of his declaration the previous night frightened her. Jabari had opened his heart and poured it out before her like spilling water onto dry sand. And like dry sand, she'd drained him, giving back only empty bitterness.

How could she marry him when her grandmother lay wasting away in a cold institution across the Atlantic? How could she subject herself to becoming a mindless puppet to him? If only he could understand how precious freedom was and how frightened she was of marrying a man as strong-willed as himself. To give up all control, as her mother had, forgoing her own needs.

Elizabeth stared ahead into the broad blue cloth of Asriyah's *kuftan* as the woman walked ahead of her. Could she ever love Jabari? Did loving a man mean sacrificing everything? It seemed so. When her mother died, Elizabeth only wanted independence because being a woman in love meant risking all, including life. Her mother had feared caves, yet she meekly followed her husband into one and ended up losing her life.

In Jabari's tent, Elizabeth quickly dressed and gazed around the front room. The same red-patterned rugs were laid on the sand and a few wood camel saddles arranged in a horseshoe shape. She recognized Sahar's saddle as well. No personality there. Nothing she could glimpse of the man. On impulse, she draped the robe over the horse saddle. His bedroom would be where he stored his personal effects, such as paper to attach a message to Isis. She couldn't trust that Badra had given her note to Uncle Nahid. Badra was too devoted to Jabari to risk going against him. Elizabeth had to try to reach her uncle again.

A thick woven curtain separated the two rooms. She stepped into the hallowed sanctuary where Jabari slept. An acacia wood trunk sat off against one wall. Stacks of plush cushions piled around a low sandalwood table. She glanced at the massive bed in the corner and looked quickly away. Then spotted her target—a portable, roll-top stationery box upon another table. Elizabeth hurried over to it, flipped the top up and found paper and quill.

She scribbled a note in English to Nahid. *Kidnapped by the Khamsin while digging for the Almha in main wadi by royal wadi entrance. I'm in the Arabian Desert south of Haggi Quandil. Hurry!*

She slipped the note into her *kuftan*'s pocket and went outside with a casual indifference.

Back in the council tent, Elizabeth glanced at Jabari as the Majli quietly discussed her. He threw his proud shoulders back. Spread his legs apart like a captain of a large sailing vessel standing at the helm. She felt a sharp pang of homesickness for Boston and the cold, crisp salt waters of home. Even the Mediterranean offered more solace than the heavy air inside the thick, black tent. Had Jabari ever journeyed to the Mediterranean? Had he ever stood at its shore, watching waves whip into light froth? Put his ear to a seashell and heard the lonely cries of his own soul echoing back to him?

Her pulse gave a butterfly flutter of apprehension as she watched him. All his attention centered on his grandfather, who appeared to wrestle with a decision. Finally the old man spoke.

"We will conduct the final test to make certain this woman is our Queen Kiya." His voice grated with ponderous solemnity.

"What are you going to do next, hang me by my toenails to see if I spin in the desert wind?" Elizabeth gave a light laugh, concealing her anxiety.

Jabari's grandfather narrowed his eyes. "There is an ancient desert tradition to find out if women with wicked tongues lie. A hot poker is placed upon the tongue and if the owner is not scalded, innocence is proved."

His lips curled in a sly grin as her eyes widened. Elizabeth's temper rose. His intimidating remarks did not scare her. She forgot her fear. Forgot their power. Almost stuck her own tongue out at him.

"What is this obsession about tongues?" Elizabeth spat back, balling her fists. "Are human tongues a Bedouin delicacy?"

Jabari pulled her close to him and spoke sharply into her ear. "Elizabeth, please keep silent. I have not told them of your sacrilege. If they discover it now, my grandfather could order your execution. The Majli are not as forgiving as I."

Hand to her throat, she gulped. All the talk of tongues almost made her lose her head.

"Follow me," he ordered. She sucked down her defiance as he escorted her to the birds' perch. Several people drifted toward them. The gathering crowd murmured with excitement.

"What am I supposed to do now?" she whispered. *Better make this look good, like I have never been around a bird before!*

"Hush," he said, putting a finger to her lips. His touch filled her with comfort despite the aloof attitude. "We must wait for the tribal shaman to arrive."

A shaman? The few times Nana had opened up about living in the desert, she told Elizabeth about the powerful Bedouin shamans. They extracted oils and essences from plants, using them in ritual ceremonies to clear the mind and cleanse the spirit.

If anyone needed her mind cleansed, Elizabeth did. The crowd parted respectfully as a thin, wizened elderly man, wearing a indigo *binish* and walking with a stout stick, approached.

He stopped before Elizabeth and peered at her.

"Queb is *fugara*, our shaman. He has lost much of his sight," Jabari explained.

Elizabeth neared the shaman and caught his hand in hers. She slowly brought it to her face and let him explore the contours and curves. When he finished, she kissed his hand with the greatest respect. Queb gave a satisfied grunt and nodded.

She caught the look of surprise on Jabari's face and felt a flash of pleasure that her action caught him off guard.

"You will handle the bird now," Queb said to her. "So we see if she obeys you, as a woman should obey a man."

Obey a man? Her temper rose again. "This bird belongs to the air, not tied to a perch," she declared.

They tied Isis to the perch just as Jabari wanted to bind her to his side. Elizabeth rebelled. If she couldn't liberate herself, at least she could free her bird. Nudging aside the shaman, Elizabeth stepped forward and unfastened the jesses ensnaring Isis. Even if Isis were her means of escape, she had to set her free, for she now saw the bird's captivity as a mirror of her own. Elizabeth held out a hand to Isis. The bird climbed on her fingers in an attitude of complete trust.

Facing the assembled tribe, Elizabeth gave a triumphant smile. She released Isis. The dove soared on the wind. Elizabeth felt her own heart ascend as she turned to track her progress across the desert. With a graceful arc of wings, the dove caught updrafts, floated on air currents.

Then she turned with the wind. Straight back to the camp. Toward Elizabeth. The white dove, freed from captivity, returned!

Shocked, Elizabeth barely felt the dove's claws as Isis

settled upon her shoulder. A collective gasp broke out among the crowd. The bird simply did not want to leave her! Yet Isis had flown to the camp before her, as if she predicted Elizabeth's arrival. Her bird's mysterious behavior scared her.

She stroked Isis's breast, troubled and baffled. Suddenly Isis flapped her wings and sailed off, landing now on Jabari's shoulder. Her jaw dropped. He seemed unaffected. Indeed, Jabari acted as if this were quite natural. Others did not for she heard the shocked gasps of awe and appreciative murmurs.

Jabari took the dove and settled her back onto the perch next to his falcon. Without as much of a wing flutter Isis allowed Jabari to tie her with the leather jesses. Jabari caressed her with affection. Isis made cooing noises of pleasure.

Elizabeth thought of her daydream. *As the dove submits to the talons of the falcon, so shall you give yourself to him.* A cold finger of foreboding touched her spine. She believed less in prophecies than in hard scientific facts, but was this a sign?

"It is the prophecy," one man called out. "The dove rests upon her shoulder as it once took refuge with Kiya. And see how the dove gentles under the masterful touch of our sheikh!"

Masterful touch. Suffragette resentment reared up. Elizabeth slammed it down. *I can use this to my advantage.* The longer these desert dwellers believed Isis was a mystical sign, the more control she'd have.

Still, all the strange mysticism bothered her.

Her troubled eyes met Jabari's speculative ones. She detected a flicker of suspicion there. What would Jabari do if he realized she wanted to grab power as Kiya in order to escape? And if she escaped? He'd only hunt her down with that strong-willed resolve of his and capture her. Jabari would never let go. All because of his honor. His duty to the Khamsin. Honor. Duty. She wanted to spit the words out onto the dry sand.

"It's a dove. It's gentle with everyone," she announced with an indifferent shrug as if none of this mattered.

Barely had she uttered the words when Jabari's grandfather stepped forward. He seized the bird with a powerful fist. Isis flapped her wings in a frenzy, then pecked his hand.

"Not everyone," Jabari said in a dry voice as his grandfather uttered a low cry and yanked his bleeding hand away.

"Considering the way I've been treated by the Majli, I'd bite your grandfather too. The bird has good taste," she offered.

Jabari's lips twitched upward in a crooked grin. "She prefers dark meat," he quipped.

She stared at the good humor in his eyes and offered a sassy smirk in return. "But no couscous."

"No couscous," he agreed. Jabari took her hand and laced his fingers through hers in a possessive grip.

"And now we have seen it," the shaman barked in his dry voice. "The final sign, proving you are Kiya returned to us."

Jabari's fingers tightened as Queb stepped forward and placed his wrinkled hands atop their intertwined ones.

"Jabari bin Tarik Hassid, you will marry the woman known as Elizabeth Kiya Summers," the shaman said.

"You have convinced our shaman you are Kiya. So be it," his grandfather said, grimacing as he stanched blood with a white cloth. He held up the cloth with a foreboding smile as if to indicate what awaited her in the marriage bed. "The marriage must be consummated by the third night of the full moon."

Two nights and she'd be married just to fulfill an ancient prophecy. Elizabeth stiffened with anxiety. She had until then to figure out an escape plan.

Chapter Thirteen

Escape was not going to be easy. Not when her intended kept her more guarded than a cache of gold.

He came for her the next morning to make formal introductions to his family. As she left his aunt's tent, his dark brown eyes were serious and his face unsmiling. Elizabeth felt encased in ice, resenting her impending fate.

A woman holding a little boy by the hand passed. Suddenly Jabari's countenance changed. Astonished, she watched him squat down and look at the child with a huge smile. And then he laughed. No, this was more a full-bodied roar of delight. Elizabeth stared, wide-eyed, as he swept the little boy into his arms. His affection defrosted her mood.

"Look at you," he said in a mock growl. "Already growing fat and strong. I suppose next you will defeat me in battle."

The little boy shyly tugged at the end of Jabari's turban.

"Kareem, my son," the woman told Elizabeth, following her gaze. "I lived in Haggi Quandil. He was starving and the sheikh rescued him. And me. I . . . slept with other men to get money to feed my children. To save me from this, the sheikh took me in as a sister. I could never repay him for his kindness."

A cluster of children clamored for attention, tugging at Jabari's *binish.* Jabari set Kareem down and made faces. Her jaw dropped as he ran from them. They chased the great sheikh of the Khamsin warriors, who pretended to fall as one poked his back with a thorn branch. He clutched his chest in a gesture of defeat. Giggling, shrieking children crawled all over him as he laughed. Elizabeth felt a rush of deep tenderness for Jabari.

"He will make a good father," the woman said, giving her a sideways glance, then called to her son, who came running.

Jabari stood, brushing off his clothing. A sheepish smile curled his lips as he walked toward her. The sheer boyish charm of that smile dissolved her into a little puddle.

"This was clean this morning," he said ruefully.

She felt her own face break into an answering smile. "Children like being around you."

His eyes followed the troop of children as they ran off. "I like being around children," he said softly. "They remind of life's joys. My mother used to say a child is a gift from Allah that blesses a husband and wife's love for each other. . . ."

As his voice trailed off, he looked away. When he looked at her, a cold stone mask replaced his ready smile.

"That is what she said, but my grandfather says a sheikh needs sons." Jabari took her hand. "He is expecting us."

Her heart twisted as she followed him and hammered even louder as he brought her to the waiting line of relatives.

"This is Elizabeth Kiya Summers, my bride, the chosen one who will carry my name and propagate the Hassid lineage."

Jabari's possessive grip on her shoulders felt more reassuring than disturbing as he introduced her to his extended family. The sheer number overwhelmed her. The man *did* have as many relatives as a camel had fleas.

Each one smiled warmly at her, embraced her hands and said what appeared to be a ritualistic welcome. "Greetings, daughter of the desert. We accept you into our family. May Allah guide your footsteps and grant you peace as you dwell within our tents."

The introduction to Nkosi, his grandfather, came last. She suspected it was the most important. The elderly man's regal posture reminded her of the authority and influence he carried. Jabari had told her Nkosi headed the council of elders.

"Most revered grandfather, I present to you Elizabeth Kiya Summers, my bride, the one I have chosen for all eternity who will continue our sacred name for generations to come."

Nkosi's gaze upon her was steady and unwavering. She lifted her chin and returned his look. He turned to a young boy who carried a small crimson pillow upon which lay a jeweled dagger. Encrusted with diamonds and rubies at the hilt, it gleamed in the sun. Nkosi took the dagger and handed it with formal reverence to Jabari. But he did not say a word.

She watched her intended's face tighten.

"You did not say the words. Do you not believe in the prophecy?" Jabari asked quietly, but with a low tone of anger.

"I bend to the will of the people for the sake of unity. But this one will not bring peace and prosperity. This insolent one, brings only chaos and turbulence to our people. She reminds me of the she-devil who weakened your father. I will never approve of her," Nkosi stated.

Jabari's grandfather did not condone the match. She darted a glance at his sullen face and suppressed a shiver.

His grandfather did not approve of Elizabeth. Jabari tensed at the thought as he sat next to his bride during the evening meal. Surrounded by his immediate family, she innocently watched the women stir a large copper pot over a campfire.

Elizabeth had no idea how deeply Nkosi's rejection of her hurt him. Since Tarik was dead, the duty fell to Nkosi as Jabari's closest male relative to hand down the sacred wedding dagger. Nkosi did not state the promise given to brides of Khamsin sheikhs, to love her as his own daughter, to accept her into his family.

Jabari wondered if his father were alive, if he would also reject Elizabeth. The idea grieved him too much to consider.

Jabari knew Elizabeth's intelligence and spirited defiance troubled his grandfather. Once he actually supported the idea of educating Khamsin women. He changed his mind after Jabari's mother abandoned his father.

Nkosi couldn't love Elizabeth. Elizabeth couldn't love Jabari. And he loved them both. Jabari watched women ladle out rice, samneh butter and Hobura bustard onto large platters. A deep gloom settled over him. He would marry Elizabeth to seal the prophecy. But without Nkosi's approval, the people would not fully accept her as their reincarnated queen or his wife. A very precarious future awaited them both.

Elizabeth sat next to Jabari, nervously chewing her bottom lip. He was too quiet. Did he guess that she had set Isis free?

Speculation abounded about the missing dove as his family talked. She had freed the bird while everyone thought she napped. When Jabari discovered Isis was missing, he gave her a scrutinizing look, but he said nothing.

Sitting with his left leg tucked beneath him, he rested his arm on his propped up right knee. She looked around and realized all the others did the same. Jabari reached for the flatbread with his right hand and broke half, handing it to her. He tore off a slice and dipped it into the platter, using it as a spoon to scoop up the meal.

She followed suit, nibbling at the food. Delicious as it was, distress turned it into dry paste. Swallowing became a burden. Looking up, she saw Nkosi studying her through hooded eyelids. His fixed look radiated with profound dislike.

Elizabeth accepted another slice of bread from Jabari, who ate silently, staring into the fire. She struggled to comprehend the man who was to become her husband. The more she considered her escape options, the more futile it became. How could Nahid find her? Three hours of open desert without water awaited her. And she had trouble tracking the intricate trail Jabari had followed.

Elizabeth thought of her impending fate. She had feelings for Jabari that disturbed her. She couldn't see her life without him, yet how could she love a man such as he? Arrogant, domineering, in love with tradition more than her. Yet she thought of how the outer layer of rock shielding him fell away as he played with the children. How he joked with her in his bedroom before they made love as if they were friends. Jabari talked with her almost as a man would talk to another man, not a woman he planned to seduce. He was gentle and fiercely protective of the women in his life—Badra and the woman from Haggi Quandil. She cast a sideways glance at his chiseled profile. So devastatingly handsome. He was ancient Egypt to her. A proud, noble warrior as mysterious and fascinating as artifacts lying beneath the sand. Jabari was a living specimen of ancient history with customs and traditions thousands of years old. And she called one of those beliefs "a silly superstition." Elizabeth winced.

If only she were as important as those ancient customs. If only Jabari could show her that who she was mattered more than what she was. Maybe if she reached out to him, made the first move, show him she did care.

The silky hairs feathering the back of his hand were cool to touch as she placed her hand atop his. Jabari regarded her with quiet contemplation. She said a silent prayer that this time her tongue would form the right words.

"Last night, I am sorry. I did not mean what I said. . . ." She bit her bottom lip as his eyes narrowed with suspicion.

Even to her own ears, the half-hearted apology sounded superficial.

Maybe if she dared to display her true feelings, she could build a small bridge across the gulf separating them. Elizabeth sucked in a deep breath and plunged ahead in English.

"What I mean is, I am sorry for what I said about your prophecy. You scared me. And I just reacted . . . the way I always do when I am scared. With anger."

At least the cold blankness fled his eyes, replaced by frank confusion. "Why do I frighten you?"

Now was the time to tell him. *Be honest. Don't hold back.* Elizabeth looked at the ground, struggling for words and lowered her voice to a whisper.

"I have these feelings for you that I've never had before." She took a deep breath. "And that frightens me. Because how can I love a man who thinks ancient customs are more important than I am? The man I love would honor me as much as he honored himself and love me for who I am, not what I represent, a reincarnated queen. He would see me as an equal, not physically, but socially. There would be such a close bond between us that if I bled, he would feel the pain. And I would not walk in back of him, but walk beside him, at his side forever."

She focused on the ground. Elizabeth could see every detail of every pebble. She counted the heartbeats thudding rapidly in her chest in the ensuing silence. Heat rose in her face.

He withdrew his hand. Her heart sank. Elizabeth forced herself to look up. For the briefest minute, his dark brown velvet eyes sparkled as if she'd handed him a challenge and he accepted. Then they shuttered, becoming blank obsidian again.

"Do you really mean this?" His deep voice in Arabic carried across the sand. To her horror, Elizabeth realized the varied conversations around the circle had stopped. All eyes gazed at her with rapt interest. Her private confession turned public.

Her spine tightened with resolve. "Yes, I do," she replied in Arabic. "I mean every word of it."

"I accept your apology and trust that your behavior will improve." His deep, resonant voice rang out, loud enough for all to hear. She followed the direction of his gaze. He looked straight at Nkosi, whose severe expression relaxed. Jabari smiled. He handed her another slice of bread. "Now eat. You will need all your strength for tomorrow night."

He began chatting with his grandfather about weddings past. Cold dread settled over her. He accepted her apology. Nothing more. The next day she'd wed a man who married her out of obligation to his tribe. His confession the previous night was as she had thought, a means to seduce her into matrimony. She opened her heart to Jabari and succeeded only in making a fool of herself.

The food in front of her clouded as tears swam in her eyes. She mustn't cry! Elizabeth bit her tongue so hard she almost shrieked from the pain. But it could never be as loud as the screams of sorrowful anguish inside her head.

"Badra, I would talk with you."

Jabari beckoned to his concubine to sit beneath the shade of a small acacia thorn tree the next day. She sank to the carpeted ground and studied him with a smile. He wondered about the change in her since arriving at the camp. Badra acted relaxed and more confident than he had ever seen her.

"You know I marry Elizabeth tonight and I must make provisions for you. I made arrangements for Farah to wed a visiting cousin from the southern tribe. His wife died and he has been quite lonely. She met him and seems quite happy with the match. Now, as for you. Khepri wishes to marry you. He has asked formally for your hand."

He watched her stiffen as if slapped. "No, Jabari. Khepri is a good man, but he desires a woman who can never learn to love him. I will never love a man. Not like that. He deserves better."

Jabari nodded, saddened by her vehemence. He had anticipated her answer. "Then if that is your answer, I am compelled to care for you. I can take you into my family as a sister. Unless you want something else . . ."

Her beautiful dark eyes lit up and she gave him a beaming smile. "Oh yes! I have no desire to leave here . . . and I have grown quite fond of Elizabeth."

He suspected as much and was glad of her answer. "Good. I need your help, Badra. Like you, she is a stranger here, but unlike you, she knows nothing of our customs. I want you to take charge of her ceremonial wedding bath at the sacred cave this afternoon."

Badra beamed at him. "Asriyah told me about it. Such a beautiful custom."

He leaned his chin upon his fist as he braced his arm on his knee. "Yes, it is. But I am making arrangements for Elizabeth to bathe in a tent. I do not want her in the cave."

Badra's lower lip curled out. "Tradition dictates the sheikh's bride is bathed and prepared in the sacred cavern."

"Elizabeth is terrified of caves. Remember when you woke me because she screamed in her sleep? It took me a long time to calm her. I don't want her upset. I will place the tent near the cave and you can bathe her there."

"I thought Khamsin traditions had to be followed?" Badra looked very troubled.

He gave her a gentle smile. "I have the power to break those traditions if I see it is beneficial."

She shot him a sly look so untypical for her. "Like teaching women to read? You have the power to break that one."

Drawing in a deep breath, he closed his eyes. "Badra, I already told you. My decision is final. I will not allow another woman either in my tribe or in my care to learn to read."

"But I already have."

His eyelids flew open. Jabari stared as she knelt and scribbled in the sand with a fallen branch. "Look! I can write my name. Elizabeth taught me."

Anger at Elizabeth dissolved at the proud look on Badra's beaming face. He studied the childish letters. His heart wrestled with this new revelation. His mother left his father when she became literate. Now Badra's learning testified to the benefits of educating women. For three years he tried to coax spirit into the phantom seventeen-year-old and erase the haunting pain in her eyes. In a short time, Elizabeth had succeeded where he failed by giving her the one thing she desired most—learning. Something in his chest eased at long last.

"Well? Will you allow me to continue?"

"Yes. I can see how much you want this. But only if you agree to take charge of Elizabeth's care for the ceremonial bath. I drive a hard bargain." He winked at her.

She giggled. "It's settled, then."

"Let us shake on it."

"What's this?" She looked at his outstretched hand.

"This is how they seal arrangements in Elizabeth's country," he said, grinning.

Badra wrinkled her nose. "Strange custom."

"Indeed. Come and hug me instead." She scooted over and embraced him. Jabari found himself marveling at how the women in his life never ceased to amaze him with their spirit.

Elizabeth spent her day in the company of Asriyah, who kept a close eye on her as she went about her chores. Now and then she caught glimpses of Jabari, but he studiously ignored her.

After a light midday snack, for the wedding feast would take place that night, Elizabeth slipped away from Asriyah. She walked briskly, hoping a stroll would clear her mind. She had barely taken a few steps when Nkosi joined her.

"You are not to be alone," he warned, taking her arm. Nkosi glanced around. "We will talk," he said in a low voice.

She glanced at him with distrust. Now what?

Nkosi pulled her to a short distance away from the tents. His sharp black gaze surveyed the site. When he appeared satisfied no one could hear, those intense eyes bore into hers.

"I do not believe you are Kiya. You are an imposter."

She stiffened. "Believe what you will. It makes no difference to me."

His eyes, as piercing as his grandson's, narrowed. "I have made inquiries. I know you are the woman helping the infidels desecrate our sacred lands. Why are you here?"

"Jabari brought me here against my will," she snapped.

Nkosi grunted and waved a hand. "I have seen the way my grandson softens when he looks at you. It is not right. He is a warrior of the wind, the leader of our tribe. You will weaken him before his men. He needs a woman who will obey."

Her temper flared. "Find one then. I'll step aside gladly!"

"But he desires you. And my grandson is a stubborn one. His spirit is restless. I sense it in him that he will not be satisfied until he has you. He is an honorable man and marries you to fulfill the prophecy. But that does not protect you."

Her distress grew. "What exactly are you saying?"

Nkosi's dark eyes gleamed. She saw the wrinkled face contort with anger. "If I see you wound his heart with your aggressive ways, you will answer to me. The sheikh is not the only power in this tribe. You may fool the tribe by pretending to be our queen so you can grab power away from Jabari. But you will never fool me."

Nkosi placed two fingers on her face, bridging her nose. The gesture made her shiver with fear. "I am watching you," he said softly, then drew back as a group of women approached them.

Deeply troubled, Elizabeth watched him stride off. Nkosi was no man to have for an enemy.

"There you are, Elizabeth," Badra called out.

One of the women spun her around, marching her back toward the tents. They carried pots, bowls, towels and garments and made wild, undulating noises with their tongues.

"I thought the marriage wasn't until tonight!" Elizabeth stared at the procession of women.

"It is, but before the ceremony, you will visit the royal *wadi* to pay tribute to the ancestors and ask their blessings on your union." The seventeen-year-old tossed back a waist-length tousle of inky curls and held out a pot of henna. Two dimples pierced her rosy cheeks as she grinned in female camaraderie.

Elizabeth gave Badra a conspiratorial wink. "Is that for Jabari? Can we paint a smile on his face? He's too serious."

Badra stopped smiling. "Jabari can be difficult sometimes," she admitted. "But he has a good heart. He is a brave and strong leader. And the most skilled swordsman of the Khamsin warriors. They say his scimitar is razor sharp when dealing out justice."

"Just the qualities I've always wanted in a husband. He can keep the dinner knives sharpened," Elizabeth shot back. Badra stopped. She stayed Elizabeth with her hand and gave her a scrutinizing look far wiser than her years.

"Do not see him with your eyes. But truly see him with your heart. That is where you find the real Jabari." Badra drew back, draping herself in formality again.

"First, the ceremonial bath. Come with me."

The light wind carried the musty animal smell of goats and sheep kept at the camp's edge. Tent edges flapped in the wind, rippling like sea water. Sitting under the shade of a thorn tree, Jabari quietly talked with his men. One nudged him and jerked his head toward her, and Jabari turned. His expression was unreadable as he watched her. She squared her shoulders and marched forward.

"I thought desert people didn't waste water."

"Frequent bathing is a Khamsin custom and part of our heritage. For thousands of years, brides of Khamsin sheikhs have bathed in this sacred cave where the spring feeds the tribe's water source."

Elizabeth halted. The cave. She felt her ancient phobia

crystalize into sheer terror. Her hands began shaking violently. This was Jabari's punishment for her behavior. He knew she feared caverns, but forced her to follow his tribe's traditions.

"I'm not going. I just can't. I'm terrified of caves," Elizabeth said in a hoarse whisper. "I told Jabari. Why is he forcing me to do this?" Tears spilled down her cheeks.

"Elizabeth!" Badra shoved the henna at another woman and clutched Elizabeth's shaking hands. "We are not going to bathe you in the cave. Jabari ordered a tent set up near the cave just for you."

The shaking eased. "He did?"

"Of course. He has known all along. You talk in your sleep."

She gathered her control and gaped at her. "My nightmare! There *was* someone in my room."

"Of course. I heard your screams and ran to alert him. He came into your room and comforted you. That's why he arranged to have you bathed here. Tradition calls for the sacred cavern, but he refused to make you do that." Badra squeezed her fingers. "Truly, Elizabeth, he is a kind man. He does care about you. He breaks Khamsin sacred custom, which is not easy for him."

Her fears crumbled into dust. If Jabari didn't love her, why would he break tradition? The man clung to custom like sand to bare skin. Doubts reared up. *He isn't that open-minded. Look at Badra. He's still denying her an education.*

"There may be hope for him yet if he overcomes customs that are archaic," she murmured, unwilling to voice her true feelings.

"He has broken another as well. Jabari granted me permission to learn to read." Badra's dark face flushed with joy.

Now Elizabeth stared in wide-eyed shock. "You told him?"

"Yes. He seemed at peace with it, as if he had struggled with this a long time."

Two traditions broken in one day. A miracle. Maybe Jabari truly did love her. Elizabeth felt a rush of emotion so fierce that it flooded her with warmth. Maybe she did love him. And that would be the greatest miracle of all.

Chapter Fourteen

Mounted on a gentle white mare, Elizabeth felt her anxiety rise as darkness fell. The small procession to the main *wadi* included an honor guard of two of Jabari's warriors, the Majli and Queb the shaman. She stared at the intricate patterns painted on her hands with henna. The desert wind blew her golden veil, secured to her head with a headdress of golden coins over her forehead. Her dowry was given by the tribe to Jabari since she had no father. The white velvet wedding dress, intricately embroidered in cross stitching with crimson and gold thread, weighed on her as much as the impending nuptials.

Only the sound of the horse's plodding hooves, the jingling of her headdress and decorations adoring the horse's headgear and the light humming of the warrior flanking her right, accompanied the little group. Elizabeth sucked in a breath through the thin gold-beaded veil that shielded her nose and mouth.

Stealing a glance at Jabari riding slightly ahead of her, Elizabeth felt awed at the dashing figure he cut. A dazzling white turban and *binish* reflected in the grayish moonlight.

The *binish,* slit from waist to ankle, showed muscular thighs clad in white trousers tucked into hand-tooled leather boots. Even without the distinctive clothing, no doubt existed who was in charge. The man smoldered with authority.

The jeweled dagger hung from his belt. Elizabeth gulped at the sight of the blade, remembering what had transpired that afternoon. After her bath, the women had questioned her about the most intimate details of her monthly courses. She found herself blushing furiously. Then they placed her naked on a table, spread her thighs and held her down. Two fingers were rudely thrust into her by an older woman who smiled with satisfaction.

"She passes the test. Our sheikh will marry a virgin. It is good the wedding takes place now, for she is at the most fertile part of her cycle," the woman had declared.

Then the same woman had set Jabari's jeweled dagger and a small bowl on the table. Elizabeth had squealed and fought them, terrified this was a Khamsin ritual to mark her as Jabari's bride. But Badra soothed her fears.

"It is Khamsin custom for the sheikh's bride to be shaved with her husband's jeweled wedding dagger. Removing the body hair enhances . . . the pleasure of the joining. Do not worry, Elizabeth. Maia is expert and will not hurt you," Badra had said.

Badra spoke the truth, for the woman's touch was absolutely gentle. Afterward, she realized she had been marked as Jabari's bride. His dagger. Removing her body hair. For his pleasure.

Soon she would give up her independence. Share her life with him. And her body. Elizabeth forced down the apprehension that clung to her as closely as the *kuftan* did. Jabari's actions earlier might have stated his affection for her. But now he seemed stiff and remote, as if he were forced into the act.

She squirmed in her saddle, feeling the pinching ache in her bottom from riding. The warrior riding next to her for protection noticed her movement and ceased humming.

"We will rest soon. It is a long way to the ancestral grounds if you are not accustomed to riding," he said in English.

Elizabeth's brows shot up in surprise and she regarded him. He was shorter than Jabari, but well-formed and had a handsome, bearded face and charming manner. He gave her a friendly smile.

"You speak English perfectly. Do all Jabari's warriors do so?" Elizabeth asked in Arabic.

"I learned English when Jabari and I studied together in Cairo. We have been friends a long time," the man replied in Arabic, flicking the reins. He gave a formal bow of his head. "I am Nazim, Jabari's second-in-command and his Guardian."

"What is a Guardian?"

"I am Jabari's protector. I swore a sacred oath to guard him with my life. All Khamsin sheikhs have Guardians."

She glanced to her left. Nazim followed her gaze.

"That grumpy man to your left is Izzah, his third-highest ranking commander."

Izzah glared at Nazim. "You talk too much, Nazim."

Nazim flashed Elizabeth a cocky grin. "As you can see, Izzah is a man of many words. I am deeply honored to be your escort, my lady. We have waited many years for your return."

So Jabari's people truly believed she was the reincarnation of their ancient queen. Elizabeth shot him a sideways glance. Somehow, this good-looking, educated warrior with his affable manner didn't strike her as a simple man who clung to superstitious beliefs.

"You believe I am Kiya, your queen returned to you, the powerful woman your tribe revered?" Elizabeth asked.

Nazim's face grew thoughtful and serious. "I believe that destiny has brought you to us, for whatever purpose Allah desires." Then he gave her a mischievous smile. "And I believe that you are powerful, for I have never seen Jabari so much under the spell of a woman before!"

She forgot her anxiety and laughed, his deep chuckle

joining hers. Jabari, riding ahead of her, looked back.

"You are very light-hearted, Nazim, for such a serious occasion," Jabari noted, but he smiled.

"Ah, sire, I am just very happy for both you and your beautiful bride. I do believe you have met your match, and that is a rare thing indeed and cause for celebration!" Nazim grinned again and clucked to his horse, riding ahead to let Jabari drop back next to Elizabeth.

After a short rest, they turned into a smaller *wadi*, which Elizabeth suspected was a shortcut to the main *wadi*. White moonlight spilled over the canyon walls, causing rippling patterns like ghost waters. The chilly desert night bit into her exposed sandaled toes. She shivered, wondering if *jinn* really did inhabit the desert. Certainly it felt so tonight.

Earlier, as the women had scrubbed her with sweet-scented soap, combed rosemary into her hair and dyed her hands, Elizabeth felt a horrid sense of loss. She would never see Nana again. She had failed in her task to find a treatment and Nana would die alone, of a horrible disease, tucked away in a cold institution.

After a while, they dismounted and all the men tugged their veils across their faces. She realized it was respect for the ceremony about to unfold.

"We walk from here," Jabari announced. Nazim and Izzah lit torches and flanked them in front as Jabari and Elizabeth walked side by side. His entire body, stiff as the canyon walls surrounding them, bore a distant, regal posture. Her nerves scraped against her skin at the thought of marrying this tower of impartial rock. She wished she could break down the granite to find the gentle man hidden deep inside.

They barely began walking when Nazim held up a hand. He cocked his head. Disquiet filled her. What was wrong now?

"Someone is digging." Nazim looked at Jabari. In the torchlight his eyes lost their joviality and turned serious.

Jabari considered and nodded. "Extinguish the torches. You two, come with me. Elizabeth, you stay here with

Queb and the Majli." Jabari withdrew his scimitar. Its sharp blade gleamed in the moonlight. He beckoned to his warriors.

Who could be digging? Maybe one of their own people making preparations for the tribute ceremony.

Or someone else . . . Someone who found a note telling of the Almha's location. Before any of the Majli could stop her, she darted past them to catch up. Elizabeth rounded the corner and nearly ran headfirst into Jabari. He reached out and steadied her, his eyes narrowing in disapproval.

"I told you to remain behind," he scolded, shielding her body with his. "Stay in back of me, right here and do not move!"

But Elizabeth had to see. She peered around Jabari's shoulder and stifled a horrified gasp.

It was Nahid, digging in the rocky sand in a frenzy like a dog unearthing a bone. Two armed Al-Hajid warriors helped him, their weapons lying on the ground. Hysterical laughter bubbled between her lips. Nahid had gotten her message all right. But instead of rescuing her, he dug for the golden disk! She cursed herself for trusting him. He probably congratulated himself on leaving her stranded so he could be the sole finder.

Her mouth went cotton dry as Nazim and Izzah unsheathed their blades, Nazim now as grim as Izzah. To her utter shock, she saw her uncle toss down the pick ax and struggle to pick up a heavy object from the pit. Finally, he lifted it up and raised it to waist level. The two warriors with him bowed.

It was a large gold circle. The Almha, at last.

At once Jabari and his warriors fell to their knees, touching their foreheads to the ground in respect, their scimitars splayed in front of them. Elizabeth supposed they thought she should as well but she was too shocked. Moonbeams winked and reflected shimmering patterns cast by the golden disk. Nahid let out a low chuckle. Even from where she stood, the greed in his face glinted like an evil promise.

Before Elizabeth could reflect upon the impact of her

uncle's deception, Jabari and his men sprang to their feet. With swift grace they charged forward, bearing their scimitars. Their loud voices echoed through the canyon in an ancient war cry. Nahid turned and dropped the Almha. It landed on the rocky sand with a clatter that echoed her heart's thudding. The Al-Hajid warriors sprang for their rifles, but before they reached them, Nazim and Jabari reacted. She crammed a fist to her mouth as she watched Al-Hajid heads roll on the stony ground. She moaned.

Then Jabari turned to Nahid and raised his sword, ready to deliver the death blow. Elizabeth leaped forward.

"No! Stop!" she shrieked, hoping her screams would bring Jabari to his senses. Elizabeth threw herself in front of Nahid.

Jabari's scimitar halted in midair, a bare whisper from Elizabeth's neck. His eyes widened as if realizing how close he'd come to hurting her. Lowering his weapon, Jabari stepped back. Nazim and Izzah grabbed Nahid. They forced him to his knees.

"Kneel and prepare to die, infidel," Nazim snarled.

Elizabeth stepped away from her uncle and turned toward her betrothed. His eyes were coal black pits of anger. "Stay away, Elizabeth. This is none of your business. This man has violated our ancestral grounds."

"None of my business? He's my uncle! Jabari, you can't kill him! Please! Please!" Elizabeth ignored the dispassionate black stare he gave her. She tugged at the front of his white robes.

"He's my only family besides Nana!"

"Elizabeth," Jabari said, and she flinched at the frost in his tone, "this man has betrayed not only our tribe, but you as well. He deserves to die."

Nahid struggled impotently against the strong hold of Jabari's warriors. Hatred flashed in his eyes as he looked at his captors. Then his expression softened as he gazed upon Elizabeth. He shook his head as if regretting his actions. "I am sorry, Elizabeth. When I got your note, I came immediately to dig for the Almha before anyone else could find it. I planned to send help to you as soon as I could. But I knew you'd want me to find the disk first, for my mother's sake. She's all that matters."

"He lies," Jabari said tonelessly. He cast Nahid a look of raging animosity. "He is trying to deceive you so you will plead for his life. He will sell the disk to treasure hunters."

"He doesn't lie!" Elizabeth put a hand to her pounding head, rubbing her temple. "Nahid did not coerce me into digging for it. Indeed, I found the papyrus telling of its existence."

Jabari's look sent rivulets of dread down her spine. "You lied," he said in a cold, hard voice that made her shiver. "You deliberately let me think this was all your uncle's wrongdoing."

"Yes, I did." Elizabeth met his steely stare. "I had to buy time to find it for myself. But I swear to you I did not want to sell it. I only needed to find the cures inscribed on the back!"

"You could have spoken the truth and I would have helped. You need not have resorted to lies," he said, thawing a bit.

"Wouldn't you lie to protect someone you love?" Elizabeth saw hesitation in his eyes and gambled on his confusion. She pressed herself against his muscular chest and threw her arms around his neck. Then tugged his veil away and her own.

"Please, Jabari. You spared me. Please don't kill Nahid. If you have any feelings at all for me, don't kill him!" Elizabeth brushed her lips against his.

He gazed down at her upturned face, the frost in his eyes dissolving. Jabari sheathed his sword and tentatively touched her cheek. "Raise him up," he ordered his men in a hoarse voice.

Elizabeth took his hand and kissed it. "Thank you," she whispered and hugged him. She felt his stiff body relax under her embrace. His strong arms encircled her as he settled his chin atop her head. Total meltdown.

Then she peeked past his shoulder and winced at his

grandfather's wrathful look. Nkosi removed his own veil and stepped forward. Jabari glanced at him and released Elizabeth.

"You dared to dig for our sacred Almha? And you, my grandson, you did not kill her but spared her life! You violated our oath!" Nkosi's face burned with rage.

"Now you will let this traitorous infidel go? Are you sheikh or a weak vassal? You are no grandson of my blood!"

Shame spread across Jabari's features as the blood drained from his face. She wanted to beat at Nkosi's chest and scream. He made Jabari's compassion into an act of weakness. Desperate to explain, Elizabeth started for Nkosi, but Jabari caught her arm.

"He is right. I violated my sacred oath and the Khamsin code of honor. I swore allegiance to the Almha as its protector. And I have failed my duty. I have no honor."

His voice, low with agonizing remorse, haunted her. Elizabeth longed to reassure him that he was the most honorable man she knew. But her actions would only disgrace him further. She grit her teeth and racked her brain for answers.

Nkosi shot Jabari a knowing glance. "There is only one way for you to restore your honor." He jerked his head toward Nahid, who scowled at the old man as if he were the devil incarnate. "Kill him. Now. Prove your loyalty to the Almha and our people."

"No, dear God, please don't!" Elizabeth cried out, her heart thudding in her chest. "Please, Jabari, don't kill him!"

"He has violated our laws and unearthed the Almha. I am sorry, Elizabeth. I must." His face filled with anguish, Jabari withdrew his scimitar. In a solemn gesture, Nazim undid the silk sash tied at his waist and held it up. Jabari's sword slashed the fabric into two. It fluttered to the ground with her hopes.

"On your knees, infidel," Jabari told Nahid in a hardened voice, once again a fierce warrior who would display no mercy. "Prepare your spirit to leave this plane." Nazim and Izzah forced Nahid to kneel once more.

She realized then what a predicament he faced. By sparing her life, he'd violated his oath. Now to prove to his people his loyalty and strength as leader, he had to kill her uncle. A hysterical sob rose in her throat.

Jabari raised his scimitar above his head as his warriors stretched out Nahid's arms. The blade whirled and flashed as he twirled it in the air in a ritualistic manner. She saw his eyes glaze over as if possessed.

"Wait!" Nkosi stepped forward, holding up a palm. "There is one way you may spare your uncle."

"How?" Elizabeth asked eagerly. Anything, anything to stop this bloodshed.

"I sense your reluctance to proceed with this marriage."

Nkosi paused, his eyes shrewd, his smile calculating. "If you agree to marry my grandson, to tame that disrespectful manner of yours, I will allow my grandson to spare his life. On your knees, as Kiya, our queen, lower your forehead on the ground and tell Jabari you humble yourself before him to prove your obedience to the sheikh now in front of us, the Majli, so that we may bear witness of your loyalty to the people. Beg for your uncle. Tell Jabari you will be obedient and submissive to him."

If he had manipulated Nahid into unearthing the Almha just for this purpose, Nkosi couldn't have orchestrated the situation to his advantage more. He saw how Jabari yielded to her pleas. She had weakened his grandson before the Majli. By groveling before Jabari, she would acknowledge his authority over her. It also ensured that the Khamsin's loyalty remained with their sheikh. A consummate politician, Nkosi wanted her to renounce any influence she had as Kiya and shift power back to Jabari.

Jabari lowered his sword. He looked at her with uncertainty, as if he doubted her compliance. Nahid remained kneeling, looking up with his lips curled in a fierce snarl.

To be a silent, obedient drone without a thought of her own, without the right to express her opinions. Elizabeth grieved the loss of her freedom, independence and fight to prove herself as an equal to men. She took a deep breath.

She sank to her knees in the rocky sand. The heavy weight of the velvet robes, the gold-coined headdress and her veil dragged her down, but not as much as the humiliating action. Elizabeth touched her forehead to the ground.

"Jabari, I honor you now as Sheikh of the Khamsin. I, Kiya, your queen, humble myself before you. I beg you now, on my knees, for my uncle's life. If you spare him, I will give myself to you and submit to all you ask. I will be respectful and obedient. I will do all this if you spare Nahid's life."

She swallowed bitter tears at her words and felt his hand rest on the top of her head as if he gave a benediction.

"Rise, woman," he said in a brusque voice. "I will stay my sword from your uncle's neck." Elizabeth raised her head and saw him looking down on her like a proud ruler appraising a lowly servant. Their roles had been charted by her action. Elizabeth mustered all the grace she could and stood, glancing at Nkosi. The old man smiled with grim satisfaction.

His honor and command reestablished, Jabari snapped his fingers and beckoned to Nazim and Izzah. "Return to camp with the prisoner while we stay here and pay homage to our ancestors."

"Wait a minute . . ." Elizabeth started to protest but heard Nkosi grunt. She sucked in her breath and grit her teeth. Lord, it was hard being a submissive female! She bowed her head. "Sire, I respectfully ask, as a humble woman who fears for her uncle's life, what will you do with him?"

"His life is spared, but he remains our prisoner."

Nahid spit at Jabari, his eyes narrowing with dark rage. "You will regret this, you spineless excuse for a warrior."

Jabari gave his men a dismissive wave. They tied Nahid's hands together and led him away. Elizabeth watched, deeply troubled. For someone whose life she'd just spared by sacrificing herself in marriage, Nahid acted too hostile.

She glanced down at the Almha lying upon the sand. Before Jabari could stop her, she touched it. The ensuing vibration in her palm called to her. Elizabeth gasped and withdrew her trembling hand. Golden moonbeams flashed at her from the Almha. She bent her head and crossed her hands upon her chest, obeying an ancient prodding. What strange force brought her here? Why did the Almha command such power? Elizabeth felt Jabari's hand upon her elbow. He gave her a long, pondering look.

Caution urged her to step back and wait as he knelt and kissed the disk with the greatest respect, then lifted it. He held it above his head and the others knelt, touching their foreheads to the ground briefly. Jabari lowered the disk. His black eyes considered her with exacting scrutiny.

"Only the Khamsin sheikh and the tribal elders may touch the Almha," Nkosi's voice boomed. "No ordinary woman is worthy of touching the sacred disk."

Of course. Forget that they considered her the ancient queen who buried it in the first place. She was still a lowly woman.

Jabari's piercing, dark eyes held her gaze. Elizabeth stepped back in shock as he held out the Almha to her.

"She is no ordinary woman, Grandfather," he stated.

Elizabeth grasped the disk's rounded edge. Together they raised the Almha above their heads to the moonlit skies. As they both bowed their heads, Jabari began reciting the ancient tribal rites of reverence to the ancestors.

Unlike many women, Elizabeth had never dreamed of her wedding day. But even if she had, never could she have envisioned such a magnificent ceremony filled with pomp and splendor. Baskets of sweet dates, figs, oranges and other fruit sat within easy reach of all the guests. Earlier they had feasted upon a delicious lamb stew Elizabeth could barely swallow.

Jabari's female relatives, dressed in brightly colored costumes of blue, scarlet, lavender and emerald and yellow danced and whirled about as men drummed upon *darra-*

bukas and plucked the strings of *rebabas*. The women's graceful bodies moved rhythmically and swayed in tune to the music. Badra had explained earlier that most desert tribes followed Muslim wedding traditions and men and women celebrated separately. "But they are not most desert tribes," she had said, winking.

Seated next to her before the large bonfire, Jabari flashed a good-natured grin at his cousins dancing before him. Elizabeth felt alienated from all the festivities.

Several small fires in golden lamp holders lit the campsite. Stars glittered above her head in the black velvet night. Wishing for some tiny connection to home, she gazed up, wondering if Nana glimpsed the same celestial bodies. Elizabeth mourned that no one could be there to represent her family. Her grandmother was in another country, imprisoned by disease. Her uncle was imprisoned for real, under armed guard far from the wedding celebration.

Alone, she faced her fate—becoming a submissive, docile wife, never allowed to voice a thought of her own. Obligated to obey her husband. No wonder Jabari's smile was brighter than moonlight. He got what he wanted.

Forcing herself to pretend, she curved her lips upward as the dancers passed. Badra had told her each dance narrated the story of Khamsin victories, love and tribal life. Such dances were rituals passed down through the generations. Now Jabari's cousins swayed before her in a graceful performance as men sang about the annual Nile floods making the fields fertile again. Elizabeth let herself flow with the movement, felt the water rippling along the Nile, the hot desert wind blowing on her cheeks, the caress of the sun against her skin.

As Jabari turned to speak with Nazim on his left, she let a deep sigh escape. Immediately he turned toward her.

"What is wrong?"

"Nothing," she fibbed. Elizabeth reached for a date, then bit. She pulled out the pit and stared at the remaining half.

Jabari removed the fruit from her hand, popping it into

his mouth. He trailed his finger across her lips. "Your lips move, but they do not speak the truth. You do not wish to be married."

Could he ever understand? Elizabeth opened her mouth to consider, then shut it. She made a promise. Nahid's life hinged on that promise. Jabari's dark eyes, expressive in the flickering firelight, searched her face. She bowed her head briefly, hiding secret thoughts from his questioning gaze.

"I gave my word of honor and I will not break it." Elizabeth lifted her chin, her sense of pride somewhat restored. "Never let it be said that women have no honor."

Grasping her hand, Jabari rubbed her palm with his thumb. "You have as much honor as any other man here. Including myself," he stated quietly. She stared at him, astounded at his statement.

He arched an eyebrow in an impish gesture. "You are the chosen one. And the chosen one's hands are cold. What would the people say? Is it a sign that the desert sun has fled the sky?" Jabari rolled his eyes upward and his lips parted in mock amazement. "Ah, it is so! The great Kiya has caused the sun god Aten to leave his berth!"

His irascible sense of humor made her laugh. "Behold the power of a woman," she sputtered in English.

"That is more like my Elizabeth," he murmured back in English. "You were beginning to worry me."

"Worry *you?*" she asked.

"You sat so silently I feared Aziz had followed us here and cut out your tongue despite my express orders not to do so."

"Oh, but Aziz would not. Not with your grandfather pulling rank above him for the privilege."

Jabari gave a laugh so hearty those around them looked his way. Seeing his mirth, they smiled with satisfaction. Jabari's cousins ceased their dancing as the musicians stopped playing.

"Of course if he did you would be pleased, so you would

not have to listen to my wicked tongue anymore," she added lightly.

His laughter stopped. Jabari's dark eyes seemed fathomless as his gaze held hers. His jaw tightened as if he struggled for control. One finger lightly stroked her lower lip.

"You are wrong. I could never let Aziz remove that wicked tongue of yours. It is what revives my weary spirit when all about me is cold and gray, lifeless and dull," he said softly.

With extreme dexterity, he plucked a date from the basket, pitted it and ate half. Jabari then brought the fruit to her mouth, tracing it against her slightly parted lips.

"It is very good. Tempting," he murmured in Arabic. "Taste and see. Such fruit is meant to be savored . . . slowly."

With black intensity, Jabari's eyes caught her gaze, commanded it, held it hostage to the pools of desire reflected there. Captivated, she let him slide the fruit around her lips, teasing her with its silky texture. Then he stopped, hesitating, as if awaiting some silent invitation to complete the act.

This was no innocent offering of food, but a symbolic gesture made by the groom, testing her willingness for what lay ahead of them that night in the marriage bed.

Show no fear, no trepidation at the unknown mysteries awaiting you in Jabari's tent. Meet his advances with the power of your own will. Dare to show that you are no timid woman who trembles before her future husband.

Elizabeth opened her mouth wider as Jabari placed the date just inside her lips. She flicked her tongue daintily over the fruit in a swirling motion, ever so slightly touching the tips of his fingers. Deep within the enigmatic swirls of his dark irises she saw desire illuminated. Elizabeth's lips closed around the date and Jabari's fingers. With exquisite slowness, her tongue gave both one last teasing dance, and then she pulled back, forcing his fingers from her mouth.

Minute pearls of sweat formed at his temple. As she chewed and swallowed, he gazed into her face with a hunger no date could ease. Elizabeth felt the power of her own sensuality.

"I do have a wicked tongue," she murmured. He licked his mouth as if tasting the date's sweet juice. Or her lips.

"Indeed," he said in the barest whisper. "You certainly do."

The corners of her mouth lifted in a delicate smile. An awesome sense of empowerment filled her as she realized the consequences of her action. Jabari had presented her with a challenge, and she did not back down, but met him on even ground. As an equal, not a submissive woman.

If Jabari truly loved her, she could make her playacting into the real thing.

Standing next to Jabari in front of the flickering firelight, the tribe assembled behind them, she faced Queb. Tall golden lamp stands, as old as ancient Egypt, flanked the elderly man. Elizabeth inhaled the bittersweet scent of sage burning in a silver bowl at Queb's feet. It mixed heavily with the smell of her own apprehension.

The *fugara,* clad in an indigo *binish,* his wizened face peering at them from beneath a simple deep blue turban, clasped a length of gold braided cord. Badra had told her Khamsin weddings, just as their culture was, were a mixture of Muslim religion and ancient tribal tradition. Elizabeth stifled a nervous giggle. Was part of the tradition to tie up an unwilling bride? Perhaps she'd be tethered to Jabari to ensure she'd not wander off in search of ancient Egyptian artifacts.

Desperate to ease the anxiety tightening her chest over the marriage rites they were about to recite, she inhaled deeply. The sage's healing properties penetrated her lungs. Her head swam a little from the power of the incense. Jabari stood erect and proud, his chin lifted high. Firelight danced in the blackness of his eyes, which reflected the solemnity of the ceremony. He was so remote and distant that she had to fight to recall the man who had placed the date upon her lips. She reached out with tentative fingers and touched the sleeve of his robe, then withdrew her hand, not wanting to display her nervousness.

Queb began reciting the sacred words from the Koran that would marry them. Forever. Mated for all eternity.

She felt a stab of misgiving, but it eased when Jabari's large, warm palm enfolded her chilled hand. He gave it a reassuring squeeze. He turned toward her, his body relaxing as he looked down upon her tenderly. Both of her hands were encircled by his as he began reciting the Khamsin vows.

"I take you, Elizabeth, most honored one, as the mate of my soul forever. You are the one chosen for me since the beginning of time. I will protect and defend you until my death, pledging my love only to you. You are an image of what I shall remember for all eternity. As this night breathes in quiet remembrance, so shall I partake of your sweetness. As time runs through our hands like desert sand, so shall our love remain as strong and fierce as the wind. The moon of this night watches over us, seals our union with silver light from the never-ending sky."

Jabari paused and rubbed the insides of her palms with his thumbs. She stared down at his long fingers. Such masculine strength, hands that could wield a sword with deadly accuracy, yet now held her own palms in the gentlest embrace. Never had she heard more poetic words. Spellbound, Elizabeth felt the tension in her body fade with acceptance. Her shoulders slackened as if she'd been dipped into a warming pool.

All her emotions stirred to life as she regarded the proud desert warrior. Jabari offered himself to her freely. He had as much to risk with this marriage as she did. And his deep, resonant voice rang forth with sincerity.

As if from a distance, she heard her own voice begin the pledge Badra made her memorize. Transfixed by the night's mystery and the power of the man before her, Elizabeth quietly spoke.

"Come, let us greet the moon of the night. It will guard us with kindness and illuminate our love. Jabari bin Tarik Hassid, noble ruler of the Khamsin, most brave and honorable warrior of the wind, I take you as the mate of my heart forever, the love of all our days past and forever. Our love shall pierce the darkness of time as the moon pierces the night with its brilliant light."

His eyes glowed with an inner intensity reflected by the shimmering moon. She could not tear away herself away from the arresting good looks. Something touched her wrist, but she barely noticed as Queb wrapped the cord around their clasped hands.

"I bind you now, Jabari bin Tarik Hassid, honored warrior sheikh, to you, Elizabeth Kiya Summers, our long-awaited queen, for all eternity. May your union produce sons with spirits as strong as the desert sun who will ride the winds of justice forever."

As if called by fate, the wind suddenly shifted and blew her veil, sending it floating about her face. Elizabeth undid the jeweled clasp holding it in place and let the veil ride the wind, far into the desert night along with the last remnant of her previous life. Jabari cupped her face and brushed his lips against hers in a kiss as she closed her eyes to the past.

Chapter Fifteen

His wife. His mate. The future mother of his sons. Jabari felt a tug of deep-seated emotion at the thought as he led Elizabeth to his tent. Accompanied by his family, making undulating sounds with their tongues as they beat joyously upon *darrabukas*, the bridal couple followed an escort of guards bearing golden torches. Jabari glanced at Elizabeth, who looked wide eyed with trepidation at all the noise. Or, most likely, what was about to unfold in the tent. He reached out and took her hand into his, wanting to comfort her, to reassure her, to ease the tension holding her slender shoulders rigid.

Nazim, walking just behind him, gave him a cheerful nudge and fell into stride on his left side. "I knew you had spotted your destiny that day when you saw her in the *samak*'s camp. I knew you would get married before me. I should have bet my horse on it," he boasted.

Jabari gave him a good-natured grin. "You are next," he warned his best friend.

Nazim recoiled with mock horror. "And disappoint all the women who have yet to experience the incredible pleasures I offer them? I have yet to find a woman whose knees do not weaken at the sight of the legendary warrior of love." He puffed out his chest.

"Such a woman may never exist. However, if that fails, I can always track down that girlish man for you." Jabari shot back and chuckled at the mortified expression on his friend's face.

Elizabeth's glance darted between the two of them. Her lovely mouth tugged upward in an amused smile.

"What is it?" Nazim asked her with a good-natured grin.

"Men. No matter what the culture, you're all the same." She rolled her eyes skyward and laughed.

Her giggles filled Jabari with unexpected joy. Grateful to his friend for lifting her spirits, he gave Nazim a friendly cuff as they reached his tent. Nazim tossed a punch back and then sobered, clasping his shoulder in a firm embrace of brotherhood. "May your marriage be full of nothing but the greatest joy, and your love as never ending as the sands," he said to both of them, but his eyes were focused on Elizabeth. Her smile fled, replaced by a distressed look, but she thanked him.

Nazim leaned close to Jabari. "Good luck. May your seed fill her belly with sons as numerous as the sands," he whispered in the traditional good-bye and stepped back. Jabari nodded, hoping Elizabeth hadn't heard him. All this formality had to be increasing her tension.

They removed their footwear at the tent's entrance. As his family shouted out congratulations, sly suggestions and hearty offers of encouragement for a boy child, Jabari pulled open the tent flap. He bowed his head to Elizabeth, who took a deep breath, offered him an impish grin and stepped inside. He liked that smile. It radiated with her plucky spirit.

Jabari knelt before the Almha settled on a makeshift altar in his tent. He beckoned to Elizabeth to do the same. Then he escorted his bride to his bedchamber, pulling aside the curtain. Flames from golden lamps cast flickering shadows against the walls. Her eyes glanced at the low, massive bed tucked into the corner and then quickly darted away. Two fierce spots of scarlet graced her cheeks. She sighed and tore off the headdress, letting it plop to the floor with a heavy thunk of coins, then swept a hand through the crown of her hair.

Her rich blond hair glowed like fresh corn silk. He thought her the most beautiful woman he'd ever seen and his heart did a crazy little dance. If only she'd meant the words she'd said during the ceremony. If only she did love him, just a little.

"Come. Sit." Jabari took her hand and settled her onto the thick carpeting before a table where a basket of dates, figs and pomegranates sat next to two heavy silver goblets. He unwound his turban and rolled it into a neat ball, placing it on the trunk. Jabari stood a moment, watching Elizabeth quietly stare into the lamplight like a moth captivated by the flame. He crossed the room, sat next to her and caught her hand in his. Kissing the tips of her fingers, he felt unsure of what to say, reluctant to reveal again what was in his heart.

The thick curtain of his bedchamber was pulled aside as Queb entered the room. Elizabeth's eyes darted up to the elderly shaman, her gaze following him as he knelt before them with a bowl containing a yellowish liquid.

Silently the *fugara* moved his hands over it, then he began muttering in low tones. Jabari beckoned to Elizabeth and motioning to the ground, indicated she should follow suit. He knelt and lowered his forehead to the ground. Much to his relief, he saw Elizabeth mimic his actions. Her respect for the shaman baffled Jabari, especially since she had such little regard for the Majli, who held a higher status than the medicine man.

When they were seated again, Queb took the bowl and poured a generous potion of the draught into one silver goblet and very little into the other. He set down the bowl and held up the goblets with formal reverence.

"May your union be joyful and blessed with sons as strong as the desert winds. As your flesh becomes one so shall your spirits mate for all eternity." He handed the goblet containing the larger portion over to Elizabeth, then gave the other goblet to Jabari. Queb stood, taking the bowl and left them alone.

"What is it?" Elizabeth broke her silence and stared at the goblet as if it contained hemlock. Her lush, musical voice held an edge of fear to it.

Jabari swirled his cup. "A fine wine laid down in the cellars of some rich English infidel whose head my grandfather cut off." He laughed, then glanced at her and stopped, wishing he could erase the anxiety in her dark blue eyes.

"Jabari, I can't drink this. I just can't."

He hastened to assure her. "It is all right. It will not harm you. Queb makes it for all bridal couples." He hesitated. "It is an aphrodisiac. A love potion designed to remove the ah . . . inhibitions of a nervous bride."

Elizabeth flushed crimson. "I assume that by the large amount he poured me, your shaman thinks I must be scared out of my wits." She frowned at his goblet. "But why do you also drink?"

He shrugged. "Tradition. It is always assumed among my people that the groom, especially if he is sheikh, is a man of great sexual prowess. Of course no one hears otherwise, most likely because of this drink that turns them into such. My warriors call it 'love insurance' for men who worry about their performance." Jabari gave her an amused wink.

At last, his words succeeded in culling a giggle from Elizabeth. His heart skipped a beat at the sight of her soft lips curving upward.

"Love insurance. How utterly poetic. Perhaps you should market it among the infidel 'fish' as your friend Nazim calls the archaeological team. They would give their right arm for it."

Jabari gave her a crooked grin, pleasantly surprised that she had picked up on Nazim's pet name for the English.

"Nazim would argue that Queb could not make the potion strong enough."

"Oh, I don't know," she murmured, staring down into her goblet with a smile. "You might be surprised one day and find that it is a far more effective weapon than your scimitar when all the archaeologists abandon Amarna in a frantic search for the nearest women so they can exercise their 'love insurance.' "

Jabari threw back his head and laughed. By Allah, she had a sharp wit.

"What is it called? It does have a name? How is it made?"

"Queb fashions it from a plant that we cultivate in our herb garden. He grinds the seeds into a powder and boils them for several hours. We call it Syrian Rue. The sacred love potion."

"Sacred love potion," she echoed.

"It can have other effects," he warned. "One can experience very powerful visions after consuming this potion."

Jabari lifted his goblet and drained it, wiping his mouth with the back of his hand, then setting the cup on the table. His breathing hitched a bit as she looked up at him with large, questioning eyes. He reached out and touched her cheek, marveling at its smoothness. Fierce desire to love her mingled with the overwhelming longing to take her into his arms and soothe away her fears. "Trust me, my love. I would not allow anything to happen to you. I will be here with you the whole time. Drink."

She nodded, tipped the cup back and drank, wincing at the slightly bitter taste. Elizabeth emptied her goblet and grimaced.

Jabari took the cup from her restless hands and set it upon the table. He laced his fingers through hers and caressed the ridges of her palms with his thumbs. She gazed up at him with those incredibly blue eyes with an air of expectation. Such fire in those twin pools of lapis . . . mingled with apprehension.

"It is custom among the Khamsin for the sheikh to offer

a prayer to Allah before the consummation of the marriage," he told her, planting a light kiss upon her hand.

Allah help him, he needed to pray right now. Never before had a woman captured his heart so completely.

After performing the ceremonial ablutions required for prayer, Jabari kneeled and touched his forehead to the carpet and began reciting the wedding night prayers to Allah in a deep voice in ancient Egyptian. Elizabeth mimicked his body position, wishing she understood what he said. It sounded so hauntingly lovely and mystical. She rolled her head to the side to regard the man beside her. Her husband. The man with the legal right to claim her body and her heart. Her eyes slipped over the long length of him, the white robes cloaking him in an air of mystery that soon would be shed. Ink black hair shone like dark satin in the flickering lamplight and curtained his face from her. His deep, husky voice bathed her with its music. An aching feeling of love swept through her and she shivered with the power of it.

It seemed but a few minutes had passed when she felt it. It was as if the world stopped revolving and slowed, allowing her to see deep within its core. Her hands and feet began to tingle, as if pricked by dozens of tiny needles. A dreamy languor claimed her limbs. She sat up, hoping the dizzy feeling would cease.

Jabari finished praying, sat back on his haunches and then stood. She followed suit, willing her limbs to hold her upright.

He eyed her with concern and picked up her goblet, handing it to her. "Are you all right? Do you need water? Sometimes the potion's strength can be powerful, although Queb deliberately weakens it for this purpose."

"Water," she croaked. Elizabeth held out her cup but her husband became a blurred image blending into the tent walls.

"Elizabeth?"

She swayed and her eyes rolled to the back of her head. The goblet spilled from her hand as she collapsed.

"Elizabeth? My love?"

Jabari's voice floated in an ethereal cloud above and around her head, a disembodied voice that faded as the vision dragged her down. She went willingly, allowing her body to sink into the dreamy feeling as she lay on a crumbled heap on the ground.

Elizabeth's head whirled and she moaned deeply. She willed the spinning to stop, but darkness sucked her into a deep tunnel.

She must remember the cure. Store the words for all eternity. Now the guards stretched her arms out, forcing her to bend her head. She thought of Ranefer's anguish. Her life was over, but through the ages, their love would lie quietly in wait until they were again reunited. She closed her eyes and heard the sword snick through the air . . . then she heard no more as she exhaled her dying breath. . . .

Elizabeth gasped for breath, fighting for life. She clawed the air with her hands, searching for a way out of the darkness choking her. Her eyelids fluttered rapidly and her hands twitched. Elizabeth felt Jabari's strong, sure arms surround her, forcing her to feel his physical reality, willing her to return to this plane of existence. She had lingered on the edge of the spirit world and now her body was slowly claiming her once more.

His lips against her temple brought back a measure of reality. Elizabeth sat up, focused on her breathing and let fresh air fill her lungs. She leaned back against her husband's chest and looked up into his concerned gaze.

"What . . . what happened?"

He stroked her hair, his mouth a narrow, straight line of worry. "You had a vision. You spoke."

"I don't remember. What did I say?"

His brow creased in a troubled frown. "You kept repeating yourself as if it were of utmost importance. You said, 'I must find the cure. I must find the cure for her.' "

"Why does this keep happening to me?" Elizabeth desperately needed to shake off the lassitude, erase the edges of her vision and make them vanish into the desert night.

Jabari did not reply. Shoulders slumped, she buried her head into her hands, taking several deep breaths. She peered at him through splayed fingers. He took her dropped goblet, removed a goatskin bag from a nail on the tent pole and filled her cup. Settling down next to her, he tilted her head up with one hand and forced the goblet to her lips.

"Drink this. It will help."

A nagging stubbornness claimed her. She pressed her lips together. No more exotic love potions or mystical drinks.

"It is only water." Jabari tilted the cup back and she drank, wrapping her hands around his as he held the goblet. He was so strong, so solid and she felt as wispy and ghostly as a *jinn*. Removing the goblet, he set it down and cupped her face in his hands, stroking her cheeks with his fingers. An expression of grief and regret crossed his face.

"I am sorry. I did not mean for it to hurt you. It was supposed to relax you and ease your fears." Jabari's mouth tightened into a narrow slash.

Elizabeth clutched his hands. "Just hold me. I need to feel your arms around me. I feel as if I'm still . . . not entirely here. As if the darkness will suck me down once more."

She leaned against him gratefully as his arms encircled her in a tight embrace. His chin rested atop her hair and he brushed a kiss on the top of her head. She sighed with relief. For some reason, Elizabeth had the keen sense that Jabari would do anything to protect her. If he could have hurled himself after her to pull her away from the tunnel of darkness that dragged her into the vision, he would have.

But he was a warrior, a man, not a mystic. A very powerful, real man. Her hands crept beneath the sleeves of his robe, feeling rippling muscles as hard as solid marble. Jabari uttered a deep groan and rubbed his cheek against her head.

"You must not do that."

Pulling away, she stared with honest confusion. "Why?"

"You are tempting me too much. I may lose . . . control. I want to love you, Elizabeth, as you are meant to be loved." He hesitated. "But I worry that already this night you have endured too much. We may wait until tomorrow night."

He frowned as if remembering something. "The elders will expect . . . proof. I can fool them. A small cut to my hand, a stained sheet." Jabari touched the jeweled dagger at his waist. "It will be enough to convince them."

Heat filled her cheeks as she caught the implication of his words. Sudden shyness seized her. "No, that won't be necessary." She stared at the ground in abject misery.

Duty again. He felt obligated to consummate the marriage, as was expected. The bedsheet stained with her blood as proof of their union would be openly displayed to the Majli.

Jabari did not love her. Desired her, yes. But love . . . no. She felt like a filly about to be bred to a spirited stallion. The marriage act would have no more emotion to it than that.

"Tonight then. Let's get it over with. It doesn't matter, you don't love me anyway," she said dully, feeling bitterly defeated and drained. "You never did. Go ahead, claim your conquest. I don't even care anymore."

Two warm palms settled on either side of her cheeks. Jabari gazed into her eyes with such tenderness that she had to blink to make certain she wasn't seeing things again. "Elizabeth, Elizabeth. My love, my only love. I have always loved you. You are part of my heart." He slid his arms around her waist.

She tried to jerk free. "Liar," she whispered, finally caving in to the tears that now fell. "You said all you wanted was a virgin in your bed."

"I lashed out at you," he admitted. "I had to mask my

feelings because you did not feel the same."

"You did? But what about my apology? I told you I had feelings for you and all you did was accept my apology and trust my behavior would improve!"

He heaved a deep sigh. "You must understand that my grandfather did not formally accept you when he handed me the wedding dagger. My family realized this. He thinks you are too aggressive. For them to fully acknowledge you as my bride, they had to see you humble yourself before me. Your apology filled that purpose, my love. They are unused to your proud, independent spirit." He brushed his lips against her ear.

"My independent spirit." The thought soured on her lips as if she tasted them and found them bittersweet. "I gave my word to your grandfather that I would submit myself before you, a dull, mindless wife without a thought of her own."

He touched the top of her head, as if probing for the brain cells she claimed now lay dormant. "My grandfather forced you to say that. Not me. Do you truly believe I would want such a woman for my wife? For my sweet desert rose to dry up and become as lifeless and spiritless as dust?"

He laughed and pulled her closer. "My love, I adore and cherish your brain, every bit as much as I cherish your lovely body. You are an oasis for my mind, for my soul, my heart. You are the only one for me. You always were, my precious darling."

Elizabeth gazed into his face. "Do you really mean that?"

"I would not have broken Khamsin custom if I did not. The sacred bath and allowing Badra to learn to read. My people's traditions are sacred to me, but you are more important."

Elizabeth tilted her head to look at him. At last she had peeled back the final stratum of this man and found the heart of him. It was like reaching a treasure buried deep inside the stony earth. She looked into his eyes and just as she had the first day they met, saw a reflection of her own soul. And the reflection she saw there was love.

"I love you, my beautiful Elizabeth." He pressed a deep kiss inside her palm.

"I love you, too, Jabari," she whispered back.

Black eyes as deep as the night sky held hers, commanded her attention. Deep within those dark pools shimmered passion and fire. "Elizabeth, more than anything, I want to make you mine tonight. I want our bodies, and souls, to mate forever. But the decision is yours, my love. What say you?"

She traced the outline of his firm lips with one finger. Elizabeth rose, pulling Jabari with her. She began unfastening the *kuftan*'s tiny pearl buttons. She let the garment fall, slipped out of trousers and the *kamis* shirt and stood before him naked. "Does this answer your question?"

His pupils dilated. Jabari drew in a ragged breath as he nodded slowly. "So be it."

He led her over to the bed, pulling back the satin coverlet and settled her upon the clean white sheet. Jabari dropped to one knee before her and cradled her face with his hands. He gazed upon her as if she were a precious item he deeply cherished.

"So beautiful. You are so beautiful." His voice was hoarse with passion. He stood and rapidly shed his clothing, letting it fall in a pile to the floor.

Elizabeth let her eyes roam over his naked body, the wide breadth of shoulders, the thick cord of muscles roping down his arms, the lean, narrow hips. Her breath caught, hitched in her throat as she gazed at the virile hardness between his legs. Remembering the harem talk, she felt herself blush. He was huge. Enormous. Quite powerfully aroused. He would tear her in half, she thought, her earlier fears rising.

"What is it?" he asked.

Elizabeth swallowed hard. "I think . . . Farah was right."

Jabari's brow furrowed, then understanding flickered into his eyes. "Ah, you have listened to her talk." He smiled.

"But you're too . . ." Elizabeth gulped, flushing furiously. "Too big! I don't see how . . ." she whispered.

A proud smile tugged at his beautiful mouth. He sat next to her, running his hands through the masses of her long hair. "It will. My beautiful Elizabeth, do not be afraid," he said gently.

Jabari's eyes grew soft. He cradled her face with his hands, brushed his lips tenderly against hers, then whispered into her mouth. "I give you the seven sacred promises of love all Khamsin warriors pledge to their brides. I promise you a thousand nights of love as deep as the desert night. I promise you an eternity of passion as bright as the distant stars. I promise you I will cherish and protect you until I breathe my last. I promise you my soul, mated to yours until the end of time. I promise you my forever love, my heart joined to yours as our flesh becomes one. I promise you will be mine for all eternity, and I will never leave your side. I promise you we will breed fine sons who will have strong spirits and brave hearts."

He kissed her, a whisper against her lips. Her heart ached with emotions at his poetic confession.

Then he gave her the softest of pushes back onto the bed. "Lay down on your stomach," he instructed.

She did as he ordered. Elizabeth turned her head and watched him climb into the bed with her, first setting a small golden bowl on a nearby table. A delicious fragrance drifted up.

"Jabari, what . . ."

"Hush, my love," he whispered. "Relax. Lie still." He lifted the curtain of her hair and flung it to one side. Then he dipped his hands into the bowl and began rubbing them against her back. His expert fingers glided over her skin as he massaged warm oil gently into her skin. Elizabeth shuddered with need, feeling the richness of desire intertwine with his great love for her.

"It is perfumed oil, a tradition in my tribe. Perfumed, flavored oil," he said, his voice a hushed, seductive purr.

Sighing with delight, she closed her eyes against the seductive caress of his hands. Jabari massaged her back, then worked downward. She let loose a startled cry, rising up as his expert touch drifted over her buttocks, kneading them, then plunged between her legs.

Kissing her backside, he pressed a finger against her spine, easing her onto the bed. "Lie down, my darling," he whispered.

Warm hands slid over the backs of her thighs, trailing rich oil in their wake. Her body went rigid with tense pleasure. A low moan rose from her throat. "Please, I cannot stand it."

Jabari gave a deep chuckle. "Oh, you will my darling. This and so much more."

So very much more. Elizabeth had no idea what he had in store for her. The thought sent a delectable feeling of sensual anticipation through him.

She turned over as he instructed and he began massaging warm oil onto her belly, working his way up, teasing her with long, sure strokes. Her skin felt as delicate and soft as rose petals. He cupped her rounded breasts and massaged them tenderly, pausing for a minute to give a delicate flick of his tongue to one pearl-like nipple. Another deep moan from his wife. Mmmm, so tempting. He needed to taste her. Jabari drew in a deep, ragged breath. He worked more oil onto his hands, then slid them down her hips, then, massaging her thighs, he parted them gently and caressed the satin flesh there. He pressed her thighs farther apart, staring with avid hunger at the sweetness awaiting him at the juncture between her legs. As was custom, she had been shaved earlier during the ceremonial preparations. There was a reason for that, Jabari thought, grinning. It heightened a woman's sense of pleasure. And he intended to bring her every minutia of that ecstasy. His fingers began stroking the softness of her, small delicate strokes meant to arouse. He heard her gasp and whimper. Her honeyed juices began flowing, eliminating need for the oil. Enormously pleased with her reaction, he increased his rhythm and pace, then carefully slipped a finger deep inside her. She arched against his touch. Jabari frowned. She was so very tight against him. He must be gentle and careful with her. He continued his tender caresses, then slid another finger into her narrow passage, attempting to stretch her little by little.

But it was no use, for the resisting flesh would not give way. Jabari sighed deeply. Ah well, at least to give her pleasure then. His eyes roamed over her feminine core. He grinned again.

She really had no idea what he was going to do with her. Of what delights he would give her. Very, very slowly.

Jabari began administering the secret of one hundred kisses, kissing her satiny skin all over, pausing at her birthmark, giving that extra attention. His appetite whetted, he eagerly anticipated the rest of the banquet.

"My beautiful desert rose, you are a feast for my hungry mouth," he whispered hoarsely against her skin. "I could dine on you all night."

He lifted one ankle and his lips worked their way down to her thigh, kissing softly. Then he settled between the cradle of her legs and lowered his head to lick her soft, rosy skin.

Immediately she bolted upright. "Jabari," she wailed, "what is this?"

He raised his head, grinning with mischievous glee at her startled reaction. "Dessert."

Jabari pushed her gently back onto the bed. Lowering his head, he lapped at her, tasting her, swirling his tongue over the delicate flesh that he knew would bring her the most pleasure. She began moaning and thrashing. He steadied her thighs with his hands, pressing them still against the bed. Mmmm. Like the juiciest pomegranate. She tasted so delightful. So delicious.

"Please stop, oh, oh, oh, I cannot take it."

He ignored her impassioned entreaties. She began rotating her pelvis, arching her hips upward. Pleased with her response, Jabari continued to dine. He wasn't finished. Not by half. Not until he heard her cry out her release, his name on her lips. He could continue this sweet torment all night. If need be.

He was licking her. Sampling her like a cat with cream. Tasting her. Wanting her. His tongue glided expertly around in intricate whorls and delicate flicks. Elizabeth's embarrassment shifted into pure moans of ecstasy. She begged him to stop. Begged him not to stop. She didn't know what she wanted. He was remorseless in his quest. No mercy. No quarter given. A true Khamsin warrior, determined to slay her with pure pleasure.

Jabari raised his head. She looked down and saw the ruthless determination in those black eyes. "Call out my name, Elizabeth. Cry it out. I want my name on your lips. Only then will I cease this." Then he began his slow, tormenting assault once more.

Her body hummed, throbbed as the crescendo built, the fire raged. She burned with need. She raged. Elizabeth curled her fists around a pillow. Her body became as taut as the finely tempered steel of his scimitar. She felt herself ready to burst into a thousand shattering pieces of delight. Over and over she cried out his name in a scream as the mounting pleasure exploded within her.

He stopped and settled next to her quivering body, gathering her into his arms. Jabari nuzzled her temple with a soft kiss.

"You please me so much, my lovely desert rose. You are all I could ever want in a woman. Your passion equals my own."

He slid over her, pinning her down with his muscled form. Jabari's hands splayed her scalp, tugging her hair, forcing her to look at him. His eyes were dark with his own raging desire.

He kissed her in a wild, savage frenzy as if a tremendous beast inside howled and demanded release. A little frightened, she pressed her hands against his chest. Immediately he stopped, his breath coming in strangled rasps as he gazed down at her.

"Forgive me, my love. I forget . . . your innocence. I promise I will try to be gentle."

He began stroking her body. His touch was light and assured, a soft zephyr upon her overly sensitive skin.

Clinging to him, she wrapped her arms around him as if fearing to let go. He was exquisitely gentle and yet beneath the careful control she sensed the burning need, the fierce longing to let the storm of emotions loose.

She looked up and grazed the side of his cheek with her fingers. "Jabari," Elizabeth whispered, "I want you. All of you. I want you to love me with all your heart. All your soul. All the emotions you hide. Let me feel your love for me."

He raised his head and looked down at her with passion. Then lowered his mouth to hers. His mouth was hard, claiming her lips with heat that did not singe. She wrapped her arms around his neck in an answering passion of her own. Jabari's hands swept through the masses of her hair. He settled himself between the cradle of her legs.

"Open up to me, my sweet desert rose. Open your lovely petals and let me come inside," he ordered in husky whisper.

She opened her legs wide to him, bracing her hands on his shoulders. A powerful hardness prodded her feminine softness. He eased a bit into her. Drew away. Then pressed forward again.

This was the moment then, to feel his powerful body pressed against hers, to surrender all. To join their flesh, their spirits for all eternity. Elizabeth felt a tremendous force tunnel through her. She lifted her hips to signal her compliance.

"My love, look at me," he commanded. Jabari uttered a deep groan and gave a tremendous, powerful thrust forward. Desire gave way to burning pain.

He stopped as she uttered a small cry and thrashed beneath him. With loving tenderness, he looked down. She saw the question in the dark pools of his eyes. Waiting for her. Letting her get accustomed to the feel of him.

Her breathing slowed. He pushed forward more. Penetrated deeper. Deeper still. His hugeness filled her to the core, an exhilarating sensation as the stinging subsided.

She pulled him down and kissed him. An unspoken communication drifted between them. Slowly, he began moving against her. With each mounting thrust, she began moving her hips to meet his demands. Equals now in the age-old dance of love. Every cell of her being sang out with fire. She found herself crying out his name again. Much like her past visions, an overwhelming dizziness claimed her. But each sensation came replete with pleasure and negated the frightening illusions she'd experienced. As he tutored her in the art of love, Elizabeth felt herself become a willing captive to passion. Jabari captured her body, imprisoned it in a cell filled with the love he professed.

"Put your legs around my waist, my darling," he ordered.

She obeyed, arching her hips upward to meet him stroke for stroke. Capturing her hands above her head, he laced his large, strong fingers through hers. His breathing quickened and came in short, stabbing pants. Jabari gave a deep groan and a mighty thrust. His body shuddered as he cried out her name and she felt him spill his seed deep within her.

He kissed her tenderly and rolled off her. Jabari hugged her to his side. She settled into the crook of his arm, her face nuzzled against his broad chest.

"Are you all right?" He caressed her cheek.

"Yes, my husband." Elizabeth gave a little laugh. "They certainly did not teach us about that at Vassar."

He chuckled and murmured, "You are everything I expected you to be, my love. Everything I could have ever dreamed of."

"And you as well," she said, stroking his cheek.

Jabari kissed her. "There is something I need to do for you. Wait here."

She laid back, watching with mounting interest as he fetched a small bowl of water. He sprinkled something into it and brought the water and a clean white cloth over to the bedside.

Elizabeth felt a sudden tinge of alarm, which faded. She trusted him completely. Jabari looked at her closed legs. She stared up, a question in her eyes.

"What's this?"

"A wedding night ritual all husbands perform for their wives in our tribe." Jabari reached between her legs and carefully pried them apart. Elizabeth felt deeply self-conscious as he touched the cloth to her legs. With a gentle hand, he began bathing the blood from her thighs. He pressed the cloth to the core of her feminine softness.

"The herbs help relieve the pain," Jabari explained.

To her surprise, the stinging between her legs eased somewhat. Jabari finished his task. Set the items back on the table and climbed back into bed with her.

She give a little sigh and snuggled into his arms. "Sleep," he whispered to her in a husky voice and kissed her cheek. "Sleep my beautiful desert rose, my lovely wife."

A shrill cry woke her in the middle of the night. Startled, Elizabeth sat upright, clutching the blanket to her. Light from the lamp cast ominous shadows around the tent.

She shuddered with dread. Next to her, Jabari stirred. He woke and reached out, embracing her.

"My darling, what is it?"

"That cry . . . I heard something, a wild animal."

"Nazim most likely. He likes to sing in the night," Jabari joked, nuzzling her temple.

She slapped his wrist playfully. "More like a cat."

"Oh, a caracal. They come around the perimeter of the camp sometimes. The dogs chase them away. They are wild desert cats."

"Caracal." She tested the word on her tongue. So many strange new things she had to learn about her husband's world.

Jabari gave a long stretch. His dark eyes gleamed with mischief. "Elizabeth, have you ever seen how a cat mates?"

"No," she said slowly, her eyes not leaving his. Jabari ran his hands through her hair and then whispered in her ear in a seductive purr, "Then allow me the honor . . . of showing you."

He pulled the covers down with an impatient tug, then flipped her gently over on her stomach, instructing her to rise on her hands and knees. Elizabeth breathed hard, a little afraid of what he would do. Her long hair curtained her face.

She felt the power of his muscled form rise above her. Jabari caressed her legs, then grasped her hips. Elizabeth let out a long, low moan as he bent over her, his tongue gliding over the back of her neck as he lifted her hair and brushed it aside with impatience.

Jabari's tongue traced a pattern along the edge of her neck. His hands rubbed her breasts, teasing the silky pearls there until they tautened with need.

"Oh, please . . . I don't think I can take it," she cried out, throbbing with anticipation.

"Oh my love." He chuckled, rubbing his body over hers. "You will, and much more. Such are the pleasures I will show you."

He carried out that threat as his sure, strong hands reached down between her legs and began a series of delicate, feathery strokes in her softness. Elizabeth arched her back and cried out from the searing heat flaming across her loins. The fire began to consume her, threatening to engulf her very soul.

"Yes, my love, yes. Let it go, do not hold back, come my lovely Elizabeth, I want your pleasure to equal mine," he said in a deep, commanding voice.

Air brushed against her skin, dancing over it, making every single cell alive and throbbing. Flames shot into every nerve of her raging body. She cried out his name as they burst within her.

Jabari gave a low, triumphant laugh and pressed a kiss

to her back, beaded with moisture. "Yes, my love you are all that I knew you to be from the moment I met you. A wild enchanting temptress cloaked in a maiden's body, just waiting to be unleashed. But there is so much more . . . I shall teach you about passion between a man and a woman.

"This is how . . . a wild animal such as a cat . . . claims its mate," he breathed lowly into her ear.

He nibbled at the tender flesh of her neck, driving her wild with the sensation. With a snarl that echoed the caracal's he suddenly thrust into her with savage abandonment. Elizabeth rocked back and forth on her knees as his hardness slammed into her, his powerful body crouched over hers, claiming every inch of her as his own. He pressed his hands upon her hips and gave one tremendous thrust after another, so deep she shuddered from the force. It was a free-spirited, heated mating of their bodies, passion calling to passion, no sweet words of love, no tender caresses, but only the raging desires of a man and women blending together in an all-consuming inferno.

Her cries echoed his own, shattering the stillness of the vast empty places of the desert.

Before dawn's first flush, Elizabeth woke. For a moment, she could not recall where she was. Then she felt the solid arms of her husband around her, curling her body next to his as he slept. Elizabeth gave a secret smile. She was Jabari's wife, in every sense of the word. Easing herself from his embrace, she leaned over her husband, marveling at his male perfection gleaming in the cast by the lamp. Long black lashes swept against his cheeks as he slumbered. Elizabeth brushed back the shoulder-length black hair from his face. His golden, bare shoulders, curved with muscle, contrasted with the whiteness of the sheet. The previous night her fingers explored the breadth of those shoulders, had dug her nails into the broadness of his back. She blushed, remembering her own sensuality.

Elizabeth slipped from the bed. Love remained a hauntingly beautiful memory from the previous night, but now other matters weighed on her mind. Now, while Jabari and the others slept, was the perfect time to visit Nahid.

A short time later, dressed in an indigo *kuftan,* Elizabeth silently crept through camp. Prayers would begin soon. She had little time before the others would wake.

Her eyes adjusted to the moonlit landscape. Ashes of the previous night's campfires lay gray against the sand. Easy enough to pick out his tent. Two fierce-looking warriors, their hands resting with ease on their scimitar handles, sat before the entrance. They rose upon seeing her and formally bowed.

"My uncle," Elizabeth said, holding her shoulders rigid and hoping her voice held an equally regal note. "I wish to see him."

"Of course," one guard murmured. He opened the tent flap and she ducked inside. A candle set on a low table flickered with light. Nahid lay on a frayed carpet on his side, his hands and legs tied together. Another rope snaked from his waist, tying him to a stake pounded into the ground.

The Khamsin had the right to imprison Nahid, but seeing him tied like an animal distressed her. She squatted down next to him and poked his shoulder. Immediately he sat up, raising his hands into fists, ready to strike.

"Uncle Nahid, it's me, Elizabeth!" she whispered.

"Elizabeth. Thank Allah it is you."

Troubled, Elizabeth looked at her uncle's tired expression. She put a reassuring hand on his shoulder.

"You found the Almha, Uncle! I have seen it!" This should lift his spirits a bit.

Nahid's eyes widened with interest. "Where do they keep it?"

"In Jabari's, our, tent. There are inscriptions on the back, but I will need to be alone with it to decipher the hieroglyphics." Elizabeth thought about this. "Perhaps later I will get a chance. But how can I smuggle a message out to Nana?"

"Is it heavily guarded?"

She shook her head, a slight smile creasing her lips. "No one would set foot in our tent, even to guard the Almha. Not when we . . ." A rosy blush covered her cheeks. "We were married last night," she explained.

Nahid gave her a look of incredulous contempt. "My utmost condolences on being bound to that heartless jackal." He shook his head. "It is a gloomy day indeed when the graceless son of camel dung marries my only niece, tainting our family's blood."

"Uncle Nahid, my marriage to him spared you. And Jabari . . . he isn't what you think. He is gentle and kind and considerate." She pulled back, baffled. "Why do you hate him so much?"

"It is not just your husband I despise." Nahid's eyes narrowed. "His race. The Khamsin are not fit to lick your shoes!"

"They are honorable. They are desert people, bound by tradition and duty."

"They're heartless dogs who think nothing of dishonoring women, including you." His face contorted into a savage scowl.

"I can't agree. I think they are wonderful."

"Don't get all starry-eyed Elizabeth. You forget why you came to Egypt. Or do you?"

Remorse made her shoulders droop. Elizabeth shook her head. "I have not forgotten. How could I forget Nana?"

Nahid held up wrists chafed red and raw by his bonds. "Let me loose and I will take the cure to her," he pleaded.

"I am sorry. I can't." She hesitated and saw him wince.

"If you want to help my mother, you must help me."

Loyalty to Jabari vied with love for her grandmother. Love won. Elizabeth struggled with Nahid's bindings. The intricate knots were too complicated for her.

"I need a knife." On a low table close to the tent wall sat a bowl of fruit and a small knife. She grabbed it and sawed the ropes loose. Nahid rubbed his wrists together and plucked the knife from her hands. His brown eyes glowed with feverish intensity. Elizabeth felt fear curdle her stomach.

He stood and put an arm around her waist, pulling her with him. Nahid pressed the dagger lightly against her neck. "Now order the guards inside. Scream for them, but not too loudly."

Elizabeth called out for help in a low voice. As the two Khamsin guards rushed into the tent, she arranged her face into a mask of terror. Not hard to do, as she felt the knife prick her bare skin. "I told him of my marriage and he wants to kill me!"

The two men approached warily as Nahid jammed the knife into her until the point dimpled Elizabeth's neck. Nahid hurled his niece at them. Elizabeth stumbled against the men, throwing them off balance. They immediately hastened to steady her. Nahid seized the advantage and kicked one in the groin. The guard grunted and dropped a hand to his injured part. Nahid whirled about and stabbed the other in the shoulder. Before they recovered, he knocked them out with a furious blow to their heads. Never had she seen her uncle, the scholar who bent over books day and night, act so fierce. Like a warrior.

"Take me to the Almha."

Her lips moved, but no sound came. Elizabeth stepped outside. The camp still slumbered.

"Hurry," he ordered in an angry whisper.

Elizabeth ran to Jabari's tent. *Please let him be asleep!* She jerked back the tent flap and silently slipped inside, followed by Nahid. The Almha lay in a place of honor, atop an altar fashioned from a low sandalwood table. Two candles, nearly burnt to the wicks, framed the gold disk. To her shock, Nahid shoved her on her knees, then followed suit and bowed his head.

He rose quickly and approached the altar. Nahid lifted the heavy disk. A glow of triumph lit his face.

"I regret what I must do, my niece. But I do this for the

sake of my people, for the sake of my mother's people whom she left so long ago. I, Nahid Wilson, descendent of Farris warriors, claim this sacred disk. The day of vengeance for the Al-Hajid has come at last! The Almha is ours!"

She felt the heavy blow to her head then nothing as darkness claimed her and she fell to the ground.

Chapter Sixteen

A cool cloth was pressed to her head. Voices murmured, some in anger, some tense with worry. Ten legions of horses galloped across her pounding temple. Elizabeth winced, reluctant to open her eyes to the pain in her head and in her heart.

What an utter fool she'd been. Duped so completely by Nahid. Emotions battered her as heavily as the pounding pain. Her wistful dream of discovering she had family after all was a cruel twist of fate. Her relatives were her husband's blood enemies!

"Elizabeth, open your eyes."

She must obey that deep, compelling voice. Easing her eyelids open, she saw her husband sitting on the bed's edge dressed in a loose white robe. Jabari looked down on her, his lips drawn together in a tight line, worry creasing his brow. Gently he swabbed her forehead.

"The wound has ceased bleeding. Are you all right?"

He didn't know. Not yet. Relief flowed through her, easing a little of the pain.

"I think so." Elizabeth put a hand to the small lump at

her temple. She looked around. A few of Jabari's female relatives, including Asriyah, stood nearby. And the men . . . Nkosi, naked fury evident on his wrinkled face.

Elizabeth wrapped her hair around one tense finger. She had gained a family and betrayed her husband, all within twenty-four hours of the wedding. Vaguely she wondered if theirs would be the shortest marriage on record. Would he simply divorce her?

Her eyes shot to Nkosi's curled upper lip. Or would they chop off her head?

The bed's softness was tempting and far more inviting than the scowls surrounding her. She couldn't play victim for long. Somehow, she had to be brave and let them know the truth. Elizabeth sat up gingerly. Jabari stopped sponging her temple and held out a golden goblet with a mysterious murky liquid.

"This will ease your headache. Do not worry—it will not cause visions."

She took the cup and drank deeply, giving it back to him. Elizabeth swung her legs over the bed's edge, holding on to Jabari for physical as well as emotional strength.

If only everyone would cease staring at her. The women with puzzled disappointment and the men with open hostility.

"Elizabeth, what happened? Two of my warriors are injured and the Almha and Nahid are gone." Her husband's voice held no recrimination, yet she sensed the underlying question.

She lowered her eyes to the finely woven carpeted floor. "Nahid has escaped with it. He hit me over the head."

Indignant mutters filled the tent room. An angry male voice called out, "How could you let him escape with the sacred disk!"

She raised her eyes to see Jabari frown as he made a dismissive motion to the crowd.

"This is not an interrogation chamber, but my bedchamber. All of you, please leave."

"My grandson . . ." Nkosi stepped forward, clasping Jabari's shoulder. "The people deserve to know the truth."

Jabari nodded, his face somber. "But not here. In the council chambers. Assemble my commanders and the Majli."

Her grip on Jabari's arm tightened. Time to tell the truth. Oh, how she wished she could sit him down alone, try to explain. But the Almha, the tribe's sacred disk, was a public matter. And her explanation would be equally public.

She watched the people file out of the bedroom, glad for a little privacy. Only Nkosi and Asriyah remained behind. Perhaps now she could tell him. A slight tug on her arm indicated otherwise. She swivelled to face Asriyah.

"Jabari needs time alone with his grandfather before the council meeting. Come with us. You may eat breakfast and freshen up in our tent," Asriyah said. Elizabeth opened her mouth to protest, but Jabari gave her a reassuring smile. Nkosi hovered near Jabari, as if he feared leaving his side.

No time at all to protest, for loving words to remind him of the passion they'd shared only hours before. Elizabeth left the tent, sick with anguish. What would happen when Jabari found out he had married a member of the tribe he hated most?

In Asriyah's tent, she barely touched the breakfast of yogurt, figs and camel's milk. A little while later, Elizabeth sat by herself facing a horseshoe of accusing faces in the Majli's formal chambers. Eleven council members and Jabari's commanders squeezed into the tent. The air was redolent with tension, sweat and dust. Never before had she felt so utterly abandoned and alone. Not even when her parents had died.

The tent flap jerked open and Jabari strode in, accompanied by Nazim and Nkosi. Clad in the warrior *binish* of indigo, armed with scimitar and dagger at his waist, he stood for a moment surveying the crowd. Hands on hips, he thrust out his chest. She marveled at the sheer power he radiated. This was her husband, whose loving hands had roamed possessively over her entire body the previous night, who called out her name at the height of his passion.

No gentleness clung to his muscled shoulders now. Jabari commanded with lean strength and confidence, determined to deal with confusion and cut to the truth with razor-sharp accuracy.

The assembled men bowed their heads briefly in respect to their leader. Elizabeth pressed her hands to the carpeted floor and leaned forward until her head touched it. For once, she did not resent the submissive gesture. She wished she could remain in that position so as not to see the pained disappointment in Jabari's face when he learned the truth.

The carpeted floor thumped with their footsteps and Elizabeth sat up to face them. She expected the trio to begin the interrogation like a panel of judges. To her utter amazement, Jabari dropped to a sitting position to her right and reached for her hand. He gave it a quick squeeze and then placed his hands on his knees, palms down. Nazim settled on her left and flashed her a friendly wink. Sandwiched protectively between the two warriors she trusted most, Elizabeth's self-confidence rose.

Nkosi spared her no winks or reassuring pats. He stared at her with hostile intent. The chief elder sat so closely in front of her she could almost count the hairs on his leathery cheeks. No mercy in that dark, stern gaze. The hanging judge.

He wasted no time.

"Did you free your uncle so he could steal the Almha?"

Elizabeth swallowed hard. To ease her fear, she concentrated on her husband's scent—a clean, fresh air of spices emanating from his *binish*. His large reassuring presence sat like a brick wall, deflecting some of the harshness of Nkosi's angry voice.

"I freed my uncle, but not to steal the Almha."

Murmurs rippled through the tent like fine silk. Nkosi held up his hand, hushing them instantly. In his proud authority she saw a reflection of the traits passed down to his grandson.

"Why then?"

"I needed the ancient remedies inscribed on the back for a family member." She turned her head toward Jabari's raised eyebrows. "That is the real reason I dug for the Almha."

"How did you know of its existence?"

Elizabeth explained the papyrus she'd found in her grandmother's trunk. "She was a Bedouin, from a tribe near here, I believe. But she left her tribe long ago."

Nkosi's eyes widened and darkened. His body tensed as if he restrained some powerful emotion. "What tribe?" he asked hoarsely.

She hesitated and looked down, making circles on her leg with her fingertip. Jabari reached over and stayed her hand.

"Elizabeth, you must answer the question."

Darting a glance at him, she winced inwardly at his grave expression. Elizabeth gripped his hand with a sense of despondency that this was the last time she'd feel his skin against hers. He squeezed back and rested his hand on her knee.

Her chest heaved in an enormous sigh. "She never said. She always kept it a secret. . . . I never knew until Nahid told me, you must understand this. . . ." Elizabeth rubbed her nose.

"You lie," Nkosi said. "I see it in your face."

She stretched out her hands, flicked out her wrists and opened her palms facing upward. Badra had taught her the gesture in the Arab world meant, "What do you want from me?"

"Elizabeth, tell the truth." Jabari's voice deepened.

"What tribe?" Nkosi demanded.

Her gaze dropped to the carpet. "The Al-Hajid."

The crowd took a collective gasp so deep it was a wonder the tent walls weren't sucked in. She felt Jabari withdraw his hand from her knee and forced herself to look at his face.

His nostrils flared as he stiffened his shoulders and

looked straight ahead. Her husband's eyes were a black abyss.

Nkosi stabbed a trembling finger at her with righteous glee. Any veneer of impartiality fled as he pointed, a gesture as impolite in his world as the one she'd made by showing Jabari the soles of her feet. His face contorted with volcanic rage. She drew back, shaking with fear at his erupting fury.

"I knew there was something foul about this woman! She disguised herself as our queen to win our loyalty and steal the Almha!" Shocked gasps greeted his accusation.

Her mouth dropped open in protest. "How can this be? I am still here! The Almha is not!"

"You did not reckon with your uncle's treachery. He is an Al-Hajid, with a serpent's heart. He used you . . ." Nkosi sneered, "as you used our people!"

"I admit, I was a fool. But I did not disguise myself as Kiya! I have the birthmark!"

"And the dove?" Nkosi demanded.

"The dove is my pet bird, Isis," she admitted. "But I, I . . ."

"Used the bird to deceive us. You did not tell us it was tame. You led us to believe it was the prophecy!"

"I needed the bird to let you believe what you wanted so I could try to escape. I never wanted to marry your grandson! I told you that before! He forced me into it."

Elizabeth could have cut out her tongue herself this time. She nearly wished for Aziz's dagger. In front of his warriors she had humiliated Jabari by stating her unwillingness to marry him. Now they'd think their marriage a sham. Her vows a lie.

"She is the curse of a woman who does not know her place. She has disgraced our sheikh with her lying heart," one of Jabari's commanders growled. Others muttered in agreement.

Nazim's boyish face twisted in anger. His amber eyes narrowed into a hostile glower as he looked at her. She had deeply insulted his best friend, something this warrior did not easily forgive. But if Nazim's reaction hurt, Jabari's caused acute agony. His eyes glazed over with pain. That firm jawline tightened while his cheek ticked violently.

But I do love you Jabari, she wanted to cry out. Elizabeth remembered the promises of love of the previous night. It seemed many lifetimes ago. Jabari locked gazes with her. His eyes were harder than the steel dangling at his side. She searched for words to make him soften with affection once more.

"I would never betray your people or your love, Jabari." Elizabeth prayed she could break through that stone wall.

"You already have," Nkosi countered, his words sounding like a seal of doom to her.

Elizabeth looked wildly about the tent. Each face registered grim disapproval. Guilty. She could see the verdict written on their faces as if scribbled onto their foreheads. The back of her neck, already tense, tightened as if expecting a death blow. Her palms grew cold and clammy. No one believed her.

The tribe, which had beaten drums and happily celebrated her wedding the previous night, now was a force united against her. In their eyes, Elizabeth was the enemy. She freed the man who stole the Almha. She was tied to the tribe they hated most. Deceived them into thinking she was their revered queen. And worst, insulted their beloved leader, stripping him of honor.

Nkosi looked at his grandson and slapped his palms upon the carpet. "What is your decision, my grandson? What will you do with this . . . traitor?" He fingered the dagger at his waist.

Jabari unfolded his powerful body and rose. He seemed to grow taller until he stood before her like a monolith. Nazim joined him. The two men stepped back, facing her, until they were perfectly aligned with Nkosi. She was alone once more.

His manner bristled with authority. Jabari's eyes seared hers with a piercing gaze. She shrank inside her *kuftan.*

"Elizabeth, you have deceived me. From this moment

on, you are no longer known as Kiya, our queen. You will remain in the tent of my female relatives. Asriyah will see to any of your needs. That is all I have to say for now."

He whipped around, exiting the tent. Nazim looked at her, his expression softer now. He nodded toward the tent door. "Come, my lady, I will escort you myself."

Elizabeth stood, looking at the floor. She simply couldn't bear to see the anger in the faces around her . . . or let them witness the pain in hers.

His lovely desert rose, his wife—his worst enemy.

The wounded man replaced the furious warrior sheikh of the Khamsin. Jabari stumbled over his own feet as he entered his tent. He sagged against the tent pole and held on for dear life.

A low guttural moan rose from deep within his breast. He sank to the carpet and buried his face into his hands.

His shoulders slumped with agonized shame. His love for Elizabeth had dishonored his beloved people. If he had never bared her birthmark while making love to her, none of this would have happened. His heart had led them into disgrace. Their most sacred item had been carried in triumph to their hated enemies.

His wife, for only one night. The tribe would force him to divorce her, banish her, or worse. He could spare her life, but they could never live with her. The Khamsin would view her as a scorpion in their midst, ready to sting again. Elizabeth was as lost to him as fleeting hope. Doubts rose their ugly heads. Her words of love the previous night were a ploy to wrap his heart in kisses and deceive him so she could steal the Almha. She shattered his trust in her. He heard the pieces break cleanly in two with the confession his grandfather forced from her lips.

A hesitant cough outside forced him to calm down. Jabari took a deep breath, sat cross-legged and straightened his spine. He stared at the empty altar, a symbol of his empty heart.

"Jabari, may I enter?" Nazim sounded uncertain.

He called out his acquiesce and did not look up as his friend entered and plunked down beside him.

"Allah, what a predicament. Jabari . . ." Nazim sighed and touched his heart, then his lips in the Khamsin warrior gesture of honor before battle.

"You must not lose heart. No one blames you."

Jabari tore his gaze away from the empty altar. "The fault is mine alone. I should have killed Nahid when I had the chance. But like a woman, I softened. For a woman, I softened. Like my father!" He struck his bent knee with a furious fist.

Nazim dropped a hand onto his rigid shoulder. "For the love of a woman. That is nothing be ashamed of. You cannot hide it from me, my friend. I would have done the same."

"Truly?" Jabari glanced his way.

"Truly." Nazim touched his heart again.

"How is my wife . . . Elizabeth?"

"Quiet. She went meekly to Asriyah's tent. She said nothing in her defense. Badra is with her now."

"Nothing? No soft words or pleas of innocence?"

"No. She seems resigned to whatever will happen."

Jabari bit his lip and scratched his chin. If Elizabeth were aligned with the Al-Hajid, she would bat her pretty eyelashes and plead for mercy. Instead, she remained quiet. Something deep inside warned him she was innocent of her uncle's crime. The only guilt she carried was trusting Nahid. But he could not defend her now. Greater matters than his marriage and his heart lay before him. He must reclaim the Almha.

Still he could not help asking, "Does she inquire about me?"

Nazim rubbed his eyes. "All she said as I walked her to your aunt's tent was this: 'At least I knew what passion was, if only for one night.' She said it in English, more to herself than me."

Jabari winced. He pushed all thoughts of Elizabeth from his mind. "Assemble my warriors for a war council. We must plan our *ghazu* carefully so the enemy has no clue of our approach."

Nazim bowed his head. "It will be done as you have said." He grasped Jabari's hand once more. "I am here for you, friend. You may always count on me. I trust your judgment. If it were up to me, she would remain your wife. I know how much you love her."

Deeply moved, Jabari could only nod. "Thank you," he said in a gruff voice to hide his emotions.

When Nazim left, Jabari entered his bedroom and went to the bed. He glanced down at the white sheet, stained red with the proof of her innocence. Stained with the evidence of their passion. He closed his eyes, remembering her sweet whispers, his name on her lips. An iron band encased his heart.

Jabari picked up the soft silk-covered pillow that still bore the indentation of Elizabeth's head. A light rosemary scent wafted from it. He inhaled his wife's fragrance, then buried his face into the pillow and let loose the agony in a muffled howl.

"Elizabeth, you must eat something. Please."

Inside Asriyah's tent, Badra held out a bowl of figs, Elizabeth's favorite fruit. Elizabeth pushed the bowl away. Her stomach pitched. All she could think of was Jabari's venomous expression. He must hate her for her treachery.

"Please, leave me alone." She glanced suspiciously at Badra. "Why aren't you ignoring me like the others do? I'm your enemy."

Badra set the fruit down and reached for her hand. "Your bloodlines have no meaning for me. You are an intelligent, loving woman. You bring joy into Jabari's life. Never have I seen his eyes sparkle so as when he is with you. You are his heart's light."

"I am no light. I've brought only darkness to my husband."

"It is not your fault," Badra insisted.

"I should have known better. I knew Nahid hid something up his sleeve." Elizabeth touched her garment's wide sleeves.

"Are you a shaman? Can you read minds? You must trust in fate, in your destiny. Allah called you here for a purpose. You must believe that, despite what happened."

"What purpose? I see only destruction."

Badra's gaze was even. "Sometimes a thing must be destroyed before it can be built whole again and made stronger."

Elizabeth's shoulders slumped. "You're not making sense."

"There is a saying. 'Ask the experienced rather than the learned.' What were your strongest learning experiences? When you made mistakes. They gave you wisdom. You did not forget."

She put a frustrated hand to her temple. "Yes. I learned the hard way . . . not to trust."

"You put your trust into your uncle because he was your family. Yet now you must place equal trust into a stranger who loves you. He is not of your blood, but Jabari is your mate. And that sacred bond cannot be broken."

"Only if he decrees it. And he must. The tribe will never allow us to remain married." She felt her heart twist at her own words. Once she craved nothing more than freeing herself from the threat of marrying Jabari and sacrificing her freedom. Now that the tribe would let her go, she loved Jabari too much to leave.

"Do not be so quick to judge Jabari," Badra said.

Elizabeth's gaze darted around the tent. They sat in the open space of the tent. The sides were rolled up to allow in the desert breeze. Jabari's other female relatives passed by, smiling at Badra and averting eyes from Elizabeth's gaze.

"How can I not be certain, seeing the way everyone doesn't even look at me? And the guard . . . don't forget him." Elizabeth jerked her head outside where one of Jabari's warriors kept watch, hand on his scimitar.

"Jabari put him there to protect you, not to imprison

you," Badra said. "He fears for your safety."

A warm comforting feeling flowed through her. He still did care. This thought gave her the courage to think. Why would Nahid bring the Almha to the Al-Hajid?

Elizabeth rolled her palm back and forth on her knee. "Badra, why do the Khamsin and the Al-Hajid hate each other?"

Badra lifted her shoulders with a sigh. "I asked this once of Asriyah. She told me that once the two tribes lived peacefully side by side. Then the Al-Hajid began to breed horses. There is not enough desert scrub to support the vast herds. That is when the trouble started."

"Economics, the bane of friendship," Elizabeth murmured.

"For Nkosi, the hatred springs from the love of a woman who rejected him. A woman from the Al-Hajid when he was Khamsin sheikh. They met when he was hunting near their tribal grounds and she was fetching water from the well. They began meeting in secret and became lovers."

Her pulse quickened. Jabari's grandfather had a secret lover from her family's tribe! "Did they ever marry?"

"No. Nkosi loved this woman with all his heart. He was ready to give up his power for her. He gave her a silver necklace as proof of his love. The necklace had a small ankh."

Now her heart skipped its normal cadence. She put a quivering hand on Badra's arm. "What was this woman's name?"

When Badra replied "Jana," Elizabeth stifled a shocked gasp. Her grandmother was Nkosi's secret lover!

"They arranged to meet at the place where they had consummated their love. My grandfather would take her back to our people and marry her. He came at dawn, just as his note to her promised he would, but she never showed. He waited and waited. Heavy-hearted, he rode back to camp—alone," Badra continued.

"What happened to Jana? Did he ever find out?"

"My grandfather made inquiries among the passing caravans. She went to Cairo and married a British officer." Badra frowned. "Since then, his hatred for the Al-Hajid has grown."

"I don't understand. Why didn't she meet him?"

Badra pursed her lips. "The Al-Hajid spread word that she toyed with his affections to insult him, to make him look weak. Perhaps she never really did love him."

"But she did. I know she did!" Elizabeth grasped Badra's arm. "I know, because she still has the necklace he gave her. I know because the woman Nkosi loved is my grandmother!"

Her friend's eyes widened in shock. "It cannot be!"

"Oh yes, it is." Elizabeth explained about the charm she'd found in the trunk, along with the wedding robes. "All this time she saved them. She must have loved him a great deal."

"But why did she never meet him?" Badra put her hand to her heart. Tears filled her pretty brown eyes. "Such a sad story!"

"I don't know. Maybe it was a misunderstanding."

"Perhaps. But look at destiny. It brought her granddaughter back to the Khamsin! It's fate that the two tribes are united."

"United." Elizabeth sniffed. "All I've done is tear them farther apart. I wish I never came to Egypt!"

"You were meant to be here Elizabeth. I know it. That's why I stole your dove." Badra gave her a sheepish smile.

Stole her dove? Elizabeth's suspicions rose. "You took Isis to the camp that day when you left the harem . . . and then you . . ."

"Let her fly to the camp. I knew she was hungry and Nazim was feeding Ghazi. And where do hungry doves go? To food!"

Her spirits lifted and she began to laugh at Badra's clever gambit. "Your *sagr* said nothing?"

Badra gave a coy smile. "I swore him to secrecy. I didn't want you to leave, Elizabeth. When I saw your birthmark that first night, it gave me the idea. I knew Jabari would bed you, for he was sick with hunger for you. And I knew he would discover the birthmark and marry you to fulfill the prophecy."

"Making certain I would stay here and you could learn to read," Elizabeth finished, still laughing. "You are quite clever, dear Badra! So quiet and unassuming, plotting all the while."

Badra stopped smiling. "I learned at an early age to be so. Fareeq stripped my innocence and abused me, but I could not let him destroy my soul. My *ka* was all I had."

She squeezed Badra's hand, marveling at the girl's inner strength. Her own strength returned. Enough self-pity.

"Can I get out of this tent?"

"As I have said, you are no prisoner. However, it's best that I escort you. Where do you wish to go?"

Elizabeth thought quickly. She had to find out first what Jabari and his men planned and when they would strike.

"Badra, I need to see my husband again. I feel as if he has been torn from my side. As though part of my heart is missing." Elizabeth did feel an actual physical ache in her chest.

Badra nodded. "I will help you. I will bring you to Jabari."

Elizabeth thought of that cold blackness in his eyes and shivered. "No, don't bring me to him. I just need to see him. I don't want him . . . to see me." She hung her head.

"Ah . . . you are afraid of what he will say." Badra placed one hand on Elizabeth's shoulder and lifted her chin up with the other. "Come, we will find him. He will be meeting with the Majli and his warriors now. We will be clever in how we do this."

Badra's cheerful grin restored Elizabeth's courage. Outside the guard made as if to accompany them, but Badra raised her hand. Her lower lip pouted prettily and she fluttered her lashes, daring to lean closer than normal protocol dictated. Her breath came in a sultry lisp. Elizabeth watched, dumbfounded.

"Please, it is all right. I will be with her. I know you are a big, strong man who can protect us, but we will be right back."

The guard nodded, a silly smile on his face as though besotted with her. When they were well past him, Elizabeth asked how Badra had easily charmed the guard.

"Flirting is part of the women's way. You learn quickly when you are a young girl that men hold all the power. However, such power can be relinquished . . . using women's wiles."

"I never learned such a lesson," Elizabeth confessed.

Once out of sight, Badra switched directions. Her sandaled feet shuffled dust as they wove behind the line of tents. As they approached the tent where Nkosi interrogated Elizabeth, Badra stopped. She bent her head toward the tent.

"They are not inside yet. But they will be."

Badra walked the length of the tent, then stopped and traced the outline of a small peephole about waist-high from the ground.

"Still here," she said with a satisfied air. "You can see everything, even the hairs on their chins! My *sagr* showed me."

"How convenient."

"I will keep watch for you in case anyone comes."

Elizabeth sank to her knees to peer through the peephole. A few minutes passed. Noises sounded inside. Shuffling boots. Men murmuring. And Jabari's deep, commanding voice calling for order.

Her heart burned with longing as she took in the handsome visage of her husband. His spine as erect as the tent pole, he sat next to Nazim, surrounded by the council and his warriors. Jabari's forceful presence commanded a grace and stature that signified leadership even from a distance. Her eyes drank in his stern, unblinking expression, the finely carved jaw, the lush, full lower lip, the proud straight nose. The previous night those lips had teasingly tormented her with the delights of one hundred kisses. At the moment, they condemned her, forced her from his side.

Her gaze drifted lower to the long, narrow fingers resting upon his knees. How could it be that only last night those hands had worked magic upon her naked skin? How could it be that the man who had been the first inside her body now sat forbidden and distant from her as if thousands of meters separated them?

She must not let her emotions cloud her logic. She must listen with her head. She could listen to her heart later. Elizabeth shook off her thoughts as Jabari began to speak.

"We will attack the day after tomorrow."

The twelve elders nodded their satisfaction as his warriors focused their eyes upon Jabari. "What is your strategy, sire?"

"The enemy will plan for us to retaliate. The Al-Hajid warriors are weakened from the constant raids on the caravans. We shall hit them when they are most vulnerable—at night."

Jabari turned toward a man at his left. "Ahmed, what say you about our enemy? What have you discovered?"

"The Al-Hajid are not united behind their sheikh. The two Majli representing Farris clan called to elect a new sheikh, but Fareeq refuses to give up power. He is backed by Taleq warriors, who outnumber them."

The Farris clan! Her uncle said he was a descendent of Farris warriors. Elizabeth felt fleeting hope. She watched Jabari cock his head, as if this news provided valuable insight. "Ah, a tribe divided by itself is weaker."

"The Farris may not fight if attacked," Ahmed said.

Jabari waved his hand in an abrupt cutting motion. "No matter. They are the enemy. If they raise weapons against us, they will yield their lives. If necessary, I will yield mine. I would gladly die for the honor of securing the sacred Almha."

Murmured approvals swept through the tent. All but Nazim, who frowned as he looked at his sheikh.

"Jabari, such talk reminds me of your father before he raided the caravan and lost his life. We will recover the Almha, but there is no need for talk of your death."

Her husband's next words chilled her bones. "What is life but one stage of existence? If it is my destiny to surrender my spirit, so be it. At least I will die a man, honoring my tribe."

Fear burned in her throat at his words and the lifeless intonation of them. As if he already were dead. Sweat soaked her garments as she thought of life without him. Her Jabari. The man who laid claim to her body and her heart and her life force. Elizabeth shivered, seeing Jabari's merciless expression. He would spare no lives. Including his.

"I wish to hear your thoughts. What have you to say, my men?"

His commanders remained silent, then Nazim spoke.

"The Al-Hajid camp lies many hours south of here. If we use the *wadis* instead of the direct route, it will take more time, but it will allot us surprise. We will attack late at night, striking when they sleep," he stated with blunt assurance.

"To see our enemy fall before our swords. I have longed for this day of revenge!" Nkosi crowed. She knew the Almha wasn't the reason. He must have loved her grandmother very much.

"We ride, Grandfather, not for revenge. Our duty as Khamsin warriors, our ancient oath, is at stake. What honor have we if we do not claim the Almha? Then we are as sheep, bleating in the night, weak and without pride, and the enemy may slay us easily. We take up our swords and fight for Khamsin honor and glory!"

Nkosi nodded, his face grim. "Without honor we are nothing. The war ceremonies will take place tomorrow night."

He darted a glance at his grandson. "Never before have we had to reclaim the Almha. Such a battle calls for the Khamsin sheikh to demonstrate his loyalty and bravery before battle. We must conduct the ceremony of the sacred tattoo."

Jabari's shoulders gave a barely perceptible flinch. "As our ancestors have willed it, so it be done."

Her husband unfolded his muscled body, his eyes glinting fiercely as he raised a fist to the air. "Who will ride with me? Who is willing to die a man, a true warrior of the wind?"

Cheers filled the tent as his commanders rose and stood with their leader, the Majli rising as well. Charisma radiated from him in a powerful aura that she could feel seep through the thick tent walls. His warriors worshiped him. They would follow their leader anywhere, even to the pits of hell.

Elizabeth felt as if she were watching an illusion unfold on stage, a play in which the actors would rise, bow and take their applause. The threatening atmosphere seemed so surreal that if she walked into that tent, the men would fade into a gray mist. Elizabeth stood and jerked her head, motioning to Badra to leave. The two women crept away and walked back to their tent.

Elizabeth thought rapidly as they settled onto the floor. "They are going into battle, the day after tomorrow."

Badra sighed. "Such a battle it will be. Asryiah told me what will happen. The Khamsin have never had to reclaim the Almha. The men will segregate themselves from the women. They will uncover their heads in respect for the ancient ways. In a spirit of brotherhood they will camp away from here. The celebrating will begin at dusk, with much singing and dancing and decorating their bodies with sacred symbols."

"What rituals are these?"

"No woman knows. It would be a tremendous dishonor."

"Perhaps she could view these rituals without being seen." Elizabeth twisted her hair into a knot at her neck.

Badra's horrified expression gave her pause. "Elizabeth! You must not even think such a thing! If you were caught . . . especially now! They could kill you. It is too dangerous."

Elizabeth gave her a wry smile. "I am already disgraced. I must find some way of speaking with Jabari and stopping this. He is ready to sacrifice his life. I can't let him do it."

"You cannot stop a Khamsin warrior from riding into battle," Badra stated. "It's like trying to stop the wind."

"I must try. For my own sake. It's my fault the Almha is gone. I have to take responsibility for my actions. I dishonored Jabari and now he talks of charging into battle foolishly like a man who has lost all hope. He said I deceived him. He thinks I did so to steal the Almha. He thinks I don't love him." Her voice cracked from the emotion raging through it. "But I do. And I can't let this happen."

Badra's glance was ripe with admiration. She pushed a hand through her dark curls. "You have so much spirit. No wonder Jabari chose you. I hope that I may someday have your courage."

"I'm not feeling very brave right now," Elizabeth confessed. "Just desperate. I have to let him know how much I love him."

She considered for a minute and brightened. "I must say though, this will be interesting. Spying on an all-male ritual. Much more daring than marching for women's rights. This will be something I can tell my grandchildren about someday."

"If you make it out alive," Badra said darkly.

Chapter Seventeen

If they found her here, they would kill her. She knew it.

The Khamsin warriors of the wind terrified her with their magnificent displays of deadly force. Bare-chested, bare-headed men clad only in trousers swung scimitars against one another in feigned duels. A bonfire's crackling flames sent immense arcs of black smoke skyward. Wild screams of male fury echoed as steel clashed against steel. From her vantage point inside Jabari's tent, Elizabeth shrank inside her *kuftan,* quivering from the awesome spectacle. These men were savage in their primitive grace. Their faces gleamed with the raging fury of a powerful desert windstorm.

This was no place for a woman. Especially one now so hated and loathed by the tribe. Elizabeth toyed with the idea of sneaking out the way she'd entered, through the back portion of the tent, when she spotted Jabari. As if on cue, men stopped fighting and cleared a path as he engaged Nazim in mock battle.

Jabari's raven hair flew about his shoulders as he leaped forward with explosive speed and precision. Sculpted muscles rippled like golden water as steel screeched against steel. His chiseled profile silhouetted by the glowing fire, Jabari dueled with merciless force.

Nazim fought furiously. His friendly demeanor had vanished. Lips accustomed to laughter now pulled back into a ferocious scowl. Elizabeth's mouth hung open, watching them, two graceful jungle cats tangling in a snarling rage. She squeezed her fingers into her ears, shutting out the violence. Nazim's tigerish grace and agility matched Jabari's. But Jabari roared. Utterly ruthless, he reminded her of a majestic lion determined to overpower. He fought as if powered by an inner force of tremendous energy.

With one move, he sent Nazim toppling to the sand. Men let out an undulating cheer, praising their sheikh's prowess.

"If I were Fareeq, I would be dead by now," Nazim said, his voice ripe with admiration.

"Your sword is far too swift and remorseless to compare to that bloated son of a desert dog," Jabari responded. "How thankful I am for the oath you swore to guard my life. You are too fierce an opponent to be my enemy."

Nazim grinned and clasped Jabari's arm. They drifted to the fire. Warriors sat on sand in a circle, pounding rhythms on *darrabukas*. Flames licked the still night as ominous war chants filled the air.

"Come, let us shed the blood of our enemy. Allah is great and will lead us to victory. Join us, o men of honor."

With the ending of each refrain, the warriors lifted their swords and stabbed the night sky, screaming bloodcurdling war cries and undulating their voices until they became one solid vocal sound, chanting the Khamsin war cry.

Suddenly the singing ceased and the drumbeats stopped. The silence chilled her. Men formed two long lines, their bodies creating a walkway that led to Jabari's tent. Alarmed, she drew back, lest her shadow reveal her presence.

Like a phoenix rising from the flames, Jabari appeared

before the bonfire. With a confident stride, he marched through the human tunnel, preceded by Nazim and Izzah. He steepled his hands, holding them facing downward in front. The little procession headed straight for Jabari's tent.

Elizabeth's eyes darted around the tent. Only a few camel saddles, a simple bedroll and some scattered maps and documents were strewn about the room. *Trapped. No place to hide.*

His two top commanders bore torches in their left hands, and deadly steel in their right. They stopped barely a few feet from the tent. Nazim stabbed his torch into the sand and straightened. His bearded, boyish face looked sinister in the flickering light. Black smears of kohl traced a ritualistic pattern on his cheeks like a bizarre tattoo. War paint. Izzah did the same and both men stood at attention, waiting quietly. Jabari walked between them and halted.

Like the others, his face sported ceremonial black tattoos. His eyes glowed with fervent intensity. Elizabeth shuddered.

A group of men, the same ones who set judgment upon her earlier in the day, and the Majli surrounded her husband in a semicircle. Nazim and Izzah lifted their swords so their tips formed an arch over Jabari's shoulders. Then Nkosi, clad in his indigo robes, his face unmarked, stepped forward and lifted a wicked-looking dagger, its honed edge flashing silver.

Jabari's grandfather stood before his grandson and held the knife with both hands above his head, as if offering it to the night sky as a primitive sacrifice.

"Are you a man? Are you the warrior of your forefathers? What say you? Are you ready to be branded with the mark of the Almha to prove your worth as a true Khamsin sheikh?"

"I am," Jabari answered in a deep voice.

Jabari settled his hands on his hips, thrust out his chest and squared his broad, muscled shoulders, coated with a fine sheen of sweat. His naked chest glistened like highly polished marble in the glowing torchlight. Nkosi raised the blade to his grandson's bare skin.

Elizabeth's hand flew to her mouth to stifle a horrified gasp. She closed her eyes. The lovely fragrance of rosemary she had rubbed against her cheeks, breasts and palms contrasted sharply with the ritual of manhood a few feet away. She peeked out from splayed fingers. Jabari's nostrils flared and his lips slashed into a firm line.

After what seemed like an age, Nkosi finished, wiped his dagger on a clean cloth and stood back. Nazim and Izzah lowered their swords. Each approached Jabari and fell to their knees before him, bowing their heads. They then stepped back, raising the blades into the air with a shrill cry.

"A true Khamsin warrior has shed his blood for our cause! May his courage give swiftness to our blades to strike down our enemies! Let us honor his strength and defeat our enemies! Death to the Al-Hajid!"

An ensuing whoop rippled down the tunnel of men as they raised their scimitars into the air in unison and let loose a blood-curdling war cry.

The cries and solemn ritual sent a preternatural shiver down her spine. This was real. Men would fight and die all in the name of honor. Would Jabari's life end with the cruel, swift stroke of an Al-Hajid blade from one of her own family?

Her hands shook uncontrollably. Great choking sobs rose from her throat as she envisioned life without him. Empty. As dead as the sands she had longed to excavate.

In her eagerness to explore the past, Elizabeth had missed all the gifts the present had to offer. Life, in the form of the man she loved, stood before her.

While his heart still beat inside him, she had to find a way of stopping this. A great war between the two ancient enemies would commence. She knew Jabari would sacrifice himself to restore his tribe's honor. And all because of her . . . because she let Nahid escape with the Almha. It was her fault. Somehow, some way, she had to remand the situation. But how?

Ride south now. Steal the Almha back from Nahid. Use your woman's wiles. Remember what Badra said.

She was a member of the Farris clan. Somehow she had to reclaim the Almha. Even if it meant risking her life.

The little group turned and walked back toward the bonfire as the men dispersed. All but Jabari. He walked straight toward his tent. Elizabeth scrambled to the back, diving behind the camel saddles, hoping the shadows offered some protection. She waited, peeping out behind one, watching as he ducked inside, carrying a torch. He stuck it into the ground and crossed the room, passing her. His eyes blazed as black and fierce as the ritual tattoos on his angular cheeks. Bending over, he dug into a small goatskin bag and withdrew a towel. Fascinated, she watched the glowing torchlight cast dancing shadows across the banded muscles rippling across his bare back. This man was her husband, a powerful desert warrior whose body was lean with whipcord strength.

At that moment, Elizabeth felt her heart leap in her chest at the sheer beauty of him, the proud virility. She believed he could battle the demons of hell and they would run in fright.

Suddenly he whipped his powerful body around, turning toward her. Jabari cocked his head, listening. Elizabeth pressed herself tightly against the rigid wood saddle.

"Elizabeth?"

She made no sound, dared not draw in a breath.

"Elizabeth? I know you are here. I smell your rosemary. Come out," he ordered in a quiet, but commanding voice.

She stepped out into the circle of light, sucking in her breath, hoping her plan would work. Badra said women's defenses were charm and wiles. Elizabeth wasn't sure how to be charming or wily, but she did possess two very formidable physical weapons, a left and right one. Tonight she planned to use both to her advantage.

Lifting the loose indigo *kuftan* over her head, she

dropped it to the ground. The sapphire-blue gown beneath the heavy covering glowed like a fine jewel in the dim light. Its sheer gauze barely hid her breasts from his startled gaze.

His hand shot to the bleeding tattoo on his chest. Jabari covered it as if her viewing it desecrated his mark of honor.

"You are forbidden from being here and witnessing the sacred ceremonies. Get out now before I release my wrath on you. I warn you, Elizabeth. I will not tolerate your disrespect." His deep voice chilled her to the bone with its iced fury.

She cringed, but held her ground. "Badra told me women cannot witness these ceremonies. But I had to see you," Elizabeth replied in a hushed voice. No sympathy from that tower of granite. Arms folded, he stood looking down at her, his face chiseled from solid ice.

"I had to see you, Jabari. I could not wait any longer. Please listen to me. I did not fool you to steal the Almha. I love you, Jabari. I have for a long time but denied it."

He made a sharp, dismissive gesture. Jabari wiped his chest with the towel. Broad shoulders flexed as he threw down the cloth. The fierce desert warrior fixed her with a steely stare. "Why should I believe you? If not for your treacherous uncle betraying you, you would have fled into the night." *Leaving me.* She heard the unspoken words as clearly as if he uttered them. They hung in the air, slapping her with the depth of his pain.

Deep within the frozen depths of those beautiful dark eyes lurked haunting shadows. Her breath hitched in a sob.

"Why else would I be foolish enough to risk coming here, knowing what a danger it was?" she whispered. "I cannot bear losing you. If I lose you, I lose my life force. My *ka* has blended with yours and cannot be extinguished unless your *ka* is gone out forever as well."

Some of the black ice in his eyes thawed, giving her the courage to continue.

"I will never leave you. I am a woman and hungry for

your love. I could not stay away from you. I love you, my husband."

She reached out and grabbed his fingertips. Elizabeth rubbed them against her soft, supple cheek, knowing her womanly scent would stain his warrior's hand.

Rigid shoulders relaxed. Black pupils dilated in the torchlight. Lips that had narrowed into a strained line softened into sensual curves as his mouth parted slightly. Closing his eyes, he raised her hand to his face, inhaling her fragrance. His Adam's apple bobbed as he swallowed. Jabari released his fingers from beneath hers and traced the outline of the gown. Elizabeth shuddered with need as he caressed her breasts with sultry slowness.

Then he jerked his hand away as if touching a scorpion's stinger. "Elizabeth," he said in a hoarse whisper, "leave. I am forbidden from touching you. Tomorrow night we ride into battle."

She grasped his hand in a pleading gesture. "Please, don't go. You must not ride against the Al-Hajid!"

He grasped her arms and leaned close, pinning her to the floor with the strength of his piercing gaze. "Why not? Is this another plea to save your uncle, that lying snake?"

"Jabari," Elizabeth faltered under the force of that cold stare. She summoned courage and continued. "Jabari, why would I save him when he betrayed me? Please listen. I can try to convince Nahid to give the Almha back. You must believe that I didn't know Nahid belonged to Al-Hajid until he stole the Almha. His clan is Farris, the same ones opposing the Al-Hajid sheikh!"

Jabari's upper lip curled. "And how did you know the Farris clan opposes the sheikh? I see you have been eavesdropping."

She drew back a step from his sudden hostility. "I only did so to try to figure out a way to help you."

"Help me?" he echoed.

The sheer incredulity in his voice irritated her. "Yes, just because I have breasts does not mean I lack a brain!" Elizabeth bit her offending tongue. *So much for a woman's charm.*

She took a long, controlling breath. "Jabari, I will do anything to help you. Please don't act as if I am an object you can shuttle aside, a stone without feeling." In a daring move, she took his palm and placed it against her breast.

"Can you feel my heart beating? It beats with love for you, my husband, my one and only love," she said softly, her eyes gazing up into his. "Your men call me a curse and say I have a lying heart. If I must, I will walk out onto the plain and shout to them that I will go reclaim the Almha. I will tell them I do so because I love you with all my heart. And if they killed me for violating the sacred ceremonies, at least I would know I died for love."

Still the impassive rock, the cold look of disbelief as he removed his hand. Very well then. Her words made no difference. Elizabeth swallowed her fear. She would prove it. Turning on her heel, she started for the tent door, steeling her spine. Jabari's men hated her. They would probably kill her for what she did to their beloved leader.

She grasped the tent door to pull it aside. Elizabeth said a silent prayer for courage, swallowed hard. She lifted the tent flap and blinked away warm tears.

Two strong, warm hands settled on her shoulders, pulling her away, forcing her to face him again. Jabari touched the edge of her eye, tracing the trail of tears with his forefinger. With extreme gentleness, he wiped them away.

"I am only a simple woman and know not of clever things such as battle and men's honor and courage. All I know is that I love you," she whispered brokenly.

"You are anything but a simple woman. Far from it," he replied in a husky voice. "With you by my side, I could conquer one thousand enemies. You have more courage than my bravest warrior."

Elizabeth tilted her head up to his and dared to clasp his forearms. She slid her palms across the glistening, sculpted muscles. With a half-groan, half-sigh, he lowered his head, his long dark hair curtaining the sides of his face. Jabari brushed his lips against hers as his arms slid around her waist.

"I love you, my husband," she whispered into his mouth, cradling the back of his neck. "Even if you push me from your side, I will never cease loving you. I made a pledge. You are the mate of my heart, the love of all my days past and forever."

"And you are the one chosen for me. I will protect and defend you until my dying days, pledging my love only to you," Jabari responded softly. He kissed her and all her torment fled in a whoosh of relief so deep she sagged against him for support.

A rustling of the tent flap pulled them apart like two swift hands. Jabari's head jerked toward the entrance as Nkosi stormed inside. His grandfather's lean, wrinkled face contorted with silent fury upon seeing Elizabeth. Nkosi crossed the room and raised a fist as if to strike her.

Immediately Jabari jumped in front of Elizabeth.

"Leave her alone," he said in a low, threatening growl.

Elizabeth peered around Jabari's arm. The old man trembled as his face flushed crimson. He narrowed his eyes.

"You dare to desecrate our sacred rituals of manhood. For this, you shall be punished."

Jabari spread out his arms as if to erect a barricade between his wife and the threat, but Elizabeth stepped from behind her husband. Nkosi grunted.

"I see she has been softening you with her weeping. Beware, my grandson. A woman's weapon is her tears. Do not trust her."

"I am not afraid of you anymore," Elizabeth stated, wiping her eyes. "I came to tell Jabari I love him. Nothing will ever erase him from my heart. No matter what you do to me, I will always love Jabari. Always."

She met him stare for stare. Tension hung in a thick cloud until a smile tugged at the wrinkled corners of Nkosi's lips.

"Such a brave, determined spirit. A warrior's heart hidden by a woman's softness. You remind me . . . so much of someone I once knew," he said softly. To her amazement, an expression of grief crossed his face. His shoulders slumped. The fierce old man seemed to struggle with deep-raging emotions. Then he gathered his control and resumed his proud stance.

Nkosi stepped back, dropping his fist. He sniffed.

"Bid him good-bye then. Do it quickly and leave before anyone else sees you. I will . . . let this slip. I was not here."

He turned to leave, then looked over his shoulder. His voice lowered to a prophetic rumble.

"But know this. My grandson rides into battle tomorrow night because you have put the Almha in our enemy's hands. If his blood is shed, it will be upon you."

Jabari picked up her *kuftan* as Nkosi ducked out of the tent. He handed it to her without looking.

"Elizabeth, go back to the women's tents. Do as I say now."

Elizabeth gave a brief nod, sadness engulfing her once more. As she slipped past him, he reached out and caught her arm. Brushing his lips against her hand, he looked down at her, sudden emotion clouding his gaze.

"So then. Do you not have one last good-bye kiss for a warrior riding off into battle? For a husband . . . who loves you with all his heart?"

Elizabeth rushed against him, lifting her face. His lips against hers were hard, fierce, demanding. Desperate need and aching longing rippled through her. She felt the echoing emotions in her husband as he wrapped his arms around her waist in a bone-crushing embrace as if he hated to let her go.

Releasing his grip, Jabari grasped her upper arms and kissed the top of her nose, then strode out of the tent, not looking back. Elizabeth bit her lip and started to tug on the *kuftan*. A strange wetness nestled against her upper body.

She glanced down at her gown and shuddered. Their passionate embrace imprinted Jabari's tattoo upon the bare skin above her bodice. Nkosi's warning rang true. His blood would be upon her.

She hunted for the towel Jabari had tossed down, grimacing as she wiped off the blood. It would not happen again. She had the power to stay their weapons, to prevent any more bloodshed. Elizabeth's gaze darted about the room. The maps!

She scanned them quickly, noting one had marks indicating various water holes and a route to the Al-Hajid camp. Tucking it into her bodice, she quickly donned the *kuftan* and silently crept out of the tent's back side. She needed a change of clothing, a saddled horse, some provisions and prayers. And a veil. Khamsin women went unveiled, but she had no idea what customs the Al-Hajid embraced. Better to go to them as humbly as possible.

With luck, she'd reach the Al-Hajid camp just after dawn.

Chapter Eighteen

"She's gone!"

Jabari looked up from his map, seething with irritation at the sound of a woman's shrill cry. Anger caved into shock as Badra rushed in and gave a quick bow before the assembled commanders. Winding her way through the men, she finally reached Jabari and fell on her knees before him.

"Badra, what are you doing here? You had better have an excellent reason," Jabari demanded. For Badra to dare to risk coming took tremendous courage. Or a horrible motivation . . .

She lay at a crumbled mass at his feet as if fearing to move. Tension gripped his shoulders. The ritual cleansing that washed the tattoos and was supposed to purify his spirit, brought him no peace. The previous night he tossed in his sleep. Elizabeth's rosemary scent lingered in the tent, haunting his dreams, watering down the blood fever he needed to charge into battle.

"Badra," he said in gentler tone, "what is it?"

"Jabari, please forgive me for intruding, but you must

know this!" Badra beseeched him, looking up. She gulped, her dark brown eyes wide with worry. "Elizabeth has fled!"

Her words slapped the breath from him. Jabari felt blood drain from his face as he dropped the map.

"When did you find this out?"

"Just this morning. I had thought her still sleeping . . . she left clothing crumbled up under her bedding with a blanket. Then I checked the horses. Her white mare is missing."

Looking around the mass of scattered maps, he realized one was missing. Elizabeth went to reclaim the Almha. Thoughts of her, alone in the desert, riding to the very men whose lives they would take, hammered at his heart. *Think like a warrior. Do not let emotion cloud your judgment! It will not save her!*

"Elizabeth has nearly a day's start on us and most likely has reached the camp," he mused. "We cannot catch her now, no matter how swiftly we ride."

"Good. She returns to the enemy. To her own. Why should we care what happens to that woman?" came one grunted reply.

Jabari's voice lowered to a threatening rumble. "That woman is my wife. Do not forget it."

His feelings for Elizabeth brought his emotions bubbling to the surface. He glanced at Nazim, his face a neutral mask.

"If we mounted an attack on horseback, leaving the camels behind . . . we could reach the camp faster."

"And the mares would be tired and unable to charge swiftly," Nazim's even reply came.

Hearing his second-in-command say it drove home the futility of chasing after her. Jabari grit his teeth and looked at Badra. Tension tightening her brow reflected his own inner turmoil.

Izzah, sitting nearby, asked to be heard. "Sire, I speak with the greatest respect. To ride now would be foolhardy. We must attack at night. Our quest is to recover the sacred

Almha. You cannot change plans for the sake of a woman."

"Especially not a traitor," another warrior muttered.

"She is no traitor," Jabari snapped. "Elizabeth did not betray us. Does anyone believe that?"

"I do," Nazim said quietly. But no one else answered.

Jaban's chest tightened at his men's sullen looks. To them, Elizabeth was the enemy. He wanted to rush out, saddle Sahar and gallop into the desert to claim his bride. But he was Khamsin chief, on the warpath against her family. And responsibility hobbled his own personal needs. As sheikh, his men came first. Jabari glanced at Nkosi, who signaled him to go outside.

Once outside, Nkosi paced a distance from the tent. Never had he seen his stately grandfather this agitated. His eyes glazed over as he stared into the distance. Finally, he spoke.

"Jabari, do not make the same mistake I did years ago. Go rescue your wife. Do whatever it takes, if you love her."

Shocked, he could only stare as he continued. Nkosi sucked in a noisy breath. "All these years, despite my affections for my wife, I had not forgotten my Jana or the love we shared. I should have gone after her. I should have led a *ghazu* against the Al-Hajid, but my foolish pride led me to believe she changed her mind about wanting me. Her granddaughter has her spirit, her fire, her love of life." He glanced up. "Your wife. Elizabeth."

His jaw dropped. Jabari could only stare in staggering disbelief. "How do you know this for certain?"

"The papyrus she found. I gave it to Jana. It is the only explanation for how Elizabeth found it. And when she confessed her grandmother was a Bedouin from the Al-Hajid, I knew."

He watched the proud old man fight to rein in his emotions. "Think with your heart, Jabari. Is the love of a woman worth surrendering your position as sheikh? I once thought it was."

Turning, he waved his hand. "Go back to your men now.

You will know what to do. I trust your judgment, my grandson."

Torn between wanting to comfort his grandfather and the need to attend to business, Jabari watched Nkosi walk away. Deeply troubled, he ducked back inside the tent. Resuming his seat, he looked at his men who awaited his word.

He spoke up, knowing what the answer would be even as his lips uttered the question.

"Besides Nazim, who will ride now to rescue her?"

Dead silence settled over the men. Jabari stood. Deep in his heart, he knew what he must do. His soul felt torn asunder as he contemplated his next action. He beckoned to Nazim. His second-in-command stood, a puzzled look of concern on his face.

Jabari reached down at his waist and withdrew his scimitar from its sheath. He stared at it a minute, lovingly stroking the dull edge of the blade. His father's sword, passed down through the generations to each successive sheikh. More than a weapon, the sword signified power and authority. For generations, the Hassid family had ruled the Khamsin tribe.

No longer. Jabari closed his eyes, feeling his heart shatter with the weight of his decision. But he could not leave Elizabeth in the hands of the Al-Hajid a minute longer.

"I am Khamsin sheikh and sworn to uphold our people's honor and guard them from all danger. I am also sworn to protect my bride. If no one will accompany me, I will ride alone to reclaim her. I do not do this as sheikh and leave my people leaderless. So Nazim, I pass the command of the tribes to you."

Shocked murmurs swept throughout the tent. Badra stared at him with widened eyes. He handed the ivory handle of his scimitar to his friend. Nazim stared at the blade. His jaw tightened. But he did not take the sword.

"Sire, I cannot. I will not."

"You must."

"Jabari, you will be killed! What good will that do Elizabeth?" Nazim's breath eased out in a frustrated, angry hiss.

"I have no choice. I pledged my oath to protect her. Every minute she is in their hands risks her life. She is my beloved and I must rescue her."

"You would risk your life, give up your leadership for a woman?" Izzah stood, his jaw dropping in disbelief.

"For my heart's desire, yes," Jabari replied quietly.

"The life of one woman is not worth the life of our sheikh. Women are inferior," another cried out.

"The life of one woman is certainly worth the life of a sheikh. Women in our tribe have as much value as warriors. Elizabeth has more courage than anyone I know. She risks her life to recover our sacred disk, although she is not bound by honor as we are. I say that does not make her inferior to men. Indeed, it makes her superior to all the men here."

Nazim drew his eyebrows together in a dark scowl. He whirled and faced the commanders with a look of contempt. "You cannot pass leadership on to me. I will not let you go alone. Give your blade to one of them."

Silence reigned. Finally Izzah grunted. "Do not pass it on to me. I ride also. You are right, sire. The life of one woman is worth the life of a sheikh. And my life as well." He looked at the rest of the commanders.

Almost in unison, they stood. "We respect your decision, sire. We will ride with you. We shall have no commander but you, Jabari bin Tarik Hassid," one said.

Overwhelming gratitude filled every pore. Jabari nodded briefly and sheathed his sword. The intensity of the moment, the fidelity of his warriors and the stubborn loyalty of Nazim filled him with pride. He felt as if his heart would swell and burst.

"Besides," Nazim said, his usual grin back in place, "I never liked that sword of yours. It has a nick on the blade."

Jabari smiled and clapped a hand on his friend's shoulder. "Ready the horses and camels. We leave shortly."

* * *

Elizabeth glanced around the tent's interior, her heart racing faster than her horse's hooves had pounded over the rocky sands earlier. Sequestered in the enemy's camp! Yet this was her family. Doubt, confusion and anxiety wrestled for control. She inhaled deeply. *You are the wife of a warrior now. How would Jabari act? Would he show fear? Would he let these men intimidate him? I think not!*

Shortly after dawn she had arrived at the camp, exhausted, stripped of defenses, her horse weary and parched. Two men had approached her. Clad in cloaks with striations of black and scarlet, they carried long scimitars pointed straight at her.

The noble idea of taking the Almha back to the Khamsin deflated upon seeing the Al-Hajid warriors' formidable weapons. Charm and women's wiles had little defense against solid steel.

After speaking to them quickly in Arabic, she told them of her uncle and begged hospitality, asking to see Nahid. They escorted to her the watering hole, then through the camp. Dozens of tents peppered the rocky sands. The warriors took her straight to the largest tent—the sheikh's, she presumed.

Now she sat alone on a worn carpet. Perspiration rolled off her brow as she wondered about the foolhardy move she'd just made. They were her family, but she did not even know them.

A rustling noise drew her eyes to the tent flap. Elizabeth sat straighter, adjusted her blue veil firmly across her nose and concealed her trembling hands beneath the sleeves of her *kuftan*.

She must not show fear. No matter what.

"Elizabeth! What are you doing here?"

"Uncle Nahid!" Relief flooded her limbs. "I think you know why I'm here. I came to take back the Almha."

Dressed in a white turban and crimson *thobe,* her uncle looked every part the desert dweller. His scowling expression did little to appease her worry. Nahid dropped to the floor beside her.

"Sheikh Fareeq ordered me to his tent. I doubt it is for a long-awaited family reunion. Where are the Khamsin?"

"Back at camp. I came alone. I do not need their intervention. And I pray I can stop this war before it starts."

"You cannot," came his haughty reply. "The Al-Hajid are prepared to defend themselves."

"Just answer me one thing. Why did you take it?"

Nahid's ire deflated as his shoulders slumped. He buried his head into his hands. "All those years growing up in Egypt, I longed to emulate the Al-Hajid. After I returned from Oxford, I finally initiated contact with our clan. Although they accepted me, the sheikh did not. For twenty years, I tried to win him over. Then Flinders hired me to begin the Amarna dig. And you cabled how you found the papyrus. I told Fareeq. He said if I brought him the Almha as proof of my fidelity, the Al-Hajid would welcome me back."

Her heart ached with pity for the little boy he once was, a boy who had struggled for acceptance by his tribe. "That's why you hired them to protect the dig site."

"Yes. I originally hired warriors from our clan, but Fareeq's warriors took over. They hold the power in the tribe. It is a dangerous situation, Elizabeth, especially now that you are here. Fareeq hates the Khamsin. The blood hatred runs deep."

"I know about Nana's affair with Nkosi."

Nahid's face filled with fury. "He sent a message to her to meet him at midnight. He never showed up."

Something didn't add up. "I heard he was to meet her at dawn, not midnight."

Nahid sighed deeply. "A group of warriors came to escort my mother back to the tribe as she waited for her lover. She was to marry the sheikh's son. He discovered her adultery and threatened her life. She fled to Cairo with a passing caravan."

Elizabeth's fleeting sympathy for her uncle turned to panic. She had not known Nana was betrothed to the sheikh's father.

Perspiration soaked her *kuftan* as droplets rolled down her back. "Uncle Nahid, we are in trouble. I didn't know Nana was the sheikh's intended! She was Nkosi's lover, so that makes her . . ."

"An adulteress." He did not look at her. "Under their laws, the sheikh could execute her. They have not forgotten. Nor does his family easily forgive such an insult."

She sucked in her breath, striving to think. "We must come up with a plan. The Khamsin are on the warpath. They are determined to reclaim the Almha."

"Our only hope is that our clan opposes the sheikh."

Elizabeth repressed a shudder. "If they fight against the sheikh, on the side of the Khamsin . . ."

Nahid glanced up. "There might be a chance. Taleq warriors assassinated the two Majli representing our clan to prevent them from electing a new sheikh. No one dares speak up now."

"Nahid, you must organize those who oppose Fareeq, then ride out and warn the Khamsin. You must make amends for your crime."

Some of his old antagonism returned as he sniffed. "My loyalties lie with the Al-Hajid. I cannot deny my people."

"What are you denying if . . ." Elizabeth cut her sentence off as voices sounded outside the tent. She placed her hands meekly onto her lap. A stout, squarish man dressed in loose trousers, a flowing white cloak, *kamis* shirt and a checkered *kaffayh* upon his head swaggered inside, several armed men trailing behind him. Fareeq bin Hamid Talib. Elizabeth and Nahid bowed their heads.

She judged him to be an older man, perhaps in his late fifties, with jowls and a large paunch. Elizabeth found herself comparing his softness to Jabari's tough, leanly muscled body. The sheikh seemed as insubstantial as tapioca pudding. But his eyes were small yellowish orbs that radiated evil. A festering, moldy odor rose from him, a mixture of stale tobacco, sour camel's milk and old sweat. Elizabeth found her gaze fixated on a few circular stains on his right sleeve. Yogurt and date juice. She could read his breakfast menu from his clothing.

He made no sound of greeting, only snorted as he sat on the floor on a broad cushion. Elizabeth wondered why he bothered with a cushion at all, as his plump posterior offered plenty of protection from the hard sand.

"Another member of the Farris clan has returned to us. Woman, I waste no time with polite courtesies, especially for the wife of my enemy," Fareeq said.

Elizabeth's jaw dropped in shock. "How do you know of my marriage?" She eyed him with growing misgiving.

He uttered a wicked, low chuckle that grated on her raw nerves like sandpaper rasping against chalkboard. "Your uncle so kindly supplied me with a warning that his niece's husband would lead an attack against our people to reclaim the Almha."

Nahid had the grace to look shamefaced as Elizabeth shot him a vicious glance.

"Foolish man. Nahid thought he could win his way over to my favor by giving us the Almha and sharing information. But I do not make pacts with Farris jackals."

Giving her a sly wink, Fareeq leered at her. "But your body is most becoming and I may bestow mercy upon you if you share my bed and pleasure me enough. If you beg now, I may consider mercy. Beg, granddaughter of the female dog who dishonored my family."

Elizabeth recoiled with disgust. Calling her grandmother a dog constituted a grave insult in Arabic. By the sneer on Fareeq's face, he knew she knew this. Suggesting she could share his bed was far worse.

A purplish tongue snaked out from between his lips as he slid it over his lower lip. She grimaced behind her veil. Those rolls of flesh about his expansive stomach, his pudgy hands groping her . . . Elizabeth thought of how skilled Jabari had been in making love to her, gentle with her innocence, yet passionate.

Her old defiance returned. Determined to show this man

she was no female who cowered before him, she did the unthinkable.

With a calm hand Elizabeth reached up and removed her veil, tossing it to the tent floor. A collective grumbling went up among the sheikh's men, but it was his reaction she watched. His deep-set, cruel eyes flashed anger. Good. She wasn't going to endure insults any longer. She thought about what Farah had said.

"I've heard from your former concubine about your . . . manhood—or should I say lack thereof?" Elizabeth said and held her thumb and forefinger barely an inch apart. "I'd rather eat camel dung than sleep with you, you fat pig," she said.

Fareeq's eyes narrowed to slits. "You display the same insolence as your grandmother. She was to be my father's wife. But like a woman, she was weak and wanton. She dared to mock my family by committing adultery with our enemy!"

"You call it thus, but I say to you it was love. I am certain my grandmother did not intentionally set out to shame your father," Elizabeth responded.

"Love!" he spat the word out like an olive pit. "What matter is love for marriage? Jana dishonored my father. Had she not slipped out of his grasp, he would have beheaded her."

"Thank Allah she did escape. And if she had not, better she die than be enslaved to such a brutal beast!"

Fareeq shook with murderous outrage, making the rolls of flesh on his enormous stomach quiver like jelly. Nahid put a cautioning hand on her arm. "Elizabeth, do you want to get us killed?" he hissed in English.

Fareeq smiled like a plump cat that swallowed the canary as an appetizer and eyed the bird's brothers and sisters for dinner.

"Somehow, I think that whatever I say will not make a difference," she replied in Arabic. "He already had his mind made up what to do with me from the moment I walked in here."

"Oh, you are so correct, worthless granddaughter of a treacherous whore. You have walked directly into my trap." He rubbed his fat hands together. "Having the whore's son here at my disposal was revenge enough. But to have her granddaughter—another worthless dog, the bride of my enemy—helpless at my feet! Allah has granted me a rare gift!"

His cheeks pulled back in a smile that made him uglier than the frown he'd worn previously. Beady eyes gleamed with malevolence. "Today my father will be avenged of his disgrace when the infidel granddaughter of Jana al-Farris suffers the punishment her grandmother escaped!"

He snapped his fingers and barked to his men. "Take her to her family's tent. Guard her closely. She will be punished. Thirty lashes. And when the Khamsin attack, vengeance is mine!"

His sinister laugh raked claws of fear over her raw nerves. "What a treat for your husband. He will ride into our camp and when he does, he will be greeted by the sight of his lovely bride . . . as my sword beheads her."

Chapter Nineteen

Helpless to protect her, Elizabeth's newfound relatives sat with her in the tent in silent mourning while Al-Hajid warriors stood guard outside. Elizabeth smiled at the dozen or so women who came to greet her and pay their last respects.

The tent flap opened and another woman entered. Short and rather stout, she was clad in a thick black *abbaya* and heavy veil. Elizabeth gazed at her. Was this a cousin?

"Peace be upon you," she said, holding out her hands.

"And upon you, my niece."

Elizabeth gasped as Nahid jerked back his veil. Her female relatives smiled at her reaction.

"It was the women's idea." Nahid smiled and wrapped the heavy veil around his face once more. "How do I look?"

"Definitely tempting," Elizabeth smirked, trying to lift her spirits by joking. "If you sway your hips just right, maybe Fareeq will carry you off to his tent."

"I'd rather die first," Nahid shot back.

Elizabeth smiled, then sobered, remembering the fate awaiting her at Fareeq's hands.

Nahid touched her hand. "Don't fret. I convinced the warriors in our clan to fight with the Khamsin. I will leave here pretending to fetch fresh water and seek Jabari. I can't save you alone. I pray he can."

She nodded, feeling sudden hope. If anyone could rescue her, it was a Khamsin warrior of the wind. Not just any Khamsin warrior, but one whose heart was brave and true. And hopefully, that heart still beat with love for her.

It had been a hard day's ride from the north on the dromedaries and now at last they had reached their destination.

About two kilometers from the enemy camp at a watering hole hidden in one of the twisting *wadis*, Khamsin warriors dismounted and watered their animals. Tethering their camels together, they attended to the horses that would lead the battle charge.

Decked in full battle gear, Sahar pranced and shook her head. Tassels dyed in rich gold, crimson and indigo on her silk bridle danced with her movements. Similar tassels and tiny silver circles resembling the sun decorated the indigo breast piece, which was embroidered with costly gold thread in an intricate design. A blue velvet saddle cloth encrusted with silver held a saddle with wide stirrups and a high pommel.

Hundreds of Khamsin warrior horses, similarly decorated, snorted with impatience. Jabari checked the scimitar and dagger at his waist. He wrapped his veil across his cheeks, leaving only his eyes exposed. He then squatted to the ground and beat out a throbbing war rhythm on his *darrabuka* in the ancient ceremony to call his horse to his side. Sahar pranced, lifting her front hooves. By beating the instruments, the Khamsin's eerie drumbeats raised the blood fever necessary to lead the battle charge.

Jabir called to Nazim and Izzah, and the trio rode off to scout out the enemy camp, hugging the mountains instead of riding in open desert. A short distance away, Jabari held up his hand to stop. They dismounted. He withdrew a spyglass from his *binish.*

Suddenly a distant dust cloud swirled and took shape as the pounding of galloping hoofbeats neared. His eyes narrowed and he tucked the spyglass into his *binish*. Unsheathing the scimitar, he held it high, ready to attack. The lone horseman neared and halted. A woman clad in a heavy black *abbaya* and veil dismounted.

She flung herself in the sand, prostrating before him and then tore off the veil. Jabari nearly dropped his sword in shock.

"My lord, I throw myself upon your mercy," Nahid pleaded.

Bemused, Jabari shook his head. Elizabeth's uncle dressed as a woman! He recalled how he'd first met his wife—dressed as a man. Did all Farris clan members go about dressing as the opposite gender? Was it some strange tribal ritual in their blood?

"Get up, man, and take off that ridiculous garb."

Nahid stood and tore off the *abbaya*, revealing wide trousers and a *kamis* shirt. "Fareeq plans to kill Elizabeth."

Jabari raised his scimitar and pointed it at Nahid's chest. "This had better not be another one of your treacherous tricks, or I will gladly end your life now!"

Nahid's dark, hooded eyes shot back and forth as Nazim and Izzah gathered near Jabari in a semicircle. "I swear to you, I would not risk my own life for such a ruse. Fareeq has declared blood vengeance upon Elizabeth for her grandmother's crime."

Jabari studied him, hiding his mounting anxiety. "Go on."

Urgency gave Nahid's voice an arrogant tone. "My clan voted to remove Fareeq, but Taleq warriors outnumber our men and protect the sheikh. My relatives cannot save Elizabeth. Fareeq will beat and execute her today as you attack."

The thought of that sly jackal daring to lay a hand on his wife filled Jabari with possessive fury. With a snarl, he twirled the blade in the air, gloating at the idea of parting

Fareeq's head from his body. "Not if I have anything to do with it."

"Fareeq is expecting you, but you still have the advantage. I convinced my clan to fight against him and join your men."

Jabari considered his words and turned to Izzah. "Watch him. I do not trust this one. Nazim, come with me."

The two men climbed the mountain, clambering over the craggy rocks until they reached a height that satisfied Jabari. Black tents dotted the horizon. He withdrew his spyglass and scanned the camp, hoping against hope for some sight of Elizabeth.

Like most desert camps, tents were erected in a elongated line facing one another with plenty of space between them. He spotted a large campfire in the middle of the camp. Nearby, a tall wooden pole with a cruel hook near its top stretched to the sky. Jabari knew it well. He'd heard stories spread through the desert, indeed, even from his own concubines, of Fareeq's favorite pastime. The sheikh used the pole to publicly whip those who displeased him, then left the prisoner hanging by his bonds to wither in the blazing sun.

His pulse thundered in horror. Tied to the pole, her long, slender arms stretched above her head, was Elizabeth. Clad only in the barest gown, her body pressed against the stake.

The Al-Hajid sheikh approached her. Fareeq reached up and ripped the gown from Elizabeth's shoulders, baring her body to the waist. She did not bend nor hide her head, but lifted her chin to him as if to scoff at his improper lack of manners. Aching pride in her spirited response jostled for space in Jabari's heart with anguish. Jabari drew a heavy breath as Fareeq fondled her bare breast with a rough hand and laughed. White-hot wrath, as burning as the scorching sands, filled Jabari's core.

Fareeq held a long, sinewy length of leather whip. Jabari's heart split as the whip slashed the air. He lowered the spyglass, clutched in white-knuckled agony.

At Nazim's troubled glance, Jabari responded in a low tone, "He is going to whip her. I must go now."

His best friend's nostrils flared. Nazim pulled back his lips in a vicious snarl that made Jabari draw back with surprise. As many times as he had fought with Nazim in battle, had seen his blood rage as he sliced down the enemy with ruthless precision, never had he witnessed such a change in his friend. It was like seeing a friendly puppy turn into a vicious wolf. Nazim reached for the handle of his scimitar in a sudden move.

"Let me go, sire. I will slay this dog of the desert who strikes your wife, our queen. My blade cries out for his blood."

"No, friend. It is my duty. You will lead the battle charge and fight while I save Elizabeth."

"I am your Guardian. My protection extends to you and Elizabeth. I will not leave your side."

"You are also my second-in-command and my fiercest warrior. I need your skills on the battlefield to lead my men."

Nazim sighed deeply. "Very well. What about Nahid?"

"I will deal with him. If the others are truly aligned against Fareeq, we shall use them." Jabari clenched his fists. "If not, they die. I will spare none."

Nazim glanced at Jabari's scimitar. He fingered the rifle dangling from his shoulder. All warriors carried one except Jabari. "You must take a gun, Jabari. The Al-Hajid are sly dogs who will shoot you as we charge into camp."

Jabari scowled. "Men of honor use swords, not bullets."

"Fine, you have honor. Jabari, take a gun," Nazim repeated in an exasperated voice.

Jabari laid a hand on Nazim's shoulder. "I am the tribe's leader and must lead by example. Sahar is swift and I have the advantage of you leading my men. Do not worry, my friend."

"You leave me much to worry about," Nazim grumbled. "You are fearless, but reckless. Do you plan to charge blindly through camp toward Elizabeth, presenting yourself as an open target?"

Jabari shot his best friend an irritated look. "Use Nahid to set the front tents ablaze, then I will ride in from the opposite direction as you charge. The diversion will give us the advantage while people try to extinguish the fire."

Nazim cocked his head. "Better yet, split off with several warriors. Surround them from both sides as the fire spreads."

He nodded, thankful for Nazim's cool judgment. How could he forget such a simple battle strategy? He remembered Elizabeth and realized anger and concern for her muddled his thinking.

"Go, Nazim. Ready the warriors. I will wait here for you."

"As you wish. Your word is my command." Nazim bowed quickly from the waist and climbed down the rocks.

Jabari stood alone, the hot desert wind whipping his indigo *binish* in a flutter that matched his swirling emotions. He closed his eyes and let his feelings battle within him.

Once his life filled with darkness as dank and deep as the tombs of the dead. Elizabeth found his soul and brought back the light. He would defend her to the death. Jabari envisioned Elizabeth's trusting eyes, deep as the desert sky, looking up at him. Felt the silky brush of her lips against his.

Heard the ugly crack of the whip as Fareeq viciously wielded it. Rage flickered. He let it slowly burn, then welcomed the bursting inferno as it consumed him in a fury as fierce as the noonday sun. Through the searing heat, his brain fed logic and formed a plan. Then, with the determination of a man who would let not even the fiercest *jinn* stand in his way, Jabari descended the hill to rescue his wife.

She must not faint nor show fear. Jabari would not.

Dressed in a delicate silk gown and pointed golden slippers that once belonged to her grandmother, Elizabeth had marched toward her fate. She had held her shoulders straight as Fareeq's warriors led her to the open circle before the tribal campfire to the flogging post. She did not shirk as they stretched her arms upward, tying her to the iron hook. When Fareeq had ripped the gown from her and groped her breast, bile rose in her throat. His sweaty, pudgy hand felt like raw meat upon her sensitive skin. She spat in his face.

Courage held her chin high, even as Fareeq shed his long white cloak, leaving his body clad only in loose-fitting black pants and a red *kamis* shirt, "to not interfere with my aim upon your back." She glanced at the scimitar dangling from his belt, remembering the death sentence awaiting her.

For several minutes he tormented her. Fareeq snapped the whip in the air behind her, so she could not anticipate when it would land on her bare skin. Terror inched up her spine and laced icy fingers around her heart. She prayed for strength and hugged the pole, bracing herself for the pain.

As the whip finally cracked a line of fire across her back, she flinched and bit her lip. An image of Jabari bravely enduring the ritual tattooing surfaced. Her husband's courage burned into her brain. Like Jabari, she would not give sound to her pain.

"Ah, you make no cry, Farris whore. But you will. Beg me to stop and I may. Beg, weak pitiful wife of that Khamsin dog." Evil, taunting laughter lashed at her as cruelly as the next flick of the whip.

She would not give this fat jackal the pleasure of hearing her whimper from the hot agony. Beg for mercy? Never.

She would hold her head high. She was the wife of the Khamsin chief and would make him proud. If only he knew.

As if reading her mind, Fareeq paused and chuckled. "You think that dog will come and save you? Perhaps he will not. He is a weak coward and you are but a traitorous woman."

Fareeq's vicious taunts weakened her more than his whip as he cracked it across her back again. Three. She should not count, for it only heightened her fear. Elizabeth laid her cheek against the rough wood of the pole, her heart heavy with thoughts of Jabari. Why should he save her? His oath was to the Almha. She had betrayed him and his people. Maybe this was her just punishment for her crime. Tears blurred her eyes. Teeth descended upon her lower lip to stop them. She must not give Fareeq the pleasure of thinking he defeated her.

Acrid smoke suddenly burned her nostrils. Elizabeth turned her head, watching thick blackness rise in the air from the camp's edge. Distant shouts filled with fear and panic echoed through the desert. Hope filled her.

Fareeq dropped the whip, grunting. He beckoned to his guards. "Go! See what that is about!"

As they ran off toward the fire, she heard a new sound amid the shouts. Gunshots. War whoops. Distant thunder echoed in her pounding brain. She lifted her head from the pole and gazed at the opposite direction of the pandemonium.

Not thunder. Hoofbeats. Hundreds. Like a stream of angry ants, Khamsin warriors spilled into the camp. Sitting tall upon Sahar, Jabari galloped toward her, letting loose a chilling war cry that promised bloodshed. His scimitar gleamed in the sunlight as he held it aloft. Her husband, the noble desert warrior, was coming to rescue her in a furious blaze of righteous vengeance.

A fierce mixture of love and pride filled her as she gazed upon his magnificence, coming toward her like a dark, avenging angel. Panic set in as she realized the danger he risked as Fareeq reached for a nearby rifle. Her breath quickened as he turned his back to her and raised the rifle to his shoulder. Jabari closed the distance between them as his men engaged Al-Hajid warriors. Pain forgotten, she could only watch in horror as her beloved galloped closer to Fareeq's gun. Men of honor, Jabari once told her, fight with swords. Fareeq had no such honor.

And neither did she.

Elizabeth smiled as she remembered how the Khamsin guard had groaned when Nahid kicked him between the legs. Fareeq thought her a weak woman. The fat pig was going to learn now just how strong she was.

He was still within easy reach. Excellent. She flexed her toes inside the confines of the golden slipper. "Take this, you rancid, stinking son of a scorpion!" she muttered under her teeth in English as Fareeq cocked the trigger and aimed for Jabari.

With all her strength, she kicked. Like an arrow flying toward its mark, the pointed-toe slipper landed with howling precision between Fareeq's legs. He screamed and doubled over, dropping the rifle. Elizabeth smiled with satisfaction.

Some days, it must be hell being a man.

Hoofbeats rang like music in her ears as Jabari approached. He twirled his blade and sliced through the ropes holding her fast. She lifted her arms up as her husband, her beloved, her lover pulled her up. He spurred Sahar and they galloped off. Elizabeth clung to Jabari as if he were a life raft in a turbulent sea. She closed her eyes.

"Nice of you to drop by. But why did you save me?" She had to ask the question as she fought the urge to collapse.

He pressed his cheek against the top of her head. "I would die before letting them harm you," he said simply.

"Jabari! Over here!" Elizabeth heard her uncle's urgent shout and opened her eyes. Jabari steered Sahar to her family's tents and lowered Elizabeth to the ground.

"My family will care for her and keep her safe," Nahid said quickly as some of Elizabeth's female relatives surrounded her.

Elizabeth leaned against her aunts and stared at Nahid. A white turban wound around his head. He wore a white *kamis* shirt, striped cloak and loose crimson pants tucked into leather boots. A dagger and a long, wicked-looking scimitar dangled from his waist. Fierce pride radiated from his tight-lipped face. The scholarly Egyptologist had transformed into a ferocious desert fighter. Elizabeth gave a ghost of a smile.

"Uncle Nahid. You look much better dressed as a warrior than as a woman," she murmured, and then let the welcoming darkness enfold her as she slipped to the ground.

His heart twisted with anguish as he beheld the unconscious, bleeding form of his beloved. Jabari slid off Sahar, lifted Elizabeth into his arms and brought her inside the tent. With loving gentleness, he laid her down on her stomach upon a nearby sheepskin bedroll on the ground. He stretched out his hand, longing to touch her fevered brow, to soothe the wicked marks upon her back. But there was no time.

"Hurry! Elizabeth will be all right," Nahid barked from outside the tent. Angry cries sounded too near for comfort.

"Take care of her," he ordered Nahid, unsheathing his sword.

"The women will. I stand with you now. And so do they." Nahid jerked his blade toward a band of men rapidly assembling behind him, dressed in the Farris clan colors of crimson and white. Jabari's eyes widened.

The rumors of clan division bore fruit. Nahid held his head high, narrowing his eyes to slits as the Taleq warriors advanced, screaming war cries.

"My clan demands justice for Fareeq's cruelties," Nahid said simply, slicing the air with his blade. "We fight until death claims us." He raised his sword and let loose a wild, undulating war cry as he led the charge toward the warriors.

"Until death claims us!" Jabari echoed, crying out his own tribe's call to arms. He touched his heart, then his lips in the traditional Khamsin warrior gesture of honor before battle and rushed into the oncoming fray.

Chapter Twenty

He fought with all the strength of his honored ancestors.

Jabari grunted and swung his scimitar, clashing it in a deadly ring of metal against metal as a Taleq warrior thrust his blade at him. He whirled and kicked, forcing the man to double over, then slashed him in a killing blow.

As soon as one dropped, another seemed to magically appear in his place. It was clear Nahid had been right—Fareeq's warriors outnumbered his own clan. They seemed as numerous as the sands. Nazim and the majority of his men were nowhere in sight.

Jabari glanced to his right, astonished to see Elizabeth's uncle. Nahid fought with the strength of a lion, in a ferocity equaling Jabari's own. Admiration renewed his own strength. Jabari parried his opponent's blade, sidestepped and slashed, making him drop to the sand with a cry. He felt the hot breath of another behind him. Without turning, Jabari sidestepped, then aimed his sword backward at his side, and stabbed back. A grunt of pain and the fall of a body followed.

He spotted a familiar figure. His heart pounded with joy.

"About time you got here," he yelled to Nazim, who fearlessly charged a Taleq warrior like a man possessed.

"Glad to see you too!" Nazim roared back, scimitar flashing in the sunlight as his opponent dropped his weapon.

"Take over for me! My battle is with Fareeq," he shouted to Nazim, who stepped forward to confront the warrior intent on engaging Jabari. He spotted his target hiding behind his warriors. Jabari growled beneath his veil and dashed through the clashing bodies, single-minded in his purpose. Fareeq saw him coming. Stumbling backward, he ran away.

"Come here, you whey-faced son of a female dog and fight like a man!" Jabari shouted.

He chased his enemy into a clearing between two tents, away from the heated battle. Spinning around, Fareeq withdrew his scimitar and thrust at Jabari, who parried it effortlessly. Sweat ran down Fareeq's bloated face and soaked his clothing. The Al-Hajid sheikh grunted and clashed his sword again against his.

As he dueled with his enemy, Jabari blocked his emotions and concentrated on analyzing his opponent. They were not evenly matched, not in height nor size. Fareeq's head barely reached Jabari's chest. He was clumsy and graceless, but he had the advantage of sheer bulk and strength. Jabari would have to rely on his flexibility and endurance. But Fareeq's small stature forced him to strike downward, which made him harder to attack. Strategy called for him to adapt. Jabari began feinting upward dropping his scimitar to the ground to press his advantage.

Fareeq dodged Jabari's attacks with surprising swiftness for one so rotund, and then suddenly aimed for his thighs, slicing through his *binish* but not the skin. Jabari kicked him in the stomach and Fareeq howled, dropping his weapon.

Kill him now, his brain dictated logically. End this.

No, there is no honor in killing a sheikh who is unarmed. Jabari's booted toe caught the edge of Fareeq's scimitar and hurled it up toward his enemy. Fareeq retrieved his blade, glowering at Jabari with hatred.

Engaged again in single-handed combat with the sheikh, Jabari suspected Fareeq would not fight with honor. True to form, Fareeq shouted for one of his warriors, who rushed Jabari from behind. Jabari whirled, parried his lunging blade, and struck a vicious blow. The warrior withdrew, grunting. He heard a noise behind him. Instinctively Jabari spun, deflecting Fareeq's sword from his back. But he could not completely block Fareeq's blade and it slashed his shoulder in a brutal upward thrust. The Al-Hajid sheikh pulled back, his beady eyes victorious at wounding his opponent.

Jabari bit his lip at the stinging pain and narrowed his eyes. "So you will fight without honor, cowardly son of a jackal. I tire of playing with you."

"I will see your life's blood flow like the Nile and then will take my delight in bedding your wife before the day is done. She will know the pleasures of a real man, not a eunuch!" Fareeq sneered and withdrew his dagger from his belt with his left hand. Now, armed with dagger in the left, scimitar in the right, he rushed at Jabari with a cry of fury, the short knife aimed straight at Jabari's groin.

Jabari dropped to the ground, rolled and lashed at Fareeq's legs, then sprang to his feet. Fareeq tripped, howling with pain and rage, and fell. He rose, wheezing, glaring at Jabari. "For this you die," he snarled and charged.

His scimitar poised and ready, Jabari held his stance. *Wait for it. Focus. Concentrate.* As Fareeq approached, bellowing with anger, Jabari raised his sword with both hands, sidestepped and let his father's blade sing through the air with righteous power.

The killing blow across the neck was swift, brutal and on the mark. Fareeq fell.

"That was for Badra and Elizabeth," Jabari said and ran back into battle to rejoin his warriors.

* * *

Drifting in and out of a pain-induced doze, Elizabeth blinked, mystified. Then she realized what troubled her. Silence. Her stomach pitched and rolled as she contemplated its meaning. Did Jabari live? Elizabeth raised herself on her elbows and looked into the face of the aunt ministering to her injuries.

"The battle . . ."

"The Farris and the Khamsin have defeated the Taleq clan."

Elizabeth sighed with relief. She laid her face on the bed and closed her eyes, fearing the answer to her next question. "And the Khamsin sheikh? Does he live?"

"That he does, my lady." Her husband's deep voice rumbled like rough velvet against her ear. Elizabeth gasped with joy and whipped her head around to gaze upon him. His dark eyes, framed by a deep blue veil, shone with triumph and love. Kneeling beside her, he took the cloth from her aunt, who left them alone.

"It is finished. Fareeq will not bother you ever again." Elizabeth closed her eyes again, flinching slightly as he pressed the soft cloth to her back.

She shuddered at the image in her mind, Jabari's sword wielded with deadly precision. Her husband did what had to be done. Like Badra had eloquently pointed out, Jabari's scimitar was razor sharp when dealing out justice.

"No great loss," Elizabeth murmured, turning her face toward him again. "Not a very pleasant fellow."

Jabari's eyes glittered with anger as he surveyed her injuries. A long tear in his *binish* showed that Fareeq had not died without inflicting damage upon her husband. Blood soaked his sleeve. Lifting up on her elbows again, she cried out.

"You're hurt!"

"It is nothing but a scratch. I have more concern for you. Are you in much pain, my love?"

Elizabeth reached up and tugged away his veil. The layer of cloth fell, showing flared nostrils and lips tight with worry. "Not as much now that I know you are here . . . alive and well."

"I will ask the Farris shaman to prepare you a draught." Jabari removed his hand from her back. Elizabeth moaned loudly and dropped to the bed, looking up at him. He bent over her, his face riddled with anxiety and concern.

"What is it? The pain?"

"Not another noxious potion! I'd rather have the pain."

"Wife, you do well to vex me at times!" Jabari tenderly pushed hair back from her cheek, stroking her head with a gentle caress. "Very well then. I know of a poultice that will ease the stinging. I will instruct your relatives how to prepare it. Then I have business of great importance I must attend to."

She buried her face into the pillow. The Almha. She had almost forgotten how she'd dishonored the Khamsin. Jabari would march back with pride to restore the sacred Almha to his tribe.

Leaving her behind, the dishonored one.

"I understand," she said in a muffled voice, feeling grief lace her as painfully as her physical injuries. "I know you must leave with the others. Your duty is to the Almha. I am still in disgrace for how I allowed it to slip away from the people."

She felt his caress against her cheek like a warm velvet glove. "Elizabeth, Elizabeth. Disgrace? You saved my life. I would never leave you. How could I leave my heart's light? Nahid asked me to witness their Majli's meeting to elect a new sheikh." His lips grazed her temple. "Do not fret. I will return soon."

Joy overlapped the stinging ache of her wounds. He was going to stay. She heard the scrape of boots dropping onto the sand, the ruffling of the tent flap pulled aside, and Nazim's cheerful voice ask, "How is your patient?"

"A much better patient than my husband," Elizabeth answered, turning her head as he knelt beside her. His dark brown hair tumbling past his shoulders, he looked as boyish as ever until his amber eyes raked over the stripes on her back. She saw them darken with anger and gave him a reassuring smile.

"See that someone tends to my husband's wounds. He is stubborn and thinks he is invincible and needs no medical care."

Nazim frowned as he took hold of Jabari's arm and examined his shoulder. "Nasty gash. Elizabeth is right. This needs immediate attention." His lips tugged upward in a wicked, sly grin. "I will attend to it myself, my lady. Have no fear. Your husband is in good hands."

Jabari's eyes widened and he drew back. "You? A goatherd has better skills in tending the wounded than you do. Allah forbid, a goat could do a better job!"

"Now, now," Nazim made a clucking sound with his tongue. "I did a fine job the last time you were wounded in battle."

"You call salt and water on an open cut a fine job?"

"Typical ruler. Fights valiantly and then cries like a babe at the thought of a little cleansing."

Jabari drew himself up and scowled. "I did not cry."

"No? Your eyes gushed more water than the Nile!"

Elizabeth snickered. Nazim's amber eyes twinkled with good humor. He grinned and winked at her as he took Jabari's arm. "Come on, sire. Be brave. I promise my touch will be softer than a babe's bottom."

"Your touch is as soft as a cactus," Jabari muttered as the men stood. Elizabeth smiled and settled into the bed, letting the weariness claim her as she closed her eyes to sleep.

Distant starlight flickered in the ebony sky. Jabari stared up at the heavens, feeling tranquil and optimistic. Led by Nazim, his warriors had returned to the Khamsin camp. Elizabeth safely slumbered inside the tent and the two tribes had mediated a tentative, but hopeful peace.

He ducked inside the tent and watched his wife rest. Firelight flickered over the paleness of her delicate face, casting shadows on her soft cheeks. An aching love filled him as he thought of her bravery, how she had risked all to save him. How she risked her life to reclaim the tribe's honor.

Such strength and courage. His heart filled with pride as he lowered himself to the bed. Jabari sat beside her, running his hand through the thick masses of her silken hair. She gave a gentle sigh and nestled deeper into the thick padding.

He lifted the poultice from her back, his nostrils flaring at the pungent odor of herbs and ancient remedies. Jabari frowned at the three stripes upon her back. He traced one with a gentle finger, then replaced the poultice. His blood boiled, thinking of Fareeq's pleasure at flogging her.

"May he burn in hell," Jabari muttered aloud.

"Indeed."

Jabari glanced up, hearing Nahid, who stood formally at the tent's entrance until Jabari bade him to sit. The two men settled on the floor near the fire.

"How is my niece?"

"She sleeps, and the healing poultice seems to be easing her pain."

"Good," Nahid said. He studied his steepled hands. "I wish to thank you, Jabari bin Tarik Hassid, for placing your trust in me and fighting to defeat Fareeq."

Jabari felt a tug of emotion as he considered Elizabeth's uncle. "It was not an easy decision for your clan to make." He thought about this. Tribal strength rested in the fidelity of its members. Fareeq's own cruelty finally worked against him.

After the battle, when causalities were counted, Khamsin warriors considered themselves fortunate. Unlike the Taleq, they lost few men. Fareeq's second-in-command, also a Taleq warrior, had been killed. Immediately the balance of power shifted to the Farris clan. The Majli had held a council meeting to elect a new sheikh. To no one's surprise, they chose Nahid. His rallying war cry to the Farris warriors led the charge against Fareeq. He had proved his valor during the heated battle.

"You will make a fine sheikh," Jabari said, resting his hand upon Nahid's shoulder.

"Now our two tribes will know peace at last, with the new blood ties forged from your marriage to my niece," Nahid rumbled.

Jabari nodded somberly. "Perhaps the prophecy did come true after all. Kiya's return heralds a new era of peace within our land. And how else could this be but for Elizabeth?"

"An extraordinary woman, my niece," Nahid responded. He held out both palms to Jabari in a gesture of reconciliation. "May I be the first to ask forgiveness for stealing the sacred Almha?"

Jabari hesitated. "None is needed. The sacred disk belongs to your people as much as mine." He embraced Nahid's hands in a spirit of brotherhood.

Releasing them, he cast a critical eye about the tent. "For so many years, the sacred disk has remained buried, its secrets guarded by my people. Now that it is in the light, I fear its awesome power. It can make men kill for its riches."

"Bury it then, as I once did." A haughty, commanding voice regaled their attention. Both men looked up to see Elizabeth sitting upright, a sheet clutched modestly over her front. "Let it remain forever in the sands, unknown to anyone. Do not let anyone claim its power."

Jabari and Nahid exchanged uneasy glances. A sense of awe came over Jabari as he stared at his wife, her slender shoulders regal and proud as if no whip had dared touch them. For a minute he envisioned her soft blond hair as dark as midnight, in a blunt-style cut of an Egyptian royal woman. In the dark shadows of the tent, she radiated queenly grace.

Then she sank onto the bed once more, as if sleeping.

Jabari quietly crossed the room and sat next to Elizabeth. He touched her arm, caressed the soft skin.

"Is that what you wish us to do? Bury the Almha?"

Like a sleepy child, she blinked and opened her eyes.

"Jabari," she said, smiling, "hello. What are you talking about? Why on earth would I tell you to bury the Almha?"

In the dark of night, they completed the deed. Nahid and Jabari, the two sheikhs of the two tribes that had once fought bloody battles, buried the secret of the ages. Once more, the golden disk lay below the sands.

In the week that followed, Elizabeth healed quickly under Jabari's tender ministrations. Naked, sitting on the bed's edge now, she flexed her shoulders, feeling the healing scar tissue stretch. Soft firelight from flickering lamps made shadows dance across the tent walls. With longing she looked at the large canvas bathtub the tribe had allocated for her. A few minutes ago, her cousins brought in buckets of steaming water.

She heard a rustling at the tent flap and pulled the blanket about her for modesty.

"I see you are feeling better," Jabari said, entering the tent with a bowl in hand, grinding some kind of powder.

She wrinkled her nose. "My sense of smell has deteriorated rapidly from all those noxious potions you've been spreading on my skin. Any more and I'm sure the tribe would have roasted me over an open fire, I smelled so much like a main course."

"Garlic is an excellent healing herb," Jabari proclaimed, sitting next to her and placing the bowl on the floor.

"I'm sure, but it certainly doesn't make it smell any better." Healing. She thought of Nana and pain laced her heart.

He regarded her. Interesting how keenly he read her mind. "What troubles you?"

"The Almha. It's buried now, but it held no answers for me."

"Answers? What answers? The key to your destiny? To ours?" Jabari grazed her knuckles with a brief kiss.

"No, not that. The cure." She bit her lip. "It is time I truly explained to you my mission here."

Elizabeth told Jabari how Jana was confined to a tuberculous hospital. Her breath came in hiccupping sobs.

Jabari wiped away her tears with his thumbs. "You should have trusted me before this," he gently scolded her. "My tribe has had treatments for many illnesses for ages."

"You have?" She stopped crying, feeling fleeting hope.

"For respiratory illnesses, we use herbs like garlic and a diet of carrots, fresh milk, green vegetables, as well as lemon juice with honey every morning and lots of fresh air and sunlight."

"Amazing," she whispered.

"It is but ancient medicine. My people are familiar with it. We have used herbs for many, many generations."

"If you write down the treatment for me, will you come with me to New York to visit her?" Elizabeth asked.

He frowned. "She will not recover in a cold, damp climate. We will bring her back here. She will have to be confined, of course, but the desert has fresher air than a stale institution."

"Your grandfather, how will he feel about that?"

Jabari's eyes grew sad. "He still loves her. I know it."

"We will have to go to Cairo first," she murmured, studying him. "Your mother lives there. Layla told me the story. Jabari, can we visit her? She is still your mother."

Elizabeth watched her husband turn to solid granite. Definitely a sore point. But she had to address it, for his sake.

"That is something I will have to consider, Elizabeth. I have not seen her since she left."

"I know she would want to see you again. Mothers never forget their children. She loves you, Jabari, she must. And I want to meet her."

"If she never left my father, he would still be alive." His voice turned to ice as he set his jaw, staring at the tent wall.

Elizabeth hated to see him hide his pain and took his hand, knowing she had to smash that rock wall again. "You can't blame her for what your father did. Every person has to accept responsibility for his own actions. You have to let go of the past, Jabari. She never meant to leave him for good. And her longing to learn must have been as fervent as Badra's. Look what happened with Badra. Can't you understand that?"

A deep sigh escaped his lips. "Perhaps. I do miss her. But my grandfather insisted that she was best forgotten."

"Like he tried to forget my grandmother. But he didn't."

Jabari's jaw slackened as the tension fled his face. "You are right. We will visit her, because you asked me to."

Elizabeth kissed his cheek. "I ask you because I don't want to see this torment in you, Jabari. The wounds of the past must heal, just as they had to heal with the Al-Hajid."

He sobered and stroked her hair tenderly. "My beloved, you are Kiya. Who else could bring peace to my heart?"

"An ancient, long-dead queen." She considered. "Maybe I am. I've never been the type of woman to meekly follow others."

"No, you are not. My love, I must know something. I know how much you love archaeology. Do you want to continue excavating?"

Astonished, she drew back and looked at him. Jabari's face reflected the dignity and mystery of the Sphinx. "Most teams will not let me join them, as I am only a mere woman."

He touched her nose with one finger. "Not a mere woman, but one with extraordinary talents. My people know of ancient sites deep in the Arabian Desert, if you wish to explore them."

Elizabeth marveled at this and settled her head against his chest. His heart beat firmly beneath her ear with a steady, reassuring rhythm. How she dreaded it ceasing as she lay in her bed, hearing the sounds of battle ring outside the tent.

"Jabari, it is enough for me to know you want this for me. My love for Egyptian history is stronger than ever, especially now that I feel so connected to the past. But I don't need to dig to unearth my roots. Now I have a far greater responsibility than the past."

"That is?"

"The present. To rule at your side and lead the Khamsin into the future." She winked at him. "And teach the women to read."

He laughed. "I know Badra will be eager to hear of it."

Jabari's lips curved into a dangerous smile. He put a finger to her mouth. "But you forget one thing, Elizabeth."

Elizabeth furrowed her brow. "I do?"

"You need lessons also. There are many things I have yet to teach you about the pleasures shared between a man and a woman. Shall we begin now?" He glanced at the large canvas bath, water still rising in steam curls.

With the care of a mother cradling a newborn, he lifted her and then lowered her into the tub. Elizabeth winced as the water hit her skin, then sank into its warmth.

She fluttered her lashes. "Care to join me?"

"No, I bathed earlier. I have something much more . . . interesting in mind." He quickly shed his clothing and retrieved a small vial. Then kneeling by the tub he poured water over her head with a small cup and began to wash her hair. She closed her eyes, enjoying the gentle massaging of her scalp. Ducking, she rinsed, sniffing the rosemary scent.

Jabari picked up the bar of soap floating in the water. Next he began soaping her shoulders. Elizabeth purred with pleasure as his hands slid over her skin. With gentle circular motions, he soaped her breasts, pausing over her taut nipples.

Her breath quickened and she moaned softly. "I think . . ."

"Hush now," he laid a finger upon her lips. His eyes glittered with triumph at her obvious delight. "Do not think. Just relax . . . and enjoy."

Elizabeth capitulated and threw her head back as his hands slid deeper into the water, slowly stroking her lower legs with the soap, working up to her thighs, then plunged into the softness between her legs. Little gasps shuttled between her lips. Her heart thundered in her chest. She closed her eyes as the sandstorm of burning pleasure filled her core.

Jabari's gentle stroking with the soap continued as he bent and kissed her with fierce hunger. Pulling away, he whispered. "Look at me. My love, look at me. I want to see your eyes as I give you this pleasure, my gift to you."

Elizabeth opened her eyes and gasped, bracing his broad shoulders. "Jabari, I . . . can't . . . it's too much . . . I can't . . ."

"Hush. Let it go, my love. Surrender to me," he commanded and her fingers tensed and dug into his naked shoulders as rich tension built and exploded in a whirlwind.

With a tender, satisfied smile, he bent and kissed her mouth. She curled her arms around his neck, sagging against him as he lifted her from the tub. Shivering, she stood on the carpet as he gently toweled her off.

"Did you enjoy your first lesson, my love?"

She sought his lips and kissed them, as she toyed with the satin curls spilling about his shoulders. "Oh yes. I suppose you think I will make an most willing student. And if I am not?"

"Disciplinary measures will be called for. I must punish you for disobeying me." He pulled her into a tight embrace and she felt the hardness between his legs. Lifting her again, he brought her over the sheepskin bed and laid her down on her side. Then he slid in next to her, his firm, muscled body molding to the length of hers. His light, assured kisses feathered her temple and worked down past her neck. Jabari let out a playful growl as he lowered his head to her breast, teasing the tender bud with several light licks.

"Is this the . . . punishment? Then I resolve to be the worst pupil you've ever had."

"Indeed," he murmured.

After two more days of "lessons," which left Elizabeth breathless and weak with love, Jabari proclaimed her well enough to travel. They bid their good-byes to Nahid and the Al-Hajid, with promises of future visits.

Jabari calculated their distance and route home by charting the stars. First, they stopped at the dig site. As they rode across the wide, flat plain and neared the excavation, several diggers looked up at Jabari, wide-eyed, and scrambled away. Dismounting, Jabari and Elizabeth walked over to the temple where Flinders Petrie squatted, frowning at a limestone tablet. He did not glance up as Elizabeth called out a greeting. He traced the tablet with one finger.

"Look at this. Fascinating. Limestone stela of Akhenaten with Nefertiti on his lap and the two princesses. Regretful that the heads are broken off. As if chopped off by a sword."

Jabari smiled widely. Elizabeth choked back a laugh.

"It's a wonderful find, Mr. Petrie," she said.

He looked at her, no trace of surprise on his face. "Elizabeth. Your uncle left me a note saying you both had to leave on urgent family business. Are you ready to work?"

How typical of the great man, she thought with amusement. She showed up with a warrior who terrorized his camp and he only wanted to know when she returned to work.

"I'm married now. This is my husband, Jabari. He is—"

Flinders interrupted her as he waved at them, peering down at the tablet once more. "Pleased to meet you. When can you return?"

"I will not be returning. Neither will my uncle."

"Too bad. We could use your uncle's knowledge and your thoroughness. The man I have recording artifacts is sloppy. No excuse for sloppiness. Well, good luck to you. I've work to do."

He strolled off. Jabari looked at her with raised brows.

"A peculiar man, single-minded to his task," he commented.

"Very much into his work," she murmured. "I think nothing surprises him. If Nahid returned leading the whole

Al-Hajid tribe, Mr. Petrie would only ask if they had digging experience."

She gave him a suspicious look. "About those chopped off heads on the tablet . . ."

He gave another mysterious smile and took her arm. "Let us go. I am most eager to return home."

Approaching the edge of the Khamsin camp, they were greeted by shouts of victorious joy. Elizabeth pulled back on her mare's reins, certain the cries were for her husband. As she sat quietly, Jabari glanced back at her. She heard it before she saw it. A flapping of wings, a purposeful flight. Elizabeth kept still as a statue as Isis landed on her shoulder.

She stroked the dove's chest and gave an audible gasp as what seemed like hundreds upon hundreds of dark-garbed figures fell to the ground, touching their foreheads to the ground.

Elizabeth raised her eyebrows to Jabari, who flashed her a devilish grin. He nodded his head toward her.

"Rise now, my people, and come greet your queen," he said in a deep, commanding voice. He dismounted. As the people stood, gawking, Jabari helped Elizabeth off the mare and took Isis from her. Badra cried with joy, rushing up to fling her arms around Elizabeth's neck. Elizabeth hugged her back with equal intensity.

"Now I know you are Kiya." Badra gave an impish smile. "Who else could defeat Fareeq with one blow and save our sheikh?"

"Who says that?" Elizabeth gawked.

"Nazim. All the tribe is talking of nothing else, how you are Kiya indeed, not a queen, but a goddess! For you felled the evil sheikh with one blow from your mighty limb!"

She raised her eyebrows at Nazim, who gave a sheepish grin. "Be thankful I did not tell of the lightning bolts that flashed from your eyes!"

Jabari chuckled and clapped a hand on his friend's shoulder. "My friend, I see I shall have a hard time tempering my wife now that you have made her into a goddess."

Nazim's amber eyes twinkled with mirth. "Someone needs to watch over you when I am not around. Why not a goddess?"

Elizabeth laughed, then stopped as Jabari's grandfather approached. Nkosi had a regal dignity about him. Despite the tribe's acknowledgment, Elizabeth knew she needed Nkosi's respect to be fully accepted by the Khamsin. She dreaded this moment.

Jabari handed Nazim the dove, telling him to replace her on the perch. Her husband sensed her discomfort and draped a reassuring arm around her waist. "Grandfather," he said formally.

"Grandson," Nkosi responded, "I must speak with you both."

They walked with Nkosi into the crowd, which pulled back with hushed respect. Elizabeth looked up as they approached Jabari's tent. They went inside and settled on the floor, a long silence stretching between them. Finally Nkosi spoke.

"And what of the Almha?"

"It lies beneath the sands once more," Jabari responded. "So much power is too tempting for but one tribe to claim it."

Nkosi nodded thoughtfully. "A wise move, my grandson."

"Not mine," Jabari replied. "Elizabeth's."

"Ah." Nkosi sighed deeply. "I have misjudged you, Elizabeth. I humbly seek your forgiveness." Nkosi seemed to struggle with the apology. She sensed just how much it cost him to say it.

Elizabeth closed her mouth and gave a little nod. "Thank you. I forgive you. I love Jabari and always will." She explained to him about her grandmother and Jabari's plan.

"Would you like for her to live here?"

Nkosi appeared to struggle with his emotions. He gazed

at the tent wall and nodded. Elizabeth touched his hand gently.

His burning eyes settled upon his grandson. "We need to go outside now. There is something I have neglected to do."

Outside the tent, she noticed Jabari's extended family had gathered in a circle. Nkosi quietly regarded them. He stretched out his hand to his grandson.

"Jabari, hand me your wedding dagger."

As her husband complied, Elizabeth's heart sank. He was taking back the dagger. Did he not approve of her after all this? But Nkosi fingered the blade for a moment, then returned it to his grandson, his eyes focused on her as he spoke.

"I accept this woman into my family as your bride and promise to love her as my own daughter. Like my father before me, I give to you the sacred dagger that has been in our family for generations. Use it to protect your bride, to guard her life and keep her safe always. May you both enjoy everlasting peace and harmony and may your union be fruitful and filled with love as deep and flowing as the Nile."

Tears scalded the back of her throat at his beautiful declaration of acceptance. Nkosi stepped forward and kissed her on both cheeks. She wiped her eyes as Jabari stared at the blade, the muscles in his cheek twitching as if he fought to suppress his feelings. Finally, he spoke.

"Thank you, Grandfather."

Nkosi broke the moment's intensity with an infectious grin that mimicked his grandson's impish spirit. "It is my pleasure. After all, I am eagerly awaiting you to make me a great-grandfather. What are you dawdling for? Go make a baby!"

Elizabeth flushed as Jabari and Nksoi roared with laughter. Her husband took her elbow, steering her toward their tent. He paused to regard Ghazi and Isis perched beneath the thorn tree.

"Look at them," he said quietly. "Sitting side by side so peacefully. The falcon and the dove."

"Like you and I. But which are you?"

He placed her hand on his chest. "The dove. Because my heart is filled with peace, peace you have brought into my life."

Elizabeth's mouth quirked up in a mischievous smile. "I am feeling quite like the falcon now. And I can't wait to prey upon you once we get inside," she said in a husky whisper.

Once inside his bedroom, Jabari pulled her into his arms. She loved the predatory gleam lighting his dark eyes. "Your Nana can wait a few days, can she not? I plan to keep you trapped in my bed, claiming what is due to me." He fingered a strand of her hair, lifting it to drop a soft kiss against her neck.

Elizabeth shuddered at the delicious promise of his kiss. "Do your worst," she whispered as she curled her arms about his neck. "Are you going to make me beg and plead?"

"I will torment you with pleasure until you cry for mercy."

"And I thought the secrets of one hundred kisses were deadly."

Jabari tightened his grip around her waist. "I think we should fulfill my grandfather's request for a great-grandchild."

A scarlet flush filled her cheeks at the thought. She felt her womb quicken as if Jabari's babe already grew there. "But know this, my beloved," Elizabeth murmured.

"What?" Jabari asked, as he pressed his lips to her neck.

"I am Kiya, your queen, and you must obey me."

Lifting his head, he gave her a puzzled look, then seemed to consider. Jabari bowed, then fell to his knees. Holding her hand, he kissed it with the reverence of a subject honoring a royal.

"And what is my queen's wish? You need only state it

and I shall respond faster than the wind to fulfill your command."

"I have only one desire: Make love to me now."

Her husband stood, pulling her with him, complying. He tore his mouth away from hers, his eyes glittering with fervor as he stripped off her clothing then shed his own. Jabari lifted her and laid her upon the bed with extreme gentleness. As he rained a trail of burning kisses down her bare skin, Elizabeth felt the fire of her own passion burst into an inferno to meet his desire.

"Jabari, I feel as if I'm rediscovering you," she reflected, her hand trembling as she stroked his cheek. "What if I am Kiya? How could I bear losing you again as she lost Ranefer?"

"My love, you told me to let go of the past. Now I am telling you. Let the past bury itself in the earth with the Almha. Nothing can separate us or my love for you."

He raised his head, looking at her with such tenderness Elizabeth felt all agonized recollections of ancient history crumble into dust. A deep feeling of peace settled over her as she envisioned the desert swallowing those memories whole. Let the past sleep deep beneath the shimmering dunes.

The sands of Akhetaten could hold many secrets. Forever.

Tempted Tigress

JADE LEE

Orphaned and stranded, Anna Marie Thompson can trust no one, especially not her dark captor, a Mandarin prince. Not when his eyes hold secrets deadlier than her own. His caress is liquid fire, but Anna is an Englishwoman and alone. She cannot trust that they can tame the dragon, as he whispers, that sadness and fear can be cleansed by soft yin rain. Safety and joy are but a breath away. And perhaps love. All is for the taking, if she will just give in to temptation….

ISBN 10: 0-8439-5690-9
ISBN 13: 978-0-8439-5690-0 $6.99 US/$8.99 CAN